Highlander Entangled

Vonda Sinclair

Highlander Entangled

Copyright © 2017 Vonda Sinclair

ALL RIGHTS RESERVED

This book may not be reproduced in whole or in part without written permission from the author. This book is a work of fiction. The characters, names, incidents, locations, and events are fictitious or used fictitiously. Any resemblance to actual persons, living or dead, is purely coincidental or from the writer's imagination.

www.vondasinclair.com

ISBN: 1981920897
ISBN-13: 978-1981920891

DEDICATION

To my amazing nieces and nephews.

You inspire me with your energy, creativity and love.

BOOKS BY VONDA SINCLAIR

THE HIGHLAND ADVENTURE SERIES
My Fierce Highlander
My Wild Highlander
My Brave Highlander
My Daring Highlander
My Notorious Highlander
My Rebel Highlander
My Captive Highlander
Highlander Unbroken
Highlander Entangled

THE SCOTTISH TREASURE SERIES
Stolen by a Highland Rogue
Defended by a Highland Renegade

www.vondasinclair.com

ACKNOWLEDGMENTS

My sincere thanks to the highly skilled Amanda Sumner of Careful Copyediting.

I'm also grateful for the following generous and helpful critique partners and beta readers: Dana S., Vanessa H., and Nicole L.

CHAPTER ONE

The Scottish Highlands, October 1617

"You cannot force my sister to marry you!" Kristina MacQueen yelled at Blackburn MacCromar, a hulking warlord with long black hair. Candlelight glinting off the metal studs in his leather armor, he stood beside her sister, Susanna—or Anna, as she was better known—in the small chapel before a priest.

Dark brows lowered, Blackburn glowered at Kristina. "Shut your mouth, bitch!" Lunging toward her, Blackburn slapped her face so hard her neck wrenched. The pain exploded and she stumbled backward.

"Nay! Leave her be!" Anna grabbed onto his arm.

Holding her stinging cheek, Kristina clenched her teeth and glared at Blackburn. Anna was pale, weak and thin, barely recovered from all the blood loss she'd suffered when she'd lost her babe at seven months… after Blackburn had shoved her down the stairs. Only months before that, Blackburn had slain Anna's husband, Chief John MacCromar, and taken over as chief.

Now, tears trailed down Anna's face and she appeared ready to collapse.

"Father, how can you perform this ceremony?" Kristina demanded of the priest. "She already refused to marry him. He murdered her husband in cold blood!"

The priest merely stared down at his prayer book as if he didn't hear a word she said.

"Don't let her move from this spot," Blackburn murmured to the guard he'd placed beside Anna. He then turned toward Kristina and pulled a dirk from the scabbard at his belt.

"Don't touch her!" Anna shrieked, trying to free herself from the guard.

The long blade flashed in the candlelight. Terror striking her like a sharp icicle, Kristina dodged backward, but Blackburn's second-in-command, Red Holme, blocked her escape. Blackburn pushed her against the wall. The rough stones dug into her back. His fingers bit into her chin as he restrained her. With his other hand, he held the knife close to her face. "You listen to me, wench," he hissed. "You will keep your mouth shut during the ceremony or you will find yourself dead. Do you understand?"

"Kristina, please be quiet," Anna begged, her face wet with tears.

"Aye, you'd best listen to your sister," Blackburn said.

Her heart hammering, Kristina clenched her teeth and narrowed her eyes. Equal parts fear and rage stampeded through her. If Anna married him, they were both as good as dead anyway. "You can't force a woman to wed you. 'Tis illegal!"

"She will agree to the marriage." Blackburn smiled maliciously.

Kristina glared past Blackburn to the priest. Was he a man of God or an imposter? "Please help us, Father. I beg of you! This man is a murderer!"

Blackburn's fingers tightened, nearly crushing her chin. "I warned you," he seethed.

She kicked and struggled against him. He held her firm and sliced the blade down the left side of her face. She screamed at the searing pain. When she yanked away from him this time, he let her go. Blood poured from the cut on her cheek and drenched her hands.

Anna's screams echoed until they were muffled.

"Hold your knife to her throat," he ordered Holme.

Before Kristina could escape, the beefy man pinned her arms to her sides, near squeezing the breath from her, and placed his blade against her throat. The sharp tip pricked the skin of her neck but 'twas naught compared to the devastating pain lashing her face.

"I like you, lass, but I always follow orders," Holme growled into her ear.

Was she going to die this day? The gash on her face was deep, several inches long, and it bled profusely.

"You will marry me, m'lady," he told Anna, "Or I will order your sister's throat slit."

Kristina coughed and gagged against the blood entering her mouth from the wound and forced herself to breathe. Nausea flooded her stomach and the sharp pain in her face was near unbearable.

She wanted to gut the bastard, and the one holding her too, but she was no match for Blackburn, Holme and the eight large guards he had stationed inside this chapel. She and Anna could not best Blackburn now. But if she lived, she would kill him.

The ceremony continued. Though Anna was crying and the guard had to hold her up, she finally said, "I do."

After he kissed Anna, sealing the hell-hated vows, Blackburn told the guard, "Carry my wife back to the keep." Blackburn approached Kristina. "I told you she would agree." He smirked.

"Bastard!"

Snarling, he grasped the front of her bloody bodice, yanked her away from Holme, then threw her against the wall. The back of her head struck the stones. Agonizing pain consuming her, she slid to the floor, and her surroundings vanished.

CHAPTER TWO

Stirling, Scotland, October 1619

"*Kristina, wake up and ready yourself for a journey!*"
In her bedchamber, Kristina MacQueen jolted awake. Had she just heard her mother's voice? 'Twas impossible. Her mother had passed many years ago. The voice had been inside her dream. What had Ma meant about a journey? Kristina had not left the vicinity of her aunt and uncle's manor house in many months.

Hearing the faint hoofbeats of many horses galloping in the distance, she sat up and listened. As each moment passed, the horses' hooves pounded closer and closer until they echoed off the cobblestones just outside the window. Her heart thumping and an eerie feeling prickling along her skin, she swung her feet toward the floor and sat on the edge of the bed.

A fist battered violently at the home's entrance door below.
"Saints. Who could that be?" she whispered. It had to be the middle of the night or the wee hours of the morn, for she heard no one moving about the house and her room was chilly. The visitor couldn't be the physician calling to treat Uncle Gilbert, who suffered from gout, rheumatism and various other ailments. Nay, he wouldn't bring that many horses with him on a house call. Maybe 'twas the creditors, come to expel them from their home. When her uncle's health had declined, so had his funds.

Could it be news of her older sister? She had not heard from Anna in many months.

Ready yourself for a journey, her mother had said in the dream.
Good heavens! Had someone come for her, to take her to Anna?

Heart hammering, Kristina leapt from the warm bed. Though

4

she couldn't see, she knew the placement of the furniture in her room and could easily navigate the space without bumping into anything. After tiptoeing across the cold wooden floor in her stockings, she approached the door and turned the knob to open it a crack, then listened. The maids were in an uproar on the ground floor below.

"What's the racket?" Aunt Matilda yelled as she tromped by Kristina's chamber and down the stairs. "Who is it?" she demanded near the front door.

"Chief Blackburn MacCromar!" The snarled response was bellowed from outside, just below her window.

A chill of terror and revulsion flashed through Kristina. "Saints, preserve us." She shut the door and barred it, her fingers trembling. She had not been near the malicious bastard in two years. He had finally come for her.

Anxiety and nausea froze her to the spot. What would he do? Would he kill her for a certainty this time?

After Blackburn had sliced Kristina's face and slammed her head against the stone wall, she had not known anything for days. When she'd awakened, she'd been blind and had not seen anything since.

Anna had been the only one there to protect her. If not for her, Blackburn might have easily finished Kristina off in her weakened state.

When Blackburn had left on a trip, she and Anna had run away. After bringing her here to hide with their aunt and uncle, Anna had fled toward Edinburgh, to lure Blackburn away from her, she'd said. What a strong and brave woman her sister was, and how she admired her. Anna had only slipped back a couple of times since, to bring money she'd earned from singing.

Why would her mother, in a dream, expect her to take a journey with such a cruel man as Blackburn?

Had he found Anna?

"Dear God, nay. Please keep Anna safe," she whispered, nausea clutching at her stomach.

Kristina had to be ready for the blackguard. Feeling along the plaster wall, she found her storage chest, the oak wood and the metal studs cold against her palms. Kneeling, she opened it and dug through the scratchy woolen and linen clothing, feeling for the small knife in its leather sheath. Finding it, she strapped it to her thigh above her stocking. She knew the blade was sharp, for she'd whetted it herself.

Was it sacrilege to hope for an opportunity to kill Blackburn? Regardless, she would protect herself and her sister as best she could.

She tied a small linen pouch containing a few supplies, silver coins and her mother's gold and garnet earrings around her waist. The earrings were the last things of her mother's that she possessed. Not wanting to be without them, she either wore them or had them close by at all times. Blackburn had stolen the rest of her mother's jewels, along with the ones Anna's first husband had given her, and sold it all. Kristina would not want him to see these earrings.

Shivering from the chilly room, she struggled to pull on two layers of her warmest clothing over the smock—no easy task, as she was unable to see and had no assistance as she usually did. Once she'd adjusted her clothing into place, she secured the wide leather belt over her arisaid.

Where could Anna be now, all these months later? "Dear God, let her be well," she whispered. "And please forgive me if I have to kill a man to protect myself."

Heavy footfalls pounded up the steps, riveting Kristina's attention. Chills of fear slid along her spine.

"Search this place!" Blackburn ordered.

Doors opened and slammed. Heavy boots thudded back and forth.

Kristina's hands trembled and her stomach knotted as she pulled on her leather boots, then her thick woolen cloak. She found her cane where she'd propped it by the bed. 'Twas long, lightweight and made of pine, not nearly strong enough to use as a weapon. She was wise enough to know she couldn't defeat Blackburn with a stick, but she did need it to get around wherever she went.

"Where is she?" the male voice growled outside her door. "Out of my way, you hag!"

Panic quickened Kristina's breathing and her heart rate. She felt as if she were headed to her own execution… and she might be. The barbaric murderer who had forced Anna to marry him two years ago could easily kill Kristina… but he might suffer a couple of stab wounds in the process.

Though she had not wanted to ever prepare for this day, she had, for she knew Blackburn would never stop searching for Anna… unless he was dead. Unfortunately, no one had killed him yet.

He was obsessed with Anna, wanting to possess her and abuse her in equal measure. But Kristina—he would not give one rotten fig for her. He had merely used her to bend Anna to his will.

Had he not done enough damage to Kristina already? Blindness. A horrid scar down her face. What had she done to him? Naught but try to protect her beloved sister.

A heavy fist pummeled her door. She jumped, then stood firm, facing it. "Dear God, give me strength," she whispered, releasing a breath.

The latch clattered, but the bar held the door securely closed. "Lady Kristina, if you wish to see your sister alive, you will open this door now," Blackburn roared.

She frowned. His words made no logical sense. If he had Anna, he wouldn't be here. Did he take her for a fool?

"I will kill your aunt! Do you hear me, you little witch?"

Aunt Matilda screamed, turning Kristina's blood to ice. Had he grabbed her?

Kristina hastened toward the door. "Leave my aunt be… and everyone else here! Then I'll open the door. Do you promise?"

"Aye."

As if his promise meant anything. She well knew she could not bargain with the devil.

Kristina drew in a deep, calming breath. She would need all the fortitude and courage she possessed to face this brute. "Are you well, aunt?"

"Aye, but don't you dare open that door, Kristina!"

She didn't listen. She unbarred the door, for she wouldn't stand by while this madman killed her aunt, perhaps her ailing uncle, and everyone else in this house.

Kristina pulled the door open by slow degrees, feeling as if she stood before a gaping abyss, vulnerable, only blackness before her. Her heart thundered in her ears so loudly she could hardly hear. But she smelled him. Blackburn MacCromar stank of sweat, horses, and whisky.

"What do you want? Where is my sister?"

He yanked the cane from her hand, and it clattered away.

Roughly, he grabbed Kristina, picked her up and tossed her over his bulky shoulder. Pain slammed into her stomach, near knocking the breath from her, even as fear spiked inside her. "Bastard," she gasped.

Her aunt screamed. Then Kristina felt her aunt's weak, arthritic grip on her arm as she tried to pull her from the monster.

"Get back, you old crone!" Blackburn turned about, shook her aunt off, then strode down the corridor.

"I'll be fine, aunt! Don't worry over me," Kristina called, trying to keep her voice steady, though she wanted to sob, her head dangling upside down. She imagined the horror on her aunt's face. "I'll send word when I can."

She heard sobs coming from her aunt and some of the female servants. Blackburn's boots clomped down the steps and along the wood floors, his men's footsteps following, as they exited the front door into the cool night air. The acrid smoke from burning pitch invaded her nostrils, making her cough. The sounds of hissing and popping torch flames reached her next. Horses neighed and snorted as he carried her among them. The scents of horses and sweaty men increased. How many men were here?

Chill wind blasted them, carrying away some of the odors and freshening the air.

"She can ride with me," a man said. She remembered that callous voice—Blackburn's second-in-command and war leader, the soulless man who'd held a knife to her throat: Red Holme.

Revulsion gave her a tremor as she recalled the nasty, lust-filled looks he'd given her before she'd lost her sight. He had tried every ploy to lure her to his bed. Disgusted by him and his malevolent aura, she'd spurned his advances.

"I brought a horse for her," Blackburn called to Holme. "Can you stay in the saddle, wench?" He dumped her onto her feet, then his voice became mocking. "Or would you feel safer riding with Holme?"

Toppling sideways against the horse, she grabbed onto the saddle. "I can ride alone." She had not been on a horse since losing her sight, but before that, she'd ridden plenty. Surely she hadn't forgotten how. And she wanted to be as far away from Holme as possible.

"Where is my sister?" she asked, keeping her voice steady and neutral.

"You will find out soon enough. Keep quiet or you'll find yourself gagged." Lifting her, he placed her astride the horse. After she shoved her skirts out of the way, she grabbed hold of the saddle and placed her feet in the stirrups.

"She cannot keep up with our fast pace," Red Holme grumbled.

"Aye, she will. Hold her bridle and keep her beside you, Ralston. I want her alive until we reach our destination."

What did he mean? What was their destination and what would he do to her there?

Within moments, the horses started walking forward, then trotting at a brisk pace. The cold wind stung her cheeks, blowing her cowl off and her hair back. Holding onto the saddle and using her legs to grip the horse, she worked hard to keep her balance, leaning slightly forward over the horse's neck.

She wondered about the man Blackburn had put in charge of guiding her horse.

"Ralston?" she said, loud enough to be heard over the hooves pounding the muddy road.

"Aye." He sounded younger than the other two men, 'haps in his early twenties.

"Where are we going?"

"You'll have to ask the chief."

Chief, hah! Blackburn had stolen the position when he'd murdered his own cousin, John MacCromar.

"How many soldiers did he bring?" she asked.

"Four dozen."

Why on earth would he need that many men simply to capture her? He obviously had other plans in mind, perhaps some sort of attack.

"Any other women in the party?"

"Nay."

Saints. She refused to think about how vulnerable she was.

As they rode, she tried to figure out the situation. None of the men were talking because of the fast pace. 'Twas clear Blackburn knew where Anna was, but mayhap she wasn't so easy to get to.

Likely, Blackburn planned to use Kristina to lure or force Anna out from her hiding place. That had to be it. Why else would he abduct her in the middle of the night and then ride like the devil? He wanted to use her as leverage. If that were the case, she had to escape and hide. But how? She could see naught, not even a faint hint of light at midday.

She had no inkling what time of night or morning it was, but they rode for about an hour.

"Halt!" Blackburn called out from somewhere up ahead. All the hoofbeats slowed, then drew to a stop. Leather creaked as the men dismounted. A flowing stream splashed nearby. The air smelled fresh and damp, like black dirt in a garden.

Though stiff and sore from sitting in the saddle so long, she dismounted without help. It had been over two years since she'd ridden much, and her muscles had weakened.

Footsteps thumped and swished toward her through damp grasses. "I was going to help you dismount, m'lady," Ralston said.

"I'm fully capable of doing so myself. Is there a place I might… have some privacy?" Her face burned with the awkwardness of the situation. She prayed the men would actually give her some privacy and show her respect.

"Aye, there are some bushes just over here." Ralston took her arm and gently but firmly guided her over the uneven ground. After her feet got tangled in the tall dead grass, he steadied her, then she took higher steps.

After they stopped, she listened, not hearing anyone close by. "Is this private and away from the men?"

"Aye. I will stand guard with my back toward you."

"I thank you." She didn't know if she could trust him, but what choice did she have? "Is it daylight yet?"

"A hint of dawn is just at the horizon."

After she'd relieved herself, Ralston led her from the bushes and toward the talking men again.

"I wish some clean water or something to drink," she said, holding her head high. She would not be cowed by these criminals.

"Do you now, my queen?"

She turned her head toward Red Holme's grumpy voice, the sound of it sickening her. Her whole body tensed. She remembered what he looked like—a tall, hulking man with shaggy red hair and a beard to match.

"Can you now see?" he demanded.

She frowned. "Nay."

"Then why are you looking at me with those eerie blue eyes?"

What in blazes was he talking about? Did she appear to be staring at him? A bitter laugh almost burst from her mouth, but she prevented it. Instead, she listened, hearing him move aside and turning her eyes toward the sound. Everyone said that her eyes appeared fine and healthy. The physician had told her whatever had caused her blindness, it was deeper inside her head and caused from the blow to her brain.

"What's wrong with you?" Blackburn asked nearby.

"She can see!" Red Holme declared as if spooked. "Look at her!"

"Are you mad? She's as blind as a damnable bat."

Her stomach turned at Blackburn's snide tone. Something small bounced off Kristina's shoulder, startling her. "What are you doing?" she demanded. "Throwing rocks at the blind girl? How heroic you are."

"Shut your mouth!" Blackburn ordered. "Your sharp tongue is why you're blind now and why your face is so hideously ugly with that scar."

Kristina ground her teeth. Bastard. She'd like to take her knife and slice his face as he had done to her. Tears stung her eyes, but she refused to let the blackguards see them.

Red Holme chuckled as he walked away, the grass rustling beneath his boots. She wished she could accurately throw a dirk at each of them.

She pulled the cowl over her head, hiding her face. Indeed, she felt hideously ugly, as he'd said. She traced a finger over the deep, puckered scar that ran down the length of her cheek, now wet with tears. No man would ever find her attractive—she knew that. Nor would any man want a blind wife who couldn't take care of a household or children. She had no illusions about marrying.

Don't think of it, she told herself. She simply needed to survive this journey and try to protect Anna as best she could.

Boots stamping through damp dead grass approached, and she tensed.

"Here you go, m'lady," Ralston said.

She wiped her tears away, hoping he didn't see. "What is it?"

"Water." He took her hand and placed it around a cold, wet metal cup.

"Is it clean?" Everyone knew disease came from dirty water.

"Aye, I drank some myself. I got it from a small stream flowing down from the hill."

"I thank you." She sniffed it, detecting no rank odors. A small taste told her it was fresh enough. After drinking all she wanted, she handed the cup back to Ralston. "Is my sister all right?" she whispered.

"Aye, far as I know." He kept his voice low.

"Have you seen her?"

"Nay." His brief answers did not satisfy her curiosity.

"Where is she? Where are we going?" Kristina asked.

"Northwest and into the Highlands."

"How far?"

"Through Lochaber and to the west coast."

Saints, how had Anna gotten so far away… and been discovered anyway?

As Ralston's footsteps retreated, she listened to the other men, trying to find out more, but they were too distant or talking so low she couldn't make out their words. If not for her blindness, she might spy an escape route, but her affliction imprisoned her as much as Blackburn did.

"Mount up!" the knave yelled, his voice echoing. "We must ride many miles this day."

CHAPTER THREE

Bearach Castle, Loch Moidart, Scotland

Colin Cameron strode into the candlelit great hall from the courtyard, where the men were preparing for an impending attack. Colin had come to help his friend and foster brother, Neacal MacDonald, the new chief of the MacDonalds of Moidart. Enemies were sneaking up on Neacal from every side.

When Neacal had sent Colin the missive, he'd said he expected MacDonald of Sleat to attack, attempting to take over the castle while Neacal's clan was recovering from the MacKenzie siege in which many of the Moidart men had been killed.

Now, a new threat loomed—Blackburn MacCromar. The man was trying to seize Anna Douglas from Neacal. All Colin knew thus far was that Neacal had eliminated a dozen of MacCromar's men singlehandedly, with bow and arrow, while protecting Anna on a remote mountain.

Colin proceeded into the solar where the maids had served supper. His friend wished to speak with him in private about the conflict.

The fireplace and a few candles lit the spacious, well-furnished room. The aromas of venison, bread, vegetables and herbs teased his senses.

Colin inhaled deeply. "Smells good."

"We missed supper in the great hall, and I wished to speak with you away from the others." Neacal's sharp blue gaze held great seriousness.

Good. Colin hoped he would enlighten him with the details.

They took seats at the table near the hearth. Prior to today, Colin had not seen his friend in a year. Neacal's return to remarkable health was astounding. The last time Colin had seen him, his friend had been near skin and bones from the horrid injuries he'd sustained while captured by his enemy, MacRankin.

Now, Neacal was lean and muscular, like a Highland warrior should be. His long dark hair hung over his shoulders, and the jagged pink scar on the side of his face only made him appear more fearsome.

Colin was hungrier than he'd realized after his long ride into the mountains to find Neacal. Besides, the food was delicious. He chewed and swallowed. "What's your plan in dealing with Blackburn MacCromar?"

"I'm going to kill the bastard." Neacal's voice was deadly serious.

"Ah. Don't you feel you're being a bit too lenient?" Colin asked with a trace of dry humor.

Neacal smirked. "Aye. He deserves torture worse than I suffered, but I'll spare him. I have no doubt he'll show up here."

"What if he wants to negotiate?"

"Negotiation happens when there is a hostage. Anna is here of her own free will, and I won't hand her over to him. Of a certainty, she won't choose to go with him. I expect that he'll grow hostile and attack once I tell him nay."

For several minutes they discussed battle strategy, ways they might gain the upper hand, and other clans who might join their force.

Colin took a long sip of ale, remembering how he'd come upon Neacal and Anna kissing in a glen between the mountains. Obviously, his friend was smitten with the lovely blonde. "Do you intend to marry Anna?"

"Of course."

Colin chuckled. "Damnation. You've become decisive of late."

Neacal grinned, giving a glimpse of his younger self. "I've always been decisive."

Colin was pleased to see him find happiness again. The change in Neacal when he was with Anna was miraculous.

He still didn't understand the lass's situation, and his friend seemed reluctant to tell him the whole story. What was her connection to Blackburn MacCromar, and why were his men trying to capture her?

"What on earth happened to her?" Colin asked.

Neacal hesitated for a moment, though Colin didn't ken why. Surely his friend trusted him. Neacal had always told him that he considered him more like a brother than his actual brother, Elrick.

Neacal drew in a deep breath. "Anna was forced into marriage with the murderous whoreson."

"Marriage?" Colin was stunned. The lovely blonde Neacal planned to marry was already married? His friend, ever the risk-taker, was playing with fire again.

"Aye. Blackburn MacCromar murdered the previous MacCromar chief, his cousin, Anna's first husband."

"Saints!"

"The marriage is not legal, but I'm certain he won't give up. 'Tis why I'll have to either take the matter before the king or kill Blackburn. In a fair fight, of course."

"Of course." Obviously Neacal had strong feelings for her if he was willing to take such risks to marry her. "You love her," Colin stated.

Neacal lifted a brow. His eyes growing more intense, he glanced away.

"Do you not?" Colin persisted, grinning.

"I'm drawn to her."

That was an understatement. He suspected his friend was mad about Anna.

"You used to be drawn to a lot of women... before." Aye, before the torture, Neacal had been a charming rogue, and all the lassies had been in love with him... the ones who hadn't been in love with Colin. They'd sown plenty of wild oats during their early twenties. "But this is different."

"Anna is different." Neacal's voice was solemn, reverent. "She gives me peace as I've never had."

Despite his friend's earnest mood, Colin couldn't resist teasing him a wee bit. "Are you certain 'tis peace? Or a raging storm of desire?"

"If you must know... both," Neacal admitted reluctantly.

Colin chuckled. "Aha. The storm, then the peace."

Frowning, Neacal stared down into his cup of ale. "She helps me forget the torture."

Colin relented, visualizing for a moment the hell Neacal must have gone through. He couldn't even imagine the severe pain. Neacal's torturers had broken several of his bones, dislocated his joints, and inflicted cuts and stab wounds. Colin didn't know how Neacal had survived it. Anyone would come out the other side of torture a changed man, nearly a completely different person. And it had changed Neacal—gone were the easy smiles and quips. Any joy in life had been destroyed, but he seemed to have discovered an intense drive to be stronger, mentally and physically, than he'd ever been before. If Anna could bring a bit of that joy back to Neacal...

"I'm glad for that, my friend. None of us can truly understand what you suffered at the hands of MacRankin, even if you tell us. 'Tis something only you know the full extent of." He wished he'd known his friend had been captured at the time. He would've charged in and pulled him out of that hell-pit.

"Anna has suffered too—'haps more than I have," Neacal said. "And I mean to protect her from that demon. He not only murdered her husband, he also caused her to have a miscarriage because of his abuse."

"Damnation," Colin muttered. Anna was a sweet, gentle lady. How could any man treat her thus?

"He cut her younger sister's face," Neacal continued.

"Why?"

"He forced Anna to marry him by threatening her sister with a knife. He cut Kristina's face, then had his man to hold a knife at her throat. After that, he shoved her down and her head hit the stone wall. She is blind because of it."

Even though he didn't ken the lass, fury rampaged through Colin at such injustice. Women should be treated with the utmost respect and care. "Hell. I hope he arrives soon. I want to personally run him through."

"Not if I get to him first."

After Blackburn MacCromar's small army had traveled for several hours at a moderate but steady pace so as not to tire the horses overmuch, Kristina felt the morning sun's warmth on her back. Indeed, they were heading northwest.

Around midday, the pace slowed and they drew up.

"Where are we?" she asked.

"'Tis a wee village." Ralston helped her dismount. "The chief is approaching."

Not knowing what to expect, she tensed.

"I need to have a word with both of you," Blackburn said.

Hating him more each time she heard his voice, she ground her teeth.

"Do not say a word to anyone, Kristina. You're my sister-in-law and that's the end of it. Ralston, make certain she doesn't talk to anyone."

"Aye, chief."

Footsteps tromped away.

Ralston placed her hand around his elbow. "Come. I'll find you some food."

She released the breath she'd been holding. "I thank you for being so kind to me."

"'Tis naught. You remind me of my sister."

"Oh, you have a sister?"

He hesitated a long moment while they walked over the uneven cobblestones. "I used to. She passed five years ago from an illness."

"I'm so sorry to hear that."

Heavy footsteps approached. "Watch that you don't get too smitten with the lass," Red Holme said.

"I'm nay smitten," Ralston snapped.

Holme was such a knave. She wanted to kick him in the groin. Back when she was younger and had her sight, she'd watched two young men fighting. One had kicked the other in the groin and the injured man had gone down groaning in pain and hadn't risen to his feet for several minutes. She knew it might be a good way to disable Holme or Blackburn if she ever had the opportunity.

When she and Ralston entered what she assumed was a crowded tavern, she smelled the scents of ale, roasted venison, and mutton stew, along with onions and other vegetables and fresh oat bread. Her stomach growled, for she had not eaten since the night before. The many voices in the room were a dull roar.

"Take a seat here, m'lady." Ralston lowered her.

She placed her hand down behind her as she sat and found a bench beneath her.

"I'll be right back."

She still wore the cowl hiding most of her face and hated that she couldn't see who might be staring at her. Most likely several people were. Regardless, she sat upright with her back straight as her mother had always taught her.

"Enjoying Ralston's mollycoddling, I see." Holme's rough, nasty voice grated on her nerves.

"Leave me be," she muttered, refusing to be afraid of him. Above the roar of conversation in the room, the sound of Holme's footsteps clomped even closer and moved in behind her. Cringing, she wanted to draw away, but she remained as upright as a tree.

He tugged her cowl back, away from her ear, then his hot, fetid breath wafted against it. She turned away.

"Don't like me very much, do you, lass?" Holme whispered through clenched teeth.

Nay, she hated him.

"I ken how to make you like me." Standing upright again, he ground himself against her back, chuckled, then walked away.

Recoiling with disgust and the avalanche of cold shivers, she averted her face and drew the cowl closer over her head. Dear God, what was he going to do to her? He'd always made it obvious he wanted to bed her.

Would he try to rape her?

Nausea overwhelming her, she clutched at her stomach, then placed her hand upon her thigh, feeling the *sgian dubh* secured there. If she killed Holme, what would Blackburn do to her? Kill her? Or would she be unwittingly putting Anna's life in danger? She had to find out anything she could about her sister.

Kristina listened, trying to pick out Blackburn's voice so she might hear a few words about why she had been taken hostage. Suddenly, her ears picked up a man's aristocratic voice to her right. His accent was noticeably upper crust. Who was he? Could she possibly gain his help in escaping these brigands? If only she could hear him introduce himself, or hear someone call his name. Or if he would come close and speak to her. She remembered Blackburn's warning about talking to no one, but she had to gain help from somewhere.

Feeling uneasy, she slowly pulled the cowl off her head, revealing her hair. She had always received many compliments on her blond curls. They were a mess at the moment, but maybe that wouldn't matter. Mayhap the man would see her for what she was, a lady in need of help.

Fortunately, the unmarred side of her face was toward the man. She hoped he might notice her and come closer so she could ask him to help. Of course, it was a big risk. He might be a worse knave than Blackburn.

But then she heard a woman's voice say, "Who is that girl, just there? She wears fine clothing but sits alone."

"I know not. 'Haps we should find out," the man said.

Thank the saints! Though her heart pounded with tension, Kristina gave a hint of a friendly smile, while also trying to hide the scarred part of her face. A chair scraped across the floor.

"Chief MacCromar, what the devil are you doing all the way out here?" 'Twas the aristocratic man's voice. He knew Blackburn? Nay!

"Chief and Lady Graham, good to see you."

Kristina's hopes fell further and further as she listened to the jovial exchange between the two men.

"Are you well, lass?" Lady Graham asked from what sounded like two feet away.

She faced the woman and shook her head.

"Are you alone? Who are you?"

"Lady Kristina MacQueen." Could she ask this woman for help? Obviously her husband was friends with Blackburn, so likely she would get no help from that quarter. Still, she had to try. She lowered her voice. "I've been taken hostage."

"What?" the woman asked from a closer distance.

"I see you've met my ward," Blackburn announced and moved in behind Kristina's bench. "My sister-in-law. She's a pitiful little thing, but sweet."

Bastard! Kristina wanted no one's pity.

"Good heavens, what happened to her face?" Lady Graham asked.

Kristina narrowed her eyes, wanting to tell her the blackguard behind her had done the deed.

"She got injured in the midst of battle a couple of years ago. Blinded, too. Poor lass," Blackburn said in a grave tone.

What a liar.

Blackburn laid a hand on her shoulder, gripping it too tightly. "We've located my wife and are going now to rescue her and bring her home."

"Oh, that is good news. Your wife disappeared some time ago, did she not?" Laird Graham asked.

"Indeed. Abducted by brigands. Thank the saints, she's fine. We shall have a happy reunion and all will be well."

Blackburn gave her shoulder one final squeeze, then the two men walked away talking. The lady said not another word to her, although Kristina couldn't tell where she'd gone. Blast! Her one and only opportunity to escape was gone.

"Here you are, m'lady," Ralston said. "Roasted venison, cheese, bread and ale. And a napkin for you. I noticed you didn't have a knife so I've already cut up the meat for you."

Her throat tightened and she almost burst into tears, but finally managed to speak. "I thank you for your kindness." He was indeed thoughtful to cut the meat and provide her a napkin, for she often dropped food or made messes.

"My pleasure." Ralston sat down on the opposite side of the table.

After they ate for a few moments, footsteps approached.

"What do you think you're doing?" Red Holme's insidious voice demanded.

A frisson of fear chilled her. Was he talking to her?

"Go eat over there, Ralston. I'm eating with the lady."

"The chief asked me to guard her," Ralston growled.

"I'm your commanding officer and I'm ordering you to eat over there!"

Bastard! Would he not even allow her to eat in peace?

Tension and anger was thick in the air as Ralston arose, took his food and left.

The opposite bench creaked as Holme sat down. "Eat up, Kristina. We're leaving soon."

The disgust and nausea returned, taking her appetite. But she knew she had to eat and maintain her strength. If she grew weak, she wouldn't be able to defend herself.

Ignoring the knave as best she could, she inched her fingers close to the trencher again and found the chunk of bread. It smelled fresh-baked. She picked it up, tore off a bite and pushed it into her mouth. Mayhap it would soothe her roiling stomach.

"Would you like for me to feed you, lass?" Holme snickered.

"Nay. I'm perfectly capable of eating." Even so, she hated when people watched her. Carefully moving her hands, she located a small piece of cheese and put it into her mouth. If it hadn't been such a long time since she'd eaten, she would refuse now. She was famished and didn't know when they would stop to eat again.

Apparently Holme was eating stew, and the scarfing sounds he made reminded her of a pig in a trough.

Trying to put him from her mind, she picked up a sliver of the roasted venison. It was still warm and smelled delicious. She placed it in her mouth and chewed, finding it tender, smoky and flavored with herbs and spices. She savored the tasty morsel.

"Eating like a wee bird, are you, lass?"

Why couldn't the boar mind his own business?

"'Tis too bad you lost your great beauty when your face was cut," he said. "Not so proud and haughty now, are you?" He chuckled with a mouth full of food while he chewed. For the first time, she was glad she couldn't see him. No doubt he looked as disgusting as he sounded.

She had never been haughty; she'd simply refused his advances. Paying him no heed, she drank the ale and ate as quickly as she could, focusing on her own survival and trying to figure out a way to help Anna, rather than become the bait to her capture.

A quarter hour later, Blackburn announced that it was time to travel. Holme left the table and she couldn't tell where he'd gone until she heard him murmuring low to Blackburn. The words were unclear, but a moment later he returned, his boots thudding—she was starting to recognize the distinct sound of them. He grasped her arm and pulled her up.

"The chief has put me in charge of you now, Kristina."

Saints! She suspected her life was about to get even more difficult. Besides that, what had given him the impression he could call her by her given name? They were certainly not friends.

Clamping her teeth together to keep her anger in, she allowed him to lead her from the tavern. She didn't know where Ralston was, but she prayed he was nearby, keeping an eye on Holme.

"Wait," Blackburn said when they were near the horses. "Kristina, I saw what you did in there. Trying to gain help from Lady Graham. If you attempt to talk to anyone else, you'll regret it. Once I have Anna back—and I will have her back—I'll beat her senseless and make you listen. Do you understand me? Anything you do to escape me will only cause your sister more pain."

Kristina felt the blood drain from her face. Ice water flooded her veins. She shook her head, tears filling her eyes. Blackburn knew well how to control her, for she would do anything to keep her sister safe.

CHAPTER FOUR

Red Holme eyed the blind lass riding beside him. 'Twas bizarre that she could ride a horse and not see where she was going. He was holding the bridle, but still... he was not entirely certain she couldn't see a little. Sometimes it seemed as if she was staring at him... straight into his eyes and into his soul. It felt unnatural.

He snorted, laughing at himself for the ridiculous thoughts.

Despite the scar on her face, Kristina still roused keen lust in him, as she always had. He yearned to wrap those long blond curls around his fingers and hold her down so he could take her any way and every way possible.

But from the first time he'd met her, she had treated him like bog scum. How snobbish she'd been, her nose upturned like a princess, golden earrings dangling from her ears. She still held that regal air, her spine straight as an arrow, but now her fine clothing was splattered with mud, and he saw no gold upon her.

It thrilled him to see her brought down to his level... lower than him, now that she was their hostage and couldn't see besides. He grinned. Somewhere along this trip he would take from her what he wanted. Once he'd humiliated her as she had him, he would be satisfied.

Blackburn didn't care about her beyond what leverage she provided to get his precious wife back. Kristina was naught but a pawn.

Blackburn veered off the trail and toward a grassy field near a loch. "Halt here!"

Holme muttered a curse under his breath. He was sick to death of following Blackburn's orders. The man was a bastard nobody, never meant to be a chief. Holme, on the other hand, was the legitimate son of the former MacKillican chief. But the title and lands of his father had been taken away by the king for a minor infraction. He'd been forced to drop his true name and take on a false one, else be arrested for the part he'd played in the battle more than ten years ago, just before the king had granted the land to another clan.

Holme was the one who was supposed to be a chief, not Blackburn… although of a different clan. Most of the men of the MacKillican clan were either dead or dispersed throughout the countryside. He retained some loyal friends from his own clan who now worked as guards for Blackburn—Dobson, Fordyce, Mungo, and Scroggie. Although the four were fearsome warriors, they were not enough to help him lay siege to Rhodie Castle, and he did not have enough coin to hire more men. Even if he did take back the castle he'd grown up in, the king would send out forces to kill him and anyone who followed him.

Still… sometimes, he would just love to have some revenge, even if it cost him his life. He was starting to realize being some other man's servant was a fate worse than death. His da would think him the lowest of cowards for not at least trying to regain their castle or to seek revenge against the thieves who now held it and who'd killed his da.

After Holme swung down from his horse, he was disappointed to find that Kristina had already dismounted as well. He'd wanted to grasp hold of her and lift her down, mayhap run his hand over her breast.

"Ralston?" Kristina called out.

"Why are you calling him?" Holme was sick of Ralston sticking by her like a leech, getting in his way.

She turned to Holme, one side of her face immaculately beautiful with fair, smooth skin, and the other side marred by a puckered, thick pink line. Her blue eyes were directed toward him, but unfocused. An unnerving chill ran through him.

"I must use the bushes," she said.

Imagining her hiking up her skirts in the middle of the field for everyone to see, Holme chuckled. Aye, he would love to see that. "Come. I'll help you." He clutched her arm.

She struggled to free herself from his hold. "Nay! Unhand me!"

Her forceful, demanding tone only aroused him more, but he released her. There were too many people around now, anyway. "Ralston, aye?" Holme asked. "Did you give him a wee peek earlier? Maybe you wish to drag him off into the bushes for some sport."

Her cheeks reddened. "Don't be ridiculous!"

Young Ralston approached, little more than a lad, 'haps in his early twenties, but he was brawny and strong. 'Twas why Blackburn had hired him. "Is everything all right, m'lady?"

"Nay, 'tis not. I have need of the privacy of the bushes again. Would you help me?"

"Of course. I see some just over there beyond the field. I'll stand guard." He took her hand and placed it around his bent elbow.

"Hold on there, Ralston," Holme said, annoyance spurring him. "She's no longer your charge. Blackburn wishes me to guard her."

The young man's blue eyes turned hard as ice. "You're harassing her and trying to take advantage."

"Is that what you think, wee pup? 'Haps you forgot I far outrank you."

Ralston clenched his jaw. "The chief wishes the lady kept safe until we reach the castle where his wife is being held."

Annoyance rising to the surface, Holme grasped Kristina's other arm. "I'll keep her safe in the bushes. Have no worries."

"Take your hands off her!" Ralston growled.

Dark rage near consumed Holme. "How dare you think to order me about? I am your commander!"

"What's the quarrel about?" Blackburn demanded, storming toward them.

"I'm merely guarding the lady, as you asked." Holme ground his teeth. If Blackburn weren't here, he'd dirk Ralston and be done with it.

"He's harassing her," Ralston said. "Not allowing her privacy to use the bushes."

Holme forced himself to chuckle, despite wanting to run both men through. "You sound like a whiny bairn, Ralston. I have far more experience in protecting ladies than you do."

"I beg of you, chief, allow me to guard her," Ralston said. "I'll keep her safer."

"Very well," Blackburn said. "I want her in good health when we reach Bearach. No bruises or cuts. If I see any on her I'll cut you both down!" Blackburn strode away.

"Watch yourself, Ralston," Holme said through clenched teeth.

"You may find a dirk in your back soon." He walked a few steps away, trying to keep his rage under control.

"Come, m'lady." Ralston wrapped her hand around his elbow.

"He is a beast," Kristina hissed in a whisper as Ralston led her away.

Eyes narrowed, Holme watched them walk up the hill toward the bushes at the edge of the field. "Beast, huh?" he muttered, then spat on the ground. He would show her just how much of a beast he could be, no cuts or bruises necessary.

After riding for several more hours up and down hills, through the sharp, cold wind, Kristina was almost ready to topple from her horse when Blackburn yelled, "Halt! We make camp here!"

"Thank the saints," she whispered.

She could smell naught but the fresh air and pine forests, nor hear anything except a few birds and the distant roar of a red deer stag. 'Twas obvious to her they were deep in the Highlands now. The autumn air had grown colder, and a light mist hissed through the air. She was thankful she'd had the foresight to put on two layers of her warmest clothing before being taken hostage.

She dismounted and heard Ralston approaching. She'd started to recognize his footsteps, lighter and stealthier than some of the other men. "Where are we? Is there a village close by?"

"Nay," Ralston said. "We're going to camp in this field near the loch."

She was too exhausted to care. She simply wanted to lie down and sleep.

While she made use of the bushes, she felt a rock beneath her leather boot. She picked it up, finding it to be oval shaped, like an egg, except larger—the perfect size to fit into her hand for a weapon. It also fit into her pouch, where she slid it. She still had her knife, but she feared it was not long or sturdy enough to do any damage to a man wearing leather armor, unless she could slit his throat. Not that she wanted to kill anyone, but she did not like the threatening, sinister tone Holme used with her. Who knew when he might get violent with her? Anytime she was near him, she felt tension and aggression emanating from him, especially after he and Ralston had argued.

She stood, straightened her clothing and carefully stepped forward. "Ralston, I'm finished."

After a moment, his footsteps approached, rustling in the grass. "M'lady." He took her arm, then guided her across the field. "If you wish, you can sit on this stone while the men pitch your tent."

Why was he so kind to her when all the other men in this party either were brutes or never spoke to her?

"I can't tell you how much I appreciate your help." Tears pricked her eyes. She didn't know what she would do without him.

"'Tis no bother at all."

She sat, finding the stone about two feet in height, flat on top, and wet from the light mist. 'Twas unfortunate the stone was not large enough to lie down upon. Leaning forward, she rested her head on her folded arms, hoping she wouldn't drop off to sleep and topple to the ground.

She said a prayer of thanks for her continued safety, then prayed for Ralston because he was so considerate, and also for Anna's well-being. Imagining Anna securely ensconced in a castle, she drifted toward sleep.

"M'lady?" Ralston's voice startled her from the drowsy reverie, and she sat up. "You can get into the tent now."

"Sounds heavenly. Will you be sleeping nearby?" she whispered, hoping Holme wouldn't hear her. "I would feel safer if you were."

"Aye, just beside your tent, but I must also take my turn at watch sometime during the night and patrol the perimeter of the camp. But I will keep an eye on your tent."

"I'm so grateful to you." She wanted to give him a reward once this journey was done, but she had little to offer him. Her mother's gold earrings were the only thing of value she had, but she could not give them up.

After he guided her toward the tent, she crawled inside to lie down out of the mist and cold. Pulling the smooth rock from her pouch, she held it in her hand. It gave her a small measure of comfort, like a talisman. She would keep it always to remind her of this arduous journey.

What seemed only moments later, Ralston awoke her to give her a bannock, some roasted rabbit and a cup of fresh, cold water. She must have been asleep for an hour or more without even realizing it, if they'd had time to hunt rabbits and roast them for supper.

Ralston seemed a good man, and she trusted him to protect her while she slept. She liked the fact that she reminded him of his sister, but she was sad that he'd lost her. Mayhap she could be his new sister. She'd always wanted an older brother and had thought she might feel safer if she had one.

Her older sister was near as tough as a man... at least, emotionally she was. Physically, of course, she was petite and had been no match for Blackburn when he'd shoved her down two years prior and caused her to have a miscarriage. He'd wished to kill the former chief's heir before he could be born. The bairn, though, had been a wee lass. No doubt Anna still grieved the terrible loss. How she wished she could be with her sister and embrace her. Tears pricked her eyes and tightened her throat, making it difficult to swallow the food. She wiped her eyes on her sleeve. "You must grow tough, Kristina," she whispered.

After eating, she became drowsy, lay down amid the blankets and dropped back to sleep. Her bizarre dreams about riding a horse endlessly turned to nightmares, and suddenly her mother appeared before her in a swirl of golden light.

Kristina! Her mother yelled within the dream, her tone alarmed.

Heart pounding, Kristina startled awake to find someone crawling into the tent. "Who are you?"

When no answer came, she sniffed the air and detected Holme's body odor. Panic near stole her breath, but she managed to scream, searching the blanket beside her for the rock she'd dropped during her sleep.

"Be quiet," he growled low, then plastered his disgusting mouth to hers, his beard scratching her face.

Her fingers touched the rock and she clasped it in her palm. She slammed it against his head, then kicked and shoved at him, managing to get out another brief yell for help.

"Ow, you little bitch," he seethed.

"What's going on?" That sounded like Ralston.

"Help!"

"You bastard!" Ralston yelled.

Holme was dragged off her, and he finally let go. The sounds of fists pounding against flesh followed, along with scuffling, growls and curses.

Dear lord, she hoped Holme didn't kill Ralston. He was the only kind man in this group of ruffians.

"Halt!" Blackburn commanded somewhere outside the tent. "Cease your fighting! Or you'll both be finding yourselves dangling from yon tree!"

Holme continued his curses and threats against Ralston.

"Stand down, Holme," Blackburn ordered. "And stay away from the lass until I have my wife back. After that, I don't care what you do to her." Footsteps tromped closer. "Kristina?"

If she pretended injury, would Blackburn treat her better and keep that beast away from her? She lay silent and still as if passed out.

"Bring a lantern." Blackburn opened the tent flap. "If you've killed her, Holme, I'll string you up by the neck! She's the only leverage I have."

"I didn't kill her."

Soon, a lantern rattled nearby and she smelled the burning fat of the tallow candle. The heat of it warmed her skin.

"Kristina?" Blackburn shoved roughly at her shoulder.

She frowned, pretending to awaken, pressed a hand to her head and moaned.

"Are you awake?"

"Aye," she mumbled.

"I think you'll survive." Blackburn left the tent. Outside, he said, "Holme, you ken what a frail lass she is. You could easily kill her. Be patient until we reach Bearach. In the meantime, I'm assigning Ralston to keep her alive."

Thank the saints.

Where was this Bearach he spoke of? She'd never heard of it. Although Blackburn was a knave, at least he would keep Holme away from her until they reached Anna. Still, she didn't want to be the bait that lured Anna from her safe hiding place—at least, she hoped Anna was safe.

After supper at the high table at Bearach Castle, Colin watched Neacal as he spoke quietly to his new love, Anna. Colin held back a grin. Such opposites they were. And yet when they were looking at each other, or talking quietly together, they lit up from within. Great love shone in their eyes and in their smiles. Who would've guessed Neacal would find a lady who looked and sang like an angel to pull him from the pit of tormented despair his life had become? Colin was incredibly happy for his friend.

Still, he could not deny he felt a wee bit envious of their romance. But at the same time, he was unsure whether he would ever want to find love again.

Colin's father, Chief Maitland Cameron, urged him to marry soon and had suggested several chiefs' daughters for him to consider. 'Twas not as if Colin was old at six and twenty. Of a certainty, he would have to marry and sire an heir eventually. But he didn't know if he could withstand having his heart chopped to bits and handed back to him on a silver platter again.

Every time he thought of his former betrothed, Lady Emma MacMillan, his gut knotted. He'd loved her to distraction. He still remembered how she'd made him feel. He'd been elated when she'd agreed to marry him. But when she'd called off the wedding, he'd felt as if he'd been caught beneath a rock-slide.

Colin didn't wish to discuss it with Neacal, especially since he'd found such a joyful love with Anna. But Colin couldn't deny he missed the feelings of excitement upon finding a lass he was drawn to. What if he never felt the intensity of passion and love again? What if he ever remained lonely? He hadn't revealed to anyone the depth of his pain from the rejection. It hadn't been that long ago, and he assumed in time he would forget about Emma. He held no ill will toward her and wished her happiness and good health.

Even though his da often urged him to go to gatherings, feasts, and dances to meet a future bride, he had been avoiding social events. Instead, he'd been focusing on a different type of clan alliances, ones that didn't require marriage to be a part of it. A sort of brotherhood of Highland clans in his area that might band together for the greater good. Less feuding and more cooperation. Too many lives were lost over silly conflicts.

'Twas true that some conflicts though, like the one Neacal now faced, were not silly in the least and they had to be opposed.

Anna arose from the table and headed for the stairs.

Neacal turned to him. "How about a wee dram in the solar?"

"Aye." Colin was tired of the music, dancing and noise of the great hall anyway. He followed Neacal from the room.

Once inside the solar, Colin closed the door while Neacal poured two small glasses of whisky.

Colin took the glass Neacal offered him, then raised it. "To you and the new love you've found. May you two ever be happy together."

They both drank.

"I thank you for your great wishes." Neacal set his glass on a small table, knelt before the fireplace and added peat. "What about you?"

Colin near groaned at that question. "What about me?"

Dusting off his hands, Neacal arose and eyed him. "You're normally in good cheer, but you looked gloomy at supper." Neacal gestured toward a chair near the hearth, then sat down in the one opposite.

Taking a seat, Colin wanted to mutter a curse. He'd hoped no one would notice his bleak mood. He certainly hadn't thought Neacal would, with his attention focused on Anna much of the time. Colin was rarely grumpy, but apparently he was feeling lonelier than he'd realized. Plus, he'd had another long day out patrolling for enemies with his men.

Colin forced a smile. "I'm well."

"I ken you are physically. You told me earlier that your da wishes you to marry and that you want to choose your own bride. Have you met any interesting ladies since I last saw you?"

Colin didn't want to discuss this now. But he'd never lied to Neacal and didn't intend to start now, regardless of how this subject grated.

"Aye. One."

Neacal eyed him expectantly. "And?"

Hell, he hated talking about feelings. But this was his best friend and foster brother. He trusted Neacal and didn't want to give the impression he was hiding anything. His friend might find out sooner or later anyway.

Colin shrugged. "She broke the betrothal, but 'tis naught to worry over."

"I didn't ken you were betrothed." Neacal frowned, looking concerned.

"You had far more important and traumatic things to deal with at the time."

"What happened? Who were you betrothed to?"

"Lady Emma MacMillan. Her clan would've been a strong ally." Cringing inwardly, Colin realized he was trying to disguise the reason he'd wanted to marry her in the first place.

Neacal raised a brow. "Are you certain it wasn't more than an alliance you lost?"

His friend was too damned perceptive. Colin blew out a breath, then sipped the whisky, feeling the burn all the way down his throat.

"Very well. If you must know, I loved her. She's beautiful, spirited and intelligent." Remembering her didn't hurt nearly as much now as it had several months ago. "A few weeks before the wedding, her father informed me she wished to call it off. After much pressure from me, her father finally revealed that an earl had fallen in love with Emma, and she with him. He offered for her. Since the man outranks me, and is wealthier besides, her father went along with her change of heart. He paid me a small recompense, but it didn't take away the sting of her rejection. Especially when she'd already told me she loved me. She must have been lying."

"'Tis a hellish situation. I wish you'd told me sooner."

Colin shrugged. "I would prefer to forget it and put it behind me." He'd kept his distance from marriageable ladies since. A war waged inside him. Should he marry a lady he didn't love simply to bear an heir—someone who couldn't hurt him—or should he risk his heart again by waiting for a lady he could fall in love with? Someone he might find blissful happiness with… or another bout of soul-rending rejection?

He hated thinking about it. In fact, he'd rather go to battle than mull it over. He'd much rather focus on the impending attack.

"Enough about me. When do you think Blackburn MacCromar and his men will arrive and attempt a siege?"

Three days earlier, Neacal's other enemies, MacDonald of Sleat and Chief Titus MacRankin—the man who had tortured Neacal—had joined forces and made a failed attempt at taking Bearach. Thank the saints, Neacal's and Colin's clans had suffered no loss of life. Their enemies hadn't fared so well. The night before, Sleat and MacRankin had been in a nearby village, then they'd vanished.

"They could show up at any time," Neacal said. "He'll not give up on wanting Anna back."

"What if MacCromar, MacRankin and Sleat show up at the same time?"

Neacal looked agonized of a sudden. "I've already thought of it. We'll be outnumbered."

Kristina and the MacCromars had been traveling for five days in much the same way they had the first day, except sometimes they took ferries along the lochs, the latest of which was Loch Shiel. They had then ridden on horseback another couple of hours. She prayed they reached their destination soon, for she didn't know how much more she could take.

Although Holme made snide remarks, threats and promises at every opportunity, he had not touched her again. Ralston stayed close by her, and each day he seemed more like a brother to her. He made sure she had food and water, as well as privacy when she needed it.

"We'll be arriving at Bearach Castle soon," Blackburn announced. "And I want all of you to obey my orders. Come, we'll talk over here. Ralston, you and Kristina stay over there."

She heard the noise of many men dismounting and trampling the grass and other vegetation, rocks crunching and clacking beneath their boots, then the low murmur of voices.

"What are they saying?" Kristina whispered. "Can you hear them or read their lips?"

"Nay," Ralston said. "But I ken he's going to use you as leverage to draw your sister out."

Even though she'd known it, panic grasped hold of her chest yet again. "What can I do? I don't want Anna to be hurt."

"I have no inkling. Damnation, here they come," Ralston murmured.

"Help her dismount," Blackburn ordered.

Kristina had no idea which man he spoke to, but one of the guards lifted her down from the saddle. What were they going to do? Icy fear raced along her veins as she stood vulnerable before them. Still, she maintained her upright posture and proud bearing.

"Here. Tie her hands and feet with this rope," Blackburn said.

Kristina's whole body tensed, the prickles of fear intensifying. "Nay. Why is that necessary?"

"Because I said so."

"I cannot see. How could I run away?" Tears pricked her eyes but she forced them back.

"You have no say in the matter! Do you not remember what

happened the last time you argued with me?"

Knave!

Two of the guards forced her hands together and bound them.

"Now, help her sit on the ground and tie her ankles," Blackburn said.

Damn him! Kristina didn't understand why he would need to do this… unless he was going to toss her in a loch.

"If you're going to drown me, at least be man enough to say so," she demanded, tears dripping from her eyes.

Several snickers followed. Blackburn laughed darkly. "I'm nay going to drown you, at least not until I have your sister bound and gagged on the horse in front of me. Once I have her, I don't care what happens to you."

Bastard! What could she do to prevent him from capturing Anna? He would treat her horribly—beat her and abuse her.

Once Kristina's ankles were tied, Blackburn said, "Throw her facedown over Ralston's lap."

"With all due respect, chief, why would you treat her this way? She is no danger to anyone."

"I didn't ask for your opinion, Ralston. Either keep your mouth shut and do your job, or you can turn over your weapons now and head back east on foot."

"Lift her up here," Ralston said, relenting.

One of the brawny guards flung her across the saddle and Ralston's legs. Pain shot through her stomach. Saints, he'd near knocked the breath from her. 'Twas the most uncomfortable position she'd ever been in. Despite the pain, she tried to inhale as deeply as possible.

"Damn the man," Ralston grumbled low, for her ears only. "I see no reason for this."

They rode a half hour farther and Blackburn yelled, "Fan out, men. Archers, ready your bows."

"We've arrived at the castle," Ralston told her.

"What does it look like?" she asked, trying to ignore the pain and discomfort of her position.

"It is made of dark stone and has high walls. It sits on a small island in a loch—"

"Quiet," Blackburn ordered through clenched teeth. "Holme, get her off the horse and make her be quiet."

"There's no need to—" Ralston began.

Someone slapped her hard on the arse.

She screamed. "Keep your hands off me!" She knew 'twas Holme who had done it.

He chuckled and dragged her from the horse. She screamed again. Suddenly she was upright, her feet on the ground and her head spinning from the quick change in position.

"Who is the lady?" a man yelled from the distance.

"I'm sure you must have guessed!" Blackburn called back. "Send my wife out to me and Lady Kristina will not be harmed."

Nay, please, Anna, stay inside.

"Kristina!" Good heavens… that was her sister's voice.

"Anna! Is it really you?" Kristina yelled.

"Aye. Release her at once, you blackguard!" Anna ordered.

Blackburn laughed, though there was no humor in it. "Lady Kristina wanted to travel with us to get you, my sweet. She misses her sister."

"Don't—" Kristina began, but a meaty hand clamped over her lips, muffling her warning.

"Shut your mouth," Holme growled into her ear.

Don't do it, Anna. Stay where you are, she wanted to scream, but couldn't. *Please God, don't let her come out here.*

"We'll come out!" the distant man called, the chief, she assumed.

Nay!

In the quiet, the sound of many horses' hooves pounding over the rocks and dirt reached her ears. They were not approaching from the castle but from the opposite direction. Was another warband coming upon them? Would they attack?

"Put Kristina on your horse and hold onto her tight," Blackburn said, sounding both riled and panicked. "Half of you guard the lady and half come with me." Several horses trotted past them.

"Hold her while I mount, then hand her up to me," Holme said.

A different guard latched his hands onto her and then lifted her to sit sideways before Holme. Ugh! She hated his stench. Even the strong salt-scented wind couldn't entirely squelch it.

She listened, trying to figure out what was happening. "Where is Ralston?"

"Don't worry about him," Holme said.

Please, God, protect Ralston.

One of Blackburn's guards shouted, "Galleys approaching!"

This caused an uproar amongst the men and much yelling as they prepared for battle. She heard the name *MacKenzies* growled a few times.

Since she could see naught, all she could do was pray for Anna's safety and her own. "What's happening?"

"Be quiet and stay still," Holme snapped.

She heard someone else shout that near two hundred MacKenzies were advancing from the sea loch.

"Dear God, help us," she whispered. She couldn't keep count of how many clans were gathering here—MacCromars, MacDonalds, MacKenzies. This might be an all-out war, and she sat in the midst of it. Holme's grip on her tightened and his breathing quickened. He snarled curses. His horse danced about nervously beneath them, jostling her.

"Do you see my sister?" she asked.

"I said to shut your mouth." Cold metal touched the side of her neck. "Since you can't see, I'll tell you... I have a knife against your throat. Any of the MacDonalds or MacKenzies come near us and you're dead."

Kristina closed her eyes and prayed for a miracle, tears streaming down her cheeks.

War cries sounded in the distance. Swords clanged together. The start of the battle.

"Saints preserve us," Kristina whispered, shivering against the fierce, cold sea wind.

"Damned MacDonalds," Holme grumbled.

Men shouted and groaned in agony and the clash of metal continued, coming closer and closer.

CHAPTER FIVE

Colin and six of his men slipped out Bearach Castle's postern gate and down to a couple of two-oared boats at the shore, on the back side of the castle. Strong wind from the west blasted them as they boarded the rocking boats.

He had to rescue Anna's blind sister before the battle broke out and before the impending gale struck. He glanced up. The clouds were as dark as gloaming, predicting a fearsome storm.

What clawed at his soul like great talons was that Lady Kristina was probably terrified, and not being able to see would make that fear a hundred times worse.

"We'll row around behind that wee island. They won't see us approaching the shore of the mainland around the bend behind those bushes." Colin pointed. It would take longer, but it would allow them to slip in unseen. "The approaching MacKenzies on their galleys will keep their attention."

Warton, looking rough and ready for battle, shoved the boats from the shore and into the water of Loch Moidart, then leapt aboard one of them. Warton was the son of his father's swordbearer or war leader. They had grown up together and he would one day serve in the same position for Colin.

A man on each boat rowed, propelling the wherries through the turbulent water, which was rapidly rising from the tide and the storm surge. They traveled around the small, bush-covered island.

Soon they arrived at the mainland shore, around the bend from the battle. They quietly alighted, their weapons and targes in hand. He hoped that the MacCromars would be so engaged in the battle they wouldn't notice Colin and his men. They ran through the bushes, then crouched behind gorse and peered out.

"She is there." Colin pointed. On horseback, one of Blackburn's men held her, a dirk to her throat. He was a large, burly man with bright-red hair and a matching bushy beard. "I'll need two of you to circle around behind her captor, then each of you grab an arm. He looks strong. Don't underestimate him. At all costs, make sure he doesn't cut the lady with that knife. When you have his arms pinioned, I'll take Lady Kristina from him." Colin placed his targe on the ground, for he wouldn't need it, and shoved his sword into the scabbard. "The rest of you, fight off the other men and serve as reinforcements."

"Aye." Warton put his weapons away. "I'll grab the bastard's knife hand. Rusty, you grab his left arm."

"Aye."

These two were just as strong and braw as Blackburn's man. Colin had much confidence in them. They crept around through the bushes behind the lady's captor. When Colin saw them slipping closer to the whoreson, he proceeded in that direction.

Rusty and Warton leapt onto the man, grabbing his arms before he knew what was going on. Once the knife was well away from Kristina's throat, Colin ran forward and caught her as she slid from the man's lap. The horse danced beneath them, almost stamping on Colin's foot.

He leapt out of the way.

Lady Kristina screamed and struggled within his arms. Colin threw her over his shoulder and ran with her, away from the battle. He glanced back to see Warton and Rusty dragging the ginger-haired man from his horse. The other Camerons hung back, defending Warton and Rusty from enemies.

"Unhand me!" The woman over his shoulder kicked and elbowed him.

Once they were behind the bushes, Colin pulled her from his shoulder and held her in his arms. "I'm sorry to treat you like a sack of oats, Lady Kristina, but I'm here to help you. I'm Colin Cameron. I'm to take you to your sister."

She gasped and stilled. "What? Anna? Where is she?"

"Inside the castle."

Tears sparkled in her blue eyes. "Oh, thank God she didn't come out."

"The chief wouldn't allow it." Colin peered out from between the bushes and saw that the large force of MacKenzies had fully joined in the battle, fighting on Neacal's side. The MacKenzie chief's younger brother was Neacal's brother-in-law. Thank the saints the MacDonalds of Moidart were no longer outnumbered.

Warton and Rusty approached, slipping quickly through the bushes with their weapons and targes.

"Damnation," Warton growled. "They've discovered our boats." Colin followed his gaze to see that three enemies waited on the shore where they'd disembarked. "Hell." Likely they had been patrolling the area. The bastards had already shoved one of the boats out into the rough water. They couldn't go back the way they'd come.

"Sir, you could keep her hidden here while we take care of them," Warton said.

Even if his men did defeat these enemies, the water was becoming extremely choppy because of the storm. It was too great a risk for Kristina.

"Nay, leave them." Colin glanced up at the ever darkening sky. "The storm is coming in quickly. The water is too dangerous now. Retrieve the rest of our men. I'll need all of you to help protect her. Rusty will stay with me."

"Aye." Warton trotted off to get the other men.

"The battle is raging," Rusty said, looking between the gorse limbs toward the sandbar causeway linking the castle to the mainland.

"Aye." Colin peered out, seeing that more and more warriors from both sides were joining the fray. He had no quick and easy way to get the lass back inside the castle and out of harm's way.

"Can you untie my hands and feet?" Kristina asked.

"Of course." He'd been too focused on keeping her safe to think about her being bound. He placed her on the ground and, using his dirk, carefully cut the thin ropes. "Are you hurt?"

"Nay. I thank you." She rubbed her reddish, chafed wrists.

"'Tis too dangerous for us to take you to the castle at the moment." But where could he take her? He knew of only one place.

Warton and the rest of his men crept quietly through the bushes and joined them. Colin was glad to see none of them were injured. Thankfully, the enemies near the shore hadn't spotted them yet.

"Come." Colin lifted Kristina into his arms again and slipped into the wood.

"Where are we going?" Warton asked quietly.

"I know a decent hiding place. Rusty, you and Patrick make sure no one follows us."

"Aye."

As they crept across the pine needles and the spongy forest floor, Colin glanced down at Kristina. 'Twas true she had a wide, puckered pink scar on her left cheek, but she was beautiful in spite of it. Or maybe because of it, for it gave her face character. It showed she had lived through a hellish experience and grown stronger because of it.

"Are you sure you're all right, Lady Kristina?"

Her unseeing blue eyes shifted toward his voice but remained unfocused. "Aye, I merely have some bruises and scrapes."

Unable to imagine what she'd endured, he admired her strength and fortitude. "You must have been terrified these last few days."

She nodded, her brow furrowed. "It has been an ordeal."

"And not being able to see must have made it far harder on you."

"Aye." She pulled her cowl over her head, hiding her face more. Mayhap he shouldn't have mentioned her blindness. Did it make her uncomfortable? Surely, she would expect that Anna had told him of her condition.

"You can relax now. We'll protect you with our lives." Colin strode faster amid the pine trees, increasing the distance between Blackburn's men and her.

"I thank you."

All Kristina could do at the moment was hold on and listen to the sounds of battle growing fainter behind them as this strong warrior carried her through what smelled like a pine forest. It was a cool, dank place that was somewhat sheltered from the wind. The men's footsteps on the forest floor were quiet thumps. She heard a few men moving along behind them and one in front.

They kept their voices low as they communicated in a West Highland dialect of Gaelic. Being from the east, she found Colin's voice and accent unusual and appealing. His deep, confident voice brushed over her senses like rich velvet. She wished more than anything she could look into his eyes. What color were they? Would she see compassion there, or pity? His voice sounded kind and concerned.

His arms, holding her securely, felt iron-hard and strong. When she turned her face toward him, his pleasant, masculine scent took over, far more appealing than the scent of pine needles. He smelled of some sort of spicy masculine soap.

She held on tightly around his neck, helping as much as she could. She hated appearing a helpless female.

"Where are we going?" she asked.

"To a good hiding place," Colin said quietly.

She knew that, but she wanted to know where, specifically.

He started climbing a hill or mountain. His breathing increased and his heart beat faster and harder against her, but his pace did not slow. The ride for her was much bumpier but she didn't mind. She thanked God for her rescuer.

Though mayhap 'twas sacrilege, she hoped Blackburn was killed in battle for what he'd done to her and Anna. He was the vilest and most vicious man she had ever encountered, and Holme wasn't much better.

After a few minutes of climbing farther and farther up what must have been a steep mountain, Colin said, "Here we are." He slowed and his breathing eased. 'Twas clear to her the ground was flat now.

She sniffed, drawing dank, musty air into her lungs. They were no longer outside, for the men's voices echoed and the wind was blocked.

"Where are we?" she asked.

"In a cave," Colin said.

"Is it dark? How large is it?"

"Aye, 'tis very dim in here. This part of the cave is about twenty by thirty feet. It has a low ceiling."

She was glad he had described it for her. As children, she and Anna had played in a cave while visiting their grandmother, near the east coast. She'd always had a fondness for caves.

"Can you stand?" Colin asked.

"Aye."

He lowered her feet to the uneven cave floor and, still holding her hand, steadied her.

Her sore, stiff legs ached from all the horseback riding. Certainly, reclining in Colin's arms had been more comfortable, but her arms were tired from holding on around his neck so tightly. Besides, she was certain he had to be exhausted from carrying her.

Through her leather boots, she felt the hard-packed dirt floor beneath her feet, along with a few pebbles.

"Will you be all right standing here alone for a few minutes?" he asked.

"Of course." Though she didn't want to, she released his warm, strong hand. She still missed her cane, but she was starting to grow used to not having it. Once she arrived at the castle, 'haps Anna could convince one of the craftsmen to carve a long, lightweight cane for her so she could move about on her own.

Colin talked quietly with his men near the cave's entrance. She caught some of their words because her hearing had grown keener since she'd lost her sight. He told one man where to position all the other men for guarding the cave. Was he a chief? If not, how did he have a small army at his command?

"Aye, sir." Footsteps hastened from the cave and outside.

All grew quiet, but she still sensed Colin nearby. Was he staring at her? She pulled the cowl more firmly over her head to hide the scar on the side of her face. Of course, he had already seen it, but she didn't want him studying every detail.

His firm and confident footsteps approached. "All is well now, Lady Kristina. My men are guarding the entrance to the cave and the perimeter."

"I thank you for protecting me. Are you a laird?"

"My father is chief of Clan Cameron."

"Are you his heir?"

"Indeed."

"Oh." Saints, he was an important man then. What was he doing risking life and limb to rescue her? Was he that selfless or did he simply love action? "What should I call you?"

"Colin." The smile came through in his tone, making her wish she could see him. Was he a handsome man? Imagining what he might look like, she felt her face heat. What difference did it make? She was the last person to judge others on looks. To her, his kindness was far more attractive than the bonniest masculine face she'd ever seen.

"Colin," she repeated. "Please call me Kristina."

"'Twould be my pleasure."

Had she only imagined the sensuality in his deep, rumbling tone when he'd said those words? Her face felt warmer than it should. Admittedly, she knew little about men and she'd scarcely had any interaction with decent, honorable men her since her injuries. Prior to that, she'd been so young she'd only talked to a few.

"Can you tell me... is Anna safe?" she asked.

"Aye, she's inside Bearach Castle, and the walls are heavily guarded."

"Thank the saints. I always worry over her, even though she is the older sister."

"Why do you two not stay together?"

"She chose to leave in order to draw Blackburn away. She didn't think he would bother with me. I've been staying with our aunt and uncle in Stirling. If Anna had stayed with me, Blackburn could've easily guessed where she was."

"I see. Well, you're both incredibly brave ladies."

Though the admiring tone of his voice made Kristina's heart swell with gratitude, she shrugged modestly. "I don't know about that. We're simply trying to survive."

"You've had a difficult time of it."

Was he referring to her scarred face? 'Twas her main insecurity for, even more than her blindness, it made her unattractive and undesirable.

The grit beneath Colin's boots crunched as he took a step closer. "Did Blackburn harm you in any way?"

Why was he asking again? Did he not believe what she'd said before? "Not this time," she said. "I'm sore from the days of riding, and I have a few scrapes and bruises, but no serious injuries."

"Neither he nor his men took advantage?"

She lowered her burning face. "Red Holme tried to." Her stomach knotted as she recalled the night the bastard had crawled into her tent. "But Blackburn set Ralston to guard me." Renewed panic spiked her heart rate. "Good heavens, I hope Ralston doesn't get injured or killed in the battle." He'd been so kind to her when all the others had been nasty. Tears pricked her eyes.

"You're close to this Ralston, then?" Colin's voice held a slight edge. "Is he a good man?"

"I think so, better than the rest, anyway. He told me I reminded him of his sister." She gave a sad smile. "No one has ever told me that before. I felt safer when he was near. He and Holme got into a fight while he was defending me."

"Is Holme the man who was holding a knife to your throat out there?"

"Aye, he's Blackburn's war leader and second-in-command. A madman. Aside from him, no man wants..." Remembering she was talking to a stranger, she pressed her lips together and dropped her chin. Even though it should be obvious why no man wanted to touch her—nor, thankfully, take advantage—at times she could not bring herself to say the words, especially to someone she'd just met. But Colin didn't seem a stranger anymore. How could she have grown used to him so quickly?

"What?" Colin stepped closer.

She lifted her chin, forcing herself to be confident. "Most men keep their distance. Fortunately, one glance at my face quickly douses the flame of their lusts," she said firmly. Why be afraid to state the obvious truth?

"'Tis ridiculous," he muttered.

She pulled back her cowl a bit. "In case you didn't notice, I have a scar on my face." 'Haps it was darker outside than she'd realized.

"So? You're still an incredibly beautiful lady," he said in a husky, irritable tone.

Her breath halted. Could he be serious? No man had complimented her looks since she'd acquired the scar. Though she'd never seen it herself, every day she felt how jagged and deep it was. Unexpected tears burned her eyes, but she blinked against them, turning away from him.

"You're in need of spectacles, then?" she asked.

He gave a brief laugh. "Nay. My vision is perfect."

"'Tis most surely pitch-black in this cave, as well as outside," she said dryly.

"Nay."

She frowned, trying to figure him out. She did not like to be teased and toyed with. "What do you hope to gain by lying to me?"

"I'm not lying." His voice was almost a growl.

Running footsteps entered the cave and one of his men spoke, breathing hard. "Here is some food I took from the enemy's saddlebags while they were busy fighting. I thought the lady might be hungry."

"'Twas very brave and canny of you, Ethan," Colin said. "I'm certain she must be."

In truth, she was famished. Blackburn had only allowed her a small piece of bread that morn. When Ralston had tried to slip her more, he'd been reprimanded.

"Please bring some fresh water for her if you can find a spring or a clean stream flowing down from the mountain."

When Ethan's footsteps retreated, Colin gently took her hand in his warm one. Tingles spread from his touch. "Here's a bannock." His voice was so deep and comforting, she shivered. He placed an oatcake into her hand.

"Are you certain 'tis not poisoned?"

"I'll try a bite of this one." He sniffed loudly, then she heard his teeth clicking together as he chewed. "Seems fine to me. They had the food for their own use, so likely 'tis safe."

She smelled the oatcake as well and detected no odd odors about it, although it was turning stale. Once she'd eaten that, Colin handed her another bannock and a piece of dried venison. Though the meat was tough, the flavor was wonderfully smoky and salty.

"We can't build a fire to cook, even if we did hunt some wild game," he said. "The enemies would see the smoke and find us. Besides, I should be able to get you back to the castle soon, once the skirmish is over."

"I pray your allies are the victors. Will Blackburn's men be able to track us?"

"Nay, my men know how to cover our tracks and create a false trail that will lead them on a merry chase."

"That is clever." Relief allowed her muscles to relax as she took another bite of the dried meat.

"How much did Blackburn allow you to eat on the journey here?"

"At first he was generous, but as we ventured farther into the Highlands, the taverns were harder to find. Then supplies ran low, and he allowed me less and less."

Colin growled a Gaelic curse. "I hope Neacal runs him through."

"As do I." She knew from listening to Blackburn and his men that Neacal was the MacDonald chief who held the castle where Anna had taken refuge. He was the main one Blackburn wished to kill. "Is he a strong warrior?"

"Aye, Neacal is one of the best. He can take care of himself. He's my foster brother and good friend." Colin spoke with confidence and warmth. She could easily tell the two men were close.

"Will he continue to protect my sister?"

"Of course. The lady has enchanted him."

"She has?" Saints! Did he mean the MacDonald chief was smitten with Anna?

Colin chuckled, but she did not know what was funny.

"In what way?" Kristina had to find out more.

"As I'm sure you ken, Anna has a remarkable singing voice."

"Aye." Kristina smiled, remembering her perfect intonation. "I wish I could hear her sing now." She wanted to ask more about Anna's association with the MacDonald chief, but felt a bit shy and out of her element. Maybe they were in love and that was why the chief was willing to go to war for her. Good heavens, what if they were lovers? She would much rather ask her sister about it. She did not feel comfortable talking to Colin about such intimacies.

CHAPTER SIX

Colin had savored Lady Kristina's smile and wished to see it again. Talk about enchanted... he was. And transfixed. The scar she was so worried about did not disfigure her. Not in the way she thought. He had grown used to facial scars since being around Neacal. Besides, Colin had plenty on his own body, though not on his face. All warriors possessed scars, and wore them like medals of honor. That's how he saw her... as a wee female warrior. It wasn't simply her scar, but her strength of spirit. Her courage came through in the words she spoke and her confident bearing. She was a tough lady.

"Do you sing?" he asked her.

"I used to."

He'd hoped she would smile again, but instead, she appeared melancholy. "I hope to hear you sing, too, then."

The corners of her exquisite lips turned down, and she lowered her chin. "It has been a long time. I'm out of practice."

"Once we get back to the castle and you are reunited with your sister, hopefully she can convince you to join her in a song."

Another small smile brightened Kristina's face. That was it. The thought of being with Anna made her smile. He could easily see how much she loved her sister. "Aye, 'haps," she said.

"Would you like to sit? I didn't bring an extra plaid, so you'll have to sit on the dirt floor until I find one for you."

"I'm certain my clothing is already dirty, so it won't matter. I'm tired."

"I hope to get you back to the castle soon. You need rest." He took her hands, which were surprisingly cold, and helped her sit on one of the cleaner spots.

"Your hands are chilled." He crouched, cupping her small

hands between his larger ones, trying to warm them.

She shivered. "Well... this cave is cold. And the wind outside has picked up. Do you hear how it roars?"

"Aye. I think we'll have an early winter." Since they'd traveled from the castle by rowboat and had planned to return straightaway, they had brought no supplies. Releasing her, he stood and searched the cave, finding nothing except rocks and dirt in this chamber. He doubted the two chambers farther back contained anything more. "I'll see if one of the men has a spare plaid." He strode outside into the wind where the trees tossed violently and the sky was as dark as gloaming. Several of his men trotted up the hill toward the cave.

"I found some water." Ethan held the wineskin aloft.

"Can you give some to the lady?"

His boyish face lit up. "Aye. With pleasure."

Colin frowned after Ethan as he hastened into the cave. Clearly Colin was not the only one who had noticed her beauty.

"The strong gale is close," Rusty said, his long russet hair blowing in the wind.

Colin nodded. "Do any of you have a spare plaid? Lady Kristina is cold."

They shook their heads, exchanging glances as if they feared he'd order one of them to hand over his plaid. "Nay."

"'Haps you could give her yours." Warton's craggy face split into a rascally grin.

Colin ignored the teasing. Though he didn't want to disrespect the lady by being half naked around her, the truth was she couldn't see him. Unfortunately. And his long linen shirt did reach almost to his knees.

"'Tis the only solution." Colin removed his belt and his plaid fell from its pleats.

Warton chuckled. "Should've known you would get naked any time a bonny lass is around."

Colin raised a brow. Yet another man who thought Kristina was attractive. He could understand her insecurities about the scar, but he wished he could convince her of how gorgeous she was in spite of it. He had a feeling all his men thought so, too.

He buckled his belt back into place at his waist and glanced down at the tail of his shirt, just above his knees. "I'm covered well enough."

He took the loose plaid into the cave, knelt, and wrapped it around Kristina where she sat on the floor.

She shivered, hissing a breath between her teeth as she pulled his plaid tight about her. "I thank you. This is so warm." She closed her eyes, seeming to revel in the heat. "Wait." Her eyes popped open. "You were wearing this!"

"How could you know that?"

She hesitated. Even in the dimness he could see her blush as she averted her face. "You will need it in this weather." She started pulling off the plaid.

"Nay, keep it. I'm not cold." He wrapped it tight about her again. How had she known he'd been wearing it? Had she heard them talking outside the cave, even with the strong winds?

The lass was perceptive, even more so than those who could see. He would have to be more careful about what he said.

He would also have to guard his heart, lest she steal it away.

Kristina listened to the fearsome wind blowing outside the mouth of the cave, the pine limbs thrashing together, and the rain pouring down for a long while.

She wondered where Ralston was. Had he survived the battle? She hoped her sister was still safe inside the castle.

She snuggled down into Colin's plaid, his enticing masculine scent surrounding her. 'Twas both comforting and exciting.

The men's voices rumbled quietly in conversation within the cave. They were discussing who would head toward the castle after the storm, scouting to see if the enemies were gone. If 'twas still unsafe, a couple of them would take first watch. Ethan would go in search of more food once the wind and rain ceased.

A chilly mist blew into the cave and she once again felt cold, despite the plaid. 'Twas much cooler now than before the gale. Though it was October, it felt like winter.

After the winds quieted, some of the men exited the cave and all grew quiet. Footsteps moved toward her, leather boots against the packed earth, grit crunching.

"Are you still cold?" Colin's voice murmured right beside her. He must be crouching close.

Good heavens, she could drown in his deep voice. "Not terribly." But she couldn't stop the shiver that coursed through her at that moment.

"Aye, you are. Lie down."

His words surprised her, confused her, and she frowned. "Where?"

"Right where you are."

"Why?"

"I'll show you, if you but trust me."

Strangely, she did trust him, though she'd only known him for a few hours. He had saved her life and seemed an honest, forthright man. When she lay back on the hard floor, he stretched out beside her and spread the plaid over them both, shocking her. She gasped. "What are you—?"

"I don't mean any disrespect, but I have to get you warm now, lest you catch an ague. Turn toward me," he murmured.

Good heavens. His words were both commanding and caring, which gave her a warm tingle. When she faced him, he drew her against the hard wall of his chest and tucked her head beneath his chin. Though she was stunned speechless for a moment, his body was deliciously warm. She couldn't help but press herself tighter against him.

"Feels good," she whispered, basking in his heat. "You're like an oven."

"Aye." His deep voice now sounded gruffer. With his large hand on her back, he pulled her closer. "And you feel chilled to the bone."

"I get cold easily."

"I wish you had told me sooner."

Their murmured conversation seemed profoundly intimate and comforting to her. "I didn't want to bother you."

"You're not bothering me," he chided. "In addition to the cold, the past few days have been very demanding for you. Being taken hostage. Not enough food. Being attacked by a madman."

No man had ever held her like this and expressed concern for her well-being. His sentiments made the warm tenderness she felt toward him expand. He near overwhelmed her, both mentally and physically. She was amazed at how hard his body was. Her own was a mere soft feather in comparison. He felt like stone beneath her fingertips.

Colin blew out a breath. "What are you doing?"

Pausing, she realized she'd been stroking her fingers over the muscles of his back and exploring. "I was but..." She couldn't say *feeling of you.* "'Tis simply that you feel so hard, like a rock. I've never felt anything like it."

He gave a brief, rough chuckle.

Her head lay on his muscular upper arm, and her nose was pressed against his chest. He smelled so manly in a very appealing way. 'Twas all she could do to keep herself from humming out her enjoyment.

She drew in a deep breath through her nose for another whiff.

"What's wrong? Your breathing sounds odd," he said.

She grinned, wondering what would happen if she told him the truth. "You smell good."

He inhaled against the top of her head. "And so do you."

Was he lying, or only saying that because she'd commented on his scent? Either way, she was thankful now that, the previous day, the mistress of the inn in Glenfinnan had taken pity on her and assigned one of the chambermaids to help Kristina take a bath. She had not dared ask for either woman's help in escaping, lest Blackburn kill them. She had simply pretended to be Blackburn's sister-in-law and ward, as he'd claimed.

Don't think of the beast, she told herself. *Just enjoy this moment...* one of the most blissful she could remember. She felt so safe, warm and protected, lying here in Colin's arms. He had a caring and comforting feeling emanating from him. Was she only imagining it? Fantasizing and hoping? 'Twas ridiculous. He could not care for her already. They'd only just met. Some innate part of her told her she was not dreaming it up, that her impression was real. She relaxed into it and let go of her fears.

She had not slept well in days, not since Holme had tried to attack her in the middle of the night, and the exhaustion combined with Colin's delicious heat and comfort lulled her to sleep and into dreams.

Colin could not believe he lay in a cave with a fairy sleeping in his arms. Kristina felt so small, soft and slight, like a feathery bird with a broken wing. How could such profound strength of spirit lie within her?

He could not help but compare her to his former betrothed.

Lady Emma had not been so delicate feeling. Not that he had held her like this, lying down, but he had held her close enough to kiss her a few times. But 'twas not Lady Emma's lips he was thinking of kissing now.

Nay, indeed.

When arousal coiled slowly through him, stronger and tighter with each moment that passed, he felt like a depraved rogue. He drew in a slow, deep breath, trying to calm himself, but this only filled his awareness with her luscious female scent. She lured him like a fresh brambleberry pie... near irresistible.

Was Kristina an innocent? She had to be, given how she'd been sliding her fingers along his back earlier, almost as if she'd never felt a man before. He hoped she hadn't. He wanted to be the first to hold her, to kiss her... damnation! Why was he thinking of that? He had to cease such imaginings. He did not want to get entangled with another lady.

He hadn't been with a woman in a very long time. That was it. Hell, his body was letting him know loud and clear who and what it was interested in.

Once the idea of kissing her had sprung into his head, it wouldn't leave. The image turned into a full-blown fantasy. He could almost feel the smooth, hot wetness of her mouth against his own. He hungered to taste her lips, but he could not. He gritted his teeth against the heightened need.

She moved restlessly in his arms, brushing against him, making matters far worse. He stifled a groan, hoping she wouldn't feel what she'd done to him.

She had been asleep no more than a half hour when she started awake. "Oh." She froze and tried to draw away from him. "Where am I?"

"'Tis me. Colin. We're in a cave."

She let out a relieved breath, relaxing again. "I remember now." She was silent for a moment. "Do you have anything to drink? I'm thirsty."

"Aye." He reached above his head and took the wineskin Ethan had filled from the stream. "Here's some water."

Sitting up slightly, she swallowed two long gulps. "I thank you."

After taking a few sips himself, he recorked the wineskin and set it aside.

She snuggled closer and released a sigh against the upper part of his chest. "I feel better now," she whispered.

"I'm glad." Good lord, how was he supposed to tolerate her sighing against him with her warm breath while pressing her slim, curvy body against him? The soft mounds of her breasts flattening against his chest were driving him mad.

Unable to help himself, he sniffed her hair again. 'Twas not a soap scent but pure sweet female. His arousal grew and it took great effort for him to suppress a groan.

"I was going to wait and ask my sister, but... I'm too curious." Kristina sounded bright and merry of a sudden but kept her voice quiet as if 'twas a secret. "What of Anna and Chief MacDonald? Is he smitten with her?"

Colin grinned, remembering how clear Neacal had made his feelings for Anna. "Aye, he is. Very much so."

"And is she smitten with him?"

"I think so. You'll have to ask her. Neacal wants to marry her."

"Good heavens. In truth?" Her voice heightened with joy. "That's wonderful."

Absorbing her good cheer, he smiled. "Aye. I pray she will agree to the match. He deserves happiness more than anyone I know."

"As does Anna."

"They've both been through hellish times."

She nodded, then grew quiet. "If only they can survive Blackburn's attack."

Red Holme slipped through the pine thicket and gradually up the steep slope, which was more like a cliff in places. Four men quietly followed—loyal, trusted friends who had been in Blackburn's army, and before that, they'd traveled with him from the MacKillican clan more than ten years earlier.

During the fearsome gale storm, they had sheltered beneath a thick rock ledge, protecting themselves from any of the falling pine limbs or trees. Still, their clothes had been drenched by the cold, blowing rain.

Holme peered down at the plaid-clothed dead soldiers lying about everywhere between the wood and the castle in the distance. He was canny enough to know a lost cause when he saw one.

"Where the hell is Blackburn?" Holme whispered so as not to

draw the attention of any MacDonalds below.

"Looked like him rowing across the loch earlier," Dobson, the man closest to him, said.

Had Blackburn escaped, then? Did he still live?

The battle was over and they'd lost, even with the help of MacDonald of Sleat. In fact, that man was dead, along with most of his soldiers.

As Holme and his comrades watched from a distance, the few remaining MacCromars were disarmed. One of the victors talked to them, too far away to hear, and pointed out toward an island.

Mayhap Blackburn had rowed out there alone. Even if he had, Holme doubted the MacDonalds would let him live.

Holme didn't care about Blackburn. Aye, he'd been under Blackburn's command for over five years, but the bastard had always incensed him. Guarding Blackburn and serving as his war leader had been a good paying position, but by all appearances, that was over now.

Something else leapt to the forefront of his mind, something that ate away at him—Holme had recognized the whoreson who had grabbed Kristina from him. Holme had not seen him since the knave had been a lad of around fifteen or sixteen summers, and it had taken Holme a few minutes, with his mind working furiously, to figure out why that face looked so familiar.

'Twas Chief Cameron's eldest son, Colin. Thieving bastards, the lot of them! Fury raced over Holme anew, burning a trail from his face downward, making him clench his fists. Hate and battle lust threatened to burst from his chest.

"I ken the man who snatched Kristina from me and so do you," Holme growled low.

"What's his name?" Dobson asked.

"Colin Cameron." Holme gritted his teeth so tightly they ached.

"Damnation, man. His sire stole your birthright and your clan's castle."

"Aye, and killed Da. He's the son of my father's worst enemy. I can't allow this opportunity to pass me by." Finally, he had a purpose and a goal beyond surviving, beyond earning money.

"Which direction did he go?" Dobson narrowed his black eyes. "We'll hunt him down and put a dirk in his heart."

"'Tis what I plan to do." Holme gave a bitter half smile. "And then I can have the lass."

"Aye."

He didn't ken which obsessed him more, the need for revenge or for lust. During the past week while they'd traveled from Stirling, that blind witch had cast a spell on him. Well, if he were honest, she'd started casting that spell the first time he'd laid eyes on her over two years ago, back when she could see as well as everyone else. She had given him withering looks, but that hadn't dampened his interest in her.

He couldn't stop thinking about her. Now all he had to do was find them. He knew Cameron hadn't taken her back to the castle yet. Holme had been watching the trail, even during the downpour. Where had they gone for shelter? Was there a cottage in the wood? He would find them, slay Colin and his men, then nab Kristina.

"He only has about a half-dozen men with him." After they had attacked him, he had glimpsed the Camerons running into the wood.

"We'll surprise them and take them down one at a time," Dobson said.

"Aye." Holme motioned the other men toward him, then addressed the one with short dark hair and a bushy beard. "Scroggie, slip back down there and find five horses, preferably MacCromar horses. If not, then you may find some of Sleat's. Don't let anyone see you. Take them around the back side of this hill, from the other direction, then hide and wait for us."

Scroggie nodded. He was the best with horses and most suited for the job.

"Dobson, Fordyce, and Mungo, I need you to help me go after Colin Cameron and his men."

"Colin Cameron?" Fordyce glowered, black brows lowered. "That's who the bastard was what stole the lady?"

"Aye. I want to make him suffer an agonizing death like my father's."

Holme moved from the deeper part of the wood onto the trail the Camerons had taken. He knew how to track, and though the rain had destroyed most of the clues, their tracks through the black mud were obvious.

Holme heard a thudding noise and stopped abruptly. "Shh, listen."

The men behind him halted, dropping silent.

A rock clattered. He jumped behind a large boulder and bushes, his friends following. Sword drawn, Holme crouched and peered out. Two Cameron men walked by. He recognized them from the earlier attack.

"We can take them," Holme whispered.

CHAPTER SEVEN

Colin wanted to take Kristina back to the castle posthaste. He didn't want her to have to spend the night in a cave. But since it was autumn, gloaming arrived early.

Ethan and Rusty had climbed up the cliff so they might peer down from the top toward Bearach in the distance and see if the battle was over.

Ethan strode toward Colin where he stood before the cave entrance. "It appears the fighting is over, sir."

Colin was glad to hear that, at least. "Could you tell who the victor was?"

"The MacDonald standard remains flying from the gatehouse tower. Just from their movements and the color of their tartan, I recognized some Camerons and MacDonalds walking around down there."

Relief relaxed his muscles a bit, but all was not resolved as of yet. "Did you happen to see the chief?"

"We were too far away to identify him."

Warton and Lawrie rushed up the hill, breathing hard. "We heard a sword fight and yells down below," Warton said. "We're thinking Patrick and Thorburn were ambushed by the enemy. We ran to their aid but couldn't find them."

Fury and alarm surged through Colin. "Damnation, surely not! How many attacked?"

"We couldn't tell. Do you want us to go search for them?"

Hell, normally he would have a couple dozen men with him, but he hadn't planned on hiding in a cave. "Nay, I need all of you here to protect the lady. They may try to reclaim her to exchange for any prisoners."

He cared about Patrick and Thorburn. They were his clansmen, distant cousins, and friends. But, as soldiers, they had known the risks of their duties, especially after a battle where some of the enemies had survived and scattered. They should've been more canny.

"Since gloaming is upon us, we'll stay the night in the cave and be extra vigilant. We'll have to fight our way back to the castle in the morn. 'Twill be dark soon, and we don't know how many enemies are lurking in the wood. We may be outnumbered."

The men nodded gravely.

Colin prayed that Neacal would send out a search party for them, especially since only five of them remained to protect Kristina, if Patrick and Thorburn had been killed. He prayed they were only injured. If not, he would miss them sorely. Both good men.

"Ethan and I will take first watch," Warton said.

"I thank you. I'll take the lady into a deeper chamber where she'll be safer." Colin entered the cave again.

Kristina turned toward him. "What's happened? Did someone get ambushed?"

Colin figured she must have heard them talking. "Aye, two of my men, Thorburn and Patrick."

A troubled frown crossed her brows. "Oh no. Do they yet live?"

"I have no inkling. I pray they do. Enemies are lurking about the wood. We'll stay in the cave this night and protect you."

She averted her face. "I'm sorry to be the cause of all this."

"'Tis not your fault. Blackburn and his men caused it when they kidnapped you and then showed up here making demands."

"Still, if your two men died, they did it while protecting me." She lifted her face again, her tears sparkling in the dimness. "And the rest of you could be in danger. Do you think they will find us?"

He didn't want to scare her, but chances were their hiding place would be discovered. All of them had to be prepared. "'Tis possible. I'll take you deeper into the cave where you'll be more protected. There are two more caverns."

"I didn't know that."

"Aye, well, 'tis not a very pleasant place, but safer than out here. If you'll give me your hand, I'll help you stand." After she lifted it, he took her small, delicate hand in his, alarmed at how cold it was, and tugged her up. He would have to warm her again, and though it made him feel like the worst rogue, he could not deny he looked forward to it.

Carrying the plaid in his other hand, he led her across the cave floor. "The second chamber is dark and low. And the third contains a small river flowing down from the lochan on the mountain. After the rain, the river will no doubt be more swollen than usual. The passage between the last two caverns is especially narrow."

"I won't mind as long as we're all safe."

Well, he couldn't guarantee the safety of all of them, but he could focus on increasing hers.

Since the first opening was only about four feet tall, they were forced to duck down to enter the cave's second chamber. Only the barest hint of light seeped in from the two entryways on either side of the cavern. He felt along the floor and found a smooth, dry spot near the cave wall, then spread out his plaid.

"Sit here." He led her forward and helped her sit. Though he couldn't see her in the darkness, he felt that her body was tense and her breathing shallow and fast. How could he get her to relax? "Neacal and I used to explore these caves when we were lads. We climbed the cliffs and did all sorts of insane things." He smiled at the memory.

"He must be a wonderful friend to you."

"Aye. Like a brother." Colin knelt before her. "Lie down. We'll sleep here."

"But… I don't know if I can sleep."

"You can rest, at least. You must be exhausted."

"'Tis true."

"Just a wee nap, then," he suggested. "I'll protect you with my life."

"I don't want you to risk your life for me anymore." Her vehement tone surprised him.

"'Tis worth it."

Kristina felt humbled and honored that Colin would take such chances because of her. What had she done to deserve being treated so kindly? Maybe it wasn't her at all. 'Twas he who was the special one.

Though she didn't truly wish to lie down, she did because he wanted her to. She was far too worried to sleep. What if Red Holme and more of Blackburn's men invaded this cave and killed them all? 'Twould be her fault. She never, ever wanted to be the cause of someone else's death. Unless it was Holme or Blackburn. She would kill them if she had to, in self-defense, or to protect Anna or Colin. Blackburn and his men had already murdered too many innocent people.

Colin lay down beside her, gently drew her close into his arms and pulled the other half of his wool plaid over them both.

"Put your hands here between us so they'll get warm." He drew one of her hands against his chest, and she moved the other one.

His deep voice and delicious heat seeped into her, so soothing yet so thrilling. Still, she felt the tension in his hard body and rigid position. Based on his breathing, it seemed his head was cocked backward slightly, as if he was listening for intruders.

He moved his head a bit closer to hers. "Are you warm enough?"

"Aye."

"Relax and get some sleep, then."

"Mayhap you should, too."

"I'll try. How long has it been since you had a good night's sleep?"

"I've only slept a few hours each night since I was captured, especially after Red Holme attacked me. I was afraid to close my eyes after that. But I know I must have slept, because I would jolt awake during nightmares at times."

"The bastard," Colin growled. "Pray pardon."

"I have called him many names myself."

"To his face?" Colin sounded surprised.

"Of course."

He snorted. "I admire your bravery."

Colin kissed the top of her head, surprising her and making her feel warm and tingly all over. Of its own will, her hand tightened in the material of his shirt. She wanted to pull him closer still. Having a man hold her was a startling new experience for her. She'd never imagined she would enjoy such a thing. Generally, she wanted men to stay a great distance away from her. But Colin was so different. Almost instantly, she'd felt very comfortable with him. His voice had calmed her and inspired trust.

She snuggled closer and fantasized they were lying in a huge, firm bed in his home, no doubt a fine castle. She sighed at how wonderful that would be.

She felt him stiffen of a sudden. "What's wrong?" she asked.

"Naught." His response was quick and his voice gruff, making her suspect he was lying. Had he heard a noise she'd missed? She listened for a moment, detecting nothing but silence. One of his hands caressed her back, soothing her again.

He was so sweet and caring. She pressed a small, silent kiss to the shirt covering his chest. She was certain he couldn't feel it. She hoped. But she wished she could kiss him all over, especially his lips. She wondered what they looked like and, most especially, what they felt like.

His hand moved upward into the back of her hair to gently massage her scalp. Delightful tingles spun down her neck and along her spine. His fingers felt heavenly. She sighed again and, with it, a soft moan slipped out, against her will.

"Kristina?" Her name was a guttural murmur against her hair.

Och, nay! He had heard it. What would he think? "Aye?"

"What are you doing?" He sounded as if his teeth were clenched.

"Naught. What are you doing?"

"Hell if I know. You're driving me mad."

Why on earth would the minute sound she made vex him so? She moved back a few inches. "What am I doing that so annoys you?"

He blew out a breath. "'Tis not annoyance, lass. Surely you ken that."

Nay, she did not ken the entirety of what he meant. She had no familiarity with men, had never even experienced a real kiss, truth be told. If he was not annoyed, what was he? "What do you mean by *mad*, then?"

"Damnation," he muttered.

"I'm sorry I've angered you." She drew farther away.

"Kristina." He stroked his palm up the undamaged side of her face. "I'm not angry, sweet lass," he murmured.

The change in his tone from irritable to compassionate brought tears to her eyes. "What then? I'm tired of this riddle. I don't understand you."

He tilted her face upward and pressed his mouth against hers. But it wasn't a simple, quick peck. Nay, indeed. His mouth did not leave hers. Instead, his lips explored hers and then suddenly his tongue was flicking against her lips and teasing her mouth. Good heavens! She had never imagined a kiss could feel like this.

When men had pressed their lips to hers in the past, all she'd felt was repugnance. But this was the opposite. Colin's mouth was delicious and appealing against hers. She reveled in this contact and wanted more. She opened her mouth as he seemed to want her to do and he delved inside, took the kiss deeper. Tingles spread from her breasts downward. The feeling of wanting was so overwhelming she knew not what to do.

His hand slid down her back to her hips and he gathered her closer against his body.

Suddenly he tore himself away from her. "Hell. I'm sorry."

She gasped for breath. After finally drawing in enough, she whispered, "Why? That was amazing."

He shoved himself to his feet. "Ow!" He hopped about, muttering several colorful Gaelic curses.

"What happened? Are you hurt?"

"Stubbed my toe on a damnable rock."

"If 'tis dark in here, mayhap you should lie down."

"I cannot. You tempt me too much."

A heated flush of happiness covered her. Very few men found her tempting. Was he being honest?

He'd certainly sounded sincere.

She smiled. "That's the first true kiss I've experienced. Thank you for showing me how wonderful that can be."

Colin was silent for a long moment. "What does that mean? Has someone else kissed you?" He sounded almost possessive, and she was unsure how she felt about that.

"Red Holme smooshed his disgusting mouth to mine when he attacked me, so I would not call that a kiss. Years ago, before I was blinded, another man pressed his paper-dry lips against mine for an instant, and I would not call that a kiss either. But what you did…" She would remember forever. It stole her thoughts and sent her to another realm. "Anyway, I don't mind if you kiss me again."

He muttered more curses, which she didn't understand. Maybe it had disgusted him as much as Holme's kiss had disgusted her.

Tears burned her eyes. "I'm sorry you didn't enjoy it. But I know not how to kiss."

"Damnation, Kristina," he muttered. "I loved the kiss. Do you not know that?"

She would never comprehend men. "Then why are you so angry?"

He laughed without humor. "Saints! I keep forgetting how naïve you are."

"Well, pray pardon! I cannot help it that I'm not experienced!" This whole conversation was mortifying to her.

He lay down beside her again. "I don't wish you to be experienced," he said with gentle compassion and kissed her forehead. "Unless I'm your teacher."

Imagining him teaching her about kissing and passion, her whole body heated. "Would you... teach me how to kiss?" she whispered.

"I will. Aye." He hissed a breath through his teeth. "Once we reach Bearach Castle." He turned to his back. "At the moment, I must focus all my attention on protecting you."

She felt completely out of her depth, and he seemed beyond her reach. "You're right. 'Twas silly of me to ask."

"Nay, not silly at all."

Hell, to Colin's way of thinking, Kristina was already so good at kissing, she near made his mind explode. Only the danger they were in kept his arousal down to a manageable level. He covered them up with the plaid and turned his back to her. She snuggled against him, making it hard to breathe normally. He couldn't remember a woman arousing him so much with a simple touch.

After a few minutes, he felt himself drifting toward sleep. Sensual dreams of Kristina filled his head.

Sometime later, battle cries echoed, waking Colin and yanking him from the comforting embrace he shared with Kristina. Alarm for her safety propelled him to his feet.

"What's happening?" she gasped.

"Must be an attack. Stay here." He grabbed the sword and targe by his side and took out his dirk.

As he bent and moved along the narrow passage, steel clashed in the outer cave. One man growled in pain. He prayed 'twas not a Cameron.

Once Colin emerged from the passage, he saw that four enemies had entered the cave and were battling his own men. A lantern sat near the entrance and dawn light filtered in, revealing the bearded, ginger-haired man who'd held Kristina at knifepoint when first he'd seen her. She'd called him Red Holme.

Colin charged him, hoping to off him quickly.

Holme deflected the strike and attempted one of his own.

"Cameron, you thieving, murdering bastard!"

Colin lifted his targe, catching the blow. "Lady Kristina was never yours." He struck again.

The man leapt back. "I'm nay talking about her."

"What then?" Colin moved forward aggressively.

"Do you remember the name MacKillican? I'll never forget what your family did to mine, Colin Cameron."

MacKillican? Colin halted, frowning. They were the ones who had been proven traitors to the crown over ten years ago, their lands and castle seized by the king and given to Colin's father for the part he'd played in squashing the rebellion. "I thought your name was Red Holme."

"'Tis not my real name."

"The MacKillican chief was the thief and murderer! He killed the king's representative." Colin sent a lunging strike toward the other man's abdomen. Holme blocked it, the swords clanging.

One of Holme's injured men fell onto the lantern, casting the cave into near darkness. The muted glow of dawn at the entrance was the only remaining light.

"Let's get the hell out of here!" Holme yelled and the three of them fled out the cave's exit, leaving their fallen comrade behind.

"Capture them!" Colin ordered, then lowered his voice. "I'll hide the lady deeper in the cave."

"Aye." Warton rushed out into the dawn light behind Rusty, Ethan and Lawrie.

Colin checked the man lying on the ground and found he was not breathing. He dragged his body outside, then returned to the cave and hurried through the passage.

"'Tis me." Colin entered the second cavern, again finding it dark as pitch and disorienting. This was what Kristina had to live with every day. He didn't know how she dealt with it.

"What happened?" she asked.

"Your friend Red Holme paid us a visit."

"Saints! I knew 'twas him. Is anyone injured?"

"One of his men was killed. The rest ran. I sent my men to capture them. I want to hide you deep in the cave until they're no longer a threat to you."

"Good heavens," she muttered. "'Tis ridiculous that Red Holme would try to take me hostage again."

"I agree, especially since his clan was the loser in the battle at

Bearach Castle. But now I'm thinking he probably wants to kill me more than he wants to capture you."

"Why on earth would he?"

"I didn't ken it until moments ago, but we have history. When I was a lad of fifteen, my father rooted out some traitors to the crown. 'Twas my first battle. We fought the MacKillican clan and won. Those not killed during the battle were imprisoned, except for some who fled. He claims to be the chief's son."

"He has always gone by Holme, not MacKillican. Is he telling the truth?"

"Most likely. He recognized me and called me by name. He looked far different back then, but I do see the family resemblance. He's starting to look more like his father now."

"So, he wants revenge against you personally for something your father and your whole clan did?"

"Aye, like I said, I fought in the battle."

"How could you at such a young age? Did your father not fear you would be killed?"

"I had been training every day since I could walk, and I was big for my age, almost the height I am now. During practice, I often bested men twice my age."

"I'm greatly impressed."

He snorted. "I was not trying to brag. Just letting you know why my father didn't worry. And neither should anyone else."

"Well, I will worry about all of us until we are safely behind castle walls."

"I will get you down to Bearach as soon as I can. In the meantime, I'm going to take you into the third chamber of this cave. 'Twill make it harder for them to find you."

She agreed that might be for the best.

Crawling along the narrow, damp passage, Kristina heard the rushing water of the small river Colin had told her about earlier. Though her skirts hampered her efforts to navigate the constricted passage, Kristina managed it well enough and after another minute, Colin helped her stand.

"The river is more swollen than usual because of yesterday's storms." Because of the water's roar, he raised his voice a bit as he spoke near her ear.

"Is the water deep?"

"I'm guessing about four feet at the moment and running

swiftly."

"And is it dark in here?" She liked to visualize places as much as possible since sight had been a part of her life for so long.

"Aye, but not as pitch-black as the second chamber. The barest hint of light filters in from the channel cut by the water, but 'tis still as dark as deepest gloaming."

After crawling, her hands felt crusted in mud and dirt. "Could I wash my hands and drink from the river? Is it clean?"

"Aye. It comes down from the mountain. No one lives up there that I'm aware of."

He led her forward. When she crouched, he held onto her *arisaid* lest she lose her balance and fall into the river. After she washed the dirt and mud from her hands and face, she drank several gulps of the icy, fresh-tasting water. Then he helped her stand again.

"Better?" he asked.

"Aye." She dried her face and hands on her wool arisaid.

After washing his hands, he led her away from the river. "We can sit here." He helped lower her to the ground where he'd spread his plaid. "I'm sorry I have no food for you this morn. Ethan was unable to find any."

"I'm fine. I grew used to not eating as much during the journey."

"Becoming accustomed to the blindness must have been far harder. How did you do it?"

"Indeed, but I had no choice. I started listening more and noticing scents." Not long after her injuries, she remembered waking up at times and hearing male voices in the hallway outside the door of her chamber. Fear riveting her, she'd strained her ears to hear what was being said, but couldn't quite make it out. "'Twas a matter of survival."

Colin sat down beside her. "I'm sorry you had to suffer through that. Blackburn should be horsewhipped."

She nodded. "I pray you will not feel sorry for me."

"I don't," Colin assured her. "I admire your strength and determination."

Her heart swelled with gratitude at his kind words. "'Tis times like this I miss my sight most."

"During times of danger?"

"That, too, but… more because I can't see you." She smiled and averted her face, wondering how forthright she could be with him. Very rarely in her life had she been around a man she found compelling and exciting. Should she sit in fear or tell him what she really thought? She had never been one to let fear rule her.

"You must be a handsome man," she said.

He chuckled. "I have no inkling whether you would think so or not."

Her face heated, and she found herself smiling at the sound of his warm laugh. Though he had kissed her the night before, she had not thought to trace her fingers over his face to feel what he looked like. She well knew he didn't have a beard or mustache and that his lips had a sensual shape. But that was the extent of it.

This seemed a strange and suspended moment in time which was completely different from her normal life. She felt like being even bolder than she usually would be.

"Can I... find out?" she wondered.

"What do you mean?"

"Could I touch your face?"

He was silent for a long moment, then gruffly said, "Aye, if you wish."

She hesitated, uncertain as to why he'd paused. What was he thinking? "That is... if you don't mind."

"Not at all." He sounded more convincing that time.

On the plaid, she arose to her knees, hoping her hands wouldn't tremble with nerves. She trailed her fingers from his shoulders up his muscular neck and found that his thick hair fell a couple of inches below his collar. "What color is your hair?" she whispered, suddenly feeling the intimacy of the moment.

"Sandy brown," he murmured.

"Were you blond as a lad?"

"Aye."

"What color are your eyes?"

"Gray."

"That sounds like an interesting color." She did not recall seeing a man with gray eyes before. Were they like steel or slate... or silver? "Light or dark?"

"It depends." The smile came through in his tone.

Oh, what she wouldn't give to be permitted to look into his eyes for five minutes. This, above all things, made her yearn for sight more than ever before.

"Close your eyes." She stroked her palms and thumbs over the lower part of his face, feeling his strong, square jaw. His new growth of beard stubble scraped her palms. She was certain it must be light brown, too—appearing, in the sunlight, like flecks of dark gold. Avoiding his tempting lips, she stroked her fingertips over his nose, finding it straight and noble. His skin felt smooth, no scars to be found like on her own face.

Moving carefully, she stroked the fingertips of both hands over his forehead. "You have a high forehead. You must be highly intelligent."

A short laugh escaped him, his breath warming her wrists. "Some would argue that point."

Smiling, she smoothed her thumbs over his brows, finding them silky. The bone structure of his brows and cheekbones painted a picture in her mind of a man with an incredibly attractive, masculine face. But she would never know for certain if she was right or wrong in her imaginings of him. Her fingers trembled.

He grasped her hands and placed warm kisses on the back of each. "Is my façade that frightening?"

"Nay, on the contrary. You are a most handsome man."

"You exaggerate." He leaned forward and pressed his lips to hers.

Heavens! He took her breath and her mind in one fell swoop. She leaned into him, and he pulled her to sit on his lap. His stubble scratched her chin and her upper lip, but she did not mind. His lips were soft and firm at the same time. Everything about him was amazing and dreamy. She relished the idyllic moment as one that neared perfection.

"Where are you, bastard?" The yell echoed from one of the first two chambers of the cave.

She froze as terror chilled her bones. "'Tis Holme."

Glaring at the darkened opening of the passage where Red Holme's voice had echoed, Colin helped Kristina sit on the ground. He arose and pulled the foot-long dirk from the scabbard at his belt, then picked up his sword from the ground. The bastard would find him and Kristina soon enough. If the man was alone, Colin should be able to take him down, although he did not intend to be overconfident. Holme might have a man or two with him.

"Kristina, stay here, in the back corner of the cave," he whispered.

"Aye."

What had happened to Colin's men? How had Red Holme gotten back here without Rusty or Warton seeing him? Damnation, he might have killed both of them. Lawrie and Ethan, too. A sinking feeling settled into his gut.

"I have a knife," Kristina whispered. "He comes near me, I'll stab him. Please have a care."

"I will." Colin was glad Kristina had a weapon, at least, but he intended to do the man in before he could reach her.

A dim light glowed from the entrance to this small cavern.

"He has a lantern," Colin murmured. He'd probably managed to use a flint to light the one that had been snuffed out earlier. Intending to use the element of surprise, Colin picked up a nearby stone.

Holme's breath whooshed in and out as he crawled closer. The lantern dangling from a hand came into Colin's view, then a head. Colin drew back his arm and threw the stone at the lantern. Rock crashed against metal. Holme dropped the lantern and growled out a curse. Near darkness reigned again, but he could still see a hint of movement.

Colin heard a swish and was surprised to see a fist-sized rock whizzing from Kristina's direction. She met her target and Holme roared, "You bastard! I'll kill you for that!"

Colin's chest swelled with pride and admiration for Kristina. With her blindness, how on earth had she managed to strike him? She was a little hellion!

In the dimness, Colin charged Holme before he could rise to his feet, sword aimed at his neck. Holme rolled aside and the sword tip rang against the stone floor. Colin struck again, hitting metal-studded armor.

Holme grabbed Colin's ankle and yanked. Everything spun as Colin flipped through the air and fell to the ground. He landed on his elbow and hip. Pain shot through both joints, but he ignored it as fury and battle lust consumed him.

Before he could arise, metal clanged against the stone beside him—the tip of Holme's blade stabbing into the cave floor as he tried to strike Colin. Using his dirk, Colin slashed upward, making contact. Holme yelped.

Colin rolled out of the way and bounded to his feet. He slashed his sword back and forth toward Holme's dull silhouette. Sparks popped off the smashing blades, providing a bit more illumination. This was a horrid place to fight—too dark and enclosed.

Holme's blade struck Colin's sword arm, forming a shallow but painful gash. "Bastard!" He slashed back, cutting Holme's wrist and eliciting a growl. Twice more their blades clashed and Holme's blade went flying through the air.

Colin drove his blade toward Holme's gut, but before he could make contact, Holme dodged aside and crouched. Instantly, he launched himself at Colin with a roar, tackling him backward. Colin's back smashed against a large stone. Amid the blinding pain, he lost his grip on the sword, and it clattered away.

"Damnation!" Colin shoved at Holme, then slashed his forearm with the dirk. Yelling, Holme knocked the blade from his hand, dragged him up and punched his jaw, knocking Colin backward. Unable to stop the fall, Colin splashed into the icy river and his head struck a stone, triggering devastating pain. "Nay!" he yelled before the rushing water engulfed him and carried him downward. In the shock of it, he forgot to hold his breath. Cold water filled his lungs.

CHAPTER EIGHT

"Colin!" Kristina yelled. "What happened?"

A laugh sounded, but 'twas not Colin's. Chills of terror consumed her as she absorbed Red Holme's hateful, gloating laugh.

"Your lover hit his head on a rock and washed down the river," he crowed with glee.

"Nay!" Crushing despair enveloped her. "Colin!" she screamed.

"'Tis too late now. He cannot hear you. If he's not already dead, he will be soon."

Dear God, please don't let it be so. She clasped another stone in her hand and hid it beneath her leg. In her other hand, she held the small dagger. She would stab this beast for what he'd done to Colin.

"Come, sweet lass," Holme cajoled. "Come quietly and I will not hurt you."

Sharp claws of hatred and anguish scraped along her nerves. "Stay away from me, you bastard!"

He laughed. "And what will you do if I don't? You can't even see me. How will you defend yourself?"

She would kill him! She wanted to shout it, but kept her mouth shut tight instead. She had to use the element of surprise.

"Show me your hands," he said.

She remained still, her hands hidden behind her skirts.

"I'm holding a sword stained with your lover's blood. I could easily kill you with it. You wouldn't see it coming. Would you like to join him in his watery grave?"

Rage burned in her gut. "I hate you! Whoreson!"

Holme cackled again.

Please let Colin be alive, please, please, please.

"Show me your hands!" Holme demanded.

Leaving her weapons hidden beneath her skirts, she brought her empty hands out.

"Stand up," he said.

She moved her hands beneath her legs again, preparing to push herself up, but she grasped her knife and the stone. She then pretended weakness as if she couldn't gain her feet.

Holme grasped her elbow and painfully yanked her upward. "Hurry. We're leaving."

She swung her arm around, aiming the rock at his head. It made contact, but not hard enough.

"Bitch!" His hand struck her forearm hard, sending intense pain through it, and she lost her grip on the stone.

He yanked her close and smooshed his mouth against hers. She turned her face away and thrust the knife toward his abdomen. It made contact with something. Leather armor? She pulled her hand back and stabbed again, lower. He growled against her ear, grasped her hand, then yanked the knife from it.

"You will pay me recompense for that, over and over. And I will enjoy every minute of it." He yanked her to him, lifting her. She hiked her knee upward, smashing it into his groin.

He growled and hissed through clenched teeth. "Damn you, wench!" He held her tightly under one vise-like arm, nearly squeezing the breath from her. Her heart pounded hard as she tried to free herself, but his strength made him immovable.

Holding both her wrists in one of his hands, he wrapped a cord around them and tied it. He pushed her facedown on the dirt floor, grit and small stones biting into her cheek. While he bound her ankles, she screamed, kicked and fought with all her might, but she could not overcome his brute strength. Next, he tied a gag in her mouth, but this did not stop her from screaming and yelling, although the sounds came out muffled.

He crawled backward through the narrow cave passage, dragging her by her feet, a few inches at a time. By the time they emerged into the second cavern, her skirts were around her waist, but she didn't think he could see her. Colin had said this chamber was especially dark.

Dear Colin, please be all right.

Holme picked her up and carried her across this chamber of the cave, then again dragged her along the slightly taller passage. She heard no one. Were any of Colin's men around? She again attempted to scream and yell, but the only sounds she could utter were loud moans. Not loud enough to carry very far.

Holme picked her up, threw her over his shoulder and slapped her derriere. "Be quiet."

She wanted to call him every vile name she could think of.

He carried her out into the fresh air that smelled of pines. She heard no sounds other than the wind hissing through pine needles, distant bird calls, and a few rocks clattering beneath his feet.

She beat her bound fists against his back, but he kept walking, very briskly, and it seemed he was climbing a hill or mountain. Every time she hit his back, he gave her arse another stinging slap. Tears of frustration dripping from her eyes, she dropped still.

Where was Colin? Had he drowned? *Dear God, please keep Colin alive and protect him!*

"Rusty! Come quick!" Warton's gruff voice yelled the words as Colin became aware. He felt like a numb block of ice being dragged by the arms, face down. He couldn't draw breath.

He gasped violently.

Water gushed up from his lungs and poured out his mouth. His body convulsed into a coughing fit.

Warton lowered him to the ground. "What happened, sir?"

Shivering, Colin coughed a few more times and gulped great breaths of air into his stinging lungs. Kristina popped into his mind, and fear for her racked his body.

"Kristina!" he roared then shoved to his feet. "Holme is in the cave with her."

"Damnation!" Warton's eyes widened. "Can you walk?"

"Aye. Go! We must stop him from capturing her!"

Warton ran up the hill, yelling for Rusty and the others. Colin followed but after a few yards started coughing again. Stopping, hands on his knees, he rested for a moment, breathing deep. Thank the saints Warton had pulled him from the river. After gaining enough breath, he climbed the hill, although at a slower pace than Warton.

At the cave, he went inside, finding Warton waiting by the passage. "Ethan is checking the other two chambers."

Colin bent and progressed through the passage to the second

chamber. 'Twas still near dark as midnight in here. "Kristina?" he yelled.

He heard Ethan crawling along the narrower passage from the third chamber, weapons clanging against the stone. "No one is in there, sir."

"Hell! He took her."

"I found your plaid and weapons." Ethan handed him the items.

"I'm glad. I'll need them." It sickened him anew that Kristina couldn't use his plaid at the moment. Was she cold? In pain? Had Holme hurt her?

They quickly made their way back to the mouth of the cave. Colin sheathed his weapons and belted his plaid into place. 'Twas filthy with the dirt from the cave, but he didn't care.

"Holme wouldn't have thrown her in the river, would he?" Warton asked. "I didn't see her."

Colin shook his head. "Nay. The bastard's abducted her."

"Up here!" Rusty called from near the top of the rocky hill. "I heard the lady trying to cry out."

"Damnation. That bastard best not hurt her," Colin growled.

They ran up the hill toward Rusty, and Lawrie joined them.

"What did you hear?" Colin asked.

He pointed. "I was a short distance down there when I heard a moaning sound from up here and rocks clattering. I followed the sound, but didn't see her."

"Holme must have gone that way." Colin nodded toward the east. "If he was carrying her, he wouldn't have been able to scale this cliff. Look for tracks. He'll probably go through the pass, and then he'll be harder to find."

Bound, gagged and infuriated, Kristina could do nothing to free herself. Holme's hard shoulder dug into her stomach. He'd climbed uphill for a long while but now he ran down what felt like a slight slope. All she heard was his boots pounding the ground and his harsh breaths.

After a few minutes, he paused to rest, still breathing hard. He cursed, then muttered, "Where the hell is he?"

Holme walked briskly for what seemed a half hour. Sometimes

she felt the warmth of the sun on her back. Other times the air smelled like dampness and pines. Now and then she heard streams flowing.

"Scroggie?" Holme growled. "Dobson? Damnation! Where are they?"

Mayhap Holme was lost and separated from his cohorts in this unfamiliar wood. And maybe he would walk in circles until Colin and his men found them.

Thinking of Colin was the only thing that kept her sane. She felt as if Holme had been carrying her for hours. Why couldn't he simply grow tired and put her down somewhere? If only she could get some relief from his shoulder rammed against her stomach.

A horse nickered nearby. Who might have a horse and could they help her? Hope swelled within her, and she tried to yell out again.

"Scroggie?" Holme sped up and crashed through the bushes.

"You got her," a man said.

"Aye." Holme breathed hard.

Disappointment near suffocated her. These ruffians were simply Holme's men, and they had horses. Which meant they would escape with her even faster.

"It took you a long time. We feared you'd been killed."

"I know naught about this wood."

"What about Cameron?" another man asked. She remembered his voice. One of Blackburn's soldiers.

"He fell in the river and hit his head. Drowned, I hope."

Nay! Colin could not be dead. Kristina refused to believe it.

"Scroggie, bring my horse. We'll ride until dark, then make camp."

"Won't be long now."

Slow hooves thumped over the grass nearby.

"Did anyone see you bring the horses?" Holme asked.

"Nay, I slipped them away one at a time. No one followed." She assumed that was Scroggie answering. She remembered Blackburn calling his name a couple of times during their long journey from Stirling. But she also knew him to be a friend of Holme, for she had heard their voices joined in conversation before.

"Hold her until I mount, Mungo, then hand her up to me." Holme dragged her off his shoulder and placed her into the arms of another man. The bastard groped her breast. She growled out a protest, muffled beneath the gag, then drove her bound fists toward his face. She made contact with the side of his head and his cheekbone. Her knuckle stung as a result, but it was worth it.

"Ow! Bitch! I'll strangle you!" His grip tightened.

"Don't hurt her!" Holme commanded. "If anyone hurts her, it will be me. But I plan to have my fun first."

Her small victory was short-lived as nausea welled inside her. She had to figure out a way to stop Holme from his horrid plan.

"Aye, sir." Mungo placed her across Holme's knees. Her stomach was aching already. The horse nickered and danced beneath them, jostling her about painfully.

Dear God, help me survive this, she prayed.

They rode at a trot for some distance. Kristina knew not how far they'd traveled. She simply tried to focus on breathing and ignoring the pain in her torso. She thought about the time she'd spent with Colin. The things he'd said to her. The way he'd kissed her. That brief time with him in the cave had been the most joyous time for her in the last several years. But that was over now. She might never see Colin again. Although she didn't want to accept that he was dead, he might be. Her chest felt crushed, for she could do naught to change that.

They rode for a couple of hours at a slow pace over the rough ground, only stopping now and again to give the horses water and let them rest for a few minutes. During those times, Holme sat her on the ground and said naught to her. She was thirsty, and the gag further dried out her mouth. Her stomach ached with hunger. But she doubted they had any food.

As they continued to ride, she was near numb from lying across Holme's knees, and her mind was starting to fog.

"Halt!" Holme drew up. "We'll camp here by this small loch. Carry her over there, Mungo."

The man pulled her from the horse and carried her for a few seconds, then laid her on the damp ground. The air smelled of wet black dirt. She rested for a moment, thankful for the change in position and the relief. Her stomach would probably be bruised and sore for days. She turned over, sat up and listened. After drawing the cowl of her arisaid over her head with her bound hands, she covertly tried to pull the gag from her mouth, but it was tied too tightly. She wanted to yell curses at the loathsome men.

"Put up the tents, Dobson," Holme ordered.

"I'll build a fire," Mungo said.

"Nay, 'twill make it easier for them to find us."

"We have to eat."

"Scroggie should still have some bannocks."

"They disappeared. Someone must have stolen them."

Holme let out a string of curses. "Build a fire, then. I doubt Cameron still draws breath, and his men won't know where we are. You two go out hunting for some game. If Cameron and his men happen to follow the scent of the smoke, we'll be ready for them. And if Colin Cameron survived his swim in the river, I want him killed first. In fact, 'tis a good idea to lure the Camerons here so we can finish them off and be done with them."

Nay! Watch out, Colin, she wanted to yell at him across the miles.

The men went about their duties mostly in silence, with a few clatters and thumps now and then. Within minutes, she smelled smoke.

On the one hand, she hoped Colin and his men would smell the smoke and come to her rescue; on the other, Holme's plan to lure them in frightened her.

Hearing no one nearby, she lifted her bound hands and again worked at the gag, using all her strength to tug it from her mouth. Finally, it came free, and she could breathe freely through her mouth again. Her jaws and the corners of her mouth were sore from the abrasive material and the unnatural position it had held her mouth in.

An owl hooted in the distance and the air was growing colder again, telling her night was approaching. She hoped it was dark enough that Holme wouldn't notice right away that she'd removed the gag. If he saw she wasn't going to scream, maybe he would leave it off. She would keep quiet until she actually needed to use her voice.

She needed to relieve herself, but she didn't want to draw Holme's attention to such a personal matter. 'Twas obvious he wouldn't give her privacy.

"Cut the ropes off her ankles and put her in that tent," Holme said, surprising her. Had he noticed the missing gag?

"What about her wrists?" Mungo asked.

"Nay. Leave them tied."

Why did he want her ankles cut loose? A chill crept over her, along with nausea, for she suspected what he planned.

She acted like a demure kitten as the man cut the ropes from her ankles and helped her stand. Holding her arm, he guided her forward. She stepped in a hole and stumbled, knocking her cowl off. He laughed, lifted her into his arms and carried her. She felt one of his dirk hilts by her leg.

"I would like to keep you company, m'lady," Mungo murmured, too low for Holme to hear, no doubt, then he sniffed her hair.

Though she wanted to gag, she forced a smile and stealthily moved her bound hands toward the knife hilt. Judging by the smooth, hard feel, the hilt was made of bone. She clasped her hand around it gently and pulled. Once she had it in hand, she hid it within the folds of her skirt between her knees.

He lowered her to the ground. "Here you are, m'lady. This tent is fancy enough for a queen."

She doubted that, for it stank of man sweat. "I thank you."

"Do you, in truth?"

Before she could answer, he plastered his mouth to hers. She turned her head away and screamed.

"What the hell?" Holme's voice echoed from several yards away, then running footsteps approached. "Get away from her afore I string you up from the nearest tree!"

Mungo scrambled away from her. "I did naught. She was whispering sweet words to me, trying to seduce me. She wanted me to untie her wrists."

"Stay away from her from now on!"

She hid the knife beneath the wool blanket covering the ground. The blade was not overly large, maybe six or eight inches long. She thought the man might not notice its absence, since it was likely not his primary dirk, which would be much longer.

As she listened, footsteps tramped closer, then heavy breathing sounded at the tent opening. "Trying to seduce Mungo in exchange for your freedom, were you?" Holme ground the words out in a furious tone.

Icy chills prickled her nerve endings. "Nay. He lied."

"Humph. Mayhap you're the little liar. And for that, you will pay a price."

Dear God, what would he do to her? Still sitting, she slid over and covertly placed her hand on the knife hilt beneath the blanket. Instead of panicking and lashing out, she had to stab him in just the right spot to do him fatal injury. And she had to somehow get beneath his leather armor.

He crawled forward.

"Stay away from me!" she warned.

"Nay. Why do you think I went to so much trouble to reclaim you?"

Because he was a madman bent on tormenting her all of her days. Or maybe he wanted revenge for perceived snubs in the past.

"Because you're a tasty morsel," he said. "You've been teasing and taunting me far too long. Years."

Ugh! How could she talk him out of his vile plan? "Have you not seen my scar? I'm ugly," she stated.

"Nay, I like the look of you, and now I want to feel the shape of you in the dark."

Nausea roiled in her stomach. "Do not touch me!" What a foul swine he was.

"I will touch you and a lot more. I can wait no longer."

She'd castrate the bastard if she had the opportunity.

He rolled her onto her stomach and tugged the back of her skirts upward.

"Nay!" she screamed.

"Shut your mouth," he growled. "Or I'll put another gag on you. You don't want to anger me, lass. I'll only make it more painful for you."

Pain? She would give him pain. She fisted one hand around the knife's hilt, then wrapped the other hand around that one for added strength. But how could she stab him from this position? She must turn over.

His hand burrowed beneath her skirts to the bare skin of her upper thighs. She thrust one elbow backward, hitting his chest.

He laughed. "Don't try to fight me. You are only a small, weak lass."

He would see about that if only she could turn over.

Some hard, bare part of his anatomy pressed against her derriere. Raw fear and revulsion made her want to retch, but she forced herself to remain calm and think logically.

"I wish to turn over," she said. "Do you not want to kiss me first?"

"Aye." He grabbed her arm and roughly rolled her over. When he came down on her, pressing his mouth to hers, she shoved the knife upward, hoping to get it beneath his armor. It made contact and she pushed the knife with all the strength in both arms.

"Ow! Bitch!" He leapt off her. "Where did you get a knife?"

She drew the weapon back and struck at him again, making contact. Cursing, he knocked the blade from her hand. He then yanked her up by the front of her bodice and struck her face with his fist. The pain exploded through her skull. When his fist hit her the second time, all went black.

"Damn that bitch!" Carrying the knife he'd taken from Kristina, Holme crawled from the tent. The hellish stab wound in his belly smarted. He strode toward the campfire to check his injuries.

"What happened?" Mungo stood by the fire, the light flickering off his face.

Holme examined the knife in his hand. It looked familiar. "Is this yours?"

Frowning, Mungo glanced down at his empty scabbard, then back at the knife, his eyes wide. "Aye."

"Did you give it to her?" Holme demanded.

"Of course not! Do you think me mad?"

"Well then, how the hell did Kristina get it off you?"

"I have no inkling."

"You weren't paying attention. That's how! A shapely lass can easily make you go daft."

"She's as canny as a mercenary," Mungo said with amazement, then glanced down at Holme's belly. "You're bleeding."

"I ken it. She stabbed me with your damned knife."

Mungo laughed. At Holme's glare, his face dropped straight. "I'm sorry."

"You should be. I should take it out of your hide." Holme removed his armor and shirt enough to see the shallow stab wound in his belly. It bled, burned and smarted like the very devil, but 'twas only a flesh wound. "Lucky for you, I'll live. Get out of my sight before I take the rest of your weapons."

Mungo hastened away.

Kristina had also sliced his wrist. Nothing killed lust faster than a couple of bloody knife wounds, even if they weren't serious. He wrapped a piece of material around his wrist to absorb the blood. Luckily he had a thick layer of fat on his belly. Good protection.

He put his clothing back on and tightened his belt to staunch the bleeding. He strode back to Kristina's tent.

"Kristina!" He kicked at her foot.

No response. Was she pretending, knocked out, or dead?

He dragged her from the tent, causing her skirts to ride up her slender shapely legs. Her eyes were closed and she was as limp as a rag. What a weakling she was! He'd knocked her out with only two strikes. Of course, his fists were large and hard as stones. And in his anger, he'd struck her extra hard. Damnation! He'd wanted to have some fun, not kill her.

He noticed a pouch tied at her waist, over her smock but beneath her outer clothing. What was she hiding in there? He cut the cord and opened the pouch. Silver coins and dangling golden earrings glinted in the firelight. The earrings were coin shaped, with a deep red stone in the center. These were the ones he'd seen her wear over two years before, and they were no doubt valuable. He could sell these, he decided, cramming them into his sporran along with her coins.

He picked her up and carried her toward the fire, then laid her down about five feet from it.

"What happened to her?" Scroggie asked, returning from the hunt with Dobson.

"She stabbed me and I hit her. She's knocked out."

Dobson stopped near her. "Are you certain she still breathes?"

Holme hadn't checked for breath. What if she was dead? A sick feeling punched him in the stomach. He knelt beside her and held a finger beneath her nose. Her weak breath whispered against his calloused skin, giving him a surge of relief. Although he wanted to strangle her at times… if he did, who would he lust over then? He'd been obsessed with her for far too long.

"Want me to throw some water on her face?" Mungo asked.

"Nay. I want her to lie here in the firelight and if any of the Camerons approach, they'll see her, lose their senses and come charging into camp to rescue her. Then, we can kill all of them from the cover of the bush, over there." Holme pointed.

"Good plan. All while our supper roasts." Dobson put three rabbits on a spit over the fire.

"Aye, we sit back in the shadows and watch for them. I want all of you fully armed and prepared for the skirmish. Scroggie, ready your bow. I want you to take out every last Cameron."

"Aye. With pleasure."

Grief-stricken that he'd allowed Holme to recapture Kristina, Colin strode rapidly through the pine forest beside Rusty, following the path Holme had left.

"Damnation! I was supposed to be protecting her," Colin muttered through clenched teeth, enraged at himself.

"You did, as best you could," Rusty said.

Nay, Colin felt like a grand failure for botching this mission. He shook his head, realizing how deeply he cared for Kristina. To imagine her at Holme's mercy gutted him. If Holme hurt or killed her, Colin would never forgive himself.

A distant yell drew Colin out of his self-castigation. He paused to listen, his gaze scanning the pine forest. Someone was calling his name. 'Twas a man's voice.

He turned around. "Listen. Someone is yelling my name from back there, behind us."

"Might be Chief MacDonald or another man from the keep," Warton said.

Aye, naturally, Neacal would either come searching for him or send someone. Amid the dusky gloaming light, they slipped back along the path to the edge of the wood. In the distance, several kilted men on foot, swords in hand, walked briskly. Some trotted. Finally, he recognized two of his own men and a few of the MacDonalds.

"Over here!" Feeling relieved, Colin waved, wondering who the rest of the men were. They had to be allies.

The newcomers increased their pace, drawing nearer through the boulders and gorse bushes. Now, he recognized the imposing, dark-haired man at the forefront, though he had not seen him in at least a decade.

"Colin Cameron?" the man asked.

"Aye."

"Saints! We've been searching for you since last evening. I'm Cyrus, chief of Clan MacKenzie."

"I remember. We met about ten years ago. Good to see you again." He gave the man a warrior handshake, recalling that Neacal had said his sister had married Cyrus's brother.

"Neacal was concerned about you and the lady. We volunteered to find you and escort you back to the castle. What happened to you?" Cyrus frowned.

Colin touched the sore gash on the side of his forehead. "Blackburn's man, Red Holme, knocked me into the river and abducted Lady Kristina. We're following his trail. He has four or five men with him and they've been riding horses for the last two hours. We found the place where they met up, back there. Thankfully, over this rough terrain, they must go slow." He turned to the man beside him. "This is Rusty Cameron, a skilled tracker."

Cyrus shook his hand. "This is my younger brother, Fraser." Cyrus motioned to a dark-haired, blue-eyed man in his mid-twenties. Colin shook his hand.

"We have eighteen more men with us," Fraser said.

"I'm thankful all of you came." Colin greeted the Camerons who had stayed back at the castle and the MacDonalds, then met more of the MacKenzies.

One of his men, William Cameron, glanced around, then asked, "Where are Tom and Patrick?"

Colin, once again, felt like he'd been kicked in the stomach. "We think they were ambushed by Holme and his men, and we've not seen them since."

"Damnation! We have to get these bastards," William growled.

Colin nodded. "Let's go."

After some of the newcomers shared their dried venison with Colin and his four men, they quickly followed Rusty into the wood as he began tracking the outlaws again.

"Earlier, we saw one of the enemies, dead near the cave's entrance," Cyrus said, keeping pace beside Colin.

"Aye. We were hiding in the cave when they attacked at dawn. When one of their men went down, Holme and two others fled. We discovered that he must've had one of his men slip the horses around the back side of the mountain. That's where they met up."

"What of the lady? Is she unharmed?" Cyrus shoved a pine branch aside.

A sense of dread settled over Colin. "When last I saw her she was. But it guts me to imagine what Holme might have done to her by now."

"We'll find her."

After they'd traveled for several more miles, mostly walking at a brisk pace, sometimes sprinting, gloaming was turning to darkness. Colin's stomach knotted with fear for Kristina. He had to find her before dark.

"I smell smoke," Fraser said in a low tone.

"And roasting rabbit," another man said.

Colin drew in a deep breath. "I smell it, too." Confidence arose within him. "That has to be them. They're close by."

"Are they truly daft enough to think we can't follow their scent?" Cyrus asked.

"Might be a trap." Colin's instincts rose to high alert.

As their eyes adjusted to the low light, they carefully picked their way along the trail, avoiding fallen tree branches and loose stones.

Soon they saw the firelight glowing in the distance. They approached cautiously, weapons drawn, glancing all about them.

When Colin had a clear view of the campfire, he saw the silhouette of a small form lying on the ground in front of it, unmoving. He took a step forward. "Kristina!"

CHAPTER NINE

Warton put a hand on Colin's shoulder. "'Tis a trap. They want us to hasten into the firelight so they can ambush us."

"Damnation," Colin hissed, trying to keep his wits about him. Was Kristina alive? He couldn't detect any movement.

Cyrus was directing his men, almost silently, to circle around behind the camp. Damn Holme and his cronies. Colin wanted to dirk every last one of them for what they'd done to Kristina.

Despite the sickening need for vengeance that near drowned him, Colin prayed Kristina still lived. Why was she unmoving and in such an awkward position?

A man's shout echoed from somewhere beyond the camp, toward the right. Was that one of Cyrus's men or an enemy? After a moment of silence, horses' hooves pounded the ground in hasty retreat.

"Go after them!" Cyrus yelled.

Several of his men raced away.

Looking about him, targe raised, Colin ran toward Kristina beside the campfire and dropped to his knees.

"Kristina?" Almost holding his breath, he turned her onto her back and placed his fingertips beneath her nose. Her warm breath tickled his skin. "Thank God." Relief rushed through his veins, near making him weak.

The firelight illuminated a large, reddish-violet spot on her cheek but no blood. Had Holme hit her? "Kristina, wake up." He smoothed his fingers gently over her forehead and hair, but she didn't respond. Anxiety clawed at his gut.

Rusty stopped beside him, breathing hard. "Is she all right?"

"She's knocked out. Do you have any water?" Colin asked.

"Aye." Rusty unhooked the wineskin from his belt and handed

it over. Colin splashed the water onto Kristina's face. She frowned and moved her head a tiny bit, giving him a jolt of hope.
"Kristina?"
"What?" she whispered, her voice scratchy.
"'Tis me—Colin." He carefully dried the water from her face with his sleeve.
"Colin, you're... alive... thank God." Tears glistened at the corners of her eyes. "Careful... Holme."
"He's gone. He ran away."
She seemed to release a breath and relax a bit.
"Are you in a lot of pain, my sweet?" Colin smoothed her hair back gently.
"My head." She touched her swollen, violet cheek.
"Did Holme hit you?"
"Aye."
Rage punched at Colin. "Did he hurt you anywhere else?"
"I don't... think so."
His stomach knotting, Colin prayed the blackguard hadn't forced himself on her. He would ask her when she felt better. For now, it might be too much, or she might not remember.
"Are you thirsty?" he asked.
"Aye."
"Would Holme give you naught to drink?"
"Nay. I didn't trust him to give me clean water, anyway."
"The bastard," Colin grated as he helped Kristina lean up and drink water from the wineskin.
"She could lay her head on this." Fraser brought a rolled-up doublet. Obviously his own, since he now wore only a shirt and plaid.
"'Tis very kind of you." Colin helped her place her head on the makeshift pillow. "Is that better?"
"Aye, I thank all of you."
"My pleasure." Fraser went with Rusty to the perimeter of the campsite where several men stood guard.
"Why did Holme hit you and how? With his fist?" Colin needed to know every detail of what happened to her, even though 'twas torturous to hear.
"Aye, he did, because... I stabbed him."
Colin felt his eyes widen. "Indeed, lass? You stabbed him?"
"Aye."

"Saints!" he hissed. "I'm proud of you."

"I stopped him from… you know."

His rage renewed, Colin leaned closer and spoke low. "He tried to force himself on you?"

"Aye, but he didn't succeed."

Colin prayed the whoreson hadn't taken advantage after Kristina had been knocked out. Surely she would realize it by now if he had. He would ask her later, once she was more herself.

"Are you hungry?" The scent of the roasting rabbits near them was certainly making his stomach growl.

She pressed a hand to her stomach, a small frown contorting her brows. "Feel too sick to eat."

Hell, he wished the healer from Bearach, Tavia, was here now with all her potions and herbs. She would know exactly what to do to help Kristina.

"You will feel better soon," Colin murmured, willing it to be so.

The men searched the whole area, but found no more men besides the one a MacKenzie had fought with and killed. Not Holme, unfortunately. Some of the men gathered around.

"Since they're on horses, even in this rough terrain, they'll be harder to catch in the darkness," Cyrus said, crouching near the fire pit.

"Only three of them left alive, in my estimation," Warton said.

Cyrus turned to Colin. "Do you think they'll come back?"

"Hard to say. Holme's real name is MacKillican. When he discovered who I was, he wanted revenge against me."

Cyrus frowned. "Why?"

Colin told him the story of what happened ten years ago.

"In that case, he may be back," Fraser said.

"When someone wants vengeance for something that significant, they don't give up easily," Cyrus said.

Colin nodded, hating that Kristina had been dragged into Holme's revenge plans. Although he'd had designs on her prior to that.

Once they'd rested and eaten the roasted rabbits and a few bannocks some of the men had brought along, a half-moon shone. He convinced Kristina to lie on her side and eat half a bannock to keep up her strength. 'Twas clear she was forcing herself to eat it.

"There is some moonlight, but I think 'twould be safer to spend the night here and head out at daybreak," Cyrus said.

"I agree." Though Colin would love nothing more than to rush Kristina back to the castle, they were several miles away by now and it would be highly difficult to traverse the rugged landscape in near darkness. Besides, he was certain the men were exhausted and needed to rest for a few hours.

Cyrus assigned some of his men to take first watch.

"Do you want to rest in the tent?" Colin asked Kristina. Earlier, he'd seen the lone tent out to the side.

"Nay. 'Tis where Holme attacked me."

Colin ground his teeth. Every time that image entered his mind, Colin wanted to smash his fist into Holme's face. "We can sleep here by the fire, then."

He lay down beside Kristina and pulled her into his arms, not caring what the rest of the men thought. Of course, she didn't need his body heat now, since they were beside the fire, but he thought she might feel safer if she could feel him... although he wasn't sure why, since he'd failed her and allowed Holme to abduct her.

"I'm sorry I didn't protect you well and that Holme got his hands on you... and hurt you."

She turned her head toward him. "You were injured and knocked into the river. There was naught more you could've done."

Regret tightened his chest. "'Tis my fault you're hurt."

"Nay, Colin. I'm so thankful you didn't drown in the river. I prayed for your safety."

He kissed her forehead. She was a treasure. "Rest and recover, my sweet. We'll travel back to Bearach in the morn." He prayed Red Holme had left the area and would not be waiting along the trail with bow and arrow.

When Kristina awoke, her head pounded as if a rock were smashing against it with every heartbeat. 'Twas the same as it had been when she'd gone to sleep. She pressed her fingers to her temples.

"Are you well, Lady Kristina?" Colin's deep and soothing voice sounded concerned as it reached her in the darkness. He was not lying next to her as he had done for most of the night. She thought it must be after dawn, because she heard the activity of several people moving around her. She smelled roasting fowl, at first uncertain whether the scent was appealing or not. She still felt a bit queasy... but also hungry.

"My head aches terribly." With her fingertips, she touched her swollen cheekbone and eye. Saints! She supposed she should not be surprised by the damage—Holme had fists like giant boulders.

"Rusty just brought some fresh, cold water from the stream. Here, try this wet cloth." Colin touched the icy cloth to her cheek. After the initial pain and shock of it, she found it soothing.

"That feels good," she whispered.

A few minutes later, Colin asked, "Do you think you could stomach some roasted grouse? Some of the men hunted this morn at dawn."

"I think so. I'm hungry."

"That's a good sign."

After she'd washed her face with the cold cloth a few times, her head felt a bit clearer. She started pushing herself up, and Colin helped her sit. He then wiped the wet cloth over her hands, washing them. She could've done it, but she liked that an attractive man wanted to help her. She would not stop him.

She hated the helplessness she felt most of the time now... well, ever since she'd been blinded, in truth, for she could not get through the Highlands by herself. In her heart, she was a strong, independent woman, but none of this showed on the outside.

"Here's a piece of grouse." Colin took her hand and placed the meat, still warm from the fire, into it. The scent was delicious.

She took a bite and chewed, finding it tender and smoky tasting. "'Tis good. I thank you."

Colin brought her fresh water to drink, then explained to her how he and his men had run into the MacKenzies, the MacDonalds and a few Camerons out searching for them last evening. Around twenty men all together. He then introduced her to Cyrus, chief of the MacKenzies, and his brother, Fraser.

"What of my sister, Anna? Did anyone see her after the battle?"

"Aye, she is well," Cyrus said.

"Thank God." Kristina could not wait to embrace her sister again. It had been so long.

After Kristina finished eating, Colin carried her into the bushes so she could relieve herself, then gave her privacy. Once she was finished, she called out to him.

He strode forward and lifted her. One arm supporting her back and the other under her knees, he carried her back toward the center of the camp. He was the gentlest man she had ever met. She rested the uninjured but scarred side of her face against his chest, wishing she could tell him how precious he was to her.

"We found this and wondered if it was the lady's," a man said.

"Did you have a pouch?" Colin asked her.

Kristina felt at her waist, shocked when she realized the pouch containing her valuables was gone. "Aye, are the earrings in it?"

"Nay, 'tis empty."

"Damn him!" she blurted, then ground her teeth. "Holme took my mother's gold earrings. Do you see them anywhere on the ground?"

"Wait here and we'll look." He seated her upon the ground. "How large are they?"

"They are coin shaped with an embossed daisy and a garnet in the center."

After a few minutes, Colin returned and crouched beside her. "Nay, lass, I'm sorry. I think Holme must have stolen them."

Tears pricked her eyes. "That bastard," she hissed. "Those were the last things I had of my mother's. I wish I'd done a better job when I stabbed him."

Colin took her hand and kissed it. "I wish I could get them back for you. Mayhap we can find them later."

Realizing she was being materialistic, she shook her head. "Do not fash over it." She and Colin were blessed to be alive. That was what she must focus on.

Readying for the journey back to Bearach, the men doused the flames with water. The hissing sounds reached her ears and the smoke drifting in the breeze grew stronger, causing her to cough.

Colin picked her up. "I need to get you out of this smoke."

As they began their journey, she heard the footfalls of many men around them, scuffling through the rocks.

Now Colin would have to carry her all the way back to the castle. Guilt weighed heavily upon her shoulders. Although she did still feel dizzy, if she'd had sight she could've walked. Judging by the way Colin moved, she could tell the ground was incredibly uneven in places.

"You must find me helpless beyond bearing," she said.

"Nay, of course not," Colin said, sounding surprised.

"Well, sometimes I do."

"What do you mean?"

She lowered her voice, not wanting to share her emotions and vulnerabilities with the other men, but she felt very comfortable talking to Colin. "I get frustrated and annoyed at myself because I can do nothing out here in the wilderness."

"No person without sight could," Colin said in a reasonable tone. "'Tis rough and rocky terrain."

"When I lived with my aunt and uncle, I could use my cane and go all over their manor house alone."

"And you will again, once you get used to the castle."

"I pray you're right." She wondered if Anna would marry the MacDonald chief. And if she did, would they welcome Kristina to live with them? She hoped so, for she would love being able to spend every day with her sister. She would make herself useful by knitting or carding wool.

"I'm certain you'll get tired of carrying me before long," she said.

"Nonsense."

"We'll all help," Rusty said. She recognized his voice. "Besides, you're a wee thing. We're just thankful 'tis not Warton who's hurt. We'd never be able to lug his heavy arse back to the castle."

The men chuckled, and Kristina couldn't help the small smile that curved her lips, despite the continuing pain in her head.

"You're not the least bit funny," Warton grumbled.

The men laughed again.

"You're all too kind. I thank you," Kristina said.

After Colin had carried her for another quarter hour, Warton said, "I'll take a turn, if the lady will permit it."

"I hate to ask it of you, Warton," she said.

"Nonsense. 'Twill be an honor and a pleasure."

"Don't enjoy it too much," Colin warned as he allowed Warton to take her from his arms.

Warton chuckled, then whispered, "He's smitten, m'lady, I vow."

Heat consumed Kristina's face. Was it true? Well, she had to admit she was also intensely drawn to Colin. But she did not think anything could come of it. She refused to think of it now. She was simply grateful to be alive and away from Holme.

Warton carried her for a quarter hour, then Rusty took over. After this, Fraser and Cyrus each took a turn. She could not believe the chief of Clan MacKenzie was carrying her. She had assumed he would order one of his soldiers to do it. Although he was a stern man with a hard voice, she sensed he was friendly and caring. And he was obviously just as physically strong as Colin.

Soon it was Colin's turn to carry her again, and she was glad. She could relax against him more easily than any of the others, and she found herself drifting in and out of sleep.

Sometime later, Warton announced, "Bearach Castle, thank the saints!"

She tried to wake up, despite the pain in her head, because she could hardly wait to embrace her sister again. But at the same time, the unnatural drowsiness dragged her back down into sleep.

As Colin carried Kristina across the sandbar causeway toward Bearach Castle, he glanced down at her swollen face. "Kristina? Are you well?"

Her only response was a murmur. What was happening? Was she getting worse?

The clanging of the portcullis being raised quickened his pace, as did his concern over Kristina. Soon the healer could see to her.

Anna ran toward them in the bailey, her green eyes wide, Neacal behind her.

"Thank God, you've returned!" Anna said. "How badly is she hurt?"

"She's had a head injury and, though she was more alert earlier, she's fading in and out. She's in great pain," Colin said.

"Anna?" Kristina whispered.

Anna took her hand. "Aye, I'm here. Let's get you into a bedchamber and Tavia will see to you."

"Let me take her up." Neacal held out his arms, his expressive blue eyes saying he knew how tired Colin was.

Although Colin was fully capable of carrying her up the stairs, he didn't argue. His good friend wanted to help, and he could probably maneuver up the familiar narrow stairs faster.

Colin followed them up to the chamber. Neacal laid her on the bed and moved back beside him, while Anna smoothed Kristina's hair back and kissed her forehead. The healer, Tavia, and her helper hastened into the room with their supplies and satchels, while a maid brought hot water.

"Go get yourself something to eat, Colin," Anna said, taking his hand. "Make certain he eats, Neacal."

"I'll eat," Colin assured her, but he couldn't take his gaze off Kristina, for she was pale and far less alert than she had been that morning.

Suddenly, Anna threw her arms around him in a fearsome embrace. "I thank you for bringing her back to me." Just as quickly, she released him and strode back to the bed, leaving tears on his doublet.

"Tavia is very skilled," Neacal said. "If she could save my life, she can save anyone."

"Aye." Colin knew that Neacal had been far worse off than Kristina after he'd been captured, tortured and then rescued by his clan. Many had thought he wouldn't survive it.

"I'm glad you arrived before supper. I'm sure you must be starving."

Colin nodded. "We ate grouse this morn."

They made their way down to the great hall, where dozens of people were gathered to eat. Colin joined Neacal at the high table, then he met Cyrus's brother, Shamus, who had married Neacal's sister.

Though Colin was hungry, his stomach ached with worry for Kristina and he could not get his mind off her. He ate, but did not taste much of the food. Some of the MacDonalds and MacKenzies acted out their final confrontation with Holme, showing the rest of the clan how things had played out, and providing entertainment. As those playing Holme and his men fled like terrified rabbits, laughter filled the great hall. But Colin could not join in their merriment. Even though he was thankful Kristina was safe and behind castle walls, he was still highly concerned over her head injury and how hard Holme had struck her.

He was glad when Anna joined them for a few minutes and reported that Kristina was resting well. Tavia was having Kristina drink an herbal tea and was preparing a small poultice for the bruise on her face.

After they'd finished eating and Anna had returned to Kristina's room, Neacal asked, "How about some whisky?"

"Aye." Colin was tired of the noise in the great hall, where a multitude of people talked all at once. It amplified the chaos inside him.

In the solar, Neacal poured two small glasses of whisky and offered him one, the amber liquid glinting in the firelight. "To Lady Kristina's good health."

Colin lifted his glass. "I'll drink to that." When he swallowed, the liquid provided a nice burn all the way down his throat to his stomach. Then they took seats near the hearth.

"Are you well?" Neacal eyed him. "I see that bruise on your forehead."

"Aye, 'tis naught." His own scratches and bruises didn't bother him. "I simply wish I hadn't allowed Holme to take her from me and injure her." Colin explained what had happened in the cave, when he'd been knocked into the river and washed downstream.

"You're lucky to have survived that, and I'm certain she'll be well in no time. Have faith."

Colin nodded. "I'm trying but… greatly concerned." He didn't ken why he couldn't release his worry over her. Was it a bad omen? Nay, that was nonsense. Kristina had to recover. He would accept naught else.

"Do I detect something else going on here?" his friend asked.

Colin shrugged, truly not wanting to discuss something he didn't understand and didn't want to feel.

Staring into the fire, Neacal sipped his whisky. "You can trust me, you know. I'll tell no one."

"I… have developed a fondness for her," Colin admitted, his heart thudding harder. "Although 'tis not something I wanted or expected to feel."

"I ken how that is."

"She's remarkable." Colin shook his head. "For someone so small, vulnerable and blind, she has an incredible strength of spirit. She's so bright, canny and resourceful."

Neacal sat forward, resting his elbows on his knees, still staring absently at the fire. "She and Anna must be alike in many ways."

Colin nodded and took another swallow of peaty whisky. "Kristina has been through hell already, and then for her to sustain this head injury… I blame myself."

Neacal turned to him, frowning. "Nay, you should not. You rescued her from Holme, Blackburn and the battle. If not for your actions, where would she be now? Probably dead. You must give yourself credit."

Colin tried to make himself believe Neacal was right. He had likely saved her life, though he had no way of knowing if she truly would've been killed in the battle. With two brutes like Blackburn and Holme in charge of her, she would've had little hope of survival without his intervention. Maybe if he told himself that over and over, he would start believing it. Now, if only she would recover quickly.

"Cyrus said Blackburn was killed," Colin said.

"Aye."

"'Tis a relief that he can never hurt Kristina or Anna again."

Neacal nodded. "He got what he asked for."

"I'm furious that Holme got away." Rage burning in his chest, Colin ground his teeth.

"Do you think he will be back?"

"I'm sure he still wants revenge against me."

"Why?"

Colin realized he hadn't yet told Neacal of Holme's real identity; he'd told his own men and Cyrus. "His true name is MacKillican."

"What?" The intensity of Neacal's blue eyes bored into him. "The same clan of traitors the Camerons defeated many years ago?"

"Aye."

"He has a strong motive for revenge."

Colin nodded. "When he saw me, he must have remembered my face. He confronted me and revealed his identity when we fought in the outer cave."

"Why did he not go back to Rhodie Castle and attempt revenge years ago?"

"I've wondered. Mayhap because he knew he would be severely outnumbered. Or because the king declared him and his few remaining clansmen outlaws when they fled. As for now, I'm thinking he was seizing an opportunity upon finding me out in the wood without many men around."

"With that sort of motive, he will not give up easily."

CHAPTER TEN

Pain drummed within Kristina's head, tensing every muscle in her body. She pressed her fist against her forehead, tears burning her eyes. "The tea is not helping!" she sobbed.
"Shh, my sweet sister, you must relax back and let me bathe your face in cold water," Anna whispered.
"We need more cold cloths to put on her head," Tavia said.
Kristina heard water splashing and then another cool cloth was draped across the top of her head.
As she relaxed and held perfectly still, the pain lessened a tiny amount. It was not quite so excruciating now. She willed it away and told herself she felt better. The thought of Colin drifted into her mind—his deep, soothing voice. She wished he were here now.
"The second cup of willow bark and poppy tea is steeped and cool enough." Tavia's voice moved closer.
"I'll help her drink it. Lean up a wee bit." Anna touched her shoulder.
Kristina did not want to move but she leaned up. The pain throbbed harder. She forced herself to drink as much of the honey-sweetened herbal tea as she could, then lay back again.
After the pain simmered down, Kristina took a deep breath. "I'm glad you're well, Anna. I worried Blackburn would hurt you."
"Blackburn is dead," Anna said with cold finality. "You never have to worry over him again."
Kristina had never been glad to hear of anyone's death before, but Blackburn was the exception. He had near destroyed her life and Anna's. They were safe now.
Kristina relaxed, her mind drifting, as if on a cloud, away from the pain.
She did not even realize she was sleeping until she awoke to the

sound of Anna's voice. "Looks like she's waking."

Someone placed a fresh, cool compress on her forehead and eyes again.

"Anna?" she whispered, wishing the pounding in her head would cease, though thankfully it had improved.

"Aye, dear sister. How are you feeling?" Anna rubbed her shoulder.

"My head still aches but not as bad."

"You can sleep more if you wish. I'll stay here with you." Anna held her hand and stroked it. Although Kristina wanted to argue about sleeping more, she found she could not resist drifting off again.

Later, a sound awoke her. She sensed someone nearby. The room was warm and cozy and smelled of food, which did not appeal.

"Oh, good. You're awake again. Are you hungry?" Anna asked.

"Nay." Her stomach ached with queasiness.

"Colin told me it has been a long while since you've eaten much more than a piece of roasted grouse, so you need to eat something. At least a few sips of this broth."

Oh, she truly did not want it, but she knew she would have to force it down in order to recover. "Very well."

"Colin is very concerned about you. He asks about you every half hour."

"Indeed?" Kristina's face heated, and her heart rate sped up. Was he truly that worried about her? "He's a kind man."

Anna helped her lean up to drink a sip of the warm and salty chicken broth. "And—in case you're wondering—Colin is handsome."

Kristina almost choked but forced herself to swallow, then coughed.

"Careful." Anna helped her to lie on her side.

Kristina had known Colin was gorgeous, maybe from the impressions she'd gotten when her fingers had taken the measure of his facial bone structure, or maybe she knew from instinct. Regardless, she did not wish Anna to know of her intense feelings for him. It was all too new and unfamiliar. She had already accepted, ages ago, that no man would ever be interested in her, and now she found it hard to believe Colin might be. Surely it was just a side effect of their being in a dangerous and frightening situation together.

"Did you hear what I said?" Anna asked.

"Aye, but since I cannot see Colin, his looks are of little importance. What of Neacal?" she asked, hoping to get the conversation off herself and Colin.

"Neacal is extremely handsome and I love him. He's such a caring man," she said softly, with much emotion. "He saved my life, more than once."

Alarmed that her sister had been in danger, Kristina frowned. "What happened? Were you hurt?"

"Nay, I'm fine. I'll tell you about it later, once you're well. For now, you must focus on getting your strength back."

"Very well. Will you marry Neacal?"

"Aye. Now that you're back, we can proceed with the wedding plans." The joy in Anna's voice was evident and it increased Kristina's own good cheer.

"I'm so happy for you. I have not even met him yet, really. Although I did hear him shouting from the battlements when first I arrived here. He sounds like a strong, commanding chief."

"He is, and he helped Colin by carrying you up here to this room when you first arrived. Do you remember?"

"Nay. I must thank him, then."

"When you're ready, I'll bring him in so you can talk to him."

"I can tell much about a person by their voice. And, at the moment, I can tell you're happier than you've been in over two years."

"'Tis true. Neacal brings me great joy and peace."

Kristina felt comfort and satisfaction for her sister. "After all you've been through, you deserve someone wonderful. You are indeed fortunate and blessed."

"As are you," Anna returned quickly.

"To have been rescued from the brigands, aye."

"And to have such an attractive and wonderful man as Colin Cameron looking at you the way he does." Anna's voice was teasing and playful.

Although delight brightened Kristina's emotions for a moment, some dark part of her squashed it down. "Since I cannot see, I'll never know, will I?"

"But you will find out about the feelings behind those looks."

Or mayhap she already had, if his kiss was any indication. Still, she missed her sight and missed seeing people's facial expressions. Her curiosity got the best of her. "How does he look at me?" she asked quietly.

"As no man has ever gazed at you before, sister—at least, no man I have observed. As if… you are a star-filled night sky, or a heather-swathed glen in summer. Or a bright rainbow over a loch."

When Kristina imagined a man looking at her thusly, as if she were beautiful, her heart ached. How could he possibly? She had felt the scar on her face many times. It was rough and jagged and people had told her it was a harsh ruddy color. "'Haps your eyes are playing tricks on you. Besides, it matters not." Kristina had to make sure it didn't matter. She had to protect herself from heartbreak. If she let herself believe Colin truly was smitten with her, and then he changed his mind and decided he couldn't tolerate her looks or deal with her blindness, she would be devastated.

Anna blew out an annoyed puff of air. "How can you say that? Do you not like Colin?"

"I like him well enough." 'Twas a grand understatement but Anna did not need to know of her feelings.

"Well enough?" Anna asked doubtfully.

"I only just met him."

"We shall see, won't we?"

"You will." Kristina found it slightly irritating how many sight expressions people used which she could no longer relate to.

"You ken what I mean. We will find out what happens. Mayhap he will want to marry you."

To counteract the sudden leap of her heart, Kristina snorted. "Come now, Anna. Surely 'tis not so dark in this room that you cannot see I still possess the scar upon my face. I hold no illusions that a handsome man would want to marry me."

"Do you think a scar matters? Neacal has many scars, as well. A larger one on his face than you have. And many scars on his body. I find him gorgeous beyond measure."

"We both ken 'tis acceptable and even admirable for a warrior to have scars. But for a woman, 'tis different."

"Regardless, you are a beautiful lass."

"Colin told me he will become a chief one day. He will want a beautiful and perfect wife, one who can see and attend to the duties of lady of the castle. One his people will admire, not ridicule."

"Nonsense. Someone can easily be hired to help with running

the castle. And everyone I know admires you."

"I don't wish to speak of this." 'Twas too painful to think about, for she knew, no matter how much she would love to be Colin's wife, neither he nor his clan would find her suitable, with her many flaws and incapacities. She had been a great burden to him out in the wilds of the Highlands. It mortified her that he'd had to wait on her hand and foot. He would want a strong, capable wife.

"Very well." Anna sounded subdued. "Would you allow me to feed you this broth?"

"Mayhap in a little while." Kristina turned over and pulled the covers up to her ears.

She was thankful to be safe behind these castle walls. But now what? All she thought about was Colin, and she couldn't have him. He might think he wanted her now, but he would change his mind once he realized how difficult she would make his life. Tears dripped from her eyes into the pillow. She craved sleep, so she could briefly escape the hand she'd been dealt, the blindness. For when she slept, she had visual dreams. Even though some of them were frightening, she still treasured being able to see inside her dreams.

When the rumble of masculine voices awoke her, she did not know how long she'd been sleeping. She lay perfectly still and listened.

"She is sleeping," Anna said softly.

"I can sit with her for a while," Colin said, his voice rough and sensual. "You and Neacal get some rest."

"Maybe for a few minutes, but I don't wish to go to bed right now."

"Very well."

"A quarter hour," Anna said.

"Aye."

My, wasn't Anna being motherly, Kristina thought. But her main concern right now was that she likely looked even worse than usual. Her hair had not been brushed in days. Her face was swollen... but what did she care? Colin had already seen her at her worst. Still, mortification burned over her, for she did not feel attractive before a man she was incredibly drawn to.

Anna's footsteps receded, and the door closed.

Although it was clear Colin was trying to be quiet, his boots clomped across the floor behind her. A heated tension burned over her. She recalled what Anna had said about the way he looked at her. Was he gazing at her thusly now? She would give anything to have her sight back so she might see him. Her heart pounded hard at his nearness. The chair beside the bed squeaked as he sat down.

"You're not asleep," he murmured, slightly amused. "Are you?"

How did he know? She frowned and turned over to face him. "Your clunking boots awakened me."

He blew out a short breath, almost as if he might be smiling. "How do you feel?"

"My head still pains me."

"I'm sorry." His voice darkened. "I blame myself for your injuries."

The guilt in his voice dug at her heart. "Nay. 'Twas not your fault."

"I should've protected you better."

He was so kind and heroic, he wriggled his way into her soul. "You did protect me, Colin. You saved my life. Without you... I wouldn't be here." She closed her eyes against the burning tears that flooded them. "I cannot express my gratitude enough." Her voice caught.

He lifted her hand and kissed the back.

"Why would you risk your life in such a way?" she asked. "You didn't even know me when first you took me from Holme."

Colin was silent for a long moment. "When Anna and Neacal spoke of you... when they told me what had happened to you in the past, about your injuries and what Blackburn had done to you, I simply wanted to help."

"You pitied me as everyone else does."

"Nay. 'Twas the opposite, in fact. I admired your mettle. A lesser woman would not have survived what you have. You have amazing strength of spirit."

"No more amazing than you. Look at what you risked for me."

The door opened and the footsteps of two people entered.

"I've returned," Anna said in a bright tone. "And I've brought Neacal with me. You said you wished to meet him, officially."

"Aye." Kristina's face burned, for she looked so disheveled. Surely she should be upright and composed when meeting a chief.

"'Tis a pleasure to meet you, Lady Kristina." Neacal took her hand into his roughened one and kissed the back. "Are you feeling better?" he asked in a deep voice with a Western Highlands accent much like Colin's.

"Wonderful to meet you, chief. I still have pain but 'tis not as bad."

"I'm glad. And please call me Neacal."

"I will, if you will call me Kristina. I understand we will soon be family... when you marry my sister."

"Indeed, and I look forward to it."

"Why do you wish to marry her?"

In the moment of silence, Kristina realized her question must have startled Neacal. But in the absence of their parents or any other family member, she was the only one left to make certain he would be a good husband to her sister.

"Truth be told, Anna first enchanted me and drew me under her spell with her song," Neacal said. "And now... she is my life. I know not if I could survive without her."

Kristina heard the adoration in his deep, soulful voice and it touched her profoundly. Neacal's love for Anna was palpable and obvious within the room's atmosphere. She had never realized she could feel such a thing before, between others.

"I am happy for you both," she said, closing her eyes against the tears.

"We would like for you to stay here at Bearach Castle with us, if you wish it," Neacal said.

Her tears welled faster. "I thank you. You're incredibly generous." But what if they found her to be a great burden?

Kristina's tears ripped at Colin's heart. He could see how appreciative and touched she was to be welcomed to stay here indefinitely. But something gnawed at him. He could not see her staying here. Instead, he only saw her by his side. Would she be interested? Would she want to leave her sister again and live with him at Rhodie Castle? Would his clan approve of her as his wife? His gut instinct told him that his father would not like the idea. He wanted Colin to marry an important chief's daughter and form a clan alliance.

Kristina's blindness did not bother him at all, but he could well imagine his clan might have reservations.

"Colin?" Neacal's voice brought him out of his deep thoughts.

His friend waited near the door.

He lifted Kristina's hand and kissed it. "I will see you in the morn, Lady Kristina."

"Very well, and thank you again. Good night."

"Good night." He bowed to Anna and followed Neacal out and along the dim corridor. "I could use a sip or two of whisky." Colin suspected he might have a difficult time putting Kristina from his mind this night.

"I have plenty." Once in the solar, Neacal poured two small glasses of whisky. "'Tis clear to me you're smitten with the lass."

"Mayhap." Colin saw no point in denying it. His insightful friend would spot any half-truths he told anyway.

Neacal grinned, offering him the glass.

"*Slàinte mhaith*," they exchanged in toast.

Colin sipped the fiery liquid and let it trickle slowly down his throat. "Her tears rip my heart out. I cannot withstand it."

"I know what you mean. I'm compelled to give Anna anything she wants. Her happiness is more important than mine own."

"Aye, we risked our lives for them and would again," Colin said.

"Indeed. So… will you ask Lady Kristina to marry you?"

The next morn, after Colin had gotten little sleep, that monumental question was still burning in his mind—would he ask Kristina to marry him? Hell, he wanted to, but many things made him hesitate. First, he had to figure out whether she would accept without actually asking her. What if she didn't wish to marry, and instead wanted to stay with her sister? What if, God forbid, she rejected him just as his former fiancée had?

Kristina truly did astound him. He wished to get to know her better, but something held him back. He sensed something was holding her back, too. It came through in some of her snippy comments, as if she were trying to push him away. But after that, she couldn't prevent her true self from emerging.

After breaking their fast, he, Neacal, the MacKenzies, and some of the other men went out searching for Tom Thorburn and Patrick Cameron, his two clansmen Holme and his cronies had ambushed days ago. Colin had sent some men to search for them after they had arrived back the day before, but no one had been able to find them.

Gray, leaden clouds drifted low over the loch, the pine forest and the rugged landscape as if the rain might begin at any moment.

When they were deeper in the wood, Neacal's brown wolfhound, Dunn, stuck his nose in the air, drew in several whiffs, then sprang forward at a lope. The men followed at a brisk pace, scrambling over the rocks and rough terrain, struggling to keep up with the long-legged, shaggy animal. A sinking feeling of dread lodged into Colin's stomach.

A few minutes later, they found the bodies, covered by leaves and pine needles, hidden in a shallow ravine in the wood. Even though Colin had known, deep down, that they were dead, a merciless mixture of anguish and fury slammed into him.

"Bastard!" Colin growled. "Holme will pay for this."

"Blackburn taught him well," Neacal muttered.

"Or maybe his father did. To think, Holme had Kristina captured and at his mercy for hours. He could've killed her so easily." Latent fear for Kristina rose up and gored him.

Neacal clasped his shoulder, gaining his attention. His sharp blue gaze speared through the dark haze of angst and rage. "But he didn't kill her. You saved her life."

'Twas true. He couldn't allow Holme's evil deeds to drown his rationality. "I couldn't have done it without all the men you sent who helped."

Neacal nodded. "She's safe now."

"Aye." Colin had to keep telling himself that. "But from now on I will have to be on my guard until Holme is either dead or imprisoned."

Later that day, they held funerals and burials for his two fallen clansmen.

Afterward, Colin bathed, needing to wash the death and destruction from his body and mind. Though he soaked in the wooden tub before the fireplace in his room until the water grew cold and the room darkened, gloom still hung over him, and he felt sullied by the lingering thoughts of Red Holme's evil.

He needed to see Kristina. If he could only talk to her for a few minutes, she would lighten his soul. He shoved himself from the tub, dried off and dressed in a clean shirt and belted plaid.

He had looked in on her earlier, but she'd been sleeping. He hoped that meant she was recovering quickly. 'Twas almost time for supper to be served, but he would visit her first. He looked forward to the time when she would be well enough to join them in the great hall for meals.

At her chamber door, he knocked.

Anna opened it. She smiled and turned back to the bed. "You have a handsome visitor, Kristina."

Colin felt his face heating. Hell, since when did he blush? He was no green lad.

"I thank you." He bowed, and when his gaze lit on Kristina's face, he found she was blushing, too. As well, she was sitting up in the bed, leaning back against pillows. Her golden hair had been washed and brushed. Some of her curls had been braided into a beautiful style. If not for the horrific bruise on her cheek, she would've looked like a princess.

"You ladies are both exceptionally lovely this eve."

"Such flattery will gain you many smiles," Anna said. "Right, Kristina?"

Her blush deepened and she grinned, magnifying her beauty a hundredfold. "Aye."

"Would you mind keeping her company while I dress for supper?" Anna asked him.

"'Twould be my pleasure." And the reason he'd come here.

"I must also scribe a missive to Aunt Matilda and Uncle Gilbert in Stirling, letting them know we're both all right. Neacal said he would have one of his messengers deliver it."

"Oh, how I miss them. Tell them I love them," Kristina said.

"I will." Anna exited, leaving the door ajar.

"You look near recovered, Kristina. Do you feel better?" The chair squeaked as Colin sat down in it. The wooden chair legs scraped over the floor as he dragged it closer to the bed. Kristina was glad. She wanted him as near as possible.

"Aye." She did feel better, especially now that he was here. "The herbal tea and cool compresses have helped. The pain is gradually going away."

"Thank the saints." He took her hand into his big, warm one. She squeezed his fingers, enjoying his strength, thankful for his presence. She wished he would never leave her side. Wished he would always be close enough to touch her. He instantly brought a calm peacefulness over her. But she could not become too attached to him, she reminded herself.

"Have you been eating?" he asked.

"Anna is making sure of it. She near pours the broth down my throat."

He blew out a breath of a snicker. "She's a good sister. With her care and Tavia's you will be up and around in no time. Hopefully, soon, you will be eating in the great hall with us."

She nodded, something far less pleasant coming to mind. Something she'd been mulling over for a couple of hours. "Anna told me about the funeral for your two clansmen. I'm so sorry for your loss and I feel horrible they were killed while protecting me."

"Nay, do not feel bad," he said in a compassionate tone. "They loved being soldiers and guards, and they considered it an honor to help rescue you."

Tears sprang to her eyes as she imagined such good men losing their lives to the brutal Holme.

"Please don't blame yourself." Colin stroked his thumb over her palm. "They would not wish you to do that."

She nodded and swallowed, trying to force the constriction away from her throat. "Will you take me to their graves, so I might place flowers there and thank them?"

"Of course, my sweet, if you wish it."

"In a few days, when I feel better."

"Aye. They would be honored, and I'm sure they already ken of your gratitude."

For the next quarter hour, he told her amusing stories of Thorburn's and Patrick's exploits and adventures. She knew he was trying to brighten her mood. But she was also saddened that the two couldn't have any more adventures. This brought to mind Ralston, the guard who had helped her on her journey here.

"Do you know if Ralston was killed in the battle?" she asked.

"Who?"

"I think I mentioned before... Ralston was one of Blackburn's guards who protected me from Holme during our travels here."

"I have no inkling if he survived. I could ask Neacal, but I would need a visual description."

Her heart sank. "Aye. And I don't know what he looked like. I would have to identify him by his voice."

"Did you... become close to him?"

"He treated me like a sister. Even though he worked for Blackburn, he seemed a good man."

"If I find out anything, I'll let you know."

The door creaked open. "Supper is being served, Sir Colin," Tavia said. A food tray clattered onto a nearby table.

"Aye." He stood, his chair making a creaking sound. "Lady Kristina, would you like to accompany me to the great hall?"

"Mayhap tomorrow. I'm not certain I'm able now. But I hope you enjoy your meal."

When he kissed the back of her hand, she relished the feel of his warm, sensual lips on her skin. Heat rushed over her, and she wished his lips were caressing hers instead.

"I will see you later, then," he said.

When he exited, she felt bereft and alone, even though Tavia was there, handing her a chunk of bread.

"Sir Colin is a handsome lad," Tavia said.

"Aye, he is."

Tavia snickered. "And how did you figure this out?"

"Anna told me, but even before that, I knew or sensed it." She didn't want to tell Tavia that she'd traced her fingers over Colin's face. Surely that was too intimate. But she wished to do it again. It seemed forever since the nights she'd slept in Colin's arms, even though it had only been a couple of days. Those two times were all it had taken for her to become accustomed to his touch and sleeping well-protected against his warm, strong body. She craved that feeling. When might she get to sleep beside him again?

Red Holme rode east through the Highlands, leading his two remaining men, Dobson and Scroggie. Damn Cameron and his men for killing Mungo at the campsite. Where had Cameron gotten so many men in a few hours' time? There had to have been over a dozen.

Holme glanced around at the dull-gray granite mountains, having no inkling where he was. Finally, the rugged mountains gave way to gentler rust-colored, bracken-clothed hills. Aye, this area was starting to look familiar. He had been here over a decade ago, and 'twas not far to Rhodie Castle.

When he thought of how the Cameron clan had stolen his birthright, fury gnawed at him, making him more determined than ever for vengeance.

Rhodie Castle had been held by the MacKillican clan for generations, given to his direct ancestor by King James II for loyalty and service. Why should the Camerons have it now, given to them by King James VI? 'Twas true that his da had refused to appear before the king or pay the exorbitant fine levied against him. And finally his da had killed the king's representative who'd come to put him in his place, but 'twas naught more than the man deserved.

'Twas all in the past. At present, if Holme couldn't have Rhodie Castle, neither would the Camerons.

Although Holme was outnumbered, as he always had been, that wouldn't matter, for he was going to use new tactics. He would pick off the Camerons one by one if he had to, until he downed Chief Cameron himself, the man who was responsible for his father's death. And of course, he would execute Colin Cameron, too.

Finally, Holme and his men crested a familiar hill and he spied Rhodie Castle in the distance, gleaming pale against the golden-brown, bracken-covered hills.

He was home, finally, after all these years. *More than anything, I want to reclaim it for you, Da.* But since King James would never allow him to hold it, he would at least ensure the thieves did not live to enjoy it. Then, his father would no longer see him as a weak coward. His father would be proud of him.

Making certain no one spied them, Holme and his two men gradually moved closer to the castle and sat amid the bushes and trees, watching the closed portcullis. Sooner or later, a Cameron would step out.

CHAPTER ELEVEN

Two days later, Colin was honored to sit beside Kristina in the great hall, for she was a woman like no other he had ever met. Though her face was still bruised a blueish-violet color, she was improved enough to eat supper with the clan, and he was thankful for that. Several clansmen had stopped by the table to welcome her and to tell her they were glad she was improving. She gave each of them a bonny smile, and he could hardly keep from staring at her.

The servants carried large platters of venison, grouse, fish, bread, cheese and various other foods to the tables.

Kristina leaned toward him and whispered, "Is anyone staring at me?"

"I am."

Grinning, she blushed. "Cease your teasing, Colin Cameron."

"'Tis true."

"Rogue," she whispered, her smile turning mischievous. "I mean others."

Wondering why she was concerned, he glanced around the hall, then back to her. "Nay, I see no one looking in your direction. Why do you ask?"

She shrugged and shook her head, sitting straight again and looking a bit uncomfortable.

"If they are staring, 'tis because you're beautiful."

Her blush deepened, and she offered a slight grin. "Nonsense. But I thank you for lying to me."

"I'm not lying," he said firmly. Leaning closer, he whispered, "You are the only woman here I wish to stare at."

Her smile seemed more genuine now. Saints! He would love to kiss her but would have to wait until they had some privacy.

Neacal's white-haired great uncle, Bhatar, stood from his seat at the high table, a few chairs down, and began saying grace.

Colin bowed his head and closed his eyes, realizing this darkness was all Kristina saw every moment of the day and night. He tried to imagine what life must be like for her—how incredibly difficult.

After the prayer was finished, Colin kept his eyes closed a moment longer. A chorus of *amen* was murmured. Then many conversations began at once, blending into a roar, the clatter of ale tankards, spoons against wooden bowls, knives against wooden trenchers. The many sounds had to be confusing and chaotic for Kristina. His greatest anxiety would be that he couldn't see who might be sneaking up behind him.

He opened his eyes and leaned toward her to speak low. "Do you ever get leery of who might be slipping up behind you?"

"I used to. But now I can hear or sense, somehow, if they do."

"In truth? That seems a useful ability. You will have to tell me more about that sometime."

Kristina nodded.

Anna, sitting on her left side, lifted Kristina's hand and placed a piece of crusty bread in it. "Here's bread, sister."

"I thank you." She sniffed it, took a small bite, and chewed. "'Tis heavenly. We could've used this in the cave, aye, Colin?"

"Indeed." He relished her companionable tone. "Would you allow me to cut up your venison?"

"I would appreciate that."

Colin enjoyed helping her. After he'd finished, he watched her carefully sliding her fingertips across the linen tablecloth until she encountered her own tankard of ale. She then picked it up, held it in both hands and gracefully took a dainty sip. Afterward, she placed it back where it had been.

He found her skills at the table nearly the same as a sighted person.

She faced him and raised her brows. "Are you still staring at me?"

Colin couldn't hold back the smile. "How did you ken I was?"

"I sensed it. You're sitting very still and not eating. I can tell you're turned toward me because I hear your shallow breathing."

"Och. I can get naught past you, can I?"

"Nay." She gave a wee half smile.

"Well, I was just thinking how graceful you are at eating, even though you cannot see."

"I've had a lot of practice." She picked up a piece of the venison and bit it in half.

A commotion began among the three guards at the entry, then one of them rushed toward the high table. "Chief," he addressed Neacal in a lower tone. "We found one of Blackburn's men lurking about in the wood."

Could it be Red Holme? Colin shoved up from his chair, ready to go choke the bastard.

"Where is he now?" Neacal asked.

"In the courtyard. We have him bound. Do you want us to put him in the dungeon?"

"Did he tell you his name?"

"Aye. Ralston."

"Ralston?" Kristina piped up, her brow furrowed in concern. "Is he injured?"

The guard looked at her in surprise.

Neacal sent a questioning glance at Colin.

"He was her guard on the journey here, and treated her well. Right, Lady Kristina?" Colin asked.

"Aye, he is a good man. I pray no one has harmed him."

"He's well enough, 'haps a few wee cuts and bruises," the guard said. "And he did ask about you, m'lady."

Colin frowned. Why? Had the guard come back for her?

"Put him in a holding cell, remove the bindings and give him fresh bread and water," Neacal said. "I'll question him in a short while."

"Aye, chief." The guard bowed and strode away.

Colin sat down again, disappointed that Red Holme was not apprehended.

Kristina turned to him. "I must speak to Ralston. He is not a bad person."

"I will go with Neacal to question him first. If he seems safe, then mayhap you can speak to him, but I make no promises."

"Very well." Kristina continued to look unsettled. She turned to her sister. "Do you think Tavia would check on him to see if he's injured?"

Colin listened in closely while sipping his ale.

"What do you know about this man?" Anna asked. "He didn't work for Blackburn two years ago, before we ran away."

"Nay. He was hired later. I know very little about him. Just that Blackburn assigned him to guard me on the way here. He got into a fight with Red Holme while protecting me."

Maybe the man wasn't terrible but… was he in love with Kristina? Why else would he risk returning for her after such a terrible battle when most of his comrades had been killed?

After supper was finished, Colin followed Neacal down the steps into the dungeon. Two guards, carrying torches, accompanied them. The smoke from the torches couldn't cover the dank, musty smell of the dungeon. At the bottom of the steps, they halted before the holding cell.

The man inside stood and approached the bars. He looked to be in his early twenties but, at the same time, burly and muscular.

"Ralston?" Neacal asked.

"Aye."

"What is your first name?"

"Finlay."

"I'm the MacDonald chief. And this is Colin Cameron, future chief of Clan Cameron."

Ralston bowed. "I'm greatly honored to meet you both."

"What were you doing lurking about outside?" Neacal asked.

"I but wanted to see if Lady Kristina is well."

"Aye, she is," Colin said. "Why do you care?"

"I feared Red Holme would kill her. The man is soulless. During the battle, I didn't see who took her or what happened. Then I noticed that Red Holme had disappeared, too."

"She's safe here now. I'll be marrying her sister," Neacal said. "And Lady Kristina can live here, protected behind these walls, as long as she wishes it."

"You didn't say why you care," Colin said, annoyance clawing at him.

Ralston sighed. "You may not believe me, but… I'm her brother."

"What?" Neacal demanded. "Anna and Kristina have no brother. Anna told me herself."

"Half-brother. She doesn't know about me. Neither of them does."

Colin frowned, exchanging a wary glance with Neacal. But he was relieved the lad had no romantic interest in Kristina. 'Twould be far better if he truly was her brother. That might explain why he had been so kind and helpful to Kristina on the trip.

"I never met my father," Ralston continued. "But my mother revealed, on her deathbed, who my father was—Chief Finlay MacQueen. They'd had a very brief tryst while he was married to someone else, and she had always kept it a secret. He didn't even know I existed. She also told me I have two sisters. I have no other family, so she wanted me to know about them."

"Why the devil were you working for a knave like Blackburn?" Neacal asked.

"My search for my sisters led me to the MacCromar clan's holdings. I couldn't ask where the ladies were, outright. That would've looked highly suspicious. I told the guards and Blackburn that I was looking for work. I figured if I was a guard there, I would see my sisters eventually. But I learned both women had run away a year before and that Blackburn was looking for Anna incessantly. I stayed on because I figured if anyone could find my sisters, it would be Blackburn. He had many men at his disposal and the funds to pay them. I had naught, and I didn't even know what my sisters looked like. I couldn't search for them alone. So, I kept quiet and observed Blackburn and his men. When I learned he was going to abduct Lady Kristina, I knew I had to protect her."

This seemed a plausible story and Ralston appeared sincere. But Colin couldn't depend upon the veracity of it, because doing so could put Kristina in danger again.

Neacal narrowed his eyes. "How do I know you're telling the truth?"

Ralston shrugged. "I have no proof. But if you ask Lady Kristina, she will likely tell you I was naught but honorable on the journey here. I helped her and protected her as much as I could."

"I will speak to her about it," Colin said.

"Aye, we both will," Neacal said. "In the meantime, I'll have more food sent down. Are you in need of a healer?"

"Nay. I have no serious injuries. I'm simply glad both my sisters are well."

Colin eyed him, realizing he did see a slight family resemblance. Ralston's hair was tawny, a few shades darker than the ladies' hair, and his eyes were a light color which was difficult to discern in the dimness and torchlight.

After climbing the steps to the courtyard, Neacal said, "Though he appears to be telling the truth, I know not whether to trust him."

"I agree." Colin felt conflicted about the situation. "Even if he was kind and helpful to Kristina, that doesn't mean he's their brother."

"'Tis true, but there is a family resemblance," Colin begrudgingly admitted.

"I noticed," Neacal muttered, glaring back toward the dungeon entrance.

"Did Anna not mention anything about a brother or her father's natural children?"

"Nay. I think this will be a tremendous surprise to her."

Colin shrugged. "If 'tis true, I hope the ladies will view the situation favorably."

"I wish we had proof, or a witness, at least. 'Tis difficult to go on a stranger's word only."

Colin watched as Anna led Kristina into the library and helped her get seated at the table. Both sisters appeared anxious.

"What is this about, Neacal?" Anna stood behind her sister's chair.

Neacal paced, then placed his hand on the mantel. "First, we need to ask how Ralston treated you on the journey from Stirling, Kristina."

"Oh." Her face brightened. "As I said, he was kind and helpful. Whether we were in a village tavern or out on the moor, he brought me food and drink. When Holme attacked me in the tent one night, Ralston dragged him out and got into a fist-fight with him. Ralston told me I reminded him of his sister. Why do you ask?"

Neacal raised a brow, sending Colin a leery glance. Were they wondering the same thing? Had Ralston been trying to feed her a suggestion so she would think of him as a brother and trust him?

Neacal inhaled a deep breath and let it out. "Do you ladies have a half-brother?"

Anna frowned. "Nay, why?"

"Ralston!" Kristina announced, her face alive with excitement.

"You know of this?" Colin asked, shocked.

"What?" Anna demanded, looking confused. "We have a half-brother?"

"I sensed it. He seems like a brother to me." Kristina grinned. "I always wanted a brother."

"What did he tell you?" Anna asked Neacal.

"He said he is your father's natural child, but he never met the man. On her deathbed, his mother told him his father's name and that he has two sisters."

"Good heavens," Anna breathed and dropped into the chair beside her sister. "What is his first name? How old is he?"

"His first name is Finlay."

Anna gasped, her eyes wide. "That's our da's name."

Kristina's mouth dropped open. "I never thought to ask his given name."

"It could be a lie," Colin muttered. "That information would be easy to find out. All of this could be a grand scheme as he tries to get closer to you ladies for some nefarious purpose."

"There is no nefarious purpose, Colin," Kristina said in a persuasive tone. "I wish to talk to him, please."

Colin exhaled an annoyed breath and glanced to Neacal to see what he thought of the idea. His scowl said everything.

"Did he tell you his age?" Anna wondered.

"Nay, but he appears to be in his early twenties," Neacal said.

Curiosity lit Anna's green eyes. "I need to know more. I want to speak with him, too."

Neacal stared at her intently, concern and worry in his gaze.

"Surely it will be completely safe with you and Colin here." Anna looked at him with pleading eyes. "You could have the guards bind his hands behind his back."

"Very well." Neacal glanced to him. "If Colin agrees."

"As long as he is bound, I don't see any harm in it. But, ladies, don't get your hopes up. He could be a very skilled liar."

"We'll bring him in here along with two guards," Neacal said. "But for your own safety, neither of you are to go near him."

A quarter hour later, two guards escorted Ralston into the library, his hands bound behind his back. Colin observed as Ralston smiled first at Kristina and then at Anna.

As Anna stared intently at Ralston, her mouth dropped open,

and her hand flew up to cover it. Colin wanted to ask her what was going through her mind. Did he look familiar to her?

Ralston bowed. "Ladies, I'm glad to see you are both well, except for… Lady Kristina, where did you get such a horrible bruise?"

Kristina turned toward him. "Red Holme struck me, but I'm recovering. How are you? Were you injured?"

"Nay. Only a few scrapes and bruises." Ralston's attention shifted. "Lady Anna… or should I call you Lady MacCromar? I'm pleased to meet you."

She seemed to get her surprise under control. "*Anna* is fine. You told the chief you are our half-brother?"

"Aye. I don't believe my mother would lie on her deathbed. A priest was there as well, giving her last rites."

"I'm so sorry for your loss," Anna whispered, her eyes still searching his face.

Ralston gave a brief bow.

"Does he look like us, sister?" Kristina asked.

"Aye. He has blue eyes, like you. And his hair is a shade of dark blond. He resembles Da a great deal, especially his strong chin and jawline."

"I knew it!" Kristina smiled. "You seemed like a brother to me soon after I met you, Ralston."

"Well, I knew you were my sister then, but I could not reveal this information. I was simply trying to keep you safe from Blackburn and Holme."

"You did a good job, and I appreciate that."

"How old are you?" Anna asked.

"Twenty summers."

Kristina drew in a quick breath. "The same age as me."

"Aye." Anna frowned, her mouth tightening.

"What month were you born?" Kristina asked him.

"September."

"I was born in March." Kristina's brow furrowed. "Our da was a bit of a rogue, apparently."

"How could he have been unfaithful to Ma?" Anna demanded.

"I know not, but you cannot blame Ralston," Kristina said.

"I don't blame him. I simply thought Da the most honorable of men." Anna appeared devastated by this news.

Colin wished he could say something to offer consolation, but he knew not what. Some men did not take their marriage vows seriously, especially when they did not have a love match. He truly believed his own father had always been faithful to his mother, for they loved one another. And that was what Colin wanted, himself.

"Even if Ralston is your brother, how do we know for certain we can trust him?" Neacal asked.

Everyone waited in suspended silence for a long moment. Anna chewed her lip, her worried gaze swinging to Neacal and back to Ralston.

"You don't," Ralston said, his expression sincere. "I will have to prove myself trustworthy."

Colin admired the man for saying that.

"I found you trustworthy during our journey," Kristina said. "Will you be staying with us?"

"I would like to, for a while, if Chief MacDonald would permit me to."

Neacal's face was impassive. "I will think on it."

"If you have work, I can earn my keep," Ralston said.

"Is there some other secure place he could sleep, besides the dungeon?" Anna asked.

"Aye. I'll have a room set up for him." Neacal's gaze shifted to Ralston. "You will be locked in and guarded for the time being. I'm not trying to be unfriendly, but you must understand that my main priority is protecting the ladies. If there is even a slim chance you could harm either of them, I must prevent that."

Later that night, Kristina lay in bed awake, thinking how happy she was that Ralston was her brother. She'd always wanted a brother. Or maybe she'd somehow sensed that she had one, somewhere, and felt his absence.

Like Anna, she was a bit surprised and disappointed in her father, that he would have a liaison while married to their mother. Still, her joy in having a brother overshadowed all of that. Her parents had both passed, and she forgave them their faults.

"Are you awake?" The male whisper came from the doorway, and Kristina recognized it immediately.

"Colin?" Excitement propelled her bolt upright in bed.

"Aye." His warm, friendly voice made her smile.

"Come in," she murmured, trying to keep her voice down.

The door clicked closed, and booted feet approached the bed.

"I had to see you again."

"I wanted to spend more time with you, too. And wanted to thank you for having Ralston brought in so we could talk to him."

The chair squeaked as Colin sat down beside the bed. "Well, he appears to be a decent man thus far. Let's hope he continues to be so."

"He will. I can sense things about people, like whether they have a kind heart or not."

"You're very canny." He was silent for a long moment. "What do you sense about me?"

His fresh-soap scent reached her, and she realized he'd recently bathed. She wished she could bury her nose against his chest, relax and drift toward sleep. Or kiss him. Aye, she was well enough now to receive one of his scorching kisses.

"I sense that you're a noble and honorable man with a good heart. You're gracious and courteous."

He lifted her hand and kissed it, and she wished he wouldn't stop there. His warm, smooth lips and contrasting scratchy beard stubble awakened her nerve endings and sent tingles over her body. She sighed, then suddenly wondered whether they might be disturbed.

She listened, not hearing anyone else. "Did Tavia and Anna go to bed?"

"Aye. 'Tis after midnight."

"Oh." Good, she was glad to be alone with Colin. "I've been awake longer than I realized. I'm excited to have a new brother."

"'Tis understandable."

"You've never told me… do you have any brothers or sisters?"

"Aye, a younger brother."

"What is his name?"

"Bryce. We've always been very close."

She lay back down, and Colin told her all about his brother and his mother and father. Finally growing drowsy, she yawned.

"I'm boring you," he said.

"Nay, 'tis not that at all. I love hearing about your family."

"Well, 'tis late. I must be getting back to my chamber." He arose from the chair.

The thought of him leaving made her feel cold and lonely. "You could rest here," she blurted.

He was silent for a long moment. "What do you mean by *rest?*"

Her face burned. Mayhap she shouldn't have said anything, but she did miss him lying beside her. "Like we rested in the cave. And by the fire pit."

He blew out a breath. "You wish me to hold you… while we sleep?"

"If you would like to. I enjoyed it."

"I did too, of course, but 'tis a bit different, being in a chamber… in a bed. Someone might walk in, see us, and assume the worst."

"Bar the door."

"You are a reckless wench." The humor was evident in Colin's voice.

He was right. When it came to him, she was reckless indeed. Her blood raced with excitement any time he was near.

"I'll be right back." A moment later, the bar fell into place.

She shoved the covers down so he could get underneath. When he returned, she heard him kicking off his boots.

The edge of the mattress dipped under his weight, then he stretched out beside her and pulled the covers over them both.

"No one will walk in and misunderstand what's going on here," she said.

Colin turned toward her, lying on his side. "I've been deeply concerned about your injury."

"I still have some pain, but I'm much improved now." She slid her arm around his waist.

He kissed her forehead, then tucked her head beneath his chin. "Am I making your pain worse?"

"Nay. Now we can sleep." Although she didn't truly want to sleep. Instead, she wished he would kiss her lips as he'd done in the cave. Her heart raced with anticipation. But maybe he thought she was still too injured for any kind of sensual contact. For now, she would revel in his warm, tight embrace. She loved the reverent way he touched her.

She buried her nose against his shirt and drew in his clean, delectable male scent. And the more she breathed him in, the more her imagination ran wild. She vividly recalled those earlier kisses, and her restlessness increased. She was unsure whether she could sleep now.

Colin cherished the woman in his arms. He had never met anyone like Kristina. She turned his heart into mush. He did not pity her because of the blindness, but he wished she could see for her own sake, so her life would be easier. Although he was certain this affliction had made her a stronger and more resilient person.

As for himself, he did crave for her to look into his eyes at times, but 'twas merely a selfish yearning on his part. One of the many yearnings he felt around her. She stirred up a much stronger desire than he'd ever felt for his former betrothed. Or maybe 'twas simply that Kristina blotted out his memory of any other woman.

All his adult life, he'd wanted a woman who inspired profound excitement in him. Kristina did that. Even though he hadn't known her long, she was incredibly special to him.

He knew he should not be here in her bed, but he couldn't resist holding her, especially when she'd asked him to. He could only lie here a brief time, maybe a half hour. For a certainty, he could not fall asleep, or he might be trapped here in the morning.

Kristina snuggled closer to him, pressing herself to his chest. She made a humming sound of pleasure. The round, firm curves of her breasts near drove him mad... even through his shirt and her smock. Arousal blazed along his veins like fiery whisky. Saints! How he wanted her. In the soft glow from the fireplace embers, her blond hair gleamed faintly.

When he stroked his hand over her back, she felt tense, not at all like she was almost asleep.

"Relax," he whispered. "Go to sleep."

"I'm trying, but you smell so good. You distract me."

She sure as hell distracted him, too. Knowing she was drawn to him only fired up his blood all the more. After sliding her arm down to his waist, she dragged herself even closer to him.

The sudden pressure against his shaft felt delicious and only compounded his yearning. Air hissed between his teeth.

"Oh, what is...?" She froze.

Damnation. Surely, she realized what she'd felt, but she might not if she was naïve and had been completely sheltered all her life.

What the devil could he say to her?

When she moved her hand to his chest and quickly slid it

downward, his breath halted.

"Lass?" He grabbed her hand... even though he didn't want to. Saints! Why couldn't he be more roguish? Placing her hand on his shoulder, he cupped her chin and stroked his thumb across her lips. "I want you. That's what," he rasped. "You're tormenting the hell out of me."

She drew in a shuddering breath. "Oh."

He was stealing a kiss whether she liked it or not. He brushed his lips lightly against hers. When her lips parted, he drew in her excited exhales. Her lips were soft and silky... and so sweet, he thought he had entered into heaven.

Fisting her hands in his shirt, she tugged at him, then lifted her face to his. She was such an innocent... he should not be doing this. But how could he resist? He stroked his tongue along her full lower lip and then between.

"Colin," she gasped and opened her mouth a bit more. Entangling her fingers in his hair, she drew him closer.

Damnation! 'Twas clear to him she wanted him, too. Placing his hand on her wee round derriere, he dragged her hips tight against his. He wanted her to feel the full effects of what she'd done to him. Her groan exploded his passion like fire set to gunpowder.

He pulled his mouth away to nibble on her ear, then placed little kisses and licks down her throat. Her sweet scent stole his sanity.

"Colin?" she breathed. "That feels so good."

When he reached the top of her smock, where the tempting swells of her breasts began, he forced himself to pull his mouth away.

"I have to stop," he said through clenched teeth, then embraced her tightly. "I'm sorry I did that."

"Why?"

"You're an innocent."

"Aye, but... I don't wish to be."

CHAPTER TWELVE

"What?" Colin rasped.

Kristina hoped she hadn't shocked him by saying she no longer wanted to be an innocent. How could she explain it to him? She would never marry. With her scars and blindness, no man wanted her as his wife. Why should she worry over her virtue? Her future was uncertain, and she made no plans for it. All she had was right now. She merely lived in the moment, day to day. Aye, she was safe here at Bearach, and she was thankful for that, but once Colin left she would have no more romance or excitement. She would only get to live life vicariously through what other people told her.

Colin stroked her hair back from her face. "What did you mean, lass?"

"No man will marry me, so why should I worry about my virtue?"

"You are mad. Of course you will marry."

"Nay, I think not." Besides, if she loved a man, why would she want to burden him and make his life more difficult?

"Surely you've had many suitors."

She gave a brief, bitter laugh. "Nay. No man had ever given me a real kiss… until you." Her voice became a whisper. "And I enjoyed it. Could we do it again?"

He groaned and threaded his fingers into her hair. His hand fisted. She felt a slight tugging at her scalp, but it did not hurt. She liked it.

Focusing on his groan, she asked, "Are you in pain?"

"Not pain, just near unbearable yearning. You make me want you so badly." He moved his hand to her derriere and drew her flush against the hard appendage at his groin. She knew very little about men's bodies, although Anna had told her a bit about love-making. She had never imagined a tarse would be so large and hard as steel. Some instinctive part of her loved the feel of it pressing against her belly. She wiggled closer to him, wishing they could be skin to skin.

She kissed his throat, and he let loose a soft moan. He captured her mouth again. Oh heavens, she could simply drown in his kiss. His tongue flicked inside her mouth, teasing and tormenting her, delicious as a sensual comfit.

What on earth was happening to her? She felt like a burning candle... melting... wanting him to touch her everywhere. His mouth upon hers was more drugging than opium tea. She crushed her breasts against his chest, loving the hard feel of him. She wove her fingers through his hair, holding his head just where she wanted it.

"We must stop, lass," he said in a harsh whisper against her mouth.

"Nay, please don't." She pressed her lips against his chin with its scratchy stubble.

When he consumed her mouth again, she was thrilled he had changed his mind. Growing bold, she flicked her tongue between his lips. He growled a curse, then drew away.

"Saints, you tempt me," he ground out. "But I must not touch you. I must not," he declared in a hoarse tone.

She felt like cursing in frustration. How could he stop? She could not bear it. Colin seemed to enjoy touching her, and she certainly loved touching him, so why should she stop? She wished him to turn her from a girl into a woman.

She wound her fist into his shirt and kissed his chin. The short, bristly whiskers pricked and scratched her lips. She flicked her tongue against his chin and, moving upward, found his lips. He was so scrumptious... she could devour him.

He turned his head aside. "Kristina? Do you ken how you torment me?"

"I'll ask naught more of you, beyond this."

"What do you mean?"

"That I want to experience passion now with you, for the first and only time ever in my life, but I ask for no promises regarding the future. I'm safe here with Anna, and so you're free of me. I live in this moment, Colin, for 'tis all I have."

"Nay, 'tis not," he growled. "You have a good future ahead of you."

She placed her finger over his lips. He drew it inside and suckled on it, sending carnal yearnings through her body, then he kissed her palm. "I shall give you something, lass. Not what you seek, but you should experience passion and desire at least once."

"What do you mean?" His words confused her, for she knew so little about passion and what she yearned for.

"I'll show you." He tugged at the hem of her smock, then stroked his warm hand up her bare calf and thigh. His palm was slightly roughened, stimulating her sensitive skin.

At his spellbinding touch, she drew in a surprised breath and held it. He kissed her again, greedily devouring her lips, distracting her and making her crave him all the more.

He moved his hand upward still to where her thighs joined her body and the exceedingly sensitive spot where she ached for him. He brushed his fingers over her, provoking a lightning bolt of pleasure. She could not prevent the gasping cry that escaped her.

"Shh. You must promise to be quiet, else you'll wake people in the rooms nearby."

"Aye, I promise," she breathed. Anything… if he would keep touching her like that.

When he stroked her again, igniting a heated reaction such as she had never felt, she clenched her fingers into his shirt, holding on for dear life. Hesitantly, she inched her legs apart. He trailed a finger along her most intimate spot, magnifying the fiery sensations. Heavens! She had never imagined she would like to have a man touching her in such a shocking place. The feeling overwhelmed her, and her back arched. She wanted to beg him but somehow refrained.

As her legs moved farther apart, he stroked her in a circle, and she could not stop her hips from rising toward him, seeking more. She grasped his hair and his shoulders, pulling him closer. She wanted him on top of her, but he stubbornly remained at her side, tormenting her with his fingers and his kisses. Her thoughts bounced in every direction, for she could not understand the startling, pleasurable sensations engulfing her, nor could she control them. Colin commanded her body like a puppet.

A moment later, she bowed backward, feeling as if she were shooting across the night sky like a blazing star. Colin closed his mouth over hers, muffling her cries. Was she dying and ascending into heaven? Such stunning ecstasy. She could scarce breathe or move.

When the euphoria diminished, she came back to herself, breathing hard, shocked at the intensity of what she'd felt.

"What happened?" she asked. "What did you do to me?"

He gave a low chuckle. "The peak of sensual pleasures."

"Good heavens. I thought I was dying." 'Twas as if she'd been flying and had just gently floated down to earth. Her body felt weak and spent.

When he kissed her forehead, she felt his smile. "Did you enjoy it?"

"Aye, but... I'm certain you must think me worse than a tavern wench."

"Nonsense. You are a passionate, beautiful woman."

"What about you? You must teach me how to bring you pleasure." She stroked her fingers down his stomach.

He grabbed her hand firmly. "Nay. I must go to my own room." Releasing her, he arose from the bed, taking away his delicious warmth. The featherbed felt higher without the muscular weight of him, and too large and empty without his tall frame taking up so much room.

"How can you leave now?" she whispered.

"I refuse to take advantage of you, my sweet." He leaned over her and kissed her forehead.

"But I want you to."

"Regardless, I would not be an honorable man if I did," he said, slipping on his boots.

"Honor is overrated."

He snorted. "At the moment, I agree with you. But I would hate myself on the morrow if I did what I yearn to do."

The next evening after supper, Colin and Neacal sat at the high table, while Anna led Kristina between the crowded tables to the other end of the great hall, toward the musicians.

Colin could not stop thinking about the scorching-hot encounter with Kristina last night in her room. It had certainly not been his plan to seduce her or make any sort of sensual foray when he'd gone in there. He'd simply wanted to talk to her and spend time with her. Her eager interest in him took away his good sense. He didn't know how he'd survived leaving her there alone, without taking advantage of what she'd offered, but he'd known he had to leave before he let desire snatch his control. He had to take her well-being into consideration before anything else.

Once Anna and Kristina reached the minstrels, silence enveloped the hall. 'Twas as if everyone held their breath in anticipation.

The violin and lute music began. A moment later, the ladies' voices arose toward the rafters in heavenly melody. Colin closed his eyes, absorbing the beautiful, soul-stirring sounds. Their voices were different and distinct, but together they created a flawless harmony. Anna's voice was higher pitched, while Kristina's was a bit lower and sensual. 'Twas obvious they had practiced for many years together. And though they'd been mostly apart for the past two years, to his ears, they were not out of practice at all.

When the song ended, the crowd boisterously clapped and cheered. Colin opened his eyes and glanced aside at Neacal. "'Twas perfection."

His friend blinked as if coming out of a trance, then nodded. "Wee pieces of heaven. 'Tis how Anna first captured my attention. I knew she was someone special and amazing when I heard her voice." Neacal turned to smile at Anna, such love and devotion in that look. A look that Colin had not seen Neacal give another woman.

When Colin shifted his gaze to Kristina, he realized if he smiled at her, she wouldn't know it. She couldn't see him. They could never exchange an intimate glance. A smile or a playful wink would mean nothing. She had lost so much along with her sight. 'Haps 'twas selfish of him, but he wanted her to look into his eyes. That was not possible and never would be.

"It infuriates me that Blackburn stole Kristina's vision from her."

Frowning, Neacal nodded. "Aye, me too. He got what he deserved, but even that cannot bring her vision back."

Colin would have to communicate his feelings for her in other ways. In words, whispered into her ear. By the way he kissed her. By the way he touched her. The luscious memory of last night burst fully into his mind. He'd had to use every ounce of strength he possessed to leave her, especially when she'd wanted him to stay.

They would be a perfect match when it came to the bedchamber. Her passion and arousal had equaled his own. Even now, his body quickened and hardened at the memory or her eager responses to his touch. But he knew she was virginal; therefore he could not despoil her.

"Do you think your father will agree to the match?" Neacal asked.

Surprise jolted Colin. "Match?"

Neacal grinned. "Aye, you and Kristina."

Of course, he'd known what his friend meant, but he was trying not to think about marriage. It made things far too complicated.

His father wanted him to marry. But would he find Kristina suitable, in terms of the clan she was from and her blindness? Or would he care enough about Colin's happiness to overlook it? His father had always taken his duty to the clan seriously. And his father had not married for love, but Colin believed his parents had learned to love one another. From what he could tell, they had always been devoted to each other.

"I know not," Colin mumbled. But if he made a decision that he wanted to marry her, he had a feeling he would come into conflict with his father. And that he didn't look forward to, because he was close to his father.

At the moment, Colin was simply trying to figure out how strong his feelings were for her, and whether hers for him were equally strong. Each day he grew more and more enamored of her, which was unsettling. He had to make sure this wasn't a brief infatuation, but was instead something that would last a lifetime.

The emotions he'd experienced since he'd met Kristina were so intense they sometimes kept him awake at night. The last time he'd felt this way, when he'd been betrothed to Lady Emma MacMillan, he'd had his hopes and dreams smashed when she'd rejected him. Would Kristina do the same thing?

Though he didn't want to admit fear of anything, that rejection was what he feared most.

Kristina had already said she would never marry, because she thought no man would want her. But what if she knew he wanted her forever? What would her reaction be?

As she and Anna sang another song, they near ripped his heart out with the stunning words, meanings and emotions carried on their exquisite voices. The deep devotion they sang about was what permeated his soul. As with most Scottish ballads, this one ended on a tragic note. Would his own life mirror this song? Would he never find happiness or lasting love?

"Take a chance," Neacal said when the song ended. He gave Colin a light slap on the shoulder, arose and left the table.

Well, he would have to take a chance, wouldn't he? If he wished to at least try for a love match. The alternative was to marry a stranger and hope for the best. He already knew plenty of people who existed in empty marriages. Business arrangements, alliances. Of a certainty, every chief needed plenty of allies. As for the marriages themselves, who knew what went on behind closed doors? Likely faithfulness was something that was ignored, especially on the part of the men. For many of the women, too, once they'd borne an heir.

He supposed he was a daft romantic.

Lifting his gaze, he watched Neacal give Anna a kiss on the forehead, just in front of the dais. He was not the only romantic in the room. His gaze darted to Kristina, who was standing near her sister. Every time he glimpsed Kristina, his heart jolted in his chest. She was the most appealing lass he had ever laid eyes upon. The scar on her cheek made her even more lovely and dear to him.

As the trestle tables were dismantled and moved to the side of the great hall so the dancing could begin, Colin arose from his chair, hopped down from the dais and strode toward Kristina, intending to ask her to dance. He took her hand and kissed the back. "I had no idea you were so talented. Your voice astounds me."

She smiled, a blush coloring her cheeks. "Oh, Colin, I thank you."

As the minstrels began a lively piece, Neacal led Anna to the middle of the dance floor. At the same time, Neacal's sister, Maili, strode toward Colin and Kristina, a wide smile upon her pixie-like face, her blue eyes luminous as a clear sky. "Lady Kristina, you have a most beautiful voice!"

Kristina beamed. "You're too kind."

Maili leaned in close and said in a low voice, "I have an idea."

"What is it?"

"A surprise for Anna and Neacal's wedding feast tomorrow. We could sing a ballad together."

Kristina's face brightened. "'Twould be great fun, but I'll need a lot of practice."

"Could you come to my chamber so we can start right away?"

"Of course. I'll have a servant tell Anna I want to retire early."

Though Colin was disappointed Kristina would not have time to dance this eve, he escorted her to Maili's chamber. Outside the door, he kissed her forehead. "I'll see you in the morn, m'lady."

"I regret that this came up," she whispered, looking solemn. "I'd wanted to talk to you more."

Her sentiments warmed his heart. "I'll look forward to talking to you tomorrow." He kissed both her hands. "Enjoy your practice."

After she entered Maili's chamber, he climbed the spiral stone staircase and exited onto the ramparts. He had wanted to spend some extra time with Kristina, but that was not to be this evening. He was glad she'd found a new friend in Neacal's sister. Truth be told, he actually needed some time to think anyway, to clear his head and figure out what he wanted.

The west wind from the sea blew hard over Loch Moidart. And 'twas much colder today than it had been only a few days earlier. Winter was certainly on the way.

He would have to return to Rhodie Castle soon, before the weather turned severe. But he didn't want to leave. Everything was completely unresolved for him. With each new moment he spent with Kristina, he was more and more drawn to her beautiful soul. But could they build a life together? Even though he knew she had a passionate spirit… was she physically too fragile to cope with a regular life as someone's wife… as his wife?

He knew not what to do. His life had become both incredibly joyful and turbulent since he'd met her. He wished he could see into the future to know how everything would turn out.

Holme and his two comrades watched Rhodie Castle from the cover of the wood, as they had been doing for days. He hated hiding out like an outlaw, stealing food from the nearby village to survive. He had to do what he'd set out to do soon or go mad with the anticipation. The need for revenge slithered through his veins like so many vipers. He kept seeing Colin Cameron's face, the way he'd looked when he'd first snatched Kristina from him—the look of a fierce and determined warrior.

Holme could be equally fierce and determined when he wanted something.

The distant clang of the Rhodie Castle portcullis being raised riveted his attention. "Nock your arrow," Holme whispered to Dobson. "Scroggie, hold the horses at the ready."

He followed Dobson a few yards farther along to a position with a better line of sight. Whoever had left the castle would have to pass this spot.

As he watched the four riders drawing closer, he realized that the middle-aged man with the graying beard who rode in the center of the three younger guards was indeed Maitland Cameron, the chief. He remembered him from years ago.

"This is our chance," Holme whispered, his heart pounding with eagerness. "Shoot the bastard in the middle—the one with the gray beard and red sash."

Aiming, Dobson drew the bow back and let fly the arrow. It struck a tree limb with a snap and went askew.

"Damnation," Holme hissed, grabbing the bow from Dobson's hand. "Give me an arrow."

Luckily for him, the horses' hooves pounding the dirt road covered the sound of the arrow hitting the limb.

After he quietly sprinted to a better position, he nocked the arrow and aimed, making sure no tree limbs blocked the line of sight. He released the arrow at precisely the right moment. It flew straight, striking the Cameron chief in the lower abdomen.

Holme couldn't believe it. He was stunned for a moment, unable to move.

Pandemonium broke out below. The chief shouted, and his horse danced about. The guards went berserk, yelling. Two of them leapt off their mounts and dragged the bleeding chief from his horse, the arrow still embedded in his lower abdomen.

Holding a targe before him, the other guard rode closer. "Assassins in the wood! Get him back inside the walls!"

"Let's go." Filled with dark satisfaction, Holme ducked low and ran toward Scroggie and the horses. Finally, he had avenged his father.

As Holme mounted, the distant shouts still echoed. No doubt all the Cameron guards would be riding through this spot in a matter of moments. Assassination of a chief was not taken lightly.

"Ride as fast as you can," Holme warned. "If they catch us, they will not let us live."

CHAPTER THIRTEEN

At Neacal and Anna's wedding the next evening, Kristina enjoyed Colin escorting her into the chapel.

"You look lovely, Kristina," he whispered as he led her toward the place where she would stand as Anna's maid of honor.

Her face warmed. "I thank you."

She did not want to release his warm, strong arm but knew she had to, for he had to stand on the opposite side as Neacal's best man.

The chapel was cold, and she missed the heat of her bedchamber fireplace. During the night, the weather had turned extremely chilly.

Bagpipes skirled from the courtyard outside as Jules, the piper, led the bridal procession from the keep toward the chapel. Many of the shrill sounds were carried away on the blustery, cold wind before they reached her ears. He continued playing outside the door of the chapel while footsteps approached. Kristina imagined Anna approaching on the arm of her mentor, the elderly musician, Eli.

Neacal did not yet trust Ralston to escort Anna, as her brother—if what he'd said was true, and Kristina believed it was. But she could understand Neacal's wariness. Both he and Colin were equally reluctant to allow Kristina to get close to him. They said they would permit Ralston to watch the ceremony from the back of the chapel, though his hands would be bound.

Once the ceremony was underway, Kristina listened as Anna and Neacal exchanged the traditional Highland wedding vows. The beautiful love they shared emanated from them like an intoxicating mist wafting over a field of heather in full bloom. She did not need to see them to know of their devotion to one another. Anna's voice caught with emotion as she repeated the vows.

Equally touching were Neacal's heartfelt vows to Anna, for Kristina knew he meant them. He would always protect her, cherish her and make her life as wonderful as he could. She did not doubt his sincerity. As joyous and grateful as she was for Anna's happiness, Kristina knew she would never be able to experience such a marriage herself, though she wanted to with every fiber of her being. 'Twas better not to dream at all, rather than dream and know the wish could not come true.

If she were a normal woman with sight and smooth skin, Colin would be the man she would select for a husband, but no man, especially a future chief, would want a blind, scarred wife to help him lead a clan or run a castle. And even if he claimed to, she would not saddle him with such a burden of responsibility. His father, the chief, would not approve, nor would his clan. In addition to her disabilities, she was also penniless, with no dowry. She had no clan alliances to offer a chief.

Kristina dried her eyes and held her head high. She refused to wallow in self-pity. She would focus on Anna's happiness and, with Maili's help, sing a special song for her sister and her new husband once they were in the great hall.

During the final prayer, she closed her eyes and blotted them, determined to feel happy. Once it was over, she lifted her head and forced her lips to curve upward into a small smile.

"I present to you Chief and Lady MacDonald," the priest announced jovially.

A cheer of excitement echoed from the rafters. Tears of joy sprang to her eyes, for she was happy the MacDonald clan accepted her sister with such enthusiasm.

She dried her eyes, and a moment later, she recognized Colin's warm, strong hand on her arm. Her smile broadened. She couldn't help it. No matter her future, Colin still made her smile.

"Are you well, Kristina?"

"Aye, of course." She was now. She hoped he hadn't seen her tears of sadness, but something told her he had... his tone of voice, maybe.

He tucked her arm into his bent elbow, next to the bulging muscle of his upper arm, and led her from the chilly chapel into the even colder wind. The cobblestones were uneven, and though she tried to concentrate on lifting her feet high enough not to trip on them, Colin's magnetism snagged her attention. The second time she stumbled, he halted and lifted her into his arms.

"Oh, goodness. I'm sorry I'm so clumsy." Her face heated at her own inadequacy. She wanted to be a graceful lady in Colin's eyes.

"Nonsense, love. These stones are so rough, I don't know how sighted people walk across them without falling."

What on earth? He had called her *love*. Pressing her eyes closed, she laid her head against his upper chest, absorbing the feel of that endearment and the heat of him. He had a beautiful, bright soul that made her feel treasured.

"Here we are." At the top of the entry steps, he placed her onto her feet and led her into the warm great hall. The delicious scents of the wedding feast reached her.

"Have I told you how gorgeous you are this day?" he whispered into her ear. His hot breath stirred yearnings inside her.

"You are too kind, sir." Finally, she was starting to be able to accept compliments from him, because she trusted him. She believed he considered her attractive, when other people didn't. Even if most others focused on her scar, Colin saw beyond it. Just as she could feel that he was handsome, even if she couldn't see him. She wanted to tell him, but a loud cheer went up for the chief and his new bride.

Colin helped her onto the dais and seated her at the high table between Anna and Maili. She had not known Neacal's sister long, but she had become friends with her quickly.

Maili grasped her hand and whispered, "Are you nervous about singing?"

"Nay, are you?"

"Aye, a wee bit. I'm not used to performing."

"But this is your clan. You should not be nervous."

"I ken 'tis silly of me, but for years they didn't accept me and my gift of second sight. I suppose I still fear their ridicule."

Kristina could understand that. She always feared people would ridicule her scar and blindness, as well. But she wanted to do this for her sister and her new husband.

After the priest said grace, Colin stood and began speaking, his deep, resonant voice echoing over the silent hall. "Let's raise a glass… to my best friend and foster brother. If anyone deserves love and happiness, 'tis you, Chief Neacal MacDonald, for you've endured more pain than any of us can imagine. And to the new

Lady Anna MacDonald, I've come to realize what a remarkable, strong and caring woman you are, the perfect healing balm to my friend's battle wounds. And I thank you for that. Neacal and Anna, may all of your days be happy ones. Great health and every good blessing to you. *Slàinte mhaith.*"

A cheer went up while many glasses, tankards and cups clanged together.

When everyone grew silent again, Kristina whispered to Maili, "Is it time?"

"Aye." Maili took Kristina's hand and stood. "Instead of a toast, we will sing a song for our brother and sister."

The minstrels stood to the side of the high table and accompanied them. Kristina had memorized the song, *Tabhair dom do Lámh,* years ago. She and Maili had only practiced the song together twice but to her ear, it sounded perfect.

After they finished, applause, shouts and whistles of approval exploded. Feeling her face heat with joy and gratitude, Kristina smiled.

Hours later, after eating and drinking all she could, Kristina remained at the high table as the din in the great hall grew—laughter, shouts and music. The clansmen carried Neacal off to join his new bride in the bedchamber.

Kristina didn't know how she would feel if she were a bride awaiting her new husband. Without doubt, she would feel excited and happy, if it was a man she wanted to marry, but also mortified that the whole of the clan would know what was taking place above stairs.

Soon the grumbling men clomped down the stairs again. By the sounds of their slurred voices, 'twas clear they had already drunk too much whisky and ale.

She had not gone up with Anna earlier to assist her in preparing for her wedding night because she would've felt in the way. Being unable to see, she couldn't help her sister undress or put on her new night rail. She couldn't style her hair. In addition, since Anna was a widow, she already knew about the wedding night activities, while Kristina did not. Anna actually preferred that she wait down here for Maili and the rest of the women to return.

Colin must have been amongst the men carting Neacal off to the chamber. Amid the lively dance music, she heard the sounds of many stamping feet as the dancing began anew.

"Lady Kristina?"

She started at the sound of Colin's deep voice just behind her left side. She turned her head.

"Could I have the next dance?"

Joy and appreciation sparked tears in her eyes. Turning her head away again, she blinked at the stinging moisture, lest he see. "I'm not a very good dancer," she said. "I tend to stamp on feet, bump into the others, and create chaos."

"I'll not let that happen. You can hold onto my hands or my shoulders, and place your feet on mine, if you wish, like a wee lass."

She heard the smile in his voice, and that made her want to smile, too. "If you promise to not allow me to embarrass myself," she said.

"Of course."

As she arose from her seat, the music slowed to a ballad. Thank the saints. This sort of dance would be far easier for her. She learned to dance more than a decade ago, and she hoped she remembered how.

Colin lifted her down from the dais, then slipped her arm through his as he led her to the dance floor. Facing her, he placed her hands on his shoulders, then clasped her waist.

"Put your feet on mine," he whispered in her ear.

Hesitating at first, she did as he asked, hoping she wasn't too heavy upon his toes. At least her slippers were soft. She matched her movements to his and it seemed they moved as one. In this slow dance, gliding around the dance floor with Colin felt good, and joy permeated every fiber of her being.

"You're a good dancer," he said, loud enough to be heard over the music.

She grinned. "'Tis because you're doing all the work."

"I don't know about that, but I do know you have a beautiful smile," Colin said.

"I thank you. Are you smiling?"

"Aye."

She did indeed hear the amusement in his voice now. "I wish I knew what your smile looked like." Just that statement alone snatched away her good mood and drew her downward, for she would never know, really. Certainly, she could imagine what his smile might look like, but she could be completely wrong.

"I'll let you feel it, if you wish," he murmured into her ear, his hot breath giving her shivers. Before she could ask what he meant, he gently lifted her off his feet, took her arm and guided her off the dance floor and away to a cooler area where the music was lower. A door clunked shut, muffling the music.

"Where are we?" she asked.

"The library." His voice was a deep, husky murmur.

"I remember now. So you're tired of dancing already?" she asked to cover her sudden giddiness at being alone with him.

"You ken better." He took her hands and raised them. He kissed the backs and then her palms. Chills skittered up her arms and across her chest, near making her sigh. With her fingertips, she took the liberty to explore his square jaw and lean face, with its short, scratchy stubble, and his sensual lips. He was smiling, and somehow she sensed it was genuine.

He leaned closer and brushed his lips across hers, then gave her a dreamy but too brief kiss.

That felt so good she slid her hands around his neck and into his thick hair, then drew him closer. She could not resist the vibrant feel of him, so exciting. He smelled of delectable wine, cinnamon and cloves.

Gently and with great deliberation, he took her mouth in a consuming kiss, making her drunk on the spiced wine taste of him.

He lifted her onto the hard wooden table, surprising her. This raised her higher so that she could more easily reach his mouth. Wickedly, he teased her tongue with his. She could not get enough of his intoxicating mouth. Every kiss made her desire him more. If his kiss was this wonderful, what would making love be like?

She pulled back an inch and whispered against his mouth, "I want you to show me."

"Show you what?" His voice was raspy and heated.

"What it is like… between a man and a woman."

"Damnation, Kristina," he hissed. "I wish you wouldn't say things like that. 'Tis hard enough to resist you as it is."

She clasped her hands onto his doublet. "I don't wish you to resist."

"You are an untouched maiden," he growled.

"'Tis why I want you to teach me. Otherwise, I may never

experience it."

"You will one day "

"Nay. I'm only interested in now," she muttered. "I want you to kiss me and... touch me. Reveal to me what a man does to a woman in the bedchamber. What you did to me before was breathtaking, but that was only a taste, I'm thinking."

"Damnation. You tempt me beyond reason," he said through clenched teeth.

"Good." She smiled, reached down and tugged his kilt upward.

He caught her hand, holding it in his, then kissed her lips again. Afterward, she was dizzy.

"Wait here," he said, prying her fingers off his kilt. His footsteps crossed the room and a lock clicked. "We don't want any interruptions."

"I agree."

When he returned, he urged her to lie back.

"What are you doing? Will we couple on this table?"

He chuckled. "You are too curious by far."

He pushed her skirts upward, past her knees and her thighs. The heat of embarrassment consumed her face while a different sort of wicked heat flamed over her body. His warm hands on her thighs, spreading them, felt positively sinful. She did not know what he was about, but she hoped he would teach her what it meant to be a woman, full grown.

Her most sensual parts were exposed to him, although she had no inkling how much light was in this room or what he might see. Before she could worry over it, something touched her delicate flesh. His mouth?

"Good heavens! Colin?"

"Shh." He blew his hot breath upon her. Then he treated her like a sweet comfit, licking and suckling on some highly sensitive place she had no name for. The sensations were extreme and exquisite, making her mad with wanting something only he could give her.

"Colin!"

"You must be quiet, or I'll be forced to stop."

She bit her lip. Though what he was doing was scandalous, she never wanted him to stop. Never! 'Twas the best thing she had ever felt. He continued with the delicious torment while she twisted, squirmed and tugged at his doublet sleeves.

She felt herself being drawn upward toward the peak of this intensity. The white-hot desire exploded, and she screamed a second before she felt Colin's hand over her mouth. *Quiet*, she remembered, turning her shouts to low moans.

Before she could recover, Colin dragged her up and wrapped her arms around his neck. She gasped for breath, trying to regain her wits. The first thing she realized was that he hadn't taken her. He had only teased and tormented her.

"I want more, Colin."

"Are you certain?"

"Aye. Of course. Please. How many times must I ask?"

"No more." He bestowed a deep, ravishing kiss on her such as he'd not yet given her.

His hands behind her bent knees, he dragged her to the edge of the table, spreading her legs wider. She heard the rustle of his clothing and sporran.

"You can tell me to stop, if you wish it."

"Nay."

"I must warn you, it might be painful the first time."

"I ken it. Anna told me."

"If you will relax and be patient, the pleasure will come after that."

She could scarce breathe for the mixture of trepidation and anticipation. "I'm ready." She wanted to get the hard part over with.

Something gently touched her tender flesh, which he had licked and teased beyond endurance. He stroked through the moisture and prodded against her. She ached with the heated arousal.

"Aye," she breathed, fisting her hands in his hair.

Before she could worry more about the pain, he dragged her hips toward him and surged forward, breaching her like a battering-ram. The stabbing pain shocked her and she cried out. He covered her mouth with his and held still.

"Kristina? I'm sorry. I would never want to hurt you," he breathed against her mouth. "Are you well?"

"Aye." She was, wasn't she? Or at least she would be once the painful part was over. She could endure it; she'd endured far worse pain in the past.

"Try to relax, love," he rasped as if barely able to control himself.

"I am. And I'm ready for the pleasure." She wanted this passion with him, for she might never experience it again.

"I will endeavor to give you every ounce of pleasure possible." The smile was evident in his voice. "But you must be patient."

She nodded.

He withdrew and pressed forward again, into her. During the stabbing pain, she forced herself to remain silent, biting her lip, hoping the stinging would diminish. She was surprised when he placed his hands beneath her hips, lifted her into his arms and drove deeper. Then paused again.

"That's it, *mo chridhe*. Relax."

Suddenly, she realized the pleasure was increasing, while the pain was decreasing. "Aye, more."

He kissed her lips, sliding his tongue into her mouth. His movements quickened, and with each thrust, the pleasure climbed.

"Oh, Colin." Her breath caught. She had never imagined this feeling. Fulfilled aching pleasure, rising higher with each moment. Sliding, plunging deeper. "Aye."

He growled a curse. The profound passion latched onto her again, and she felt as if her mind flew toward the moon. Colin shook against her, grinding himself deeper, and heat flooded her.

Her face pressed to his, they gasped for breath. Good heavens! What an astounding sensation. It did not seem real or possible.

Withdrawing, he kissed her cheek. "Did I hurt you?"

"Nay. No more than I asked for, at any rate. 'Twas amazing!"

"So you *are* hurt?" He adjusted her clothing back into place.

"Only a wee bit tender." She smiled, for the pleasure had blotted out the pain.

Loud revelers passed the door outside, making Kristina jump. Thankfully, they did not try to enter the room, and their talk and laughter faded. Though the music and dancing from the great hall was still boisterous.

"I'd best take you up the back stairs to your chamber," Colin said.

"Aye."

After opening the door and checking the hallway, he returned and picked her up. "The steps are uneven. Hold on and I'll carry you."

She nodded, slipping her arms around his shoulders.

His hands at her back and under her knees, he moved quickly

up the stairs. His thighs must indeed be strong. She hoped they didn't meet any servants or clan members. She did not want to be the gossip of the castle.

In the upper corridor, he quickly but quietly walked along, carrying her.

"What are you about, Colin Cameron?" asked a deep voice to their left.

Kristina's heart felt as if it vaulted into her throat.

CHAPTER FOURTEEN

At the sound of the voice, Colin spun around, Kristina still cradled in his arms, to find Fraser MacKenzie lounging curiously against the wall near a sconce, a smirk upon his lips.

"Fraser. I didn't see you there. Lady Kristina grew tired, and I'm carrying her to her chamber."

Fraser pushed away from the wall and stepped forward. "Is this true, m'lady? Or is this rogue set on defiling you?" he asked in a droll tone.

Kristina bit her lip, but a wee grin peeked out. And even in the low light, Colin could see her blush. "Stop your teasing, Fraser!"

He snickered.

"You're but jealous because she's impervious to your charm," Colin jested to cover his own discomfort.

Fraser snorted. "Nonsense. No lass is impervious to my charm."

Ignoring him, Colin set her to her feet and opened the door to her chamber. "Here you are, Lady Kristina. I'll send in a maid to help you. Can you manage on your own until then?"

"Aye, I've learned my way around the room. I thank you for the help."

Colin closed the door and turned to Fraser. Blast the man and his interruption. "Come, let's find a maid."

"I saw the look on her face." Devilment gleamed in his blue eyes.

Hell, Colin hoped she didn't look like a woman who had been well pleasured. Mayhap he meant the blush. "You embarrassed her."

"Not that. The other expression. I'm certain you saw it for yourself."

Colin gave him a blank look, hoping he didn't betray their secret. "I know not of what you speak."

"The lass is in love with you."

That brought Colin up short, for 'twas his fondest wish. "Do you honestly think so?"

Fraser chuckled. "Of course. Do you not see it?"

Colin frowned. "If I did, we wouldn't be having this conversation."

He knew he was falling for her, but was Kristina truly in love with him? If so, 'haps she would accept if he proposed to her. Now that he'd given in to his desires, he not only wanted to ask her to marry him, he needed to. Mayhap that was why he'd let his desires overwhelm him, so he would have no other choice but to ask her to be his wife. 'Twas what he wanted most in the world. So... now, regardless of his fears of rejection, he must propose as soon as possible, this night—once Fraser was elsewhere so he could slip back and speak with her.

"Mayhap you should go help her disrobe," Fraser suggested. "I'm certain she would like your help more than a maid's."

Well, of course, he would love to do that, but since he had an audience, he certainly wouldn't. "I think not. What are you doing, lurking about up here?"

Fraser shrugged. "I but went to my guest chamber for a... sip of my favorite whisky."

"This is the ladies' corridor."

A sneeze sounded farther along.

"Who's down there?" Colin whispered.

Fraser's eyes widened in exaggerated surprise. "'Haps 'tis a maid."

Colin hastened toward the alcove, Fraser following, and did indeed find a pretty young maid hiding there. 'Twas no accident both she and Fraser were here. "Is this knave taking advantage of you?" Colin asked.

Her face darkening in the lantern light, the maid shook her head.

"Lady Kristina could use your help," Colin said.

"Aye, sir." She curtsied and hastened to Kristina's chamber.

"Bastard," Fraser hissed drily.

Colin snorted with laughter.

"That lass was trying to seduce me," Fraser said.

"I'm certain," he said doubtfully.

"I'll make a bargain with you. When she comes out, look the other way while the maid drags me to my chamber, and neither of us will watch you walk into Lady Kristina's chamber."

"I had no intention of going in there," Colin said, hating to lie, but he needed to protect Kristina's reputation.

"But you would like to. And now that I've mentioned it, you can think of naught else."

Colin lifted a brow, glaring at the younger man. He was not like Fraser, was he? Chasing the skirts of any lass who gave him a long glance? Nay, 'twas Kristina, only, who turned his head. He could not deny he was fascinated by her. And now that they'd shared the greatest of intimacies, he had every intention of keeping her in his life.

"As long as that maid kens well what she's getting herself into, and is in agreement with it, I'll say naught," Colin said.

"And I'll not mention I saw you carrying Lady Kristina." Fraser stuck his hand out for a shake, but Colin ignored it.

"I have carried her before," he said defensively.

"But not up here." Fraser raised a brow in challenge. "You're besotted with her. 'Tis no secret. Everyone kens of it."

"What?" How could everyone know that?

"Aye, the way you look at her as if she's the sweetest angel."

Colin rolled his eyes. He'd had no idea his face was so expressive. He would have to guard against that from now on.

The maid exited Kristina's room. "Her ladyship said she did not need my help." She curtsied and hastened up the stairs.

Colin frowned, while Fraser eagerly chased after the maid.

Surprised, Colin glanced around, seeing that the corridor was empty. Listening for a long moment, he heard no one about. He then crept to Kristina's door and knocked lightly.

"Who is it?" she asked.

"Me. Colin."

"Enter."

He eased open the door and stepped inside, finding a low hearth fire lighting the room to a dim glow.

"Why did you send the maid away?" he asked.

"I was afraid she might see... um, you know." Kristina pressed her lips closed tightly.

Damnation. He'd forgotten there would be blood. He was not

accustomed to deflowering virgins."

"I'll help you."

"Are you certain? Surely 'tis unusual for a man to help a woman in this way."

"I don't mind. In fact, I want to assist you in any way I can. I hope you can trust me."

"Of course I do."

He was honored and humbled that she did. After barring the door, he poured cool water from the pitcher into the basin.

"Anna told me... a woman would bleed the first time," she whispered.

He took her hand and drew her closer to the basin. "'Tis true, and I'm sorry I caused you injury."

"Nay, don't be. 'Tis what I wanted—to be a full-grown woman. Never regret it. I realize now that I could've simply told the maid 'twas my monthly courses. But I panicked and was not thinking clearly."

He smiled, loving Kristina's forthrightness. He doubted any other woman would've spoken about such feminine issues to him. "I'm glad you sent her away, because I wanted to help you. Now, I must remove your clothes."

She nodded.

Trying his best to tamp down his arousal, he slowly and gently removed each article of clothing from her body.

Once she was nude and standing before him boldly, without trying to hide, he took in the stunning beauty of her slim curves. "You are exquisitely lovely, *mo ghraidh*."

She shook her head and covered her red cheeks. "You have need of spectacles, I'm thinking."

"Ha." He had a difficult time taking his eyes off her in order to squeeze out the cloth. Once he did, he knelt before her. Despite his best efforts, need tightened his body yet again. "Spread your legs a wee bit so I can wash between."

"I can bathe myself." She held out her hand.

"I want to." He also wanted to make sure she had not bled excessively and that it had stopped. "If you will allow me." He placed her hand upon the tall bedpost for balance.

"Aye." She moved her bare feet farther apart.

When he stroked the cool cloth up her inner thigh, she sucked in a surprised gasp. "'Tis cold."

"That should be soothing." He rinsed the cloth in the cold water and applied it again.

"It does feel good," she confessed.

"Is the pain gone?"

"Aye," she breathed and closed her eyes, her lips parting.

"You are so beautiful," he whispered. Against his will, powerful arousal surged through him. Her innate sensuality and her trust in him were like an aphrodisiac.

He dropped the cloth into the basin, then pressed a kiss to her hip bone and one to her lower abdomen. Damnation, how he wanted her in every way.

Drawing in a deep and surprised breath, she tangled her fingers in his hair. "You're a remarkable man, Colin."

"And you're an astonishing woman." It took all his willpower to draw away from her.

After turning down the covers, he lifted her and placed her into bed. He then covered her up and gave her a quick kiss. A longer one would destroy his resolve to leave her be for now.

Some of his logic returning, he realized he should not leave her naked. "Where is your clean smock?"

"I have no need of it. Come, remove your clothes."

"What?" He gritted his teeth against the powerful surge of arousal.

"Shh. Someone might hear you," she whispered. "I would like it if you would join me."

"Saints," he hissed. "You do tempt me. But much as I would love to take you again, I cannot this soon. You're too sore, and you must recover."

"I feel fine."

"Nay. I refuse to." Glancing around, he saw a folded white linen smock lying on a nearby trunk. After retrieving it, he said, "Here, sit on the edge of the bed." He drew her into a sitting position.

"Why?"

"So I can dress you."

Once he had pulled the smock over her head and placed her arms into the sleeves, he pulled it down. Realizing this was the perfect time for the most important thing he wanted to ask her, he knelt before her and grasped her hands in his. He kissed the backs of them, wishing she could know how much he cherished her.

She smiled sweetly. "You are such a gentleman, Colin. And a

treasure."

If she truly felt that way, mayhap she wouldn't reject him.

Once he was on the precipice of asking, his throat closed off and his tongue felt like a leaden weight in his mouth, unable to move. He cleared his throat and inhaled deeply, as if drawing in courage.

"Lady Kristina, would you do me the honor of… becoming my bride?"

Her mouth dropped open and she was silent for a long moment. "What?" Her unseeing eyes were wide and startled. Before he could respond, she shook her head, tears glistening on her lashes. "Nay."

Her answer had come so quickly it shocked him. "Why not? I thought you…" Nay, he could not finish that sentence. Devastation locked the rest of the words in his throat, near suffocating him. 'Twas just as he'd feared it would be.

"Colin, you do not have to marry me just because we… you know. I've already told you, I would never wish to burden you or any man with my affliction." She wiped the tears from her cheeks.

Though he understood what she was trying to tell him, he shook his head. Did she not understand? "You would never be a burden to me." As he saw it now, she was the only woman for him. He pulled in a deep breath to dispel the constricting disappointment. He had to convince her to change her mind. "'Tis not because we shared a bed, so to speak, that I want to marry you. 'Tis because I love you."

"Oh, Colin," she whispered. "I love you, too."

He scowled in confusion. "Then why will you not marry me?"

"'Tis impossible for me to be a suitable and able-bodied wife. Surely you know that."

"That may be what you believe, but 'tis not true. You are a remarkable, strong and resourceful woman who can do many things on your own. How could you possibly think you're not suitable?"

"Many reasons." Tears dripped from her eyes, each one like a knife blade to his soul. "You do not even know if your clan or your father would approve of me and accept me. Being blind, I cannot oversee a castle. I have no wealth or alliances to bring to your clan. They would see no benefit in it."

"I don't care what they think," he growled.

"Well, I do," she said stubbornly. "You don't know what it's like to not be accepted. To have people laugh at you or make rude comments about a scar on your face. People must think I'm deaf, too, for they say whatever they're thinking, no matter how mean and bitter. I do not want to make your life miserable or cause you to be ridiculed. I love you and I wish you to have a wonderful life."

Her words were so ridiculous, fury inundated him. "The only way I can possibly have a wonderful life is if you agree to be my wife," he snapped. "And if you truly loved me you would not be rejecting my suit right now."

She buried her face in her hands and sobbed.

Regret gutted him. He arose, sat on the bed beside her and pulled her against him. He placed a kiss on top of her head, her silken hair tickling his lips. "Damnation, lass. I'm sorry," he whispered.

"I'm sorry, too, Colin. How I wish things could be different. How I wish I had my sight back."

His heart ached for her. "You are perfect just as you are."

Shaking her head, she pressed her eyes closed, more tears trailing downward.

He wiped them away with his thumbs. "Why will you not listen to me? Why will you not be reasonable?"

"Why will *you* not?"

He blew out a frustrated breath.

"'Tis my fondest wish to be a good wife for you, Colin, but I cannot. I have too many limitations. I will not have you carry me everywhere I go in unfamiliar places. I will not have you be the laughingstock of your people for having a disfigured and blind wife who cannot be of any service to you or your clan."

He did not expect her to be of service. He but wanted to cherish her, take care of her and protect her all of his days.

"Kristina—"

She put her hand up and shook her head.

Damnation, what could he say or do to convince her that she was good enough? She was exceptional in every way. Why couldn't she understand this?

"If I get the approval of my father and my clan, will you agree to marry me then?"

"That will not bring back my sight, Colin," she whispered. "That will not dissolve the scar from my face."

"The scar doesn't matter. Most people have scars of one sort or another. As for your sight, 'tis not necessary. We have plenty of servants and a housekeeper to oversee the castle."

She shook her head. "Both will matter far more than you realize. I've lived with these difficulties for two years. You have not."

Frustration overwhelming him, he muttered a curse and pushed to a standing position. "This is not over. We will talk again tomorrow." He left the room, slamming the door on his way out.

Moments later, he entered his bedchamber, closed the door, and tossed aside his sporran.

Hell. He wanted to strike something. Never had he been so vexed with someone he loved this much. 'Twas like last time, when his fiancée had rejected him, except this time was far worse. He was profoundly in love with Kristina, but that did not seem to matter to her.

All of her arguments were valid points, but not one of them would prevent him from marrying her if only she would agree to it. He wanted to take care of her.

How could she tell him she loved him in the midst of rejecting him? He shook his head.

'Twas her own beliefs about herself that stopped her. Her own doubts and fears that she could never measure up.

Colin spent a fitful night in his guest bedchamber, and it seemed he had only dropped off to sleep for a few minutes when a knock sounded at his door. Holding his plaid before him, he arose and answered it.

Neacal waited there, looking pale and morose.

"What is it?" Colin asked.

"A messenger arrived from Rhodie. Your father has been shot with an arrow."

Shock, like a lightning bolt, struck him. Was he having a nightmare? "In truth? Does he live?"

"Aye, but he is very ill."

Rage replaced the shock. "Who did this?"

"The messenger did not ken. While they were on the road, an arrow flew out of the wood and struck your da in the lower abdomen. No culprit has been found yet."

"Good God." Dark fear for his father's life consuming him, Colin yanked a shirt on over his head, then belted his plaid into place. "I must go home."

"Of course. I'll go with you and help you find the assassin."

"Nay. I wouldn't hear of it. You only got married yesterday. And I'll have almost a dozen Camerons riding with me. I'll send word in a few days if I need your help." He sheathed his weapons, grabbed the rest of his belongings and strode toward the door. "Tell Kristina I'm sorry I had to leave without saying good-bye."

"I will."

She would not wish to see him anyway. He'd planned to make another appeal for her hand this morn. But what good would it do? She would only reject him. Gloom dogged his steps as he descended the stairs and left the keep.

Neacal accompanied him to the bailey, where the Camerons were already saddling their horses.

"Where is the messenger?" Colin asked.

"There. Tosh Cameron." Neacal motioned to him.

Colin's distant cousin wore a worried scowl as he strode toward them.

"What happened? Is Da in a bad state?"

"Aye, he was shot here." Tosh pressed a hand to the side of his lower abdomen.

"Do you have any inkling who did it?"

"Nay. The chief was riding out with his bodyguards, as he always does. An arrow flew from the wood by the road. The bodyguards quickly brought him back inside the walls, then chased the culprit. They found hoof tracks and a few broken twigs, but not much else."

"Did they follow?"

"Aye. They followed the tracks to the road, where they could not tell in which direction they had gone because of the many tracks from other traffic. They split up and rode in both directions but came up with naught."

"Damnation. How could the bastard have disappeared so easily?" Rage blazed along his veins. "We'll be leaving in a matter of minutes."

"Take the men you brought for the Bearach garrison," Neacal said.

"Nay. I have plenty of men, both here and at Rhodie. I wouldn't want to leave Bearach vulnerable." Especially with Kristina here. He wanted her well protected.

"Be sure to send word of how your father is within a few days," Neacal said. "If you need help, I'll bring most of my men and leave a few guards here."

"I thank you." Colin gave him a warrior handshake. Neacal was so like a brother to him, he felt as close to him as he did his real brother, Bryce. "You're a good man. Please take care of the ladies."

"I will. And I pray your father recovers with all haste."

Kristina had not been able to sleep after Colin had left her chamber the night before. She'd lain in bed awake for hours, crying, castigating herself. How could she do this to Colin, the most caring and compassionate man she'd ever met? How could she do this to herself?

Her heart was breaking by her own hand, she knew. Still, she loved Colin too much to be selfish. If he did marry her, he would soon regret it, especially when he realized she could do very little. His father or his clan might even force him to either get an annulment or give up his inheritance. She couldn't do that to him. Marriage was not taken lightly amongst members of the upper class. Very rarely were love matches to be had.

Someone knocked on the door, startling her from the turbulent thoughts. Who could that be? She'd already sent two maids away, one who had poked and puttered about, annoying her to no end. She did not want to arise, nor did she wish to break her fast. Being near Colin would be torture. Could it be him knocking? She wanted to be with him so badly, but she couldn't. She felt as if her soul was ripping in two.

The knock sounded again, louder this time.

"Who is it?" she called.

The door opened. "'Tis me. Anna."

She was glad, for she did not want to argue with Colin again. "What are you doing here? You're supposed to be in seclusion with your new husband."

"I have bad news." Anna's voice was so serious it sent a flash of fear through Kristina.

She sat up. "What is it?"

"A messenger arrived early this morn with news that Colin's father has been shot with an arrow. Colin hastened back home to see how his da is."

"Och. Nay!" For a moment, it was as if 'twas her own father she was hearing about. "Was it a battle?"

"More like an assassination attempt. An arrow flew from the wood and the culprit was not found."

"Good heavens." Her heart was breaking for Colin. "I pray his father recovers."

"As do I."

"Colin did not even say good-bye." But why would he after her rejection? He probably never wanted to speak to her again. Tears pricked her eyes.

Anna took her hand and squeezed it. "There was no time. He had to hurry. He asked Neacal to tell you he was sorry to leave without saying good-bye."

Bless him. He had actually thought of her. A tear trailed down her cheek, and she wiped it away. "His father is in poor condition, then?"

"I'm afraid so."

"Colin must be incredibly worried. He's close to his father."

"'Tis true," Anna said. "There is something else I wish to speak to you about."

"Aye?"

"Did something happen that I should know about?" Anna sat down on Kristina's bed by her hip.

Surely she could not know about the intimacy she and Colin had shared. Had he told Neacal or someone? "What are you talking about?"

Anna sighed. "Very well. I'll just say it. This morn, the maid found a bloody smock beside your bed. Since I haven't seen any cuts on you, I have to assume one of two things. Either it isn't yours or you lost your virginity."

Good heavens, she'd completely forgotten about the smock Colin had removed from her last night. She lay down and placed a hand against her stomach. "'Tis my courses, and it is rather heavy this month. My belly pains me terribly. That's why I'm still abed."

Anna was silent for a long moment. Did she believe the lie? Kristina had to admit she rarely lied and was probably terrible at it.

"I asked the maid about this," Anna went on. "She said you did not ask for any cloths to absorb the flow, and that the bleeding has apparently stopped."

The maid did uncover her while she was half asleep, urging her to get up and break her fast. Yanking the covers up again, Kristina had told her she planned to sleep in.

"My courses are always brief," Kristina said.

"One night? If only we could all be so lucky."

"Indeed, I am lucky."

"I don't believe you."

Kristina blew out an annoyed breath. "Very well, then," she snapped. "If you must know... I did share an amazing experience with Colin. But I didn't want anyone to find out."

Anna gasped. "Even me?"

"You won't approve."

"I'm not judging you, sister." Anna took her hand. "I but want to help you. Was it your choice?"

"Of course. I knew I might never get to experience passion if it wasn't with Colin."

"Do you love him?" Anna asked softly.

Certainly she did, but did everyone need to know this? She shrugged, bitterness converging upon her. "What does it matter? I have no illusions about love and marriage. I know I cannot marry a future chief."

"Why not?"

"Anna, in case you haven't noticed, I'm blind and hideously scarred. Can you imagine someone of prominence taking me to meet his father, a chief, and his mother? He would be a laughingstock." Disappointment tightened Kristina's throat.

"You're talking nonsense. Your vision has naught to do with your suitability in being a wife. Nor does your scar, of course."

"As you already know, I'm a burden to anyone I live with."

"You are not. I love you, wee sister. I want you by my side always, but if you can find happiness with Colin, I will wish you well. You have so much love to give."

Kristina could not imagine how she would perform all the necessary duties. Having been blind for two years, she well knew what she couldn't do now that she could previously. "How would I...?"

"What?"

"If we had children, how would I care for them?"

"That's easy," Anna said gently. "Nursemaids and servants."

"How would I manage a castle?"

"A steward. A housekeeper."

"In other words, I would have to shirk all my duties and let other people do them. Don't you see, Anna? I feel unworthy of Colin. He is exceptional, tall, handsome, capable, respected and admired. I don't wish to bring him down. I don't want people to question his sanity in marrying someone like me."

"They wouldn't. Once they get to know you, the whole clan will adore you just as I do. You are strong, bright, intelligent, caring and compassionate."

Tears burned Kristina's eyes, and she shook her head. "You are too kind."

"Neacal says Colin is smitten with you."

Kristina truly felt he was, but that didn't make things easier. "Colin asked me to marry him," she confessed, her heart breaking anew.

"Good heavens. That's wonderful! What did you say?" Anna sounded so joyful, such a contrast to how Kristina felt, that her sorrow compounded.

"Nay."

"Why?"

Kristina exhaled loudly and turned onto her other side, away from Anna. "I've already told you. 'Tis over now. He's gone back home. He will soon forget about me." Her throat ached. She wished Anna would leave the room so she could cry her eyes out yet again.

Anna blew out a breath. "I doubt that. An important consideration… you could be with child."

She had already thought of that. "'Tis possible. We'll find out soon, I imagine. I'm sorry I've disappointed you, Anna."

"You haven't. You've disappointed yourself though. You've chosen misery instead of happiness for no reason."

"There are plenty of reasons." Annoyance jabbed at her, for she knew she wasn't imagining things. "For instance, before I was injured I had several suitors, and since then, none. No man with his wits about him wants to be saddled with me."

Anna stroked her back, no doubt trying to soothe her. "Colin isn't like those men. He cares deeply about you."

Kristina knew it was true, but that had never been in question. "And I care about him, which is why I refuse to drag him down." She had to talk about something else before she went mad with frustration. "How was your wedding night?"

Anna let loose a brief chuckle. "I ken what you're about. 'Twill do you no good to change the subject. But last night was incredible, of course. I'm so happy with Neacal, and I want to see you happy, too, with Colin."

Regret overshadowed her mind, like dreary storm clouds. "I don't even dare dream of it. 'Tis impossible."

"We have both survived despite impossible odds... injury, pain, grief and terror, but it has not destroyed us. I've always seen you as incredibly strong, but now I see this one fear of yours has you trapped."

CHAPTER FIFTEEN

As gloaming cast purple light over the golden autumn landscape, Colin and his men rode closer and closer to Rhodie Castle, but three or four miles yet remained in their journey. They had ridden hard all day to make it this far, but they could not push the horses more at this point. They must keep to a slower pace.

Without Kristina by his side, Colin felt a gaping hole inside him. Plus, the dread and anxiety over how he would find his da's health cast bleak darkness over his mind. He could not remember feeling so fearful and devastated. Everything had become deadly serious. If his father could not survive this wound, Colin's world would crash to the ground. And without Kristina as his wife, his life was not worth living anyway. What reason would he have to go on?

His clan.

Even after the hell Neacal had suffered through two years ago, his main reason for continuing on was his clan. He'd committed himself to leading them to the best of his ability.

Colin could do no less. He would look to his friend and foster brother as a mentor.

One of the men shouted, and Colin's horse reared.

"What the devil?" Colin struggled to maintain his seat. He then noticed an arrow protruding from the saddle near his thigh. "Take cover! 'Tis an ambush!"

Why hadn't Colin been paying more attention to their surroundings?

Two more arrows whizzed toward them from the nearby wood, and the men lifted their targes, deflecting them. Colin was unable to see how many men lurked there. Probably not many if only two arrows were being launched at a time.

Regardless, he wasn't taking any chances with his men's lives or the horses. He vaulted from the saddle and quickly drew his horse farther along toward large boulders, then behind them. His men followed.

"Is anyone injured?" While holding the bridle of his spooked horse, Colin looked the men over. All were either still in their saddles and dismounting or already on their feet as they joined him behind the rocks.

"An arrow grazed my arm." Warton leapt from his horse and ripped at his bloody sleeve to see the torn flesh. "Who are these bastards?"

"Likely the same ones who shot my father." Rage burned like a fire in Colin's stomach. "We must capture or dispatch them." Colin checked his horse and found that the arrow's point that had struck his saddle had penetrated the horse's flesh about an inch. It bled, but not too severely. A flesh wound that would heal quickly. He stroked the horse's muzzle to calm him while observing the trees some thirty yards distant.

He yearned to capture or destroy each of the outlaws, but running into the dark wood after them would be suicide. From here, he couldn't see even one man.

"Rusty, see if you can shoot any of them." Colin kept his voice low. "Their archer must have a clear view of us betwixt the trees."

Rusty was one of the best with a bow and arrow, and his eyesight was keen.

Two more arrows darted toward them, missing by several feet. One struck the stones and bounced off, while the other drove into the dirt.

"Cowards!" Colin shouted. "Come out and face us!" He narrowed his eyes, watching the wood. A blur of plaid moved among the bushes at the edge. "There. Do you see him?" Colin pointed. "Shoot him."

"Aye." Rusty nocked the arrow, drew back and propelled it toward the trees. The plaid vanished behind the bushes and shouting followed.

"You got him!" Feeling a small surge of victory, Colin hoped the downed man was the assassin who'd injured his father. Rustling reached his ears. It sounded as if the other outlaws were fleeing through the dried leaves of the forest floor. "The rest are getting away. Capture them!"

The Camerons ran on foot toward the wood, leaving three in

charge of the horses.

"You two, disarm and guard the assassin," he told Warton and Ethan, then advanced with the rest of his men, chasing the fleeing murderers through the wood. Their feet crunched over the dried leaves and pine needles. At the back edge of the forest, the land turned grassy. Colin stopped, his gaze searching for fleeing men, but he saw nothing. Where had they disappeared to? Around the bend? Down the hill to the next patch of trees? Not knowing how many they'd be up against, he didn't want to split up his forces more than he had already. He wanted to keep the rest of his men safe. Besides, gloaming would soon turn to night.

"We need to reach Rhodie before dark. Let's see if the man Rusty shot still lives."

As Colin and the others approached, Warton and Ethan stood watching the outlaw lying on the ground. He was attempting to draw the arrow from his thigh, but that could be a fatal mistake, for it could cause him to bleed to death. The man's bow and quiver lay several feet away, as well as his other weapons.

"Who are you and why did you ambush us?" Colin demanded.

"Go to hell, you Cameron bastards!" the downed man growled through gritted teeth, his face contorted in pain.

"Did you tell him our name?" Colin asked Warton.

"Nay. He knew immediately who we are."

"What's your name?"

The man kept his mouth closed, his nostrils flaring, his glare venomous.

"Who do you work for? And what do you have against us?"

"I'll tell you naught. If you're going to kill me, then go ahead and do it!" he roared.

"We're not going to kill you, even though 'tis what you deserve. But you will be a guest in the Rhodie Castle dungeon until you tell me why you and your comrades were trying to kill us."

"I said I'll tell you naught!"

Likely, the man would confess what he knew in a day or two, if he lived. Colin would send the healer into the dungeon to remove the arrow and medicate his wound. "Did you or one of your clansmen shoot Chief Cameron?"

The man narrowed his eyes but kept his mouth shut. Of course they had been the culprits. Although Colin wanted to smash his fist against the man's face, he kept his impulses under control.

"Cut the arrow shaft shorter," Colin told Warton. "Have the men bind his hands and feet, then load him onto a horse. We must reach Rhodie before dark." Otherwise, they would be too vulnerable out here in the darkness. The outlaws could return.

When Colin and the rest of the Camerons rode into the torchlit bailey at Rhodie Castle a few minutes after dark, his brother Bryce, younger by two years, was there to greet him.

"Bryce, how is Da?" Colin swung down from his horse.

"Not good." His brown eyes grim, Bryce gave Colin a warrior handshake. "I'm glad you came quickly."

Colin nodded. "I must go see Da. Then we'll talk. In the meantime, can you oversee the men escorting the prisoner to the dungeon and ask Deidra to see to his arrow wound?"

Bryce nodded and glanced at the men unloading the injured man. "How did you end up with a prisoner?"

"Bastard was shooting at us. He may very well be the one who shot Da."

"What?" Bryce growled.

"Aye. Rusty and Warton will fill you in on what happened."

"Damnation." Bryce stormed off in their direction while Colin climbed the steps toward the great hall, his stomach knotting. After nodding a greeting to the solemn-faced clansmen seated at the tables, he ascended another flight to the laird's chamber. He pushed the old carved oak door open and found only his mother and father inside the bleak, candlelit room.

"Oh, Colin." His mother shot up from the chair and embraced him, tears streaming from her reddened eyes. "I'm so glad you've come."

"How is he, Ma?" He held her tightly while she wept. Though his heart was breaking, he forced himself to be strong. Looking over her shoulder, he saw that his da lay unmoving on the bed. His face was very pale above his gray beard. Saints! To see him in this condition was like a strike to his own vitals.

"I'm so afraid," his mother whispered, pulling back and turning to look at his da. "I've never seen him so ill before. He has a fever, and Deidra says his wound festers terribly."

"Is there naught she can do to help?" Surely, there had to be something that could save his father's life.

"She removed the arrowhead, stitched the wound and applied a poultice. You ken she is the best healer in these parts, but 'tis a deep wound."

"Mayhap the poultice will help in a day or two." Colin wished more than anything that he could relieve his mother's worries, but the same hopeless fear latched sickeningly onto his stomach.

"He does not respond. 'Tis as if he is in a deep, dreamless sleep."

Fearing this was indeed the end of the road for his father, Colin kissed the top of his mother's head, her tawny hair shot through with a few strands of gray. "We will pray."

"Aye. 'Tis all we can do."

He sat down on a chair by his father's bedside and leaned forward. "Da, can you hear me?"

No response. Da's face appeared far too ashen, but his breathing was deep and even.

"We're going to figure out who did this," Colin vowed.

A half hour later, Colin met his brother entering the great hall.

"The whoreson won't speak a word," Bryce growled.

"I figured as much."

"Based on what Warton and Rusty said, sounds like the same band of miscreants who shot Da from the wood nearby."

"I agree."

"Which clan could they be from? We've had no intense conflicts for a few years."

"I thought hard on it the whole way here. I cannot think of anyone who hated Da enough to assassinate him. What would they have to gain by it?"

Bryce shook his head. "Several of us had a meeting on it earlier. We came up with naught."

Colin turned, spying the healer on the other side of the great hall. "Did Deidra pay a visit to the prisoner yet?"

"Nay, she was busy." Bryce walked with him toward her.

"Deidra, what can you tell me about Da's injury?"

The middle-aged woman with gray hair shook her head, looking dejected. "'Tis a bad one, Colin. The arrow went through the lower side of his gut. I may be a good healer, but I'm nay that good. I did the best I could on him, but I'm thinking even an Edinburgh physician couldn't heal him. It'll take a miracle."

Dread weighed heavily upon Colin's heart. He couldn't imagine life without his da. "Is he suffering?"

"He does nay seem to be in any pain, but who can know, in truth? I wish I could do more. I'd best go check on him again."

"When you finish with him, can you come to the dungeon? We brought in a prisoner who has an arrow in his leg. He may very well be the man who shot Da."

"And you wish me to heal such an evil man?" she snapped, her gaze sharp as a spear.

The woman's vehemence rendered Colin speechless for a moment. "Aye, we must question him and find out which clan he's from. Several men in his party fled. We need to stop them before they attack again."

"I'll think on it." She stormed away and up the stairs.

Colin could well understand Deidra's anger, and he was tempted to feel the same way himself, but he wasn't barbaric enough to withhold the help of a healer from anyone, even from a man who'd tried to kill his father. He believed in upholding the law. If the archer recovered, he could be turned over to the authorities. But first, Colin had to find out what the man knew.

He and Bryce strode outside to the bailey, then descended the steps into the dungeon.

Lying on the floor, the man writhed and groaned in pain.

Colin stopped before the cell door. "We've asked the healer to come down and help you."

"I want naught to do with a healer!" the man shouted.

"Which clan are you from?"

"Go to hell!"

Ignoring him, Colin asked, "Why did you shoot at us? What grudge do you hold against the Camerons?"

Eyes closed, the man lay still, not uttering another word.

"Damnation. I think he passed out," Colin muttered.

"Hope he doesn't die before we get a name from him," Bryce said.

Tears burning her eyes, Kristina lay in bed awake long after everyone else was asleep. The castle was quiet. What a mess she'd made of her life. She could not get Colin out of her head or her heart. She missed him sorely and prayed his father would recover from the wound.

What a daft ninny she'd been to reject Colin's marriage proposal, but she'd had no other choice. Because she loved him beyond anyone and anything, she could not saddle him with a useless wife. How she wished she was capable of scaling mountains and doing things beyond what the average woman could do. Why had her sight been taken away? What had she done to deserve this punishment? She could not comprehend why some people had easy lives, while others were kicked down at every turn.

Feeling sorry for herself, she cried herself to sleep and dreamed.

"What do you truly want, my child?" The whisper sounded like her mother's voice.

"Ma?" she asked, opening her eyes within the dream.

Her mother stood beside the bed and a bright golden light emanated from her, as well as from behind her, as if the sun were shining in the bedchamber window. Kristina loved how she was always able to see within her dreams.

"Are you truly here, Ma?"

"Aye. Whatever you want, Kristina, just ask God and your angels for it and believe. You do not need to suffer any longer."

"Angels?" Kristina frowned, confused. "I did not know I had angels."

"Of course, sweeting. Everyone has guardian angels for help and protection."

"But… what I want is impossible. I want to spend my life with Colin and be a good wife to him. I cannot do that without my sight."

"Nothing is impossible. Ask God's angels to lift your prayer for healing your eyes to heaven. And then believe you have already received this."

"But that would be…"

"A miracle?"

"Aye."

"Miracles happen every day, but you must believe with such a strong *knowing* that it is no surprise to you when your prayer is answered." Her mother smiled. "You have a strong and beautiful spirit, Kristina, and Colin is your soulmate."

Gasping, Kristina woke up instantly to the blackness. She sat up, disappointed that the eyesight she'd had in the dream was gone. Her mother's image had been blindingly bright and warm in the dream. So real.

"Ma?"

Silence filled the chilly room. Was her ma's spirit still with her? Were her guardian angels by her side as her mother had said? She could not feel them.

And what her mother had said about Colin being her soulmate... good heavens! Could it be true? How could she be a soulmate and wife to such an exceptional man? She did not believe she had it in her. How could she possibly rise to such a lofty position?

She felt lonelier than ever before. Cold and alone.

Her mother's spirit had visited her in the dream. She had no doubt of it. 'Twas too real to be only a dream.

She lay back down, turned to her side and thought about what her mother had said about angels and asking them for help.

"Angels, are you there?" she whispered.

After a few moments, her loneliness drifted away and she felt cocooned in a warm, loving embrace. Could there be real angels holding her now, or was she only imagining it? Either way, she felt better... calmer, not so afraid. No longer alone. Her mind drifted into daydreams where she imagined herself with Colin, and for the first time she could see him in this fantasy. He was gorgeous, with tawny hair and eyes the color of silvery gray clouds.

Colin, I love you. And more than anything, I want to be a good wife to you.

He smiled at her and kissed her cheek. The fantasy was so vivid, she even felt his breath upon her skin.

"This is what I want, God... angels... anyone who is listening," she whispered. "To spend my life with Colin and see his face. Thank you for hearing my prayer."

As she floated toward sleep, she visualized herself walking with Colin, hand in hand, up a beautiful, heather-covered hill. Everything around her was so bright and vivid—the purple heather, the green grass, the blue sky reflecting off the loch. But she could hardly take her eyes off Colin's wonderful smile to view the stunning scenery. 'Twould be truly magnificent to have her sight back, for then she would have a fulfilling life with Colin. She could be his helper and mate. Her dreams would come true. She knew they would.

Upon waking the next morn, Kristina immediately remembered her dreams and her fantasies as if she had lived them during the night. It had been so grand having her sight back in the dreams. But now reality struck. Her vision was not miraculously restored. All was darkness around her. A moment of disappointment sank into her.

Do not lose faith, my child.

The words had been inside her head, like a thought. But not her thought. Again, it was like hearing her mother's voice. Saints! Strange things were happening. She needed to speak to Maili. She had the gift of second sight. Mayhap she could explain what Kristina's unusual dreams and the voice in her head had meant. Was this normal or was she losing her sanity?

After dressing and breaking her fast in her room, Kristina sent the maid to find Maili and ask if she could speak with her. A short time later, a knock sounded at the door.

"Come in," Kristina called, looking forward to talking to her new friend.

The door opened and closed.

"A good morn to you," Maili said in a bright and cheerful tone. "The maid said you wanted to talk."

"Aye. Good morn. Thank you for agreeing to meet with me."

"Of course. Anytime. I value your friendship. How are you feeling?" The chair by the hearth squeaked as Maili sat down.

Kristina knew what she meant—how did she feel since Colin had left? Miserable. But she was sidestepping that topic for the time being. "I'm not sure."

"What do you mean?" Maili's voice held much concern.

"You have second sight, do you not?"

"Um, aye," Maili said tentatively.

"I had a dream last night, and I'm hoping you can help me figure out what it means."

"Of course." She sounded far more relaxed now. "I will try. I often have dreams in which I see something that is happening at a distance or in the future."

"My mother passed many years ago when I was a child, but I saw her clearly in my dream, as if she were really here. She was surrounded by a golden light, and she relayed a message about angels." Kristina explained what her mother had said about asking angels for help.

"It sounds like a visitation dream," Maili said. "Angels and spirits are real, even though we normally cannot see or touch them."

"Do you think angels could heal my eyes so that I might regain my sight?"

"'Tis possible. Angels are extensions of God, and they do God's work. This includes healing and many miracles."

"Although I've dreamed of my mother before, and heard her speak to me, this dream was so real and detailed, 'twas unsettling."

"I'm certain it was. Maybe your mother's spirit delivered the message from above so you wouldn't be afraid. And now you can communicate directly with your guardian angels."

Kristina nodded, though she was still unsure if angels were truly beside her. "I also dreamed what Colin looks like. I have never seen him with my eyes, so I don't know if the image was right. But if it was, does that mean I'm developing second sight?"

"I don't know. Mayhap. I only know of my own experiences. Either way, do not be afraid."

A bright streak of light, like lightning, flashed across Kristina's black field of vision.

CHAPTER SIXTEEN

Kristina gasped and covered her eyes with both hands as tears welled. Had that burst of light been real or in her imagination only? "What is it?" Maili asked urgently.

Kristina lowered her hands, blinking away the burning tears, but the light was gone. Only darkness surrounded her again. "A brief flash of light."

"In truth? Maybe 'tis a sign." Maili moved to the bed beside her. "Let me see if I pick up anything for you." After holding both her hands for a few seconds, Maili said, with a smile in her voice, "Oh, you and Colin share a magnificent and special love."

Kristina's whole body flushed as conflicting emotions swirled within her—joy for the love but sadness because she could not grasp hold of it.

"You ken this, do you not?" Maili released her hands.

Kristina nodded, blinking back tears.

"Why do you cry?"

"I want my eyesight back more than anything, for then I could..." She snapped her mouth closed. Even though Maili was a new friend, mayhap Kristina was saying too much. Did she really want everyone to know the situation with her and Colin?

"Aye, go on," Maili urged.

"Anna knows this, but no one else. Do you promise to keep it a secret?"

"Of course. I consider you a sister also, just as I do Anna."

"I appreciate that." Kristina blotted at the renewed tears that threatened because of Maili's kindness. "Well, the truth is... Colin asked me to marry him—"

Maili gasped, then giggled. "Oh, that's wonderful."

Kristina held up her hand. "I have not finished. 'Twould be my fondest wish to marry him, but I refuse to do so without my sight."

On horseback, Colin, Bryce and ten of their clansmen followed the tracking dog, a small terrier. The dog took a meandering path through the leaves and pine needles, his nose to the ground. Colin had cut off a piece of the prisoner's doublet sleeve for the dog to sniff occasionally. But there was a good chance it wouldn't work, for the other men in the gang might not smell like the archer. He hoped their scents were somewhat alike since they were accomplices. Aside from that, it had rained the previous night, which had likely destroyed any scent left on the leaves or ground.

Although Colin had spent several hours by his father's bedside the night before, he could not sit still during the day. All the waiting and wondering drove him mad. Besides, he had to find the bastards responsible.

Much as he would love to capture the group of outlaws, especially their leader, even this victory would not help his father recover. Only God could help him now.

This morn, Da had shown no improvement, nor did he appear to be any worse. Deidra continued to apply the poultices and do all she could for him.

Once Colin had fully explained to the healer that if the injured archer died, they might never find the man behind his father's ambush, she had agreed to help him. She'd removed the arrow from his thigh, stitched him up and applied a poultice. Her helper had given him a cup of tea to ease the pain and help him sleep. But the man had been out of his mind with fever this morn. His recovery was uncertain. Even during his moments of awareness, he had not revealed any names or information that would help Colin find the rest of the outlaws.

Now, Colin observed the gray terrier as it trotted through the wood. Something shining brightly on the ground in a small patch of sunlight caught Colin's attention.

"What is that?" After riding closer, he leapt down from his horse and picked up the gleaming object—a golden earring, the sort that dangled, coin shaped with an embossed flower and a small red stone in the center. Kristina's earring!

"Saints!" he hissed.

"What is it?" Bryce dismounted and moved closer to see what lay in his palm.

"I think this is Lady Kristina's earring. Damnation! That means..." Colin's chest felt crushed of a sudden. "Red Holme." He'd stolen Kristina's earrings from the pouch.

Cursing, Colin shoved his hand through his mussed hair and stared toward the heavens, feeling as if a spear had gutted him. "Red Holme shot Da."

Colin glanced around the wood, seeing no one, then muttered a curse. Why had he not sent a missive to his father warning him Holme—or rather MacKillican—was back? He had not considered that the bastard would come to Rhodie. Colin had assumed he would lurk at Bearach and continue trying to kill him or to capture Kristina again.

"Red Holme?" Bryce frowned. "Who's that?"

"'Tis a name he invented. He is a MacKillican."

"Hell. I remember that name," Bryce growled. "The traitors to the crown who held Rhodie years ago."

"Aye, you were a lad, too young to fight in the battle. Red is the son of the last MacKillican chief. A few weeks ago, he was at Bearach, fighting on the side of a man named Blackburn Mac-Cromar. When Red Holme saw me, he recognized me from the battle over ten years ago. He tried to kill me but ended up fleeing here to take his revenge and rage out on Da by shooting him like a coward from the bush."

"Saints," Bryce hissed.

Colin hadn't recognized the archer. He didn't think he was one they'd fought in the cave near Bearach. If Holme had recruited him along the way, he could have several more men than the two he'd left the Moidart area with.

"The archer in the dungeon is naught but a pawn, someone he enlisted recently. I have to get this bastard," Colin said through clenched teeth.

Wearing a black cloak and perched atop a cliff in the wood a mile or two from Rhodie Castle, Red Holme watched the search party below. It consisted of a dozen men, headed by none other than Colin Cameron himself. How he hated the thieving whoreson.

Holme narrowed his eyes, his muscles tensing.

He hoped MacAlpin, the archer, hadn't revealed his identity. When MacAlpin had signed on, he'd sworn to never reveal Red Holme's identity, nor his own, if captured. The man had been the son of his father's head archer, another man dead now because of Colin's father.

Holme had been lucky to find MacAlpin living in a village a few miles away from this area. The man had wanted a way to escape the life of menial labor he'd been doing for the past few years.

The Camerons had gotten a lucky shot when their arrow had struck MacAlpin. Holme had hated to abandon him, but there had been no other choice. His followers well knew it was every man for himself. Holme wasn't going to risk losing his opportunity for revenge just to save MacAlpin's life.

All of these Camerons had to be eliminated. Every last one.

At the moment, Holme only had four men—Scroggie, Dobson, and two more from the disbursed MacKillican clan he'd found in the same village where he'd run into MacAlpin. He'd hired them using the money from the sale of one of Kristina's earrings. Alas, he had lost the other one, but no matter. What he couldn't buy he would steal.

The Camerons were following a small shaggy dog that sniffed the ground. Fortunately for Holme, he was downwind and far above them.

He silently lifted his bow from the ground. Should he shoot Colin Cameron now and be done with it? Or wait and kill several dozen of his clansmen along with him? Craving revenge, he ground his teeth but forced himself not to move. Victory would be sweeter when he could watch them all fall.

Where was Lady Kristina? He had not seen her traveling with the Camerons. He'd made sure before the last ambush. He'd been certain Colin was so besotted with her he would marry her, but... maybe she hadn't survived that last strike to the face Holme had given her.

If she was dead, she deserved it!

Although he tried to force himself to believe that and to be angry with her... something gnawed in his gut. What was it? Regret? Deep down, he hoped she still lived. Strangely enough, he liked the prickly, disfigured witch. She retained a beauty and strength he admired. She reminded him of himself—half normal and half damaged. A survivor despite all odds.

But he would likely never see her again. Revenge against the Camerons was far more important than having a lass beneath him. He was willing to give up his life to gain the revenge he'd craved for a decade but had been too afraid to pursue. Fear no longer ruled his life. His father, God rest his soul, would finally be proud of him. But Holme didn't think he would have to give up his life, in truth, for he had a plan.

Having grown up in Rhodie Castle, he knew every nook, cranny, secret passage and escape route. Upon viewing the castle from a short distance away, he saw that the Camerons had made additions in the past decade, but the main keep appeared the same. Now he simply had to bide his time and wait for the perfect opportunity to slip inside.

Holme grinned, imagining all the Camerons screaming and running for their lives. To his way of thinking, Colin and his father deserved every pain they received, as did the rest of the clan. And he planned to unleash a wrath upon them such as they had never imagined.

At Bearach Castle, Kristina sat at the high table during supper, eating and listening to the musicians while Anna and Neacal sat nearby, conversing quietly. On her other side, Maili and her husband, Shamus, also talked. She missed Colin all the time, but especially at times like this when each of the others had a loving companion but Kristina did not. Every day she missed Colin more than the day before… and more than she had thought possible. She'd believed it would get easier with time, but the opposite was true. And it had only been five days.

A messenger had arrived the day before with a missive from Colin, saying his father still lived but was critically ill with fever. And they had not caught the assassin. She prayed his father would improve soon.

In that moment, all sound faded away, for Kristina noticed something with another of her senses… her vision. It almost seemed that she could see the flame of a candle to her right. She blinked, pressed her eyes closed, then opened them again. Aye… her heartbeat sped up with excitement, for she could see the dim flickering flame of what had to be a candle. Tears filled her eyes, and she knew not what to do. She feared the image would fade away if she moved. What if it was only temporary?

She turned her head toward the left and saw the more distant impression of another flame burning there.

A pale, blurry form moved across in front of the high table—a servant refilling her wine goblet.

"I thank you," she murmured to the servant, and then burst into tears of gratitude for her returning sight.

Thanks be to God and his angels.

"Good heavens, Kristina, are you well?" Anna placed an arm around her shoulders.

On her other side, Maili also embraced her. "What has happened?" she whispered.

Kristina shook her head. She did not want to tell them here and now. "Can one of you help me to my room?"

"Of course." Anna stood.

"I'll come too." Maili took her arm and helped her down from the dais.

Holding her hand, Anna led her up the narrow turnpike stairs. Every time Kristina saw a faint movement or a blurry corner or object, renewed tears of joy filled her eyes.

Once in her chamber, Maili closed the door behind them.

"What caused you to cry?" Anna asked.

Kristina burst into tears… nay, laughter. Laughter and tears at the same time.

"Good heavens." Anna helped her to the chair so she could sit.

"Are you laughing?" Maili asked, sounding bemused.

Kristina nodded. "You will not believe this. I can see!"

"What!" Anna gasped.

"In truth? When did this happen?"

"At supper, I started seeing the candle flame, very dimly at first. And then I saw the blurry form of the servant's pale clothing."

"Oh, 'tis a miracle!" Anna embraced her. "Thanks be to God."

Maili knelt before her. "Can you see me?" She moved her hand from right to left.

"Aye. I see your hand moving."

"This is astonishing. Oh, I'm so happy, Kristina!"

"Do you think my vision will keep improving?"

"I believe it will," Anna assured her.

"Indeed. Remember your dream?" Maili asked. "You must have been talking to your angels."

"I did." Kristina told Anna about the dream in which she had talked to their mother. "That wasn't the first one. I've had a few where Ma told me things in dreams."

"'Tis amazing. She has not visited my dreams. Although John has. My late husband," Anna added for Maili's benefit. "Shall I go get Tavia and have her examine you?"

"If she isn't busy."

"I'll be right back." Anna left the room.

Once the healer had examined Kristina, she said, "I have seen sight return one other time. Could be a miracle or it could be that last blow to the head knocked something back into place for you. I don't ken the how of it. Only the Lord does. Either way, 'tis a wonderful blessing."

"Aye, indeed," Kristina said. "And I'm so thankful."

After Tavia left, Anna said, "Can I tell Neacal?"

"Could you wait? I want to be sure 'tis permanent."

"Aye, but 'twill be hard to keep it from him. And I'm certain it is permanent. It makes sense in a way. A head injury caused your blindness, so 'tis reasonable to think a head injury could also cure your blindness. Oh, you must tell Colin! Surely you will reconsider marrying him now."

"I know not if he will have me, after my rejection. He may never forgive me."

"Who is this Lady Kristina you spoke of earlier? The one whose earrings Holme had stolen?" Bryce asked while they ate a quick supper in the great hall. Though Colin had little appetite, he forced himself to eat the venison stew and bread.

Hearing Kristina's name was like a kick to the gut. He'd just been thinking about her, as he did at least a hundred times per day, remembering the joyful times they'd shared.

"She is Neacal's new wife's sister. Blackburn and Holme had taken her hostage in Stirling and brought her to Bearach to try to force Anna to come with them. With the help of our clansmen, I snatched her from Holme. She is blind and scarred from Blackburn's severe abuse two years ago." Colin relayed the rest of the story as briefly as possible, trying to keep the emotion out of his voice.

"Poor lass. I'm glad you were able to save her life."

"Aye. She's a strong and remarkable lady." If only she'd wanted to spend her life with him. If only she would've let him prove that her blindness didn't matter. She was so precious to him. Having her by his side right now, during this difficult time, would've made a world of difference.

"Is she beautiful?" Bryce asked.

"Aye," Colin answered without thought.

"I suspected as much."

Colin tensed, wishing he'd kept that last observation to himself, then scowled at his brother. "What's that supposed to mean?"

Bryce lifted a brow. "I have a gut feeling the lass means more to you than you're letting on."

Colin glanced away. 'Twas true, but he was not ready to reveal all to his brother. Everything inside him was too raw and painful to talk about. If he didn't keep it all buttoned up tight inside, he was afraid he would disintegrate.

"I don't wish to speak of it." Feeling annoyed, Colin shoved back from the table and stepped down from the dais. He strode across the great hall and out into the light drizzle at gloaming, headed toward the dungeon. He had to focus on something other than Kristina. Finding Red Holme was the only thing he could control right now. And no matter how difficult a task it was, he had to accomplish it.

Of course, he loved his brother and trusted him, but now was not the right time to speak of Kristina. He'd wanted to tell his father about her before anyone else and ask his advice, but that was not possible.

After descending the steps, he let his eyes adjust to the gloom and torchlight of the dungeon. Upon his bedroll, the archer shifted and grimaced. Hearing footsteps, Colin glanced around to find Bryce coming down the steps.

They both watched the archer for a long moment. "Are you awake?" Colin asked.

"I curse the very name of Cameron." The archer turned his head and glowered at him.

"The curse will be mirrored back to you," Colin said, forcing himself to remain calm. "I know Red Holme is behind both ambushes. And his real name is MacKillican."

The man's eyes widened briefly, but Colin saw it.

"Red Holme shot my father! Did he not?" Colin demanded. "Or was it you?"

"You're all bloody thieves," the archer growled low.

"Where is Holme now?"

"How would I know? I've been in here for days!"

Rage and desperation clawing at his soul, Colin grabbed hold of the iron bars and shouted, "Where has he been staying? You will answer if you want to make it out of here alive!"

"Go ahead and kill me now, you whoreson!" the man roared.

Colin ground his teeth, sore tempted to give the man what he asked for. He felt exhausted of a sudden, completely drained. He could not remember ever feeling so defeated and frustrated. He hung his head. He could not think of all the challenges and disappointments facing him now, or he would never crawl out of this dark abyss.

"Come." Bryce laid a hand on his shoulder. "Get some rest. Mayhap he will talk later. You've gotten very little sleep this week."

That was true enough. Besides, he could not stand this dank, suffocating dungeon one second longer. He turned and forced himself to climb the stone steps. He should drink himself into oblivion so he could forget it all for a while. But he was not that type of man. His family and clan might need him at any moment.

As they crossed the wet, torchlit bailey, a wild-eyed, anxious servant rushed toward them. "Her ladyship requests your presence in the laird's chamber."

'Twas after midnight and Colin sat alone by his father's bedside, listening to the older man's labored breaths. Bryce and his mother had been beside him for hours earlier in the night, after the healer had said his father's fever was worse and his breathing weaker. His ma was even more sleep-deprived than Colin, and she was not as strong as she used to be.

Bryce had tried to convince Colin that he would stay up while Colin slept. Colin had refused and assured them if anything changed, he would wake them. He wanted another chance to pray for his father's recovery. Without doubt, Colin had prayed more in the past week, since arriving back home, than in his entire life.

How could he be struck with two punches of devastating news in such a short span of time? First a rejection from the woman he loved, then news that his father was critically injured. The two people he was not certain he could live without.

His father was the man he trusted, admired and depended on most in the world. Colin had always sought out his wisdom when making important decisions. But now he couldn't. He'd so wanted to tell him about Kristina.

He observed his father's sleeping face, then leaned forward, wondering if his father might hear his words despite seeming far away.

"Da, I met a beautiful lass. Her name is Lady Kristina MacQueen. I want to bring her to meet you. I want... to marry her, but she doesn't think she's capable of being a chief's wife. She has the most caring heart and... she is strong. In fact, she's the strongest woman I've ever met. She has survived terrible treatment by her clan. Because of her severe injuries, she lost her sight, but that matters not to me in the least. Her spirit shines like a beacon in the night. I know she is the only woman for me. I asked her to marry me, but she has refused. I so wanted to discuss this with you and ask you if you would approve of her as a bride for me. She has no dowry and can bring no alliances to our clan. You must recover so you can give me your advice."

"Colin," his father whispered.

Shocked, Colin wondered if he was imagining things. He moved closer and took his father's hand. "Da? I'm here. Are you awake?"

The older man's eyes remained closed. "Love," he breathed, forcing the word out.

Though they had always been close, his father had never told him he loved him. Colin's throat felt near choked off, but he forced in a breath. "I love you, too, Da. Please stay with us. I need you now more than ever."

"Strong chief, son." His da squeezed his hand.

Nay! His father could not be saying what he thought he was. Colin swallowed past the large lump in his throat as his father's fingers went lax.

Holding on tightly to his da's hand, refusing to let him go, Colin said another prayer.

"I blame myself, Da, and I'm sorry," Colin whispered. "I'm

sorry I didn't send a messenger to tell you Red Holme, the son of the last MacKillican chief, was out for revenge. I had no inkling he would come after you." Colin knew he should've left Bearach the instant he'd gotten Kristina back safely. He should've been here to protect his father.

For hours, Colin sat close to the bed, holding his father's relaxed hand, listening to his breathing. Thoughts and images entered his head—the good times he had spent with his father. In his earliest memories, his father had been a strong and noble man, so robust, tall and commanding. He took his responsibilities seriously, but at times, when no one was looking, his father was playful. He seemed to delight in his sons. He would whisper funny things to Colin and Bryce during supper at the high table, making them laugh and earning them scowls from Ma. Da had taught them how to ride horses and fight with a sword and targe.

Colin must have drifted off to sleep with these pleasant, soothing memories. The sounds of a female yelling shocked him awake. He bolted from the chair.

"M'laird!" Deidra stood on the other side of his father's bed, shaking him. "Och! Nay!" she wailed.

"Is he gone?" Colin felt as if he were choking, breath refusing to enter his lungs. Not seeing his father's chest rise and fall, he touched his face. "He is still warm."

"Aye, but he does not breathe," Deidra sobbed. "Your poor ma will be devastated."

"He must have only just passed, minutes ago." Damnation, why hadn't Colin been awake? Ma and Bryce should've been here. He'd promised them he would wake them.

Colin felt as if his soul were being ripped to shreds. How could he go on without his father?

CHAPTER SEVENTEEN

In the solar at Bearach Castle, sunlight beamed in the narrow window beside Kristina where she and Anna sat on the window seat. She was thrilled to use her returning vision to see her sister's beautiful face for the first time in over two years. Although Anna was still blurry, Kristina could see her blond curls, her rosy cheeks and the green color of her eyes.

"Oh Anna, you look wonderful." Tears filled Kristina's eyes. "You look so happy and healthy now." Two years ago, Anna had been gaunt and pale from loss of blood, and her eyes had been haunted with grief and fear.

Anna smiled. "With good reason. Neacal brings me great joy. And my body has healed from all the abuse and injuries Blackburn tortured me with years ago."

"I'm so pleased for you." Tears flowing from her eyes, Kristina embraced her sister.

"When are you going to allow me to tell Neacal you can see?"

"Soon. I but wish to make certain 'tis lasting." Kristina feared Neacal would send a missive to Colin telling him. She wanted to muster up the courage to tell him herself.

After Anna pulled back, Kristina said, "I want to see what you look like, too, Maili." Although she could see a dim impression of Maili, she wanted to view her closer in the slice of rare, bright sunlight beaming in from the southwest. When the two switched places, she realized Maili's hair could not be more different from Anna's.

"Your hair is so dark and lovely." The sunlight gleamed off her thick, silky brownish-black hair.

Her friend smiled. "I thank you."

"And your eyes are pale blue. You look just as impish as I'd imagined."

Maili laughed. "Sometimes Shamus tells me I look like one of the faerie."

"Aye, you do indeed. Would one of you bring me your silver mirror? I would like to see my own face."

Maili's grin fell as she turned to Anna. Kristina could easily feel the increase in tension from the two women.

Anna hesitated. "Are you certain you're ready to see the scar?"

Kristina nodded. "I ken 'tis a bad scar. But I must learn to accept the sight of it, whether I like it or not. To pretend it doesn't exist is but lying to myself. You know how important honesty is to me, as well as facing reality."

"Aye, 'tis true."

"I will go and get my small hand mirror, if you think 'tis all right," Maili said.

Anna nodded. Once their friend had left the room, Anna said, "Truth be told, your scar is not so bad. It is minor compared to Neacal's. So please don't overreact or become melancholy about it."

Kristina shrugged, trying to pretend she was not fearful and anxious about seeing what she looked like after such an injury. "Do not worry over me, sister. I'm stronger than you realize."

"I ken you are very strong. Also, remember that Colin loves you just the way you are, flaws and all."

Kristina wished Anna wouldn't bring up Colin. 'Twas hard enough living day to day without him. But now that her fondest wish was coming true—her sight returning—naturally she would be concerned about what Colin and everyone saw when they looked at her.

Her life was on the precipice of changing completely for the better. If Colin truly did love her, she must somehow grow used to the fact he loved her even if one side of her face was ugly. She must accept it and convince herself it was true.

After Maili returned and closed the door, she placed the small silver mirror into Kristina's hand. At first, Kristina was afraid to look into it. She closed her eyes and held the mirror to her chest. She prayed she would be able to accept the way she looked and not be too discouraged over it. She dried her tears on her sleeve, opened her eyes and slowly lifted the mirror.

First, she looked at the undamaged part of her face. Although it was still a bit blurry, she viewed her blue eyes and her blond hair and brows, her fair smooth skin. In the past, people had often called her bonny, but she had always thought Anna prettier. This side of her face looked much the way she remembered. Still, it was strange to look at herself after such a length of time.

Without thinking, she turned her head, bringing the other side of her face into view. At first, she was startled by the wide and jagged pinkish-rose line that ran down her cheek. She held her breath as she examined it in as much detail as possible, given her blurred vision. Trails of small dot scars and short lines—where the healer had stitched up the cut more than two years ago—ran down either side of the main scar.

"See? 'Tis not so bad," Anna said in an overly optimistic tone, which only annoyed Kristina.

"If 'twas on your face, you would not be so cheerful."

Anna's smile vanished and annoyance flashed in her eyes. "Kristina," she admonished. "You do not have to be so cynical. I would much rather have a scar on my face than to have lost my beloved child."

Kristina felt the impact of her sister's words like a punch to the chest. 'Twas true, Anna had suffered far worse when she'd had the miscarriage after Blackburn had pushed her down the stairs.

Kristina's eyes filled with tears, and guilt near suffocated her. "You're right. I'm sorry for being so vain."

Anna clasped her in a tight embrace and wept upon her shoulder. "I'm the one who is sorry. I should not have said that. We have each suffered in our own terrible way, but now things are improving. I simply want you to find happiness as I have. Once Colin returns, you can surprise him with your restored vision."

Maili sat on her other side in the window seat. "Although the sight of the scar is new to you, Colin is used to seeing it. You would not seem the same to him without it."

"Aye. I just have to grow used to the fact he has only seen me like this." Kristina stared into the mirror again. He must indeed care for her if this hideous scar did not repulse him. "But what if he doesn't return? What if he never wishes to see me again?"

'Twas late, and Colin sat alone in the solar of Rhodie Castle, staring into the hearth flames. His world had shattered around him. His beloved father was gone. Rain poured down outside, matching his mood.

Guilt ravaged Colin, cutting into his soul. He should've been here to prevent this tragedy, to protect his father. If only he'd come home right away after seeing Kristina to safety at Bearach.

His father should've had more guards surrounding him anytime he'd been outside the walls. If only Colin had been wiser and not so caught up in the doomed romance with Kristina. He'd wasted time there with her, fantasizing they could have a future together. Valuable time he should've used to help save his father's life.

Now he was chief of his clan, something he'd always regarded with dread... not because he didn't want to lead his people, but because it would mean his father had passed on, never to return. So many things had been left unsaid. At least he had told his father about Kristina.

Love. That was the word his father had said immediately after.

Colin frowned. Had he misinterpreted why his father had said the word? Of course, he knew his father loved him, but maybe his message was even bigger than that. Mayhap he'd meant if Colin loved Kristina, then that was all that mattered. Or maybe, being half in this world and half in the next, his father had meant that love was the most important thing of all in life. Not prestige or power or possessions. Not alliances or dowries. Love, friendship, family.

Still, one of the people he'd been closest to in the world was gone, and nothing he did now could bring him back. No amount of regret would allow him to go into the past and protect his father, even though 'twas what he wished more than anything.

He would like to talk to Neacal about this, for he'd lost his father a little over two years ago. He would understand what Colin was going through. Colin had sent a messenger to deliver a missive to Neacal only hours after his father had passed, but 'twas doubtful he would arrive in time for the funeral tomorrow.

And Kristina... damnation, every time he thought of her, a new gash opened up in his soul. To have two such painful open wounds at the same time. Why had this happened to him? Was God testing him to see his mettle?

He did not know if he could endure it.

Tomorrow, after the funeral, he would continue the search for

Red Holme, but for tonight he would forget. At a nearby table, he poured himself a large dram of whisky and downed it in one swallow. It burned like hellfire all the way down his gullet. Returning to the hearth, he slumped onto the settle.

Not one given to excessive drinking, he felt the burn of the whisky in his veins and then the lightheadedness. He had forgotten to eat supper, he realized. His stomach was empty, and so were his heart and soul. He was naught but a hollow shell. Trying to calm the spinning of his head, he slid down and turned to lie on his back. Finally, numbness settled over his body and mind.

The door opened, and Neacal stepped inside the solar at Bearach. Although Kristina could not see perfectly as of yet, and her brother-in-law stood in a distant and dimmer part of the room, she did notice that he was tall and lean, with broad shoulders and long dark hair.

"There you are, *a shùgh mo chrìdhe*," Neacal said to Anna. "And Lady Kristina." He bowed.

What a gentleman he was to bow to her, even though he thought she couldn't see him. They would have to tell him about her vision soon or he would feel slighted, she was certain.

"Why were you looking for me?" Anna arose to greet him.

Taking her hands, he kissed her cheek, then drew back. "Colin sent a messenger with bad news. His father passed from the injury."

Kristina felt as if she'd been knocked flat. "Och, nay. Colin must be devastated." Her throat tightened, and tears burned her eyes. How she wished she could be there with him now to support and comfort him.

"Did you find out what happened? Who ambushed him?" Anna asked.

Neacal hesitated. "The messenger said... 'twas Red Holme."

"What?" Anna exclaimed.

Speechless, Kristina gasped. The shock of hearing the name caused her physical pain. She felt somehow responsible. Had Holme attacked Colin's father out of anger because Colin had rescued her?

"As you both know, the Camerons and Red Holme's birth clan,

the MacKillicans, have a long history of conflict. It had naught to do with either of you."

Kristina blotted her eyes with her sleeve. "I still feel 'tis my fault."

"Nay," Neacal said. "Colin wouldn't want you to feel that way. I'm going to take a couple dozen men and see if Colin needs my help in finding the blackguard."

"He helped both of us. We want to come with you," Anna said.

"Nay." His tone was firm. "'Tis not safe. Holme has not been caught. He could be lying in wait along the road."

Anna turned. "Kristina, we need to tell him."

Knowing Anna was right, she nodded. 'Twas time to reveal to all she could see. And to apologize to Colin and help him in any way she could... whether he forgave her or not.

"Tell me what?" In the silence, Neacal glanced back and forth between them.

"Kristina's vision has returned." Anna smiled. "And she has changed her mind about marrying Colin."

"Anna! I did not say that... yet." Kristina's skin burned from the top of her head to her feet. Although she did want to marry Colin, she didn't know if he would want her now.

"Saints! You can see?" Neacal faced her. "When and how did this happen?"

"'Tis a miracle," Kristina said. "Or 'haps because of that last time Holme struck me in the face. I noticed my sight returning a few nights ago. Everything is still a blur, but I can see well enough to walk alone now."

"This is indeed good news," Neacal said with excitement. "Colin will be happy to hear it."

Kristina assumed either Colin or Anna had told Neacal of the marriage proposal. "I want to tell him I'm sorry, but I don't ken if he will ever forgive me for the pain I've caused him. You have known him the whole of your life. What do you think?"

After a moment of contemplation, Neacal said, "I cannot speak for Colin, but I'm certain he would love to see you. I've always found him to be a forgiving person."

Tilting her face down, she stared at her lap. "Besides that... even if I can see again, I still have this awful scar on my face. Naught will ever change that."

"'Tis not so bad," Neacal said. "'Haps you have not yet seen the scar on my face." He moved forward and knelt before her in the sunlight. "Do you see?"

Though her view of him was fuzzy, she was seeing Neacal for the first time, close up. He was a handsome man with long, brownish-black hair and blue eyes. But he did indeed have a jagged scar, larger than hers, on one side of his face.

"For a man, a scar is a badge of valor and courage," she said. "For a woman, 'tis but an ugly mark. Unfortunately, women are judged on beauty or lack thereof."

Neacal shook his head. "Colin told me he thinks you are the most beautiful woman he has yet seen, scar and all."

"When you love someone, scars don't matter." Anna laid an affectionate hand upon her husband's shoulder. "Neacal's scar only makes him dearer to me, and I'm certain Colin feels the same way about you."

Neacal stood, pulled Anna close and kissed the top of her head.

"Imagine the situation reversed," Anna said. "What if your face was unblemished and Colin's was scarred? Would you love him any less?"

"Of course not," Kristina blurted. She did not have to think on it.

"I understand how you feel," Neacal said. "There was a time when I presumed Anna would not want to look at or touch my scarred face and body, but then she showed me that my worries were for naught. Colin has always had a deep concern and compassion for you, even from the first moment I told him of your situation."

"Aye, and he is already used to your scar, as we discussed," Anna said. "So I think we should go to Rhodie now, before the autumn snows begin. Otherwise, we'll have to wait until spring. Besides, we need to go to his father's funeral."

Frowning, Neacal let out a tense breath. "I will have to think on it and make certain I can protect you both."

"With two dozen soldiers serving as guards, surely we would be safe. Do you have such little faith in your men?" Anna asked.

"Of course not. I simply don't wish to put either of you at risk. With the last contact Kristina had with Red Holme, he was bent on kidnapping and hurting her."

"'Tis true." Anna hung her head. "And I would not wish to put her in any more danger. I'm just concerned that since Colin is now chief, his clan will pressure him into marrying soon, just as your clan urged you to marry quickly once you became chief. If we wait until spring, it might be too late."

"She could scribe him a missive and I'll deliver it to him," Neacal suggested.

That was true, but Kristina could not imagine how she would express her deep regret in rejecting Colin's suit, and also her heartfelt condolences on the loss of his father. Words on paper seemed a cold, lifeless substitute to touching him or holding him in her arms.

"I must apologize in person," Kristina said. "And I want to be there for him during his time of grief. Even if it puts my life in danger, 'tis a risk I'm willing to take, especially if I have a small chance in receiving his forgiveness."

"Have you truly changed your mind about marrying him?" Neacal asked. "I'm sorry to say this but… if you haven't, there's no need to go. 'Twould only cause him more heartbreak and pain."

She liked that Neacal was forthright with her, and she respected him for it. "Aye, I have always wanted to marry Colin. I was merely trying to spare him the burden and embarrassment of having a disfigured and disabled wife."

"I'm glad you've realized that would never be the case. You bring him great joy, and he told me he is proud to have you on his arm."

Tears burning her eyes, Kristina hung her head. "I'm sorry. I never meant to hurt him. I love him."

Anna pulled Kristina into her arms for a tight embrace. "There is no need to cry now. You love him and he loves you. 'Tis simply a matter of getting you to him. And your worries will be laid to rest."

"I'm still concerned about you ladies going along in our party," Neacal muttered. "Red Holme is vicious and unpredictable."

Colin's chest and stomach ached as his father's funeral procession got underway. He donned a strong façade for the sake of his mother and his clan. At the front of the procession, three pipers played the Cameron chief's march. The shrill sounds of the bagpipes echoed off the stone walls, and the icy wind carried them away toward the mountains.

His mother held his elbow as they followed four strong clansmen carrying his father's casket upon their shoulders across the bailey. His ma sobbed and, losing control at times, wailed out her grief. He knew 'twas real and not the keening for show practiced by many clans. Listening to her was hellish for him. Her agony magnified his own, and the chill wind near froze the tears welling in his eyes.

Bryce came upon their ma's other side, helping her to walk when she faltered.

"I can get a wagon for you to ride in," Colin murmured to her.

"Nay." She shook her head emphatically. "I'm not as weak as you think I am."

Well, he was glad for that, at least. He just hoped she was being honest.

The whole clan, even the crofters from miles around, followed and gathered into the long, slow funeral procession toward the chapel a short distance outside the castle walls, sitting in the midst of the burial ground.

After the casket was carried inside, the clan filled the chapel to overflowing.

Hundreds mourned the loss of his father, for he had been a much admired, respected and beloved chief, a strong leader. After being notified by messenger, clansmen and women from the far reaches of Cameron lands had arrived only that morning to pay their respects and tell stories of how the late chief had helped and honored them over the last few decades. Many recounted tales of the battles they had fought alongside the former chief, extolling his bravery and valor.

Colin had hoped Neacal would be able to make it to the funeral but, as of yet, he hadn't arrived. 'Twas expecting too much, he knew, for 'twas a long journey.

Sitting on the hard oak pew, Colin shifted and glanced across his mother's head at Bryce, who sat on her other side and looked just as miserable as Colin felt. Once the minister, Reverend MacAbee, had spoken at some length about what a good man Chief Maitland Cameron was, he said a prayer.

When the prayer ended, Colin opened his eyes, finding himself once again faced with the most tragic moment of his life. His father was gone and he was never coming back. Colin had no choice but to accept the finality of it, and he had to be strong for his clan.

Never had Colin imagined he would lose his father so young. He had expected Da to one day, twenty or thirty years from now, be an ancient elder with a long white beard.

'Tis as it should be, my son.

It was almost as if Da whispered the words into his ear.

Nay, it never should've happened like this—not an ambush. Murder. The dreadful and heartrending tragedy of it struck him yet again, constricting his lungs.

The clansmen carried his father's casket outside into the whipping wind where a grave was being dug on the spot they had chosen earlier, next to Colin's grandfather's grave.

A short distance away, a lone piper played a lamenting ballad as mourners gathered around the open grave. Colin had never endured anything so painful and final as watching his father's body being lowered into the earth while his mother clung to his arm, sobbing. He prayed this loss would not be too taxing on her. Although his mother and father's marriage had been arranged by their parents, they had been loving toward one another since his earliest memories. He only hoped he could have a marriage as happy as theirs had been, but 'twas looking doubtful.

Using his sword, Red Holme hacked at the large, thorny gorse bushes, bramble briars and dried thistles guarding the secret passage exit gate. Dobson helped him, along with one of the new men, Robertson. Scroggie was back with the horses and the additional man he'd hired recently.

Hell, he would have to sharpen his sword again after this. What they needed was an axe for wood chopping. But they didn't even have a Lochaber axe at the moment.

This gate was about a quarter mile from the castle walls and, by the looks of it, no one had been out through the gate in over a decade. He doubted the daft Camerons even knew of its existence. This prickly vegetation had hidden it for many years, and he was glad. If he could get the iron gate open, he could easily slip up the secret passage and into the castle without anyone knowing of it until it was too late. He grinned.

One of the wicked gorse thorns stabbed into his finger. He swore profusely and stared down at his bloody finger.

"Bastard Camerons," he hissed, clenching his teeth against the pain, hating them more and more each day. "Cut the bushes out of there," he ordered Dobson and Robertson.

Holme smirked when he remembered where the clan was now, in the kirk at the chief's funeral. He'd watched the funeral procession from a distance and determined this was the best time to find the secret passage among the thick, thorny vegetation and vines.

They had already stolen a small boat and concealed it beneath a heap of dried bracken ferns near the river. That way, they could hide their horses farther away, but still escape quickly.

A half hour later, most of the prickly bushes lay aside, exposing large stones. He remembered when he and his few remaining clansmen had slipped back and concealed this gate many years ago, hoping to prevent the Camerons from using it as escape route if they ever decided to lay siege to the place. Now he could use it in reverse to attack from the inside, if the gate and lock had rusted into oblivion in the last decade.

"Move the stones," Holme commanded, annoyed this was taking so long. They had to finish before the funeral was over or risk being seen.

Fortunately for the two men, removing the rocks was fairly easy, as most of them rolled or slid away with minimal effort. Once the rusty, three-foot-tall gate was exposed, Holme grabbed the iron bars and shook them, yanked at them, but the gate didn't budge. He growled a curse and looked at the latch through the bars. It held firm, and he saw no way to open it from the outside. Designed as it was, as an escape route for the chief if the castle was under siege, the gate's latch only opened from the inside.

Holme stood. "We'll come out this way, but we must get into the castle another way."

"But how?" Dobson asked. "'Twould be suicide to approach the portcullis if Colin Cameron sees you."

His canny mind spinning, Holme grinned. "I have an idea."

During the second day of their journey, Kristina had been chilled for many hours. The weather had turned colder, and the wind blew harder. She had even seen a few snowflakes, but they melted once they reached the ground.

They were fortunate in that Cyrus MacKenzie and his brothers, Fraser and Shamus, along with all of their guards and clansmen had wanted to accompany them. Ralston also journeyed with them, but Neacal continued to keep their half-brother at a distance and guarded at all times. Ralston had caused no trouble, and Kristina wondered when Neacal would begin to trust him.

Maili rode beside Kristina and Anna, in the midst of all the men. Tavia, her helper, and three maids also accompanied them, for they knew not how long they would stay at Rhodie. In the event anyone was hurt in an ambush or battle with Holme, Tavia would help them to the best of her ability. The length of their stay would largely depend upon the weather and how quickly Holme was captured. She did not imagine Colin or Neacal would give up before the murderer was behind bars or dead. The MacKenzies seemed equally determined to nab him and his band of outlaws, as did Ralston.

After the ferry had taken them to Glenfinnan, they stayed the night at the inn, then rode out the next morn. Neacal predicted they could make it to Rhodie before dark despite the snow flurries. In truth, she did not mind the journey. She simply relished every moment of observing things she hadn't in a long time. She had not seen sunlight or snow in over two years. She was thankful for being able to view every single thing, even though all was blurry at any distance.

When they stopped in a shady wood, she marveled at the lush green moss covering the gray rocks and tree trunks. 'Twas like an enchanted fairy wood.

When next they halted to rest and water the horses, they were in a glen by a loch. She noticed purple flecks among the tan grasses. She stepped closer and crouched to see what they were.

"Look, Anna. 'Tis heather!" Kristina pointed at the few sprigs of the late-blooming flowers. She had not thought to see them at this time of year.

"Your favorite. How lovely. I'm so glad you can see them now."

"Aye." Kristina knew she was probably acting like a wee bairn, but she could hardly contain her joy over being able to see. The wee pinkish-violet blooms were so dainty and delicate. If only she could see this whole hillside of heather in full bloom, she would probably weep with joy. She would never take her vision for granted again.

After riding for a while longer, she noticed something large, shadowed and blurry looming up beside them. She squinted. "Good heavens. Is that a mountain?"

Riding in front of them, Neacal turned back and said, "Aye. 'Tis Ben Nevis. The top is already white with snow."

She'd heard of it—the tallest mountain in Scotland.

Despite being glad about the return of her vision and seeing things she had never seen before, she knew Colin was living in the pits of despair. She wanted to embrace him and give him comfort so badly. She hoped he would be pleased to see her and to learn her vision was coming back.

What if he was angry instead? What if he could never forgive her?

Colin drew up near the wood and dismounted, following the wee terrier again. The rest of the men in his party halted, too. His breath fogged in the falling temperatures. Frustration quickening his steps, Colin strode forward, searching the light trace of snow on the ground. His boots crunching on the half-frozen leaves, he slipped into the wood, looking for any sign Red Holme had been here recently. But he saw naught, and the terrier kept moving quickly, nose to the ground.

Damnation. Where was Holme hiding? He was sure the bastard must be thrilled if he'd learned Colin's father had succumbed to his injuries and died. Had Holme slipped around to the grave and danced upon it? Did he still want Colin dead, or was killing the chief enough revenge to satisfy him?

Colin shook his head, doubting Holme would stop his quest of vengeance until Colin and maybe even his brother were dead. How could the whoreson be so elusive of a sudden? He must have one hell of a hiding place. Didn't matter. Colin would be damned if he was giving up finding the murderer. He owed it to his father. 'Twas the final thing he could do for him—bring his killer to justice.

Footsteps approached upon the crusty, snow-covered leaves. He glanced around to find Bryce moving toward him.

"We must go back to Rhodie." His brother wore a disgruntled frown, snowflakes clinging in his dark hair. "We've been out here for over two days in the cold, searching. The men need to rest."

"Go back, then," Colin growled. "But I'll not give up on finding Holme."

"We're not giving up," Bryce snapped. "We've seen no sign of him the whole time we've been out here. He's probably long gone by now."

Colin shook his head, eyes narrowing. "You do not ken him. He craves revenge more than his next breath. He wants me dead… and probably you, too. I'm sure he'd like naught more than to see all us Camerons dead."

Bryce drew in a deep breath and blew it out as if annoyed and exhausted at the same time. "I ken you're right, but mayhap there's another way."

"Tell me then. I need good ideas for catching a murderer."

Bryce glanced skyward. "'Twill be near gloaming by the time we reach Rhodie. I say we return now, get some rest so we can think clearly, then have a meeting. We can come up with a strategy to keep all of us safe inside the walls. If Holme truly does want to exact more revenge, he will come to us. We can double the number of guards posted upon the ramparts and other places."

Colin turned and glanced back at the rest of the Camerons, waiting nearby with the horses. They did look tired and discouraged. He nodded. "Very well. We'll go back for now. But tomorrow we must come up with a canny strategy, for Holme will not give up."

Wearing a black cloak and carrying chimney sweep tools—canes and whalebone brushes—Holme approached Rhodie Castle. No one would miss the real chimney sweep he'd put out of his misery and stolen these trappings from. Scroggie followed along behind him, affecting a limp and carrying the rest of the tools—a ball, sacks and ropes. Both their shaven faces were covered in black soot, helping to ensure no one would recognize them.

As they passed the chapel and cemetery with its freshly filled-in grave, Holme smirked. He'd finally given Maitland Cameron what he deserved, but Holme wasn't finished yet—not until he'd eliminated a few dozen more Camerons.

This was the closest Holme had been to the castle in over a

decade. His heart pounded in a fast, excited rhythm. Could he get inside the walls with no one the wiser? He almost smiled, relishing the challenge.

He already knew that Colin and more than twenty Camerons were out searching the wood and various other places. Holme and his men had found a canny hiding place in the village a few miles away, a place Colin and his men had searched the day before. But they hadn't found the hidden cellar of the byre used by Holme's former clansman.

Now, one of the tall, brawny Cameron guards approached the portcullis. "What do you want?"

"Need yer chimneys cleaned?" Holme affected a dialect like a peasant from the east. "We'll give ye a good price. Winter coming. Naught worse than a chimney clogged with soot and resin. Could catch the castle on fire."

"Wait here. I'll ask the steward." The guard strode away.

"What do you think, Red? Think they'll let us in?" Scroggie whispered, then let out a snicker.

"Aye. I believe they will. No one wants a chimney fire. Colin has been gone for a couple of days, but we'll be inside when he returns."

A well-dressed man wearing a plaid approached with the guard. Holme assumed he was the steward.

"Are you two chimney sweeps?" He eyed them critically.

"Aye. Can ye nay tell by our spotless clothes?" Holme held out an arm and chuckled good-naturedly. They were covered head to toe in soot. Did the daft man not see their tools as well? Surely they looked the part.

Holme had watched chimneys being cleaned, and he knew how it was done. Didn't mean he would be any good at it, but he could pretend long enough to get his revenge.

"Where are you from?" the steward questioned.

"Inverness. Too much competition there."

"What's your fee?"

"Room and board for a sennight, plus twenty shillings."

The man scratched his bearded chin for a long moment, still considering them. "Wait here." He strode away, then returned a quarter hour later. "You're in luck. We do indeed need our chimneys swept. I'll show you where you can bed down at night."

Red Holme felt like cackling with glee as he strode through the portcullis. 'Twas far easier than he'd ever imagined being welcomed into Rhodic Castle. It wouldn't be long before Colin and his brethren were dead.

CHAPTER EIGHTEEN

At gloaming, snow flurries still flittered through the air as Colin stood in the burial ground, by his father's grave. They had ridden three hours and arrived back moments ago. Bryce and most of the other men had gone inside the castle walls. Four guards, including Warton and Rusty, stood around Colin at a distance of twenty paces, giving him the privacy he needed. The other two had been his father's bodyguards, but now, since Colin would soon be inaugurated as the new chief, they were assigned to guard him.

He stared at the simple wooden cross with his father's name cut into it. Soon it would be replaced with a carved sandstone grave slab befitting a chief. He stared at the black sod and the dried heather and greenery his mother had placed there. He knew his da lay beneath, but was still unable to fully comprehend it.

"I'm sorry, Da," he whispered. "I let you down. I allowed our enemy to come back here and massacre you." Regret speared him. "If only I'd been thinking... If only I'd realized..." But, nay, Kristina had snagged all of his attention at Bearach. He had been so taken with her, he'd been able to think of little else. He felt like such a daft fool.

No more. He would dedicate his life to bringing his da's murderer to justice.

"Riders approaching!" Warton announced.

The four guards closed ranks around him. "Mayhap we should escort you back to the castle," Rusty said.

Colin glanced down the hill, seeing a party of three dozen or more people arriving, most on horseback. They appeared in no hurry, or maybe their horses were tired from a long trek.

Colin shook his head. "'Tis not Holme. He wouldn't have that many men."

As the party increased its pace and moved closer, he saw Neacal and his men, along with the MacKenzies. And several women?

"What the devil?" Narrowing his eyes, Colin glared. Aye, some of the riders wore long skirts. Surely Neacal hadn't brought Anna and... "Kristina," Colin whispered. Indeed, she was on the horse beside Anna's. Why had she come? He muttered a curse, feeling gutted once again. Why did she wish to rub salt in his wound? Dangle before him the very thing he wanted most in the world but could not have?

Mayhap she has changed her mind.

The ridiculous thought teased and taunted him, near making him lightheaded. She had already ripped out his heart. Putting it back into his chest was not going to be such an easy task.

As Kristina and the others in their party approached Rhodie Castle, she barely discerned the blurry forms of men on a hill in the distance, near a small stone kirk with a steeple. She squinted, trying to see better. They stood in the burial ground, surrounded by many grave slabs and tombstones.

Her heart drummed hard with the tumultuous combination of nervousness and excitement, because she might see Colin for the first time within a few moments—but also with sadness because of his loss.

With the snowflakes flickering in the twilight, 'twas too dim and indistinct for her to see clearly. And even if she could see the men, she wouldn't know Colin on sight. Still, she had a gut feeling one of the men was him, visiting his father's grave. She had so wanted to be here to support him during the funeral and burial, but that had been impossible. They'd traveled as quickly as they could after hearing the tragic news.

Minutes later, as they approached the kirk-yard, the five men strode away from the new grave and exited the burial ground through the gate. Melancholy consumed her as she recalled, yet again, that she would never meet his father, whom he'd held so dear.

Even though she'd never seen Colin with her eyes, only with her hands and her heart... and in her dreams, she knew which man he was. The only one who drew her attention. The only one who stared directly at her. Tall and handsome with sandy hair. Although she could not quite perceive his expression, she felt his dark and tormented pain, and it near broke her heart. She hung her head and stared at the snow-dusted ground, feeling something powerful in Colin calling out to her, raking through her soul.

She refused to look at him now, although she wanted to more than anything. Nay, she wanted to tell him in private about her returned sight and didn't want him to find out before then. She hoped he would be glad. Her heart rate sped up, and her icy hands sweated within her gloves as she held the bridle loosely.

When footsteps approached, she felt his anguish even more. Her ability to detect others' feelings had amplified during her years of blindness.

"Thank you for coming, Neacal." Colin's voice slid down deep within her, bringing her soul to life, but at the same time, his grief frayed her control. The wind chilled the tears welling in her burning eyes. She watched the men from the corners of her eyes.

"I'm sorry we're late." Neacal dismounted and gave Colin a warrior handshake. "I wish we could've arrived before the funeral, but the ladies wished to come and pay their respects, too. We could not travel as fast."

"'Tis understandable. I'm glad you've all come." His voice was deep and desolate, devoid of all cheer. Kristina had never heard this tone of voice from him before.

"Your father was a great man, Colin," Neacal said. "And a revered chief."

"I always thought so, and I thank you."

"You have my sympathies." Cyrus MacKenzie shook his hand, as did his two brothers, who had also dismounted.

"Have you found Red Holme?" Neacal asked.

"Nay."

"We're here to help," Cyrus said.

"I appreciate that. Come, let's go to the keep and get out of this snow," Colin announced. "You must all be tired and hungry."

Kristina was disappointed, but not surprised, that he hadn't come closer and spoken to her, to allow her to express her condolences. Inching her line of sight upward, Kristina allowed herself to look directly at Colin's back as he walked away, toward the Cameron horses, his guards following.

Colin's shoulders were broad, but now slumped, as if the weight of the world rested upon them. She understood how he felt, for she had lost her own father a few years ago. Everything had changed after that. Not only had she lost her dear sweet da but also her home, when a distant relative had inherited and asked her and Anna to leave.

Now she wanted to be here for Colin. She wished she could hold him and comfort him in some way. But she was unsure whether he would even want it.

They rode the short distance through the snow and toward the castle's portcullis, which was quickly raised, and into the bailey.

Kristina admired the way Colin's tawny hair gleamed in the torchlight, lying upon his shiny chainmail armor. What an extraordinary man he was. She prayed that he would forgive her and accept her back into his life.

They halted, and all the men began dismounting. Neacal helped Anna to the ground and then Kristina.

The bailey was so crowded, she did not know where Colin was. She wanted to speak to him forthwith, to let him know her vision had returned before someone else told him, and before he figured it out.

Anna spoke beside her, "I'm sorry for the loss of your beloved da, Colin."

"I thank you."

Kristina stood frozen in surprise, for she hadn't known he was so near. She wanted to look at him so badly, but dared not yet, not until she could tell him of the miracle. With her eyes still closed, lingering in the safety of the familiar darkness, Kristina waited, tears flooding her eyes and trailing down her cheeks, growing icy in the cold wind.

"Lady Kristina, I thank you for coming." Colin's hard, dark voice was so close in front of her. Dare she look at him now? Her heart thundered with fear.

She reached a trembling hand out to him and he took it. "I'm so sorry, Colin." Sorry for everything. Sorry he'd lost his father and that she'd broken his heart.

He kissed her gloved hand "Shh, don't cry, lass," he whispered, then walked away.

"Wait," she called out, but he didn't. "I must tell him now," Kristina whispered to Anna. "I don't wish him to hear it from someone else, nor discover me staring at him."

"Colin," Anna called out, then waved.

"Just a minute."

"He is speaking to Warton," Anna whispered. "I'm sure he will be here in a moment."

At least he had spoken to her with kindness and kissed her hand, but Kristina still felt unworthy of him. He should have a beautiful, perfect bride, someone with unmarred skin. But every time she thought of that, she wanted to rip the hair from the perfect lass she visualized in her mind. Apparently, she had a possessive side she'd never known about until now. Aye, she wanted Colin for her very own. But she also wanted the best for him. She wished him a happy life and didn't know if she would make him happy. She did not want to disappoint him. What if his clan could not look at her scarred face without feeling disgust? What if they hated her?

What if Colin never trusted her again?

Striding across the bailey, Colin felt an intense mixture of emotions such as he'd never felt before, not the least of which was anger at himself. Why couldn't he simply ignore Kristina? Why did he allow her to affect him so profoundly?

He could hardly believe she was here. One part of him wanted to talk to her longer, to find out why she'd come. Another part dreaded the moment. His heart thudded with excitement as he approached the two ladies. Anna watched him, but as he drew near, she moved toward Neacal a few yards away. Clearly, she wished to give them privacy, but he was unsure if he wanted it. He could not allow himself to be drawn under Kristina's spell again. He had to keep his wits about him, stay sharp, and catch Red Holme as soon as possible.

But, hell… Kristina looked even more beautiful than the last time he'd seen her. She wore a dark cloak with a cowl over her head. The snowflakes sparkled in the torchlight.

"You wished to speak to me, m'lady?" Not wanting her to know how she disturbed him, he tried to keep his voice impersonal.

She raised her head, and their gazes locked. What the devil? Her eyes were not vacant or staring into the ether. Saints, but she was looking at him! He frowned as he searched her eyes… and she searched his. Though tears glistened on her lashes, she watched him closely. The sensation was so startling, he felt as if a cannonball dropped onto his stomach. Had she deceived him the entire time? Had she been able to see from the first?

"Can you see?" he blurted.

"Aye, 'tis what I've come to tell you, Colin, along with paying my respects."

"How? When?" His voice was perhaps more demanding than he'd intended.

"'Tis either a miracle or a reaction to that last blow to the head Holme gave me. A few days after my headache went away, just after you left, I saw a flash of light, and then candle flames. Each day since then, my vision has improved."

"Saints," he hissed, hardly able to breathe. Her blindness had been her excuse for rejecting him. Did this mean…? *Hell, don't even think of it,* he told himself.

Her bewitching blue gaze was still locked on his, her pupils dilated in the dim torchlight. "Most things are still blurry, especially at a distance, but I'm starting to see better close up."

He was shocked speechless. He still didn't see how it was possible. "A miracle?"

"'Haps. Or the injury."

"Aye." He remembered… and still blamed himself for that, too.

"Enough about me," she said. "I'm so sorry you lost your father. I want you to know I'm here for you if you need to talk. As you know, I lost my father several years ago."

Colin nodded. "I'm sorry you lost your father, too," he said, simply to cover his sudden annoyance and discomfort.

"I thank you."

"Are you going to introduce me, brother?" Bryce said beside him, dragging him from the spell her eyes had cast over him.

"This is my younger brother, Bryce," Colin said, then motioned to Kristina. "And this is Lady Kristina."

Bryce bowed over her hand and kissed it. "So, you are the renowned Lady Kristina who Colin is so secretive about."

Colin ground his teeth. "I haven't been secretive."

Bryce smirked.

Kristina glanced at him with uncertainty. Saints, he could not get accustomed to the fact that she could see. The awareness in her gaze reached deep into his soul. It felt as if he were connecting with her on an even more profound level than before. He could stare into her expressive blue eyes forever.

Colin glared at Bryce. "I'm certain the lady is exhausted and hungry. I'm going to escort her into the great hall, that is, if she would like."

"Aye. And it was wonderful to meet you, Bryce."

"A pleasure." He gave an abbreviated bow.

She slipped her arm around Colin's, and they headed toward the steps. Through his clothing and chain mail armor, he relished the gentle pressure of her hand on the inside of his elbow. His body stirred in response, which infuriated him. Why was his body enslaved by hers?

"You have a beautiful home," she said, raising her voice to be heard over the din in the great hall as the servants and clan prepared for supper.

"I appreciate it." Colin was surprised to find his mother coming toward them.

"My maid told me Neacal had arrived with his new bride." His ma offered a small smile, the first he'd seen on her face since he'd been back.

"Aye."

She glanced at Kristina, who still held his arm, and he prayed Ma wouldn't mention Kristina's scar.

"And who is this lovely lass?"

"Meet Lady Kristina. She is Neacal's wife's sister. Kristina, this is my mother."

"I'm glad to meet you, Lady Cameron." Releasing his arm, Kristina leaned in and kissed his ma's cheek. "But I'm so sorry for your terrible loss."

"I thank you. And please call me Hester."

Colin moved aside and turned, finding Neacal and Anna behind them. "This is Neacal's new bride, Anna."

Neacal, Anna and his mother exchanged greetings. She then met Maili.

Kristina still stood close beside him. His mother looked pointedly at the spot where Kristina's elbow brushed his arm, then glanced up at him and gave him a wee mischievous grin. How could she be smiling in the midst of grief? Was she that glad to see that a lass was interested in him?

"'Haps you ladies would like to refresh yourselves before supper," Colin said, hoping to draw his mother's attention away. "I'll see if I can find the housekeeper." He glanced across the great hall and spotted the plump, middle-aged woman. "Mistress MacAuley," he called and lifted a hand.

She hastened toward them. "Aye, Master Colin… I mean, m'laird."

To Colin, that form of address was like a kick in the gut. His father was still supposed to be the laird.

When he hesitated a moment too long, his mother spoke up. "Could you please find rooms for the ladies and see that they are well taken care of?"

"Of course. Come, my ladies, I have just the rooms. They were cleaned yesterday after some of the guests left."

Anna, Kristina and Maili followed her up the steps.

His mother gave him an oddly curious look, then walked away. He had not mentioned his association with Lady Kristina, but she must have figured it out. His mother was ever insightful.

Colin turned to Neacal. "Would you like some ale before supper?"

"Aye."

Seeing a kitchen maid nearby, he said, "Could you bring some ale into the library?"

"Aye, m'laird." She curtsied, then rushed away.

Colin headed toward the library. "Where are the MacKenzies and Ralston?"

"Talking to Bryce in the bailey."

After the maid brought a pitcher of ale and poured two tankards, she left.

"I truly appreciate your making the journey here, Neacal. It couldn't have been easy in this weather, especially for the ladies."

"I didn't want them to come, but they insisted. And I hate that the visit is due to such a tragedy."

Colin nodded, still feeling consumed by grief, but at the same time glad to see Kristina, Neacal and the rest of his friends.

Neacal raised his tankard. "To your father—may he rest in peace. And to you as the new chief."

"I thank you." Even though he felt undeserving of such a lofty role, he would keep that to himself for now. Colin clunked his tankard against Neacal's, then drank. After seeing Kristina, he needed whisky, but this ale would have to suffice since he hadn't eaten in several hours.

Colin motioned toward a chair, then took a seat himself. "How fortunate Lady Kristina has regained her sight."

Neacal sat. "Aye, 'tis a miracle. I only found out about it days ago. Anna said Kristina didn't want anyone to know at first, afraid it was temporary."

Colin stared into his ale, feeling more confusion and conflict than he should. "I'm happy for her."

"Truly?" Neacal gave him a skeptical, questioning look.

'Haps Colin sounded less than happy, but 'twas difficult to be enthusiastic when he had never felt such grief and heartbreak. He simply wished he knew what was on her mind. "Why did Kristina come?"

"To pay her respects and tell you she can see again." Stating the obvious, Neacal raised a brow.

"Aye, but are those the only reasons?" Colin dug deeper, for he sensed his friend holding back.

"At Bearach, I suggested she write you a letter, which I would deliver." Neacal shook his head. "She would have none of it. She insisted she must come here and talk to you."

Colin exhaled a tired breath, trying to release some of the tension. "I don't know if she told you but… before I left Bearach, I asked her to marry me. She refused."

Neacal frowned. "She told Anna, who told me. I was deeply disappointed to hear of it. I know you have strong feelings for her."

Damnation! How he wished he could control those strong feelings. "Did she give you any further clues as to what's on her mind?"

Neacal avoided his gaze. "You would need to ask her."

His friend knew something more, blast him. If she'd changed her mind about marrying him, Colin was tempted but… "I cannot allow her to take my focus away from capturing Holme."

"'Tis not my place to speak for her, but I don't believe that's her intention."

"Of course not." Annoyance grated at Colin. "That's simply what she does to me. She drives me mad and distracts me. 'Tis why I stayed at Bearach too long and allowed Holme to come here and kill my father. If only I'd started home the next morn after I delivered Kristina to Bearach, my father would still be alive."

Allowing his fury to burn beyond his control, Colin now felt the mad urge to throw his tankard against the stone fireplace. Instead, he placed it on the table, arose and paced.

Neacal shook his head for a long moment, looking saddened. "'Tis not your fault. You cannot blame yourself."

"But I do, a thousand times over."

"You had no inkling Holme was coming here."

"I should've guessed," Colin growled. "If only I'd been in my right mind instead of thinking about Kristina every moment."

Neacal blew out a breath. "Well... I ken how you feel. I blame myself for my father's death, too. He died because of the injuries he sustained in rescuing me from that torture chamber. But I've been able to forgive myself. I think my da would want me to do that and get on with my life. We cannot go back and change the past."

Grief ripped at his heart yet again. "But I wish I could, more than anything."

"Aye, me too. But life is not perfect. We must learn our lessons and go on."

Feeling dejected, Colin slumped onto the chair. "I do not ken how to."

Neacal leaned forward. "I'm here for you, brother. For anything you need help with."

Even though they were not brothers by blood, they certainly were by spirit, as well as foster brothers.

"I appreciate that," Colin said. "I already told the elders I won't go through with the inauguration until Red Holme is dead or captured. If I cannot succeed at that, I don't deserve to be chief."

"You will. I have no doubt of it."

Colin shrugged. "I can only hope." He shook his head. "I cannot get used to being called laird or chief. That title has always been my father's."

"I felt the same way the first few weeks. I never expected to be chief," Neacal said. "'Twas supposed to be my older brother's position. When he was killed in that raid, I was ill prepared for the role. Plus, half the clan and most of the elders were against me early on, but I have blundered through."

"You're doing a fine job leading your clan."

"And you will, too. Your da taught you well. He taught both of us much when we were lads."

Colin's chest ached so deeply he could hardly draw breath. "I miss those days."

"As do I, but the present can be just as good, if you let it. I had to accept that the past is in the past and all I have is the present. Either I can give up and amount to naught, or I can do my best, keep my head up, and look the future. Anna helped me gain the will to go forward. She gave me a reason."

"I'm truly glad you found her."

"What about you and Kristina?"

Colin's heart sank. "There is much unspoken between us."

"You could talk to her after supper."

"Mayhap." Did he truly wish to put his heart on the rack again?

"Do you still care for her?"

Colin frowned. How could his friend even ask that? "Of course. That's the problem. She doesn't want what I do."

"You won't know whether she's changed her mind until you ask her."

He'd dealt with enough pain recently; he didn't need more rejection. "I have no need to be unmanned again so soon."

"Give her a chance to explain herself." Neacal looked far too hopeful. What did he know that he wasn't sharing?

"Clearly you know her mind better than I do," Colin muttered.

Neacal shrugged. "I asked her a few questions before I allowed her to come along, but I'll not tell you what she said. That's her place."

Anticipation tried to break free, but he tamped it down and buried it beneath surliness. "Let me guess—since her sight has returned, she's changed her mind about marrying me."

Studying him, Neacal quirked a brow. "You say that as if 'tis an awful thing."

"Nay. I'm glad she has her sight back, but her blindness was never a problem for me. The problem is the way she changes her mind. What if we become betrothed, and suddenly she loses her sight again? She could easily break the betrothal. If we were to marry, and she loses her sight again, she might very well leave me and return to Bearach to live with Anna... to spare me the *burden*, as she calls it."

Neacal looked troubled as he glanced away, for he knew it could happen.

"As I said, I don't need the distraction. I'm going out tomorrow all day, hunting for Red Holme. I will not rest until he's dead."

"I'm going with you."

A knock sounded at the door.

"Enter," Colin called.

One of the manservants opened the door and stuck his head in. "Her ladyship sent me. 'Tis time for supper, m'laird."

"We'll be right out."

The servant bowed and closed the door.

"I hope you will at least talk to Kristina," Neacal said.

Colin gave a brief nod. He was certain he would have to talk to her at some point, but he was not ready as of yet. He felt torn, and the intensity of his emotions angered him. He wanted to feel naught but numbness. He did not need this now. He needed to focus on bringing his father's murderer to justice.

As they left the library, Colin's stomach knotted. He was not looking forward to facing Kristina again so soon, and in a crowded social gathering where he would have to pretend all was well… unless she decided to take the meal in her guest chamber. Upon entering the great hall, he saw this was not the case. She was already seated at the high table beside Anna, three seats down from the laird's chair. He was both disappointed and relieved.

Her eyes met his as he approached, then she glanced away. Saints, he could not grow used to the fact that she could see him. Excitement quickened his heart rate.

After one of the elders said grace, the meal was served, but despite his stomach growling, he had little appetite. Nor could he stop himself from glancing down the table or over Anna's head to see if he could catch a glimpse of Kristina.

He, Neacal, Bryce and Cyrus discussed strategies for capturing the elusive Holme. When he found his attention straying, wondering what Kristina would say to him, he wanted to kick himself. He looked forward to talking to her, but at the same time he dreaded it.

Red Holme and Scroggie pushed their way into the crowded great hall of Rhodie Castle, among the arriving MacDonald and MacKenzie clansmen. He doubted any of them would recognize him. He'd made an early retreat from the battle they'd fought in at

Bearach. Besides that, before he'd taken on the chimney sweep disguise, he'd shaved his red hair and bushy beard. Soot now covered most of his face, and a cowl covered his head.

He'd tried to keep out of sight when Colin and his closest guards had arrived back, but some of the male servants had been in a tizzy about the beautiful ladies arriving. He'd tried to see if Lady Kristina was among them, but the bailey had been so crowded he couldn't see who they were. But now he intended to find out.

The great hall was packed with several long tables to accommodate the many visitors and clansmen.

When the lady of the castle entered the great hall, all the men and servants stood. The next lady to enter was Anna, then Kristina.

Holme's breath halted as he watched her follow her sister toward the high table, unable to believe his good fortune. His heart raced with excitement and lust. He was glad she wasn't dead. Now, he would have another chance with her.

But something was different about her. No one was leading her. How was this possible? Could she see?

"Well, I'll be hanged," Scroggie whispered. "If 'tis nay the blind wench."

"Shh."

A dark-haired lady followed. Once they were all seated, everyone at the low tables sat on the benches and resumed their conversations. But Holme could not take his gaze off Kristina.

Damnation, but she could see! No one was helping her do anything. She picked up a goblet of wine and drank from it. No feeling around for it. Her actions were so different from the day he'd sat across from her while eating in that tavern.

When Colin Cameron and his friend entered, all the servants leapt to their feet again. Holme didn't. He merely glared through the crowd as the bastard claimed the laird's chair. All the servants resumed their seats. Why was Kristina not sitting beside Colin? Two people sat between them. Were they having a lovers' spat?

Because many days had passed since Holme had eaten a good meal, he stuffed himself with bread and venison during the meal and guzzled ale, all the while keeping an eye on Kristina.

She was even lovelier than he remembered. And he could not get over the fact she could see.

Kristina's presence here changed Holme's plans. He had to find a way to slip her out. But how? She would scream and create a great uproar.

When Holme had eaten and drank all he could hold, he murmured to Scroggie, "Let's go outside." Once they were in the near empty bailey, Holme whispered, "Our plans have changed."

"Are we nay going to burn the castle down now?" Scroggie asked.

"Of course we are. But first, I'm taking the lass out of here."

"How are you going to do that?"

"I haven't decided yet."

Holme couldn't help that his interest was still piqued by that witch. He wanted deep and profound revenge against the Camerons, but he also wanted Kristina under him. How could he get both?

CHAPTER NINETEEN

Kristina paced in her guest chamber. She, Anna and Maili had left the high table so they could retire early and rest from their long journey. But Kristina could not relax. She'd refused to allow the maid to help her undress. First, she needed to speak to Colin. She'd only said a few words to him when they'd arrived, and none during supper because he sat so far away from her.

How could she get him away from the other men? They were no doubt still discussing battle strategies. With good reason, of course, but she needed a few minutes of his time to let him know the main reason she'd come here.

His manner toward her had been less than friendly. She could understand his anger and knew she deserved it, though surely he realized she hadn't meant to hurt him.

When she heard men's voices in the corridor, she hastened toward the door and silently opened it a crack. Though the corridor was dim and blurry from her vantage point, she could easily tell 'twas Neacal's and Colin's voices. Once Neacal disappeared into the room where Anna had gone to bed earlier, Kristina opened the door and stepped out.

"Colin." She tried to keep her voice low.

He halted and turned. She squinted, trying to see him better in the low light. His face was mostly in shadow, but the light from the candle sconce glinted off his square jaw. Looking at him quickened her blood just as touching him did. She had always been powerfully drawn to him, but seeing him now, she was even more attracted to him. She could not have even dreamed up a more perfect man for her—mind, body and spirit. But she had almost destroyed any chance she had with him.

"Aye?" he asked.

Dare she grab hold of courage and go after what she wanted, or should she flee back into her room and cower in the dark? She had never been one to cower, even when standing before a yawning abyss.

The fact that she could see him—in addition to his chilly demeanor—made him seem almost like a stranger to her. *'Tis Colin*, she told herself.

"Could we talk?" she asked.

He hesitated, and she feared he would say nay. In that moment of silence, she felt something powerfully intense emanating from him, but couldn't put her finger on what it was.

"We can go into the solar." His voice was cool and detached, so unlike the Colin she'd known intimately only a fortnight ago. How she missed the warm and affectionate tone he'd used with her at Bearach.

She approached him and he motioned her forward, down the poorly lit corridor, then walked beside her.

Pausing, he opened a door and held it for her. She entered a dark-paneled and stone room lit only by a low-burning hearth fire. A large table and wooden chairs sat upon a woven rug. Two cushioned chairs sat near the fireplace.

She nervously smoothed her skirts. "I thank you for agreeing to talk to me."

"I'm hoping you will do most of the talking."

His words stung. What the devil did he mean by that? He no longer wished to talk to her at all? Was he even interested in her apology?

After he'd closed the door, he moved toward a small side table and poured a small glass of amber liquid. "Whisky?" he offered.

"Nay, I thank you." She clenched her hands, willing them to stop shaking. Somehow she had to get him to listen to her, but knew not what to say first.

He picked up another bottle, removed the cork and sniffed. "Mulled wine?"

Although her stomach was too knotted to want anything, mayhap a few sips of wine would help her relax. "A wee bit."

He poured the red wine into a crystal goblet, then handed it to her. Even though the room was dim, when he drew near, she could easily see the anger and pain in his gaze. It sliced her to the core.

"Colin, I'm—" Her voice caught within her tight throat.

"Drink first," he urged in a slightly less acrid tone, then took a long swallow of his whisky. He turned away and added two pieces of wood to the fire.

She forced herself to take a sip of the wine, barely noticing the cinnamon and clove flavors. 'Twas delicious, but she was too upset to enjoy it. Her hands were so unsteady she feared she might drop the valuable crystal glass. She gulped another sip for courage, then placed the goblet on the large table.

He was still crouched at the hearth, jabbing at the wood and embers with a fire poker, causing the flames to burn brighter.

She swallowed hard and took a deep breath, forcing herself to plunge ahead before her courage fled. "Colin, I want to tell you how sorry I am for all that's happened."

"What do you mean?" His voice remained unfriendly. His question was only slightly less than a demand. Over his shoulder, he sent her a brief glance.

"First of all, the loss of your father is devastating, and I want you to know I'm here for you. Also…" She drew in another deep breath, her heart pounding. "I want to apologize for saying nay to your marriage proposal. 'Twas never my intention to hurt you, merely to spare you—"

"The burden?" he snapped, interrupting her and flinging a glare at her. "I ken it." He rose to his feet and stared into the fire as if he could no longer tolerate the sight of her.

Tears pricked her eyes. "I'm sorry I've hurt and angered you. I ken you will never forgive me—I don't deserve your forgiveness, in truth—but I wanted you to know that I regret everything. I wanted to see you, to apologize in person and let you know my vision has returned."

"And now that it has, all has changed, aye?"

She frowned, not knowing how to answer that surly question. Of course, everything had changed. She could now be an able and suitable wife for him—if his clan approved of her—but he did not seem inclined to want to hear the truth. Would it only provoke him further?

"Now you wish to accept my proposal of marriage?" he clarified, his incensed gaze pinning her to the spot.

Even though her feelings were crushed and fear consumed her, because he could easily reject her now, she drew on some inner strength and nodded. "Aye."

He blew out a breath and turned angrily aside. "God forbid, but what if you lose your sight again?"

She froze and closed her eyes, imagining the horror and disappointment of such a thing. She did not want to go back into that dark world.

"You would leave me," Colin rasped, and the raw pain in his voice shredded her soul. He turned away to pour another dram of whisky.

Would she do what he said? Nay, she couldn't. Now that she had experienced what it was like to live without him in her life—though it had only been a fortnight—she did not ever want to be without him again.

"Nay, I would never leave." She took two steps toward him, but forced herself to stop. She wanted to grab onto him and make him feel the love she held for him.

After downing the whisky, he set the glass on the side table and studied her with a critical eye. "How can you be so sure? What would be different from before?"

"Because I realize now… how much I love you."

"You said that before, while refusing to marry me. Love was not enough for you."

"'Twas not that."

"What then?"

His sharp words cut to the bone, and she felt again as if she were lost in the dark, for she could not see her way out of these entangled emotions. "I was daft before, back at Bearach, and I ken I deserve your hatred."

"I don't hate you, Kristina," he growled, sounding very much like he did.

She closed her eyes, and the tears she'd been holding back tumbled down her cheeks.

Without warning, he dragged her to him and kissed her. She gasped in shock as the passion exploded. Joy and arousal spread through her like wildfire in a dry forest, and she locked her arms around his neck. He would forgive her; he had to. She didn't want to exist without him, without his consuming kisses, without his possessive embrace.

Colin could not get enough of Kristina's delectable mouth. Damnation, how he'd missed her since he'd left Bearach. His heart hammered with excitement, for she fired up his soul as no other woman ever had.

"I could never hate you," he whispered against her lips. Nay, indeed, he loved her. Wanted her. Needed her. But when he thought about the possibility of her leaving him if her blindness returned... he would not be able to endure it. If she left him, she would take his heart and soul with her. If she had rejected him once so easily, regardless of the reason, she could do it again.

He pressed his forehead against hers. "I don't know if I can trust you."

She nodded. "I deserve that," she whispered. Her blue eyes—focused, aware, and filled with tears—cut into his soul. "But I want you to know, Colin... I love you and I always will." She turned and fled the room.

"Kristina," he said, but she was already gone. The tears streaming down her cheeks had gutted him. Did she truly love him, or was she only besotted in a very fleeting way? Why had love not been enough reason for her to marry him before, but now it was?

His heart ached with the love he felt for her. But if he believed her, if he trusted her, and she pulled the rug from beneath his feet again, he did not know how he could survive it.

Something deep inside his soul urged him to go after her, but an equally strong feeling froze his feet to the spot. He knew what it was—fear. He was not proud that he was afraid a woman would crush his spirit again.

He stepped out into the corridor, yearning to go to her door and knock. If he did, that would be the same as saying he wanted to marry her. Unable to do that as of yet, he halted.

'Twas true he craved her with every thread that wove through his soul, but he was pulled strongly in two directions. Bypassing her door, he headed toward his own room, the one he'd used since he was a lad.

As he neared the laird's chamber, it seemed as if someone was watching him. He halted and frowned, wondering if 'twas his da, paying him a visit in spirit. He shook his head at the daft thought, then continued on his way.

After entering his chamber and closing the door, he took a seat on the settle by the fireplace. He glanced at the bed, a desolate, lonely place. 'Twas doubtful he would get any sleep this night. Not after the conversation he'd had with Kristina... and the kiss.

Saints, how he wanted her.

He did forgive her. But he could not lose himself in her again, not now. Not until he was convinced she would never reject him again.

One thing was certain, the first task he had to complete was capturing Red Holme. 'Twas his responsibility, his duty, and the final thing he could do for his father. Naught could distract him from that.

Red Holme crept up the narrow back servants' stairs from the great hall, Scroggie following. He knew he would never have legal possession of this fine castle... but neither would the Camerons. Certainly not that whoreson Colin.

Holme had easily eliminated Maitland Cameron, and now 'twas time to eradicate the rest of them. An excited thrill racing through his veins, he smirked in the predawn darkness, then slipped along the keep's second floor, trying not to step on squeaky boards. He didn't want to alert them too early. Still, he carried a soot-covered canvas and some bags, while Scroggie carried a chimney brush. If discovered by a servant or one of the sleepless Camerons, they wanted to look as if they were going to work early.

'Twas about a quarter hour before daybreak. He knew some of the kitchen staff were already up, baking bread, but most of the Camerons were still sleeping in their beds, unawares. He smiled, imagining the Camerons trying to find an enemy who had vanished.

A door opened and softly closed farther along the dim corridor. Unable to identify anyone in the gloom, Holme halted, and he and Scroggie silently crept back to the alcove where he'd lurked last night, near the end of the corridor. From there, he had watched Kristina when she'd gone up after supper. That was how he knew which room she occupied. Now, quiet footsteps receded down the main stairs before he could see who it was. Obviously, the person was trying to be quiet and not wake everyone. Could have been a maid.

"Are you ready?" he whispered to Scroggie.

"Aye. Let's get her and be gone from here."

At Kristina's door, Holme tried the latch, but the door wouldn't budge. He muttered a curse under his breath. Quietly, he tapped his knuckle against the wood. Mayhap she would think 'twas her beloved Colin and open the door eagerly. He grinned, hardly able to wait to see her and touch her again.

"Who is it?"

Trying to recall what Colin sounded like, Holme disguised his voice, deepening it. "'Tis me."

A few moments later, the latch rattled, and Kristina inched the door open a crack. He didn't give her time to say a word. He barged into the candlelit room and clamped a hand over her mouth while Scroggie closed the door behind.

She tried to scream, but little sound emerged. Shoving at him with her inferior strength did little… until she kneed him the groin, sending a bolt of pain through his vitals. He almost dropped to his knees.

"Omph. Damn you, slut," he hissed quietly. "Help me with her," he whispered to Scroggie. They picked her up, restraining her legs, and deposited her on the bed.

She yelled beneath his hand and punched him in the cheekbone with her fist. A surprising amount of pain radiated from the spot. He grunted. The bitch! He'd had enough of this. When he flipped her facedown on the mattress, she slammed her elbows back against his belly, then attempted screaming again, but the sound was not loud enough.

He placed his mouth against her ear. "Be quiet or I'll kill your beloved Colin. I have him tied up in the byre."

She grew quiet and still.

"Now, that's better." Quickly, he pulled out the strips of tough canvas he'd already cut to length and tied a gag in her mouth. Next, he bound her wrists behind her back and tied her ankles, while Scroggie held her.

"Don't worry, my sweet. I won't let you burn to death. I'm going to rescue you." Holme rolled her up in the large, sooty canvas he'd brought. "You will be safe with me outside. You can thank me later." Grinning, he took the fire poker and, as quietly as he could, broke out the narrow window so the fire would have plenty of air. Through the hole in the wavy glass, he could see a couple of servants below in the bailey.

He dragged Kristina, bound up in the canvas, toward the door, then he turned to Scroggie. "Let's head to the laird's chamber. Make sure the corridor is clear."

"Aye." Scroggie stuck his head out the door, looked both ways, then motioned.

Holme held the candle's flame against the bed covers. After waiting a moment to make certain the covers caught afire, Holme picked up Kristina and tossed her over his shoulder.

They hastened down the corridor to the empty laird's chamber. Scroggie opened the door, waited for Holme to enter, then closed it again.

Holme laid Kristina down on the floor for a moment, where she kicked and squirmed about, thumping the floor. "Hold her down and keep her quiet."

Scroggie grabbed her legs and forced her to be still, while Holme opened the door of the secret panel behind the firewood box. He took the candle from Scroggie and tossed it onto the laird's bed.

"Make certain the fire is well caught. When you enter the passage, close the secret panel door behind you," Holme whispered. They would be long gone before anyone discovered the fire.

Panicking and near suffocating with the gag in her mouth and rolled up in a thick, stinking oiled canvas, Kristina attempted to draw in breath. Oh, dear God! How had Red Holme gotten inside the castle walls?

She had not recognized him at first. When he'd barged into her chamber, he'd looked like the grim reaper in that black cloak, his face covered in soot.

Holme picked her up, flipped her across his shoulder, further knocking the breath from her, and descended steps.

What had he done to Colin? Had he truly been captured by Holme? *Please God, let him be all right.*

"Help!" she yelled, or attempted to, until her throat was raw, but the sound could not carry far, muffled as it was. She focused on breathing in as much air as possible and combating the lightheadedness. What little air she inhaled smelled dank and mildewed, like a cellar.

Where the devil was he taking her?

Holme turned, bumping her head against a stone wall. The canvas provided very little padding, and a dull pain throbbed through her skull. *Ow! Bastard!* She wished she could knock him on the head with another rock.

"Scroggie?" he growled low. "Where the hell is he?"

A long moment of silence followed.

Holme strode forward and called his accomplice's name again.

"Coming." The voice was distant, then closer. "I couldn't get the damned door closed."

"Forget it. Is the fire burning?"

"Aye. The whole bed was ablaze." Scroggie chuckled.

"Good."

They were burning Colin's home! Sobs near choked her. She'd wondered what he'd meant earlier about not letting her burn to death.

Please, God, help Colin, Anna, and all the others to escape the flames! She prayed they wouldn't waste time searching for her in the fire.

After walking briskly for what seemed like several hundred yards, Holme placed her roughly on the ground. "Help me open the gate."

Rusty iron screeched.

"Shh. Put some oil on it," Holme grumbled.

After a few moments, she again heard scraping metal, but 'twas much quieter this time.

He dragged her a few feet, then hoisted her again and flung her across his shoulder. "Let's hurry to the river. 'Tis dawn." He trotted with her down a slope, jarring her painfully against the solid bone and muscle of his shoulder.

She was surprised to hear they were already outside the castle walls. She'd heard them say they were going to the laird's chamber. They must have used a secret passage.

Able to see naught but the faintest hint of dawn light through the thick material enshrouding her, she heard water flowing. Holme placed her on something hard that rocked this way and that. A boat, she realized, as the men climbed aboard, their boots clunking against the bottom. Once the boat was untied, it tottered and swayed, making her dizzy as it floated downstream.

Good heavens, how would anyone find her?

Colin strode across the bailey at dawn. Because of his

conversation with Kristina, he'd gotten little sleep last night and wanted to ride out in search of Holme now. Of course, he would have to wait until the men broke their fast. But he needed to check the armory to see how many arrows they had.

"Fire!" a servant in the bailey yelled and pointed.

Startled, Colin glanced upward in disbelief at the smoke escaping the bedchamber window on the second floor. "Saints!" That was Kristina's chamber. "Nay!" he roared.

Icy fear piercing his gut, he raced up the steps to the great hall, finding many men asleep on the floor. "The second floor is on fire! Bring buckets of water!" He ran up the turnpike steps and along the corridor. "Fire! Everyone out!" he yelled in an effort to wake all his guests at once.

Holding his breath, he shoved open the chamber door to find the room in flames. "Kristina?" Terrified she might already be dead, he hunched low and hurried into the room. "Kristina!" He coughed against the smoke burning his lungs. The bed was completely in flames but he did not see any signs of a person on the bed or in the room.

Where had she gone?

"Kristina! Where are you?" This room contained no side dressing room. He searched but couldn't find her or her remains, thank God. She must have left before the fire started. Upon exiting the room, he encountered some of his men with large buckets of water.

"Have any of you seen Lady Kristina?"

They shook their heads, rushed into the room and dumped water onto the fire.

"Where is Kristina?" Anna yelled, trying to scramble past him and into the room. He grabbed her by the upper arms and dragged her away from the smoke billowing into the corridor. "She's not in there! I searched."

"Are you sure?" she cried.

Neacal arrived and pulled her farther back. "What's happening? Where's Kristina? How did the fire start?"

"We don't know."

Bryce ran along the corridor. "The laird's chamber is on fire!"

"What the hell? No one was sleeping in there." Thank God, his mother refused to sleep in the room since his father had become ill and passed. "Make certain my mother is out of here," he told

Ethan, who'd just emerged from the stairwell.

"I'll get her now." He turned and hastened away.

"Can you make sure all the women are out, including the servants?" he asked Neacal.

"Of course."

"Find Kristina!" Anna yelled back, tears in her eyes, as Neacal rushed her down the stairs.

"I will," Colin called. He had to. He couldn't lose her again, especially now that she'd changed her mind about marrying him. Even if he couldn't trust her to never break his heart again, he still loved her more than life itself.

At the moment, he had to banish all emotion from his mind and think logically. For two rooms so far apart to be ablaze, the fires must have been started intentionally.

He passed Rusty and Warton. "Check all the rooms to make sure everyone is out of here," Colin ordered. "Upstairs, too. Get the guards and servants organized to pass buckets of water up here to drench the smoldering wood. I have to find Lady Kristina."

"Aye!"

Who would've started both fires? As Colin ran to catch up with Bryce in the laird's chamber, a man's face popped into his mind. "Red Holme," he growled. Of course! That bastard was the only person he could think of who wanted to kill as many Camerons as possible, while at the same time capturing Kristina for his own twisted purposes. Did he have a man on the inside, or was he here in the castle, himself?

Bending low to duck beneath the smoke, Colin entered the laird's chamber. "Kristina, are you in here?"

His father's bed was all that was on fire thus far. Bryce picked up the large woven rug from the floor and beat it repeatedly against the burning mattress, putting out all the flames.

The smoke was so thick, Colin could hardly see. Holding his breath, he checked the side dressing room. He yelled Kristina's name again, but she was not in this room, either, of course. Why would she be? Still, he glanced around, searching for any trace of her.

"I wager Red Holme set the fires!" Colin told Bryce. "Wanting to burn down Rhodie because he can never have it, while hoping we'd all perish in the fire. And then he abducted Kristina. He has a perverse fascination with her."

"How the hell did he get in here?" Bryce opened the window. "The guards have been vigilant."

"'Haps he paid one of the servants or guards to do his dirty work for him." Coughing against the acrid smoke, Colin stuck his head into the corridor to draw a breath of fresher air. "Have the men bring buckets of water in here and pour it on the smoking mattress! Then take it outside," he yelled to two guards nearby, and they dashed away.

Going back into the chamber, Colin found Bryce peering beneath the bed. Colin glanced aside, noticing the chimney sweeps' brush lying on the floor near the fireplace. Why was it still here? The steward had told him he'd hired chimney sweeps and that they'd cleaned the chimney in this room earlier. Stranger still, the built-in wooden box used to stack firewood beside the fireplace was pulled away from the rest of the wall. He frowned and yanked at it. The box, attached to a wooden panel, swung open on concealed hinges and revealed a small wooden door ajar behind it. He opened it and found narrow steps leading down. He had never seen this before.

"What the devil? Bryce!"

"Aye."

"There's a hidden door. Did you know it was here? Maybe they took Kristina out this way!"

Bryce cursed. "I didn't know about it. I'll go get a lantern." He hastened from the room.

"Hurry!" Colin descended several steps, as far as he could see, but 'twas pitch-black below. As he took out his dirk, a blinding thought occurred to him. "The chimney sweep!" He cursed. That had to be it.

Bryce returned in record time, holding a small lantern aloft.

"One of the chimney sweeps is Holme!" Colin took the lantern and followed the stairs down into the darkness.

"How do you know?"

"I'm guessing. Their brush was lying by the fireplace. I haven't gotten a look at either of them. Did you notice if one has red hair and a bushy beard?"

"They were both clean shaven. One is big and burly, while the other man is shorter and has a limp. They're always covered in soot and wearing cowls."

"Damnation! That's it. Holme shaved his beard to disguise

himself." Descending the damp steps, Colin breathed the mold-scented air, his lungs still burning from the smoke. "These steps go deep beneath the castle."

"No doubt intended as an escape route for the laird if the castle was under siege."

"Aye. Holme grew up here. He would know of this hidden stairwell. He must have kidnapped Kristina and brought her out this way."

"If we hurry, we can catch up to him."

Once the steps ended, Colin hurried along the low, narrow tunnel, dodging the debris, for several hundred yards. Bryce followed closely behind him. Dawn light filtered in at the end, and the small iron gate was open. Damnation! How could they not have known this was here?

They crawled through the opening and emerged onto a bush-covered hill near the wood. He couldn't even see the castle from here. Gorse bushes, brambles and other vegetation, which had hidden the gate, had recently been cut away and dragged aside, along with large stones. A light layer of snow now covered them. Holme and his men had clearly worked hard on this. Whoresons, the lot of them.

A new pathway of broken ferns and disturbed snow led downhill. Colin sprinted along the trail, which ended at the river.

Muddy boot imprints smudged the snow on the riverbank. "God's teeth! Holme has put her on a boat and taken her downstream. The falls!" When Colin visualized Kristina in a boat going over the high waterfall and crashing on the rocks below, he felt as if the life force drained from his body, leaving him colder than the icy air surrounding him.

"Holme should know how dangerous the falls are, since he grew up here," Bryce said. "If he'd wanted her dead, he would've already killed her. Clearly, he wants her alive."

Thank God his brother was the voice of reason.

"Aye." Colin breathed a bit easier. "Let's hope. If he does, he'll drag the boat ashore upstream of it and take her overland. Let's go get the horses."

The two sprinted back toward the castle, where a bit of smoke still escaped skyward. He prayed the fires had been put out.

Ralston ran to meet them. "Did you find Kristina?"

"Not yet. We believe Red Holme took her downriver. We need

horses."

"I'll go with you. After Anna told me what happened, I searched part of the castle and some of the outbuildings. No sign of her."

"I thank you for the help."

"You don't have to thank me. She's my sister. Red Holme must be stopped."

"Aye." Saints! Colin couldn't believe the steward had welcomed Red Holme into the castle. When he'd told Colin he'd hired a couple of chimney sweeps during his absence, he hadn't thought anything of it. They used their services at least once per year.

By the time Colin, Bryce and Ralston reached the open portcullis, the stable lads had led all the horses beyond the walls because of the fire and smoke. The agitated horses snorted and laid their ears back. Thankfully, some of them were already saddled.

"The fires are out." Cyrus MacKenzie strode toward them. "Did you find Lady Kristina?"

"Nay. But we know Holme has taken her down the river. We're riding to intercept them."

"We'll come with you." Cyrus turned and yelled, "Fraser! Bring all the men and the horses."

"I appreciate your help in extinguishing the fires," Colin told him.

"'Twas not such a hard job once everyone cooperated with the buckets of water."

Within ten minutes, Colin, Bryce, Ralston and fifteen MacKenzies, including Cyrus and Fraser, rode along the river, their horses galloping. He'd asked Shamus to inform Neacal and Anna were they were heading.

Colin prayed Holme knew about the waterfall and got Kristina to safety before they reached the dangerous area of the river. Still, he would not be able to breathe easily until he laid eyes on Kristina and knew she was unhurt.

He now regretted many of the things he'd said to her the night before. She'd left the room in tears after she'd told him she loved him. How could he be so daft as to let her walk away? He wanted to kick his own arse. She had apologized for all the pain she'd caused him. It had been difficult for him to forgive her, but if he'd known this was going to happen, he would've forgiven her a lot sooner.

If he'd gone to her room and spent the night with her, Holme would've never gotten his paws on her this morn. She would've never been in danger. This was his fault, just as everything else was.

When they reached the area of the river just before the falls, his mood plummeted further, for no boat waited on shore. If they had disembarked here, where was the boat?

Colin dismounted, along with several of the other men. A sinking feeling settled into his gut. His legs felt leaden, for he feared what he would see.

Fraser ran to the cliff's edge where the water plunged over the falls in a loud roar. He turned back toward them, his face ashen. "There's a boat smashed on the rocks below!" he yelled.

CHAPTER TWENTY

Fear for Kristina's life driving him forward, Colin dashed to the edge of the ravine where the waterfall plummeted downward. A small brown wooden boat lay splintered on the giant rocks. "God's blood!" His stomach aching with dread, Colin clambered and slid down the snowy embankment, his friends following.

"Kristina!" He waded into the icy water up to his thighs, his eyes scanning the rocky area for any sign of her. He saw nothing, no broken bodies, no clothing. But she could be underneath the water or already washed downstream.

Dear God, nay!

Even though the river wasn't in spate, a hard rain had fallen a few nights ago, and the water roared where it crashed onto the rocks. The rushing current would be strong enough to wash away any sign of her in minutes. He stared downstream, unsure whether to go farther southwest and look for her there or search here. Hell, he couldn't even think. Fear for her life had him near paralyzed.

Two of the MacKenzie clansmen shouted from the cliff above them on the opposite side of the river. They waved and yelled but Colin could not understand their words amid the thunderous waterfall. They motioned for them to come. Had they found Kristina?

Please, God, let her be all right.

Colin and the rest of the men climbed the bank.

"We found sign of horses in the wood," one man shouted, then pointed to a copse of trees about thirty yards away.

"Thank God." Colin leapt into his saddle. The others followed suit and they all carefully rode across the river at a wide, shallow point.

Once they were away from the noisy falls, 'twas easier to hear the MacKenzie clansman.

"First, we noticed the disturbed weeds and grass beside the river, then we followed the footprints through the snow to the wood, where we found tracks of four or five horses and piles of dung."

On horseback, they dashed toward the wood. After drawing up abruptly, Colin leapt off the horse.

'Twas true, the black dirt and leaves were kicked up. The men had tried to cover the horse dung with leaves and pine needles, but it hadn't worked. They must have been in a hurry. "Looks like the horses were held here for a few hours," Colin said.

Cyrus nodded.

"The horses ate here." Ralston pointed at the short-cropped grass at the edge of the wood where the snow had been nosed aside.

"Do you think 'twas Holme's men?" Cyrus asked.

"Aye. Let's follow them." Colin mounted again.

They trailed the tracks from the wood onto a narrow, muddy wagon road between hills, then increased their speed to a gallop. They couldn't be far behind Holme and his men, maybe a half hour.

He prayed Kristina was alive. But what if Holme had already injured her again, like last time?

Gripping the bridle in one hand and Kristina with the other, Red Holme kicked the horse into a full gallop along the muddy road flecked with small patches of snow. The wriggling lass was still wrapped in the sooty canvas and lying across his lap. He'd heard men's shouts behind them at the river. The Camerons were giving chase, damn them! He'd hoped they would all be burned to ash by now, or at least delayed by the crashed boat in the river.

Holme had to take Kristina farther away. If he could get her back to Stirling, she would be much easier to hide at a run-down inn on the outskirts. He was friends with one of the proprietors who would not report him for keeping a lass against her will. He grinned. Then he could enjoy her under him for days. But they were still a few days' ride from there.

At the moment, Holme and his men were coming upon a

whitewashed stone kirk and a wee village too small to hide in. Anyone who saw them here might give the Camerons information.

Abruptly, Holme's horse slipped in the mud and snow, stumbled and careened onto his side, falling and tossing Holme and Kristina to the ground.

"Damnation!" Holme roared, pain blasting through his left knee. He hoped it wasn't broken.

Although his knee had struck a rock at the side of the road, Kristina had broken most of his fall.

His four men turned and cantered their horses back. "What happened? Are you hurt?" Dobson asked.

Holme cursed again and pushed himself to his feet. He limped forward, testing out his knee strength. He'd have a large bruise, no doubt. "I'll live," he grumbled. "Catch the horse and see if he's injured," he ordered. After falling, the horse had bounded to his hooves again and trotted several yards away.

Scroggie caught Holme's horse and led it back, then examined the horse's hooves. "He's thrown a shoe."

"God's blood! We don't have time for this! The Camerons are on our tail. I'll take your horse, Scroggie. You hide and, once the Camerons are gone, take my horse to the farrier in the village, there. Then, meet us in Stirling in a day or two."

Frowning, Scroggie nodded.

Dobson stood staring at the canvas the lass was wrapped in. "Is she still alive?"

"Aye, of course. Why do you ask?"

"She hasn't moved or made a sound."

Holme limped toward her, remembering she had broken his fall from the horse. She was a fragile little thing. He hoped she hadn't broken her neck, because he did want to have some fun with her. He unrolled her from the canvas and turned her onto her back, finding she wore naught but a soot-stained white smock she'd obviously slept in the night before. It conformed enticingly to her every curve. Her pale skin was smudged as well. Her beautiful blond hair was unbound and tangled about her shoulders. He saw no blood upon her but she lay unmoving, as limp as a wet rag, her eyes closed.

"Kristina?" Holme nudged her with his foot. She did not respond. Was she dead?

Annoyance and regret punched at him. Hell, he didn't know

why he liked her so much. She was not a strong enough woman for him. No doubt a bedding from him would kill her, if she wasn't already dead.

Grunting at the pains shooting through his knee, he crouched next to her and placed his finger beneath her nose. In the cool morning air, he felt a slight stirring and warmth coming from her nostrils. "She's breathing. She was injured in the fall. That's all." That made him feel a mite better.

"Horses!" Dobson yelled as he stared in the direction they'd come from, his agitated gelding stamping about.

Holme heard the distant sound of hooves pounding the earth, growing closer and closer. "Hell! 'Tis the Camerons." They had not come into view yet.

Holme cursed, picked up Kristina and tossed her over his shoulder. Gritting his teeth against the pain in his knee, he trotted with her toward the kirk, the closest structure in the area. "Take the horses into the wood behind the kirk!" he yelled to his men. "Then, scatter and circle back around. Kill every Cameron you see! They'll never suspect I'm in the kirk."

He opened the door, went in and closed it. He placed Kristina onto the wooden floor, then dragged a heavy oak shelf laden with items in front of the door.

He drew his sword, fury and the need for revenge quickening his blood. Kristina might be near death, but he forced himself not to care. His main concern was Colin Cameron. "If 'tis him, he's a dead man," Holme growled.

As Colin and his search party rode around the bend, a man was running on foot, leading two horses around the back of a kirk toward the wood.

Colin veered off the road onto the snow-covered area near a small stream. Hooves had torn up the snow, grass and black dirt. Some sort of soot-blackened canvas lay on the ground.

Colin leapt from the horse before it even stopped, placed the targe upon his forearm and drew his sword and dirk. He ran behind the kirk, his friends following, their boots pounding the earth.

Four men, leading five horses, headed into the wood.

"Halt!" Colin ordered. "Or we'll fill you with arrows!"

Releasing the horses, the men stopped and spun around, their swords and targes drawn and ready for battle.

Colin halted, his gaze running over them. He thought two of them looked familiar but didn't know their names.

"Where is Lady Kristina?" he demanded. "And Red Holme?"

The men's faces paled, for they obviously realized they were greatly outnumbered. One by one, they dropped their swords and dirks.

"Where did he take Lady Kristina?" Colin shouted, glancing behind them and farther along into the wood, but seeing no one.

"The door of the kirk is blocked." Ralston yelled behind him. "I tried it."

"He's inside," Colin growled. "Tie them up." He hastened to the front of the kirk with Ralston. Bryce and a few more followed.

Colin beat on the heavy oak door. "Open the door, Holme! Do you think God and the kirk is going to protect you now? After you've done so many evil deeds?"

"Go to hell!" Holme shouted from inside.

Colin ground his teeth. "Give me Lady Kristina unharmed and I won't kill you."

"Ha! Come in alone and see if you can take her from me. Coward!"

"I'll be glad to! Open the door." Battle lust surging, Colin was ready to run the man through.

"Tell your other men to back away, or I'll kill her now!" Holme shouted.

Colin glanced around at Ralston and Bryce. Could Holme see them through the small glass windows?

"I'll slip around back to see if I can crawl in a window," Bryce breathed.

Colin nodded.

Weapons drawn, Ralston and the MacKenzies slipped farther along beside the church, out of sight, in the event Holme opened the door.

"I'm alone now!" Colin called out. "Open the door and fight me, man to man."

Scraping sounded, as if a large piece of furniture was being dragged across the wooden floor, then the door inched open. The building was dark inside.

He had no inkling what sort of weapons Holme had. The bastard could shoot him with an arrow for all he knew. Colin moved to the side of the door, so he would be out of the line of sight and lifted his targe and sword.

"Welcome, Cameron! Come on in," Holme taunted.

Why did this feel like a trap? He glanced back and met Ralston's gaze. He stood about ten feet away now. Looking intense, Ralston nodded.

Colin assumed that meant the young man who claimed to be Kristina's brother would be his backup. If everything he'd said was true, naturally he would want to rescue his sister. He had never done anything to cause Colin to mistrust him.

Colin turned his attention back to the open door and yelled, "Kristina?"

Inside, Holme laughed. "She cannot answer you. She's knocked out cold. Nearly dead. You'll have to hurry if you intend to save her life."

Dear God, nay! Fear and rage infused Colin's veins. As he took a step to charge through the door, someone yanked him back, sending him stumbling off kilter, and bypassed him.

"Damnation, Ralston," Colin growled low.

The younger man was already charging through the door, sword, targe and dirk in hand. Colin dashed after him.

Inside the building, swords clanged and the two men grunted and growled curses. A high, open shelf containing several items sat to Colin's right. Holme stood behind it. Ralston struck out powerfully, and his blade stabbed into Holme's shoulder. Face still covered in soot, Holme roared in pain and sliced his blade across Ralston's thigh. Ralston stumbled backward and fell.

"Holme!" Colin shouted, trying to take his attention from the younger man so he wouldn't deal a killing blow.

Blood ran from Holme's sword hand. Baring his teeth, he shrank back behind the shelf.

Before Colin could wonder what his strategy was, a blade slashed between the shelves toward Colin's gut. He brought his targe down just in time to block the sword's tip. Putting his shoulder and whole weight behind it, he shoved the targe against the heavy wooden shelf, toppling it onto Holme. The whoreson roared, his blade thrashing, but the shelf trapped him, constraining his movements. Colin positioned his sword and stabbed between the shelves, connecting with flesh. Holme shouted out in pain and fury. Colin further took advantage of Holme's trap of his own making, stabbing again and again until the man grew silent and still.

"I think he's dead," someone shouted. "I'll check him."

Pulling himself back from the intense battle rage, Colin glanced around to find Bryce behind him. Cyrus and Fraser knelt near Kristina, who lay unmoving on the floor. Her eyes were closed. Soot stained her white smock and pallid skin. Cold terror chilled Colin, and he dropped his weapons. "What the hell did he do to her?" He hastened toward her.

"She's alive," Cyrus said.

"Thank the saints." Colin fell to his knees beside her.

Fraser had already cut the gag off her and was now cutting the wrist bindings with his small *sgian dubh*.

Sitting nearby, Ralston muttered a curse through clenched teeth while two of the MacKenzie clansmen bound his bleeding thigh.

Colin turned his attention back to Kristina, worried that Holme had injured her terribly.

"To be knocked out like this, she must have a head injury, but I don't see one." Cyrus ran the tips of his fingers over Kristina's skull, beneath her hair. When he reached the back, he cursed.

"What is it?" Colin asked, an ache in the pit of his stomach.

"A large swollen knot on the back of her head." He withdrew his hand and looked at his fingers. "But no blood. Whatever hit her did not break the skin."

"I wager he had her rolled up in that damned sooty canvas I saw outside," Colin growled.

"Without doubt."

"Kristina?" Colin gently picked up her hand and ran his fingers over her arm to see if it was broken.

Cyrus felt along her other arm, then pulled up her sleeve to reveal her upper arm bent at an odd angle. "A broken arm. No telling what other injuries."

Colin cursed and ground his teeth, glaring back at Holme's bloody body beneath the shelf. "That bastard."

Using a sash, Cyrus bound her broken arm to her body to prevent further injury to it. "Do you want to check her legs to see if they're broken?"

"Aye," Colin said, praying they weren't.

"We must get her back to the castle quickly so the healers can help her. We'll make sure the horses are ready to go." Cyrus and Fraser left, while two of the MacKenzie clansmen helped Ralston limp outside.

"Can you bring the plaid blanket from behind my saddle?" Colin asked Bryce, the only man remaining.

"Aye." He hastened out the door.

Colin lifted the smock's hem and pressed his fingers along Kristina's cool, pale legs, finding no obvious broken bones or any other injuries, thank the saints. He drew her smock down again. He needed to get her wrapped up and warmed as soon as possible.

Bryce returned with the wool blanket.

"Her legs appear to be unharmed. I simply hope the ride back to the castle doesn't worsen her injuries."

"We'll have to be careful," Bryce said.

Colin felt as if his soul were rent in two as he carefully wrapped Kristina in the blanket, lifted her from the floor, and carried her outside. The other men rushed around him, dragging Holme's body from the kirk, rounding up the horses, and getting their prisoners ready to take back to Rhodie. Three Camerons would hang back to notify the local village and minister of what had happened in the kirk and help clean up.

Colin stood by his horse, looking down into Kristina's pale, impassive face. "Please, God, keep her alive," he whispered. "I love this lass more than life itself. I cannot live without her."

A half hour later, Colin and the search party arrived back at Rhodie. Thankfully, no more smoke trailed toward the sky, but the castle mattered little to him compared to Kristina. He simply hoped no one had been injured or killed.

Two of the MacKenzie clansmen had raced quickly back to the castle and notified everyone of what had happened, so the healers would be prepared for both Kristina and Ralston.

When Colin entered the bailey, Neacal waited near the entrance steps, ready to take Kristina from him. He frowned with concern. "She has not awakened?"

"Nay." Colin handed her down to him, then dismounted. "Was anyone hurt in the fire?"

"Naught serious."

Anna rushed down the steps toward them, tears in her eyes. "How is she?"

"Still knocked out from the blow to the back of her head. I'm taking her to my bedchamber. Can you tell Deidra we're here?"

"Aye," Anna said. "We'll be right up."

Colin took Kristina in his arms, carried her into the keep and upstairs to his room. The smoke scent was not as strong here, and a warm fire burned in the hearth. He gently laid her on the bed.

"Kristina?" he murmured.

When she still didn't respond, his gut knotted.

Anna, Deidra and her two helpers hurried into the chamber with their supplies.

"Her legs do not appear to be broken," Colin said. "But she might have other hidden injuries."

"We'll check her over." Deidra removed the blanket.

"I'll wait over here." Colin turned his back to stare out the window at the leaden, gray sky and snowy mountains.

He prayed they would find no other wounds. The head injury and broken arm were bad enough. The women worked quietly, murmuring amongst themselves for several minutes.

"The men said Holme was dead," Anna murmured at his elbow.

Colin glanced at her, nodding.

She blinked back tears. "What did he do to her? Beat her?"

"I have no inkling. But we figured he had her rolled up in a sooty canvas. He probably took her from the bedchamber in it. 'Twas lying beside the road."

"Did he toss her from the horse?" Anna's green eyes flashed with rage.

Imagining that, Colin's whole body ached and his fury flared again. "Knowing Holme, aye. Or, considering they were riding like the devil, she could've fallen off. Either way, 'tis most likely why her head wasn't bleeding—the canvas at least protected her in that way."

"I'm thankful to you that Holme can no longer hurt anyone else."

"Thank your brother also. Ralston shoved me aside and rushed in first. That's why he was injured."

Her eyes widened. "Good Lord. He must truly be our brother."

"I believe he is."

Anna moved back toward the bed, but knowing Kristina was

still uncovered and likely unclothed, Colin did not turn.

"What have you discovered?" Anna asked.

"She has several new bruises that are starting to swell and turn violet, especially her shoulder and the upper part of her back on one side," Deidra reported. "But, thankfully, no cuts. And no more broken bones, besides her arm."

The absence of cuts was good news. Less chance of infection. But still, hearing about the bad bruising made Colin want to strangle Holme, even though the bastard no longer drew breath. How could any man treat the lass in such a horrific way?

"She wasn't—" Anna's voice caught. "The knave didn't force her, did he?"

"I saw no signs of rape," Deidra said.

Thank the saints for that. Colin hadn't seen any indications of rape either when he'd checked her legs earlier, but he was glad to have it confirmed by the healer.

"What about her ribs?" Anna asked.

"Let me see." Silence followed. "I don't feel any broken ones, but they could be cracked. I'll have to check them again when she wakes."

Colin closed his eyes, wishing he had been the one who'd sustained the injuries instead of Kristina. Although she was resilient and strong in spirit, she was physically too fragile to endure such rough handling. Still furious with Holme, he clenched his teeth.

"We have her covered now," Deidra said.

Inhaling a deep breath to dispel his anger, Colin turned around, again struck by her wan skin. "When do you think she will awaken?"

"Cannot say." Deidra frowned. "Hopefully this eve or tomorrow."

"What can I do to help?" Anna moved closer to the bed.

"Mix these herbs into a poultice. We'll put it on her head to reduce the swelling."

While Anna stirred dried herbs in a bowl, Deidra and her assistants set Kristina's arm.

Colin scowled, glad she was asleep for that, because the pain would be excruciating if she were awake. Still, he prayed she would awaken within the next hour or two, for it would bode well for her speedy recovery.

He paced from the window to the door, over and over, feeling helpless as he watched the healers work. He mentally urged Kristina to open her eyes, grimace or flutter an eyelash. Anything. But she lay motionless.

A strong, comforting hand clasped Colin's shoulder. He glanced aside to find Neacal standing next to him, looking troubled and solemn.

Colin wanted to thank him for being there but suddenly found his throat was too tight to speak.

"How is she?" Neacal asked.

"She is breathing well," Deidra said. "I'm thinking she simply needs time to rest and recuperate. Time for the swelling in her head to go down."

"Come," Neacal said to Colin. "I'll pour you a dram."

"Let me know if anything changes," Colin told the women.

"Aye, m'laird," Deidra said.

"I will stay by her side, too," Anna said.

Though Colin didn't want to, he followed Neacal from the room. He encountered his mother, who was getting ready to enter the room, along with a dozen other people waiting in the corridor, including Maili and Shamus.

"She hasn't awakened yet," he told them, then went into the solar with Neacal.

Colin closed the door but found no comfort in the room as he usually did. Stark fear and desolation permeated him. "Damnation, I cannot bear losing her, too."

"You're not going to lose her," Neacal stated firmly while he poured whisky into small glasses.

"I pray you're right."

Neacal handed Colin a glass, but there was no jovial toast this time. Colin tossed the amber liquid back and swallowed swiftly, the fiery liquid burning his throat. He needed it to dull the sharp pain in his soul. "How could this happen? Why? She recovers from her previous injuries, regains her eyesight and now this."

"Colin, she will recover. Have faith."

His chest felt constricted. "I cannot breathe without her."

"I ken it. 'Tis how I feel about Anna. Thankfully, she wasn't injured, but when Blackburn abducted Anna, I almost went mad with worry and fear for her life."

Colin nodded. "Kristina has already suffered too much, even before this."

"She is a resilient woman with a fierce spirit."

'Twas true and one of the things he loved about her. In fact, she possessed so many traits he loved, he could not recount them all.

"Did you resolve things with her?" Neacal asked.

Regret felt like a leaden weight upon Colin's shoulders. "Not yet. I talked to her briefly last night, and she apologized but..." Colin shook his head. "I was daft and did not let her know I forgive her and still want her to be my wife. I told her I couldn't trust her. Damnation! I cannot seem to make the right decisions."

Neacal scowled. "You're being too hard on yourself."

"If I'd forgiven her and spent the night with her, none of this would've happened."

"You had no inkling Holme was within the walls."

"But I should have." Colin poured himself another dram of whisky. Aye, a clan leader should know who was inside the walls of his castle.

"She will awaken soon, and you can tell her how you feel."

"But what if she awakens blind again? She'll never marry me then."

Colin sat alone by Kristina's bedside for the second night in a row, the low-burning hearth fire and a single candle the only light in the room. She had not moved. Instead, she lay on her side, limp, lifeless and pale. The sheet and blankets had been pulled up over her shoulder. Her broken, splinted arm was cradled on a pillow, while she lay on her unbruised shoulder. The healers determined this would be the best position for her, to take the pressure off her head injury.

When Deidra had changed out the poultice earlier, he'd seen the bruised and swollen knot on the back of her head. 'Twas an appalling shade of blue and purple within her blond curls, and it pained him to see it. At the moment, it was covered with a fresh herbal poultice and a linen cloth.

"Why did this happen?" he whispered.

Everything happened for a reason, the wise ones said. What was the purpose of this?

He didn't understand why suffering happened.

Remembering how his father had responded after he'd talked to him, Colin leaned forward, took the hand of Kristina's uninjured arm and kissed the back, then stroked her palm.

"Kristina, I don't ken whether you can hear me, but if you can… I need to tell you I'm here for you. I love you and I forgive you. More than anything, I want you to be my wife. If only you will wake up and recover, we will be married when you're able. That is… if you will have me."

She shifted restlessly and grimaced. Despite her obvious pain, joy and thankfulness filled him. 'Twas the first time she'd moved since her injury!

When she dropped still, he leaned closer, studying her face in the low light. "Kristina?"

She did not respond or move another muscle. Her face relaxed.

He stroked her palm and her fingertips. "I'm sorry you are hurting, my sweet."

No response.

"Are you awake?"

Nay, she was not, but the movement had to be a good sign.

Leaning back, he listened to her even, steady breaths, thanking God for each one.

Colin didn't realize he'd dropped off to sleep when he was startled awake by the sound of wood thumping against the floor.

He straightened, finding he still sat in the chair at Kristina's bedside. Dawn light glowed at the window. He swung his gaze toward the door, where someone stood.

"Ralston?"

The burly young man limped forward on a pair of ancient crutches. He stared at Kristina. "How is she?"

"Earlier, she moved a wee bit." Colin sat forward, taking her hand and stroking the palm, listening to her breathing. "Lady Kristina?" he murmured.

She did not move an eyelash.

Ralston shook his head, looking as worried as Colin felt. A sinking feeling latched onto his gut, but he was determined to be hopeful.

"How's your leg?" Colin asked.

"'Twill be fine soon, I'm thinking. Tavia is a good healer."

"I've not yet had an opportunity to tell you 'twas a rash and daft thing you did, shoving me out of the way and running into danger like that. 'Tis why you were injured."

Ralston shrugged. "I could nay let you get yourself killed, now could I?"

Colin frowned, wondering what exactly he'd meant by that. It sounded more like something his brother would say.

"I did it for Kristina," Ralston clarified. "She loves you, and if you were to get killed, she would be devastated. She came here to marry you, after all. I ken you love her, as well. You will always take care of her... far better than I ever could as her penniless half-brother." Ralston's expression was bleak but determined." I wasn't there for my sisters during their worst ordeals, when those two bastards were tormenting them, but I'm here now. I wish to make it up to them. I want to see them married to men who will treat them like queens."

Colin was shocked speechless for a long moment. "You're a good man, Ralston. I appreciate everything you've done to help Kristina... and me."

"I thank you, m'laird, and I was glad to help."

"Please, call me Colin."

"I would be honored." He bowed, then straightened and lifted a brow. "Will you be marrying my sister, then?"

"If she'll have me."

Kristina must have been dreaming, for she heard the most divinely beautiful music. Had she died and gone to heaven?

Nay, she recognized it now. 'Twas Anna's flute music. No one played the way she did. Kristina focused on it and imagined the lovely sounds saturating her body. On and on they went, swirling through her like glowing, spinning stars, touching every part of her being. 'Twas almost like an angelic healing power in the form of sounds.

She felt cocooned within the warm, downy embrace of two angels' wings, while pure unconditional love surrounded her. All pain disappeared from her body, and it seemed she was floating, suspended in the warm air.

The flute music stopped, but the love surrounding her remained.

And then she heard the whispered words in her ear, "*I love you, Kristina. Please awaken and stay with me.*"

Who had said that? The deep voice was so familiar.
Colin!
Where was he? She wanted to tell him she loved him, too, but no words would emerge from her mouth. Her eyelids were too heavy to lift.

After playing another tune, Anna lowered her flute.
"'Twas the most beautiful music." Colin's mother sat in the chair by Kristina's bedside.
"I thank you."
Colin stood behind the chair. "I believe it will help her."
"I certainly hope so." Looking worried, Anna leaned over Kristina and kissed her forehead. "Rest well, sister. I will see you in the morn."
Colin bid her and Neacal good night as they left the chamber. After closing the door, he sat down in the chair beside his mother's.
"She is such a lovely, sweet lass, Colin," his mother whispered, then patted his hand. "You love her, do you not?"
His mother knew him too well. He'd never been able to hide anything from her.
"Aye. I wish to marry her, if only she will awaken and agree to it."
"Love matches are the best." His ma gave a bittersweet smile. "Although I didn't know your father before I married him—I had only seen him twice—I quickly grew to love him. And I thank God each day that I had a wonderful marriage to a good man. He was always kind to me and he made my life happy all these years. I wish the same for you."
"I believe Da approved of her."
Her eyes widened. "Did he say something?"
"One night while I was sitting by his bedside, I told him about her and the situation—how she'd been abused and injured. I didn't think he could hear me, but then he said *love*."
His mother drew in a quick breath, tears welling in her eyes. "He had not said a word since his injury," she whispered.
Colin nodded. "I think he meant that love was the most important thing when it comes to marriage. Not alliances or

dowries."

"Of course. I knew him well after these many years. If he knew how you felt about her, he would approve of the match, especially with her being a chief's daughter and of your social station. Your da would wish you to be happy. Anna told me that Kristina was blind for two years and miraculously regained her sight a few days before arriving here."

"Aye. It happened after I left Bearach. When she was blind, I asked her to marry me and she refused, not wanting to be a burden to me."

"Oh my. She seems such a good and honorable lady."

Colin frowned, annoyed his mother would see Kristina's side more than his own. "Of course, but 'twas not enough of a reason to refuse me. Would you have refused to marry Da if you'd been blind?"

His mother considered for a moment. "Mayhap, but I would have regretted it if I could've known then what a wonderful marriage we would have. Lady Kristina does not wish to be selfish. She's a principled lady."

"Well, I think that was one reason she came here... to let me know she'd changed her mind and now wishes to marry me. Do you think the clan elders will approve?"

"I know not. But I will speak to them on your behalf."

Two nights later, Colin gazed down at the lovely sleeping lass who had so entangled his heart. She still had not awakened, though she had moved a few times, as well as frowning and grimacing. He prayed she was not in terrible pain and unable to let them know. Of course, there was naught they could do about it if she couldn't swallow the herbal tea.

The longer she remained knocked out, the more his stomach knotted with worry.

He picked up her hand and kissed her exposed palm. "Kristina, no matter what happens, I want you to know I love you," he murmured. "But please, I beg of you, remain with me. We can have a wonderful life together. I can easily see how bright our future will be."

Kristina's eyelids fluttered, and her mouth opened as if she might speak.

His heart drummed with excitement. Filled with expectation and hope, he stood and stroked her cheek. "Wake up and smile at me, beautiful Kristina."

Frowning, she opened her eyes a crack and tried to move her injured arm and turn onto her back. She cried out, and tears trailed from her eyes.

"Wait, Kristina." He tried to hold her in place. "You must lie still. Deidra! She's awake." He kissed Kristina's forehead. "Thanks be to God."

Deidra pushed herself up from the pallet by the fire and rushed to the bed, the kerchief on her head askew. "'Tis the miracle we've prayed for. How do you feel, m'lady?"

Eyes closed and face contorted, Kristina gritted her teeth.

"I believe her arm is giving her great pain. She tried to move it."

"I'll make some herbal tea with poppy." Deidra set about mixing herbs and pouring hot water.

"Colin?" Kristina's voice was weak and raspy.

Thrilled at hearing his name upon her lips, he leaned closer. "Aye, *mo ghraidh*. I'm here."

"My arm hurts. What happened?"

"'Twas broken. Just rest and don't try to lift it so the pain will ease. Deidra is making some tea for you."

"Aye," Kristina breathed, lying quietly but still frowning.

"How does your head feel?" he asked.

"Hurts, too," she whispered, then seemed to slip back to sleep.

Thank you, God, for bringing her back to me. Colin wanted to leap with joy but had to restrain himself. His eyes burned with unshed tears of gratitude. He swiped his sleeve across his eyes lest Kristina or Deidra see his emotion. Men weren't supposed to cry with happiness, were they? What difference did it make? He wanted to shout from the battlements, but that would wake everyone in the castle in the hours before dawn and terrify them.

Staring into Kristina's lovely face, he held her hand and kissed it again, though he wanted to kiss her from head to toe. Aye, they would have a wonderful future together. He could easily imagine it.

"Here we are, m'lady." Deidra turned from the bedside table with the wooden cup. "I've cooled it and weakened it a wee bit with cold water. But it should be steeped enough to give you some pain relief. I've added a touch of honey so 'twill go down easy." She glanced at Colin. "Could you help me raise her up so she can drink?"

Remembering the pain she'd been in when she'd first awakened, Colin cringed, but he knew she had to drink it to feel relief. He moved to the back side of the bed. "Kristina, I'm going to lift you up."

She moved her head a fraction of an inch and frowned with her eyes closed.

"Are you ready?"

"Aye," she whispered. "If I must."

He helped her sit up, her small frame even lighter than it had been. She hadn't eaten in days.

"Ow." She ground her teeth.

The knowledge that his actions were causing her pain gutted him. "I'm sorry, *mo chridhe*, but you must drink the tea."

"Just a few sips, m'lady, and you will feel better," Deidra urged. "Can you drink some so the handsome lad holding you will smile?"

Colin grinned, watching as Kristina swallowed several sips of the tea.

"All right," Deidra said. "That should help the pain go away soon."

Colin lowered her gently to the pillow.

"I'll return in a few minutes." Deidra set the cup down, then left the room.

Returning to the front of the bed, Colin sat on the chair and watched Kristina. Her eyes were open, but she was not looking at him. Dread prickled at the back of his mind.

"Kristina?"

"Aye?" Even then, she did not look at him.

He frowned. "Can you see?"

Tears welled in her eyes and spilled down her cheeks. "Nay."

CHAPTER TWENTY-ONE

Colin gently took her hand in his warm, strong one. "Kristina, my love, you cannot see?" he whispered. "Are you certain?"
"Aye... unless the room is pitch-black."
"Why didn't you say something right away?" he asked.
Kristina did not want to utter the words. *I am blind again.* The most horrid, awful words in the world. She did not even want to think them. They were even worse than the pain stabbing through her head. She closed her eyes tightly and prayed for the darkness to abate and for her vision to return. Oh, it had been wondrous to see Colin's face, and everyone else's, during the last two weeks, not to mention the heather and the snow and the beautiful colors.
Please God, please angels, don't take my vision from me again. But she knew they were not at fault. 'Twas Red Holme who had done it, though she did not remember what had happened, beyond him abducting her from her chamber.
After taking her hand from Colin's, she pressed at her eyelids and massaged them, begging her eyes to work. Upon opening them again, she realized they would not. Her sight was gone.
Colin lifted her hand and pressed a warm kiss to her knuckles. "I love you, Kristina. And I want you for my wife either way, whether you can see or not. Will you marry me?"
"Oh, Colin," she sobbed, her heart breaking. How could he ask her that now, at the depths of her despair? She'd had her wondrous, precious vision back, but Holme had stolen it away again, damn him. Her sight was the thing she wanted most in the world so she could see Colin and be a good wife to him. But now... "I love you, Colin, but you must give me time to think."
"Please don't do this again," he muttered. "Does my love mean naught to you?"

"It means everything to me!" Despite her splitting headache, she had to make him understand. "'Tis why I want my vision. For you. I love you more than life itself."

"Then that's all that matters. You don't have to be perfect in order for us to have a happy, full life together."

"I don't expect to be perfect, but I want my sight back. You've never been blind. You don't know what 'tis like. I only got to see your handsome face a few times… for just one evening. And now, that is stolen from me. I have never seen your smile." Kristina allowed the sobs to overcome her. She mourned not only her lost vision but also her dismal future.

Colin wanted to kick himself for being such an arse when she'd first arrived here. "I'm sorry I didn't smile, but I had just lost my father. 'Twas grief, not you, that caused my bad mood."

"I know," she whispered, blotting at her tears with the bedsheet. "I had simply hoped to give you some comfort in the midst of your misery, but you didn't seem interested in talking to me or even being near me."

Hell, why had he done that? Why hadn't he insisted on sitting by her at supper? Because he'd been angry, hurt and unforgiving.

"You're right. I was a stubborn, daft idiot," he growled. "But, in truth, I did want to be with you… more than anything. 'Twas simply that your rejection stung. And you're not the first lady to do that to me. I was betrothed once, last year, but at the last minute, she changed her mind and decided she would rather marry someone else."

"Oh, Colin. I'm sorry. I didn't know."

"I think that's why it was so hard for me. Two rejections in a row are not easy for a man to take. Can you forgive me?"

"Aye, of course I do, Colin," she said softly. "You were in pain."

His throat constricting, he leaned over and kissed her forehead. After a moment, he sat back and cleared his throat, hoping his voice would sound normal. "I've never been so happy as when you awakened a few minutes ago. You've been knocked out for four days. I feared I was losing you. You hold my heart in your hands. You are my life. Do you understand what I'm saying?"

At that moment, Anna, Neacal and Tavia burst into the room. Although the interruption annoyed Colin, 'twas probably for the best. He needed to give her time to think. Pressuring her about marriage was not going to help matters.

"Oh, you are awake, my sweet sister." Anna hurried to the other side of the bed and kissed Kristina's cheek.

"Aye, but you need to know... I am blind again." Tears sparkled in Kristina's eyes.

"Och. Nay," Anna whispered in denial. She frowned, tears gleaming in her eyes. "You're alive—that's the most important thing. Your vision could return, as it did last time, after a few days or weeks."

"I know not," Kristina said in a dejected tone that near broke his heart, for he knew it meant she was unlikely to agree to marry him.

"You mustn't give up hope," Anna urged.

"I'll try." Kristina closed her eyes and, after a moment, seemed to drift off.

"I think she went to sleep," Tavia whispered.

"The herbal tea Deidra gave her is working." Colin was glad she was out of pain, at least, both physical and emotional. Mayhap he should request some tea himself, so he could forget the mental anguish.

He glanced aside at Neacal, who stood near the door looking troubled. Colin was certain he must be remembering the conversation they'd had a few days ago about Kristina's blindness possibly returning.

"Do you wish me to sit with her for the rest of the night?" Anna asked.

"Nay, go get some sleep. I'll take a nap in the morn while you visit with her."

"Very well. Send someone to get me if you need me."

"I will."

Anna left the room with Neacal.

Colin forced himself to focus on the gratitude he felt for her awakening, and not on her returned blindness or her reluctance to marry him.

When next Kristina awakened, her arm ached and darkness surrounded her. At first, she thought it was night, then she remembered her vision had been destroyed again. She pressed her eyes closed and clenched her teeth in disappointment, as well as frustration and anger. A sharp pain bolted through her head.

Groaning, she forced herself to relax again.

"Glad I am that you're awake again, m'lady." She recognized Tavia's friendly voice. She had liked Tavia from the first moment she'd met her, weeks ago at Bearach. "Are you in pain?"

"Some." 'Twas not so bad if she held still, but her body was exceedingly tired of lying on one side. She yearned to lie on her back, but knew if she moved, the pain in her arm would be unbearable. Her head, too.

"Do you think you can drink a sip of broth?"

She could hardly tolerate the thought of food, but knew Tavia would not let up until she drank some. "I will try."

"I'm glad to see you awake again, Lady Kristina." Colin entered the room, his boots clunking on the wooden floor. "How do you feel?" Was he truly as cheerful as he sounded, or was he only pretending for her sake?

Either way, her heart leapt in excitement upon hearing his voice. "Grand," she muttered dryly, but could not prevent the corners of her lips from lifting a wee bit.

He snorted. "'Tis wondrous that you still have your sense of humor."

What choice did she have? She must accept her fate once again. She had never been good at feeling sorry for herself.

"Will you help me lift her, m'laird, so she can drink a few sips of broth?" Tavia asked.

"Aye." Colin moved around the bed and behind her. He slid his warm hand beneath her side. "Am I hurting you?"

"Nay." She loved feeling his hand there, but she braced for the pain she knew would follow once he moved her.

He raised her up and the dull throbbing in her head increased, but worst of all, a sharp pain stabbed through her broken arm. Holding her breath, she forced herself not to cry out. She didn't want him to think he'd hurt her.

"Here we are, m'lady. The broth is warm, but not too hot."

Ignoring the pain as best she could, Kristina forced herself to breathe normally. She smelled the broth before the wooden cup touched her lips. Her stomach almost rebelled, but she knew she had to drink it in order to start recovering. A bit of the warm, salty liquid slid into her mouth, and she swallowed. 'Twas very hearty and tasted like venison stew. Two sips were all she could tolerate before the nausea rose up. "That's enough."

Colin lay her back down in bed and she waited for the pain to drift away. As she relaxed, the sharpest pain did subside, but the dull ache in her arm and head remained.

"I'm happy to see you're getting better." The chair by the bed creaked as Colin sat down. He did sound merrier than the day before.

"I thank you for helping me and staying by my side."

He kissed the back of her hand. "No thanks needed."

She wished more than anything she could see Colin's sweet, handsome face right now. Surely, he wore a pleasant expression.

After he drew back, it sounded as if he was sifting through the coins in his sporran. "I have something for you."

"What is it?" She was indeed curious, for she loved gifts and surprises.

He took her hand and placed a small item in her palm. When she closed her fingers over it, excitement buoyed her, for the object felt very familiar. To be certain, she turned her hand over and took the item between her fingers and thumb to feel it carefully with her fingertips—a cool metal disc with a small gem in the center and a hook on another part of it. "'Tis one of my mother's earrings!" Filled with warmth and gratitude, she blinked back happy tears.

"Aye."

"Oh, I thank you. Where did you find it?"

"In the wood, not too far from here. I only found one of them, and I didn't ken until that moment that Red Holme was the one who'd shot my father."

Her tears of joy turned to those of sadness. Imagining the devastation he must have felt at that realization, plus thinking about how Holme had stolen away her sight again, an ugly mixture of sorrow and fury grated at her. "Where is Holme?"

"Dead." Colin was glad he could give her this news. He'd forgotten she didn't know already. "He can never harm you again."

Kristina closed her eyes, frowning, looking troubled. "I wish I'd never opened the door to him that morn, but I thought…" She dropped silent.

"Aye, what?"

"He said *'tis me*, but it sounded like your voice. He tricked me."

"Damnation," Colin said under his breath, again regretting he hadn't been with her that morn. If only he'd forgiven her the night before. "I'm sorry I wasn't with you to prevent him abducting you."

"Do not blame yourself."

Well, he did. He couldn't help it.

"I remember now how I got hurt," she whispered.

"You do?" He wanted to know what Holme had done to her, but at the same time he braced for the anger.

"Aye. Holme had me rolled up in an old canvas and lying on the saddle in front of him. 'Twas painful the way the saddle jabbed up into my stomach. The horse was galloping and seemed to lose its footing. I went flying off onto the ground. My head and upper body slammed into something hard. Must have been rocks. At the same time, I felt crushed as Holme landed on top of me. That's all I remember. I passed out."

Imagining the whole scene, Colin clenched his jaw against the renewed anger. So, her current injuries had been caused by an accident. He was glad Holme hadn't beaten her again. Still, he shouldn't have handled her so roughly.

"I killed him shortly after that in a fair fight. In a kirk."

"A kirk?" she gasped.

"Aye. I hope the Almighty can forgive me for that, especially since I was trying to save your life."

Her brows furrowed. "I'm certain you are already forgiven, Colin," she said softly. "Were you hurt?"

"Nay, but Ralston was. He'd charged ahead of me." Although Colin was still annoyed at Kristina's brother, he couldn't help but admire his bravery.

"Oh, saints! Is he all right? What happened?"

"Aye, he's on the mend. Sword wound to his leg."

"I would like to talk to him. I also wish to thank you for risking your life to rescue me."

"There's no need to thank me." Colin only wished he could've gotten to her sooner and spared her the injury.

"Aye, I must. You're the most amazing and generous man I have ever met. I can never repay you for all you've done for me."

If only she would agree to spend her life with him, that would be more than enough repayment. But he feared she would never agree to it. Still, he had to try.

"I know how you can repay me." His heart pounded with trepidation, for he was diving right into a topic he shouldn't.

"How?"

"By marrying me tomorrow."

"Tomorrow?" Her eyes widened. "Saints!"

"Your sight or lack of it has naught to do with anything. I love you and I want you by my side either way. To me, you are perfect."

Kristina closed her eyes tight. "I'm far from perfect, Colin Cameron. But… aye."

He waited for her to explain what she'd meant. "Aye?"

"Because I cannot live without you… because I love you more than life itself, I will be selfish and marry you." Blinking back tears, she smiled.

Joy propelled him from the chair. "Thanks be to God!" Hardly able to contain the chuckle that burst out, he leaned over and kissed her forehead. "'Tis not selfish, my love. 'Tis most generous of you, for you make me the happiest man on God's green earth."

"You make me incredibly happy, too." Her grin widened, and she wiped at her tears. "But you must wait until I can crawl from this bed and put on a decent gown."

"I don't wish to give you time to change your mind," he teased, squeezing her fingers.

"I'll not change it. But I hope you know what you're getting yourself into." A trace of dry humor threaded through her tone.

"I do know. And by the way, my mother likes you."

Kristina's brows shot up. "She does?"

"Of course. She gives her blessing for us to marry."

"'Tis kind of her, but what about the council of elders?"

That was one thing which still concerned him. "I have not spoken to them yet." Truth be told, he'd been avoiding them.

She wore a worried expression. "What if they disapprove?"

"Then I suppose Bryce will find himself chief."

"Nay! I cannot allow you to give up the position."

"I doubt they will object, especially when they find out my mother approves of the union. And I believe my father did, too. Since you have agreed to wed me, I can now meet with them and gain their approval."

"What is all the excitement?" Anna entered the room, followed by Neacal and Ralston.

"Tell them," Colin urged Kristina. Since she'd been the reluctant one, he wanted to hear the words coming from her mouth.

She grinned. Though she still lay abed, she appeared radiant.

"Do you promise to keep it a secret?"

"Of course," Anna said.

"Colin and I are to wed."

"Oh!" Anna bounced on her toes. "I'm thrilled for the two of you."

Smiling, Neacal gave him a warrior handshake. "Congratulations, my brother."

"I'm glad you've both finally agreed you'll be perfect together," Ralston said. "Took long enough."

"Ralston," Kristina said. "Colin told me what you did, risking your life and getting injured because of me."

"'Twas my pleasure."

"Indeed?" Kristina said doubtfully. "How are you feeling?"

"I'm well. My wound is healing nicely, thanks to Tavia. 'Tis you I'm concerned about."

"Have no worries. I will be out of this bed soon. Will you escort me down the aisle, brother?"

Ralston beamed. "Och. 'Twould be my great honor. I thank you for asking me."

Kristina grinned. "I'm happy you found us."

Colin was glad, too, that the three siblings were together. Ralston seemed to fit in just fine with his two half-sisters, and Colin appreciated that he was a protective brother.

"I think you should tell them," Neacal murmured to Anna, his arm around her shoulders. Given his joyful expression, it had to be excellent news.

Her face reddened, and her gaze darted to each of them. "I don't think this is the right time," she whispered. "They've just announced—"

"Aye, go ahead and tell us," Colin urged, hoping his hunch was correct.

"What is it, sister?" Kristina appeared concerned.

"Well, since you're all here." Anna smiled, her face bright with excitement. "Neacal and I are going to be parents."

Amid the many embraces and good wishes, Colin hoped the elders would approve of his marriage to Kristina so they might one day soon also announce the impending arrival of their own bairn.

The next evening, Colin, Bryce and their mother filed into the library, along with the council of six elders.

Colin had privately told his mother and brother that Kristina had agreed to marry him. They were happy to help him convince the elders of her great suitability as a wife for him. He was indeed thrilled that Kristina was improving quickly and had been sitting up in bed all day.

Once they were seated around the table in the candlelight, Ewan, his father's second cousin—and the youngest of the elders at three score and ten—said, "I hope you're ready for the inauguration, lad. 'Tis highly unusual to wait this long after the former chief's passing, may God rest his soul."

"I ken it, but 'twas a special circumstance. I had to bring my father's murderer to justice. And now, I want to let all of you know I've found a bride."

Above his short gray beard, Ewan's eyes widened. "What?"

"Who?" his great uncle, Alan Cameron, asked.

"One that his father approved of and that I also approve of," his mother said.

Alan's bushy white brows quirked. "Are you going to tell us who she is?"

"Lady Kristina MacQueen," Colin said, his gaze darting from one frowning elder to the next. Did they remember who she was? Mayhap they had not met her. Or were they frowning because they objected?

"The lass who was kidnapped by that Holme knave?" Ewan asked.

"Aye," Colin said.

"But... the blackguard may have forced her," Alan said.

Colin shook his head, but before he could utter a word, his mother spoke up.

"Nay, he did not. The healers examined her."

Alan frowned. "Forgive me, m'lady, for being so frank, but to ensure that any child she bears is indeed Colin's heir, we should wait a few months."

"She is not with child." His mother smiled confidently.

Ewan scowled. "How can you be sure?"

Colin wished to know the same thing, for he had some concern Kristina could be carrying his own bairn from their one carnal encounter.

"If you must know, the healers confirm she is having her normal monthly courses now."

Uncomfortable about the topic being discussed in such a public setting, Colin cleared his throat.

"Is she an untouched virgin?" Ewan questioned.

Dear lord. 'Twas the topic Colin had hoped to avoid.

His mother glanced at him, a mischievous gleam in her eye. "You would have to ask Colin."

His face heating, he blew out a breath and rolled his eyes. But if they knew the truth, mayhap they would encourage a quicker wedding. "Thank you for that, Ma," he said dryly. "Indeed, we have already... shared a bed, so to speak. And whether she carries my child or not, I feel the most honorable thing to do is to marry her as soon as possible."

His mother raised her brows, though she was clearly not shocked, for she still hid a slight grin.

"I'm sorry." He shrugged. "I was in love with her then, as I am now. I proposed to her just after. Anyway, the healers examined her both times she was abducted and she had no sign of being raped."

"And she is agreeable to the marriage?" Uncle Alan asked.

"Indeed. Her sister and Neacal will stand in as her guardians. Also, their natural brother, Ralston."

"And it matters not to any of us that she's blind," his mother said.

Alan's eyes flared. "What? She's blind?"

"What of it?" His mother waved a hand. "She can be a wonderful wife and mother without her sight. She is a caring, lovable and good woman. She has a strong spirit. That's the important thing. She will help my Colin as he leads the clan and, I'm sure, bear him healthy children. I'll be glad to help with the running of the castle and overseeing the servants. 'Twill give me something to do. I wish to make myself useful."

Colin turned to his mother, wanting to embrace her for her generosity. "You would do that, Ma?"

"Of course. I've done it all these years and I enjoy it."

"How is she getting on? When will she be healed enough for the wedding ceremony?" Ewan asked.

"A month?" his mother suggested.

"Nay, I think a fortnight will be plenty of time," Colin said.

His mother chuckled. "'Haps you can marry her this night in her chamber."

"That would be my preference, but she will not hear of it."

"That will give us time to prepare for a proper wedding feast," his ma said.

"We can hold the inauguration first, in a few days, weather permitting. Are you in agreement?" Ewan asked.

"Aye."

"Good. Your father would be pleased."

Colin thought so, too, as he recalled the last words his father had murmured to him—*strong chief, son.*

Even though 'twas painful beyond words, he had to follow in his father's footsteps and endeavor to make him proud.

He simply hoped Kristina would be recovered enough to attend the inauguration.

CHAPTER TWENTY-TWO

Because of heavy rain and sleet, the clan was forced to wait longer than expected for Colin's inauguration as chief. Kristina was glad, for it gave her extra time to recover. She had been getting out of bed and walking for three days, and her pain was diminishing. She so looked forward to attending the first official ceremony of her future husband.

Wearing her heavy woolen cloak, she was waiting on a settle near the hearth when she heard someone enter the room. She recognized Colin's footsteps immediately and smiled.

"How are you feeling, *mo chridhe*?" He sat down beside her and took the hand of her uninjured arm and kissed it. His warm, tantalizing lips on her skin gave her a delightful shiver.

"Much better, now that you're here. The pain is far less than just a few days ago."

"I'm glad. You look exceptionally beautiful." He pressed a sweet kiss to her cheek.

Her face heated at his compliment. "I thank you, but 'tis Anna, Maili and the maids who should receive any praise for working a miracle."

"Nonsense." Colin leaned close to her ear and whispered, "You are equally lovely with your hair down and not a stitch on."

Good heavens! Her face felt scorched, then. It had been a long while since she had been intimate with Colin. On their upcoming wedding night, she feared she would feel awkward and out of her element. She hoped she could please him.

"Are you ready to go?" he asked.

"Aye."

"Some of the clansmen have prepared a cushioned and decorated wagon so you can have a comfortable ride out to the sacred tree where the inauguration will take place."

"How kind of them! Why would they do that?"

"Well, I'm certain you ken how clan gossip can be. Although I've made no announcement, because I was waiting until you recovered enough to join us at supper, word has spread that you will be my bride."

"Saints! What is their reaction?"

"Do you not notice how often they stop by to check on your recovery?"

"Nay." As far as she could remember, only her family, friends and the people she knew had visited her.

"They do. They peer in at the door when 'tis open or, in other parts of the castle, they ask Deidra or Tavia how you are faring. They love you. Even the stodgy elders ask me about your recovery."

Joy further lifted her spirits. "I'm thankful they accepted me as a bride for you."

"They admire your strength and tenacity. And the whole of the clan kens you have stolen my heart," he murmured in an intimate tone that curled her toes.

Kristina had never felt so elated. "You well know you have stolen my heart, too."

He gave her a dreamy, hot, but too brief kiss on the lips, then drew back. "Saints!" he hissed. "I could kiss you for hours."

She forced herself to draw in a breath. "I wish you would. I've missed your kisses."

"Don't tempt me. We must hasten out to the bailey or they will come looking for us. Hold on around my neck with your good arm." Careful of her broken arm in the sling, he lifted her and kissed her cheek, then carefully carried her down the narrow turnpike stairs. She relished his warm breaths against her hair and the side of her face.

Once they emerged into the cold, open air of the bailey, a cheer went up from dozens of people.

Colin laughed. "They're excited about our upcoming union," he murmured in her ear.

Tears burned her eyes. Knowing that his people—whom she didn't truly know—were rallying around her touched her heart. She wished she could embrace each of them.

"Here we are, love." Colin placed her on a fluffy feather bed that had been squished into a wagon and covered in blankets. "Anna and Maili will ride with you."

The wagon shifted as the two were helped aboard by their respective husbands.

"How do you feel?" Anna asked her. "Is the movement or the cold air making your pain worse?"

"Nay. 'Tis fine." Though she still felt weak and a bit dizzy, her headache was tolerable today. Tavia had given her a half cup of willow bark tea. She hoped it wouldn't make her sleepy, for she wanted to be awake for the whole inauguration, plus the feast and *cèilidh* afterward.

Far out in front, two pipers played as they set off, creating an exciting and jubilant mood. The wagon rumbled over the rough cobblestones of the bailey and splashed through the puddles of the rutted road. Horses' hooves thumped in front of them and behind. She had never attended a chief's inauguration and wasn't sure what went on precisely, though Anna had told her each clan had its own traditions and customs.

Despite being a cool, breezy November day, the sun shined warmly on her face. She had only one regret. "I wish I could see." Tears pricked her eyes. "What does this place look like?"

Anna put an arm around her shoulders. "The horse is pulling this wagon out a grassy ridge toward a huge oak tree. It looks ancient."

"Sleet lies in wee piles on the grass," Maili said, gently squeezing her hand. "A glimmer of frost sparkles upon the tree branches, the dried leaves and the brown bracken fronds."

"Colin, his brother, Neacal and Cyrus ride in front of the wagon on their horses," Anna explained. "Shamus, Fraser and Ralston are riding behind us. Colin's mother and some of the other women are riding on another wagon. The rest of the clan is walking behind us."

When they stopped, the horses snorted and the leather creaked as several dismounted. Though Kristina could tell a crowd surrounded them, all were mostly quiet. She barely heard a few murmurs and shifting feet upon frosted grass.

"Colin is now seated upon a large square stone beneath the old tree," Anna whispered in her ear. "Reverend MacAbee stands on one side and an elderly bard with white hair and a long white beard on the other. The male clansmen are forming a large circle around the tree."

After the minister said a prayer, the bard began reciting Colin's lineage back through hundreds of years of Cameron history. It amazed Kristina that he could remember so many people's names and the details of their lives. Then, he bragged of Colin's heroic deeds, starting with his most recent one of defeating the clan's enemy and rescuing the fair maiden.

Kristina's face burned, for she felt everyone's gaze upon her, but was flattered by the description, honored and humbled that they could overlook her extensive scars.

"Colin Cameron has already proven himself a powerful and most honorable leader. He would not accept the role of chief until he'd brought his father's murderer to justice. This is a man we can all depend on to protect us and provide for us," the bard said.

All grew quiet, but she heard footsteps and other movements.

"What is happening?" Kristina whispered.

Maili leaned close. "Two of the clansmen are draping a blessed plaid ceremonial mantle upon Colin's shoulders and fastening it at his throat."

"I accept the position of chief of the Camerons," Colin said in a commanding voice. "Bring me the sword of my forefathers."

Kristina was so proud of Colin at that moment she could hardly contain herself. He would be a caring, strong and generous chief. She sat up straighter, determined to be a capable and competent wife for him. She would support him and help him in any way she could.

"Warton has just placed a large, two-handed Highland sword into Colin's right hand," Anna whispered into her ear. "Another clansman has placed a white staff in his left hand. And now, the minister is anointing Colin's head with oil."

"All hail our new chief!" the bard announced.

A deafening cheer went up. The clan's joy and excitement was so intense it brought tears to Kristina's eyes.

Anna laughed. "Some of the clansmen are carrying Colin upon their shoulders."

Chuckling, Kristina wiped the moisture from her eyes. Oh, if only she could see Colin's face now. Surely, he was smiling and laughing, too. Or did he feel melancholy or bittersweet, missing his beloved father? She would have to ask him later, for there was no time to talk to him now.

"The clansmen have deposited Colin onto his horse," Anna reported.

The wagon jolted forward and turned in a tight circle as they headed back toward the castle. She knew now 'twas time for the feasting to begin.

An hour later, Kristina sat beside Colin at the high table in the great hall. She was eating a brambleberry tart and enjoying her future husband's funny comments in her ear. The whole of the clan was talking and laughing boisterously.

Colin stood from his seat and dinged his wine glass to quiet the noisy gathering. "Would you like to hear a story?"

"Aye!" several clansmen yelled. Whistles and hollers erupted, then everyone in the packed hall grew silent in expectation. Storytelling was a big part of every *ceilidh* Kristina had attended. Everyone, from the young children to the elders, loved listening to the tales.

"When I went to Bearach Castle several weeks ago to help my foster brother, I had no inkling a beautiful, strong and special lady would steal my heart." Colin lifted her hand and kissed it.

More whistles, whoops and shouts exploded from the crowd, and Colin chuckled.

Kristina could not contain her beaming smile, despite her burning cheeks. She was thrilled with his devotion to her, and he was incredibly generous with his compliments.

"We were readying for a battle with the enemy MacCromars and the man who called himself Red Holme, in truth an enemy MacKillican. Four dozen of them marched from the wood and lined up next to Bearach Castle. Their many archers nocked their arrows. Most infuriating of all, they had a hostage, Lady Kristina MacQueen. And Red Holme MacKillican held a dirk at her throat."

Much muttering and grumbling from the crowd ensued. Kristina was humbled that so many of the men were willing to stand in her defense.

"The outlaws were trying to force her sister—the lovely, talented Lady MacDonald—from the castle. I decided I had to rescue Lady Kristina. Six strong, loyal men went with me," Colin continued. "Tom and Patrick—may they rest in peace—along with

Warton, Rusty, Ethan and Lawrie."

A renewed sense of regret filled Kristina that two men had lost their lives protecting her. She had not even known them, but she felt their absence and grieved with their families. Before she had left Bearach, Neacal and Anna had accompanied her to their graves, to take flowers, pay her respects and express her gratitude for their sacrifice.

"We slipped from the castle in two small boats and circled around behind the enemy," Colin said, his strong voice echoing over the hall. "The battle had already started when we stole through the bushes toward Holme on horseback. Warton grabbed his right arm, while Rusty grabbed his left. When Lady Kristina slid from the grips of the knave, I caught her in midair and spirited her away from the battle raging around us. The enemy blocked our return to the castle, so the seven of us secreted her away to a cave in the wood."

Several people clapped and whistled.

"'Twas obvious to me within a few minutes of meeting Lady Kristina, the daughter of the former MacQueen chief, that she was an astonishing woman of great kindness, compassion and strength. She and her sister are survivors who endured great hardship and abuse at the hands of Blackburn MacCromar and Red Holme MacKillican, two men who have gone on to the hereafter, where they must face their evil deeds. I have to admit, even from that first day, Lady Kristina captured my attention and my heart. I knew I would never be the same again. I am the luckiest man on earth, for she has agreed to marry me."

A great cheer went up, which surely rattled the rafters.

Tears sprang to Kristina's eyes. Humble gratitude filled her that his clan would accept her so easily, even with her many flaws.

Colin helped her stand, then kissed her cheek. She laughed and blinked against the tears.

When the clan grew quiet, Kristina curtsied. "I feel most fortunate and honored to be wedding your chief and joining your clan."

The crowd applauded yet again. After they sat down, many toasts followed, along with clansmen and women congratulating them.

Then, the storytelling resumed. Warton told of the battle in the cave against Red Holme and his men. After this, Cyrus detailed how they had caught up with Colin and helped him rescue Kristina. Each person who was involved told a portion of the story, filling in details Kristina hadn't known about, for she'd been knocked out. Often, they described things she'd been unable to see.

Oh, how she loved these true stories. She was glad the clan could know the details of what they'd gone through.

Once they finished, she felt as if she'd relived the whole episode. She had been through a lot with Colin and was grateful to him for helping her so much.

After this, Anna sang a beautiful love ballad for them. Based on the silence in the great hall while she was singing, she held the crowd spellbound, as she always did. After the last note hung in the air a long moment and the music stopped, enthusiastic applause ensued.

"The crowd is having fine entertainment this eve," she said to Colin.

"Indeed. How are you feeling? Are you tired?" he murmured. She savored his intimate tone.

"Nay, I have been sitting here, resting. I love the way you told the story of how we met."

"Och. I did not do it justice, in truth. I wish my words were more elegant, but I never claimed to be a poet or bard."

"It sounded perfect to me. But then, everything about you is perfect for me."

"I wish I could kiss you right now," he whispered hotly into her ear.

She grinned and her face heated. "I wish the same thing."

"You'll have to let me know when you're ready to retire for the evening. Then, mayhap I can steal a kiss when I'm carrying you to your chamber."

That sounded wonderful, and she was eager to get some private time with him. "I'm certain I will grow tired before the dancing starts."

A few moments later, the minstrels started playing a lively jig that no crowd of revelers could resist. Wood clunked and dragged against the floor. She was thrilled, for she knew the clansmen were dismantling the trestle tables and placing them against the wall, along with the benches, clearing the dance floor.

Kristina forced out a fake yawn and covered it with her hand. "I'm afraid I've grown very tired," she said, loud enough for those around her to hear. "Would you mind escorting me to my room?"

"I would be most honored," Colin said.

"I'll come with you," Anna announced.

"Very well," Kristina said, hoping her sister didn't prove a strict chaperone.

"I'll come, too," Neacal said.

Colin helped her stand, then lifted her down from the dais and carried her toward the stairway. She considered telling him she was perfectly capable of walking, but knew that would not deter him. Besides, she enjoyed his effortless strength and the way he indulged her.

As he climbed the steps, she kissed his bristly cheek.

"You're going to make me trip," he growled playfully.

She snickered.

"You two behave yourselves," Anna teased behind them.

Once in the corridor containing the bedchambers, Colin took her to the room she used. Inside, he placed her gently upon the padded settle near the warm hearth.

"You're spoiling me too much," she said.

"Nay, you deserve it."

How sweet and generous he was. She wished she could give him a scorching kiss now. "Where did Anna go?" she wondered, hoping they could have some privacy.

"I'll check." His footsteps padded away from her across the rush mat. "I don't see her in the corridor. Mayhap she went to her chamber with Neacal. Do you want me to go look for her?"

"Nay!" Kristina snickered, then whispered. "I think she wants to give us time alone without setting tongues to wagging."

"I hope so." After closing the door softly, he returned and knelt before her. "I'm craving a kiss from you very badly. Do you think you're well enough?"

Anticipation coursed through her veins. "'Tis what I've been waiting for all evening, dear sir."

He rose to his feet. "First, I'm going to do something."

"What?" She heard the sound of cloth sliding.

After kneeling before her again, he took her hand and drew it to his face, where she felt a soft linen blindfold over his eyes. She inhaled sharply. "Why did you do this?"

"So I can experience what it's like for you."

He would join her in the darkness? Her throat constricted and a hot tear trailed down her cheek.

His hand stroked over her face, encountering the tear.

"Why are you crying?" he whispered.

"Because you..." She shook her head, unable to explain how profoundly he touched her. "I love you," she said instead, for that's what it was. Everything he did made her love him more.

"I know not how to explain how much I love you." He kissed her half numb cheek, the one closest to him. The one with the scar.

Her throat caught on a sob, for she felt his love so strongly. She turned and buried her face in his chest.

"Shh." He kissed her temple. "How can I seduce you if you are crying?"

A surprised laugh escaped her, along with the tears. "Rogue," she accused.

"I believe you hold a fondness for rogues."

"Just one."

"You say all the right things, m'lady." He moved, opening his sporran, then dried her tears with his handkerchief. He handed it to her and she blotted her nose.

"Better?" he asked.

"Aye. Stop making me weepy," she chided.

He laughed.

When Colin pressed his lips to hers, it seemed an eternity had passed since the last time he had kissed her this way, with gentle but persistent passion. His lips moved with slow, sensual deliberation, exploring every part of her lips with his own.

His tongue brushed against her lips, inciting a quickening of desire that stole her breath.

Being careful of her arm, he lifted her and placed her gently on the bed, then lay down beside her. "Do not tell anyone," he whispered against her mouth.

"I won't. Did you lock the door?"

"Aye." They lay snuggled warmly together, face to face, breathing the same breath, his lips sipping tenderly at hers. His hand at her waist, he tugged her closer. Suddenly, she sensed his great restraint in the midst of consuming passion. Thrilling tingles sparkled over her skin. Her arm around his neck, her hand buried in his thick hair, she drew him closer.

"I was teasing about seducing you," he said.

"Blast," she muttered. "Why do you torment me so?"

He laughed. "Do you think you'll be well enough for seduction by our wedding night next week?"

"Of course. I'm ready now."

Kristina was so excited she could hardly sleep the night before the wedding, but she did manage a few hours.

During the past week, her head pain had diminished to almost nothing, which she was thankful for.

Colin had asked one of his clansmen, an expert carver, to fashion a cane for her. She was thrilled to have it and she'd been walking around the castle beside him, Anna or Maili, learning her way around.

"A snow during the night has blanketed the whole countryside," Anna announced as she entered Kristina's bedchamber.

"I'm sure it must be beautiful." Kristina sat up and swung her legs over the edge of the bed, dejected that her blindness had not abated before her wedding day.

"Aye, but 'tis also exceedingly cold."

"I had so hoped to be able to see my handsome Colin as I marry him. I yearn to look into his eyes now as never before."

"Oh, I know, sweet sister." Anna patted her hand. "I will tell you this much… the expression in his eyes says he adores you."

Kristina smiled, happy despite her disability. "And I adore him."

"Do you have any pain this morn?"

"Nay. I feel much better. By the way, Ma visited me in a dream just before I woke up," Kristina said.

"Indeed?" Anna sounded surprised. "What did she say?"

"Naught. She simply smiled very serenely, and I could see and feel how happy she was for us."

"I'm certain she is. She will be with us in spirit this day. I need to tell you, because of the deep snow, the wedding ceremony has been moved to the great hall. 'Twill be much warmer anyway."

"Very well. Is Colin disappointed?"

"Nay. 'Twas his idea, and the minister agreed it would be acceptable. Now, I'm going to send the maid for some food to break your fast, then we can get you ready for your big day."

Musicians played as the bride emerged from the stairwell. Colin was stunned speechless, unable to believe how beautiful Kristina was. Realizing this was the happiest day of his life, he grinned until his cheeks hurt.

Ralston and Anna escorted Kristina across the great hall toward him where he stood in front of the high table, beside Neacal and Reverend MacAbee.

Kristina's long blond curls were loose upon her shoulders and interwoven with blue ribbons and dried heather. She wore a lovely gown of blue and a tartan sash of white, red and blue. The bodice fitted to her slender body perfectly, while the skirts and lace petticoats billowed out. Her arm in the splint and matching plaid sling did not detract from her elegant clothing.

Best of all, she wore a bright smile and a blush. Her happiness and love were clear for everyone to see.

When she stopped close in front of him, Colin took her hand. Since she could not see him, he wished to make a connection with her, so she would know 'twas indeed him. "You are so beautiful," he whispered in her ear.

Her smile widened and she squeezed his hand. The joy upon her face thrilled him and appeared to match his own. He wanted to kiss her now, but he knew he had to wait until the ceremony was complete.

As he repeated the vows after Reverend MacAbee, Colin could not take his gaze off her. His love for her was the most extraordinary and intoxicating thing he had ever experienced.

When it was her turn, Kristina repeated the vows in a strong and sure voice, all the while smiling.

"You are blood of my blood and bone of my bone. I give you my body that we two might be one. I give you my spirit 'til our life shall be done."

He absorbed the sacred wedding vows coming from her lips as one might relish the warm spring sunlight after a long cold winter. He prayed the rest of their days would be just as joyful as this one.

"I now pronounce you man and wife," Reverend MacAbee announced jovially. "You may seal your vows with a kiss."

Colin wanted to devour Kristina's lips, but he restrained himself. Although... once he started kissing her, he found it difficult to stop.

Whistles and yells erupted from the clansmen. Colin smiled and pulled back. He did not want to overdo it and embarrass her. But she was already blushing. He would much prefer giving her the good kisses in private anyway.

Next, 'twas time for more feasting and toasts, as well as the singing and dancing.

When Colin and Kristina took to the floor for their first dance as husband and wife, he allowed her to stand on the toes of his boots, as they had done in their only other dance, so the steps would be much easier for her. They were both giggling like bairns by the end of it, and the laughter was contagious, for everyone in the great hall joined in.

A short time later, Anna and the other women came for Kristina. When she blushed profusely, he laughed. They ushered her upstairs to the chamber she had been using, the same one he'd slept in the whole of his life until he'd given it over to her. He looked forward to spending their wedding night there, and was elated he would never have to sleep without her again.

"And now for the best part." Neacal grinned and playfully slapped his shoulder.

Colin chuckled. "Aye, I can hardly wait."

"Whisky?" Fraser offered him, lifting his flask.

"Nay, I want to remember every moment of this night."

Neacal raised his tankard of ale. Shamus, Bryce and the other men joined in. "To the wedding night!"

After drinking a swallow of ale, Colin glanced around at his circle of close friends and his brother. "Who will wed next? Bryce, Fraser or Cyrus?"

"Ha! Not I," Fraser was quick to say.

Bryce snorted. "I have no need of a wife."

"I think it should be Cyrus," Fraser said. "He's in much need of a wife, an heir and a spare."

Ever serious and intense, Cyrus lifted a dark brow, then shrugged with indifference. "If I find a lady from the right clan who measures up to my expectations."

"And those expectations are quite lofty," Fraser mumbled. "He will settle for naught less than a duke's daughter."

"Don't be ridiculous. An earl's daughter should suffice." Cyrus sipped his ale.

Shamus, Neacal and Colin chuckled, exchanging glances, for they knew finding the ideal wife had naught to do with who her clan or parents were and everything to do with her heart and soul.

Feeling giddy, Kristina covered her head with the counterpane when Neacal, Shamus, Fraser and the other men brought Colin to the bedchamber. The men were boisterous, with much teasing and laughter, which mortified her. No doubt they had already drunk too much whisky.

"Are you sure 'tis your new bride beneath the covers, there?" Fraser asked. "Could be the blacksmith's mother."

Her mouth dropped open. Fraser was such a rascal.

"I'll make certain 'tis Kristina," Colin assured him.

She pressed a palm to her burning face. How embarrassing that everyone knew what they were going to be doing in a few moments' time.

When the lock clicked and she heard no more voices, she uncovered her head. "Did everyone leave?"

"Aye." Colin chuckled.

At least they didn't stay to witness the consummation, as was customary in some places. No doubt they trusted Colin to get the job done.

She heard cloth sliding hastily over skin and then the mattress dipped as Colin got into bed. Though she was wearing a specially embroidered nightgown, he was obviously naked. She wanted to see him so badly.

"You are the most beautiful sight I have yet beheld." He stroked her hair behind her ear.

"'Tis not fair," she whispered. "I want to see you, too."

He drew her hand to his face. "You can see me with your fingers, as you did the first time."

She smoothed her fingertips over his strong jaw, covered in very short, scratchy stubble, and then over his high forehead and brows.

Placing his hand along hers, he pressed his warm lips to her palm. "I could put the fire out, if you like, and cast the room into darkness. Or I could blindfold myself again."

She grinned at how sweet and considerate he was. "That is not necessary."

"Good, because I relish looking at you right now. I'm certain we will share a lot of wonderful times in the darkness of night." He kissed her forehead.

"I hope so." Sliding her hand around his back, she pulled him tight against her. "I've missed this," she whispered. "I've missed holding you and sleeping together, like we did in the cave and at Bearach. I want to tell you again how sorry I am for—"

He placed a finger over her lips. "There's no need to speak of it anymore, *mo chridhe*. All is forgiven and we have a new start. This is the beginning of our wonderful life together. You make me so happy, I don't even recognize myself."

Touched and thrilled by his affectionate words, she smiled. "Well, I confess, I didn't ken 'twas possible to feel as much joy as you bring me. You've made my life perfect, even though I'm very imperfect. I feel selfish and guilty for having who I truly want."

"Not that again," he admonished. "You are an extraordinary woman and the clan is overjoyed to have you as their new lady. They ken how caring and compassionate you are."

"As are you."

She hadn't had the opportunity to explore his nude body before and was very much looking forward to it. She trailed her fingers down his hard chest, feeling the ridges of muscle and manly hairs. She moved her hand lower still, over his rippled abdomen, enjoying the intimate indention of his navel and the trail of hair that progressed downward. Heated excitement flamed over her body.

He moaned and clasped her hand, lifting it to his neck.

Disappointed, she asked, "Why did you—?"

"You don't wish me to be done before we even start, now do you?"

She didn't fully comprehend what he meant but had no time to ask him, for he kissed her deeply and completely. His lips were firm and possessive and his tongue sensual and delving. He tasted of pure masculine enticement blended with a hint of ale.

She curled her fingers into his thick hair and focused on how his lips felt upon hers. Decadent and seductive. Her heartbeat skipped and hurtled at an excited pace. Tingles sparked along her nerves like hundreds of points of light.

In her imagination, she brought her memory of Colin's face to the forefront. 'Twas the same way he'd looked in her dream.

Handsome and manly with a strong jaw, shoulder-length golden-brown hair and light-gray eyes. She also remembered the way he'd looked at her in the bailey when she'd first arrived. His eyes had been intense, like a lightning strike of sensual awareness.

He placed wee, hot and tickling kisses down her throat, then nipped at her collarbone. She laughed, loving how playful he was.

"I have to remove this smock. 'Tis in my way."

"Aye, please do." She raised herself up, and he gently pulled the sleeveless linen gown from her, being careful of her splinted arm.

He settled back down and pulled her tight into his arms. Feeling his heart thumping against her breast, she relished the fiery, solid feel of him all along her body.

His impressive erection pressed firmly against her, inflaming her arousal. She slid her hand down and stroked her fingers over him, amazed that he felt as hard as stone and the skin of his shaft was silken and hot.

"You feel wondrous," she whispered.

"But not as good as you." He groaned and rolled between her thighs, surprising her with his quick actions. Waiting, he lay above her, intoxicating her with indulgent, soul-deep kisses. Slowly, he trailed his mouth downward over the sensitive skin of her neck and chest, placing wee kisses here and there.

His breath warming her skin, he brushed his smooth lips over her nipple, then drew it into his heated mouth. He sent her arousal through the roof, and intense need speared her. Gasping, she arched her back. She had forgotten how powerfully he affected her, stealing her ability to think.

She simply wanted him to take full control of her; she trusted him that much. He was her soulmate... and now her amazing husband. She had to be the most fortunate woman in all of Scotland.

"Take me now, Colin. Make me your wife in truth," she whispered.

Colin moaned, loving the sound of that so much, he almost lost the tenuous grasp on his control. "Are you certain you're ready, love?" It had been a while, and he didn't want to hurt her again.

"Aye, more than ready." Kristina dug her fingernails against his arse, spurring him on.

"Let me see." Already so aroused he could hardly stand it, he stroked his hand downward, between her thighs and over her delicate flesh. "So wet," he breathed, sliding a finger into her scorching moisture.

Arching, she cried out. "Now, Colin."

"Aye." He stroked his shaft against her, teasing her a few seconds longer.

Unable to withstand his self-inflicted torment any longer, he stopped at her entrance and thrust his hips. Gritting his teeth at the immense indulgence, he forced himself not to drive to her depths, but instead to allow her to grow used to his size again.

She moaned, her body arching into his. "Feels… so good. More, please."

"Aye, lass." He withdrew and pushed forward again, deeper this time, hoping he was not causing her pain. The luscious friction of the withdrawal near seared his mind. His instincts urged him to drive deep, and he could no longer ignore them, especially when she begged him for more. Quickening his pace, he plunged into her over and over. Her impassioned moans, gasps and cries provoking his actions.

But he could not lose complete control, for he wanted her to experience the peak of pleasure, too. As he thought to slow down and wait for her, she cried out, and her delicate female muscles fluttered around his shaft, surprising him in the best possible way and launching him into an explosive release. Ecstasy rained down on him like a thousand fiery arrows, piercing his soul with a rapturous bliss. Tugging her tightly against him, he rode out the onslaught. As the aftereffects washed over him, he moaned in amazement.

"Kristina," he groaned against her throat. "You astonish me."

She giggled. "Oh, Colin. Nothing has ever felt so magical. I love you."

"Not as much as I love you."

"Ha! Do you wish to get into an argument over it?" She tried to hide her grin, but he saw it.

He laughed. "Since we're married, every night can be like this, my sweet."

"And every day, too." She grinned wickedly.

EPILOGUE

When Kristina awoke, she remembered that this night would be Hogmanay, the most festive night of the year, and tomorrow would be the beginning of the New Year. Even though Scots had not been permitted to officially celebrate Yule for several decades, the Camerons found a way to make the whole season festive. All week, they had indulged in much music, dancing, drinking and feasting, yet tonight would be even grander with bonfires outside the walls.

Anna, Neacal, the rest of the MacDonalds and the MacKenzies had left for their homes a few days after the wedding. There had been a break in the weather, and they had taken advantage of it. Kristina had wanted them to stay until after Hogmanay, but she understood they needed to return to their own castles and clans.

Kristina's broken arm was healing nicely and growing stronger, but she still wore a light splint for support. By the spring, she would be strong enough to ride beside Colin to Bearach Castle to visit Anna and Neacal, and she planned to be there when her niece or nephew was born in June.

Kristina smiled, remembering that, the night before, she and Colin had retired to the laird's bedchamber early so they might have their own private Hogmanay celebration. Though they had been married for a month, the honeymoon wasn't over, and she hoped it never would be. Each day, she loved her new husband more and more. His kindness and generosity always amazed her.

Opening her eyes, she felt Colin behind her, but he was not close enough. She turned over so she might snuggle into his warmth, for the room had grown chilly. Something caught her attention—a vague light.

"Saints!" She blinked and shifted her eyes. The faint glow was the rectangular shape of a window, and it remained.

"What is it, love?" Colin murmured in a rough voice.

She could scarce breathe for fear she was only imagining what she saw. "Is it daylight?"

"Aye, we slept late."

She pointed at the luminous spot. "Is the window there?"

"Aye." He paused. "Can you see it?" Excitement suffused his voice.

She burst into joyful tears. "Aye! I see faint light."

"Thanks be to God." He kissed her forehead and pulled her into a tight embrace. "'Tis what I've been praying for."

"This was how it happened last time. First I saw light, and then other things." Kristina pressed her eyes closed, saying a quick prayer of thanks for her returning vision. "Oh, Colin! I can't wait to see your face again, my handsome husband."

"Och. Hope I don't frighten you."

She playfully smacked his shoulder. "You know you're gorgeous, you rogue."

He laughed. "Nay, I do not. But you are the most beautiful woman in the known world."

"I thank you. I simply cannot wait to see everyone in the clan and our grand home. Along with the sunlight and the flowers in spring. 'Tis a fitting start to the New Year, don't you think?"

"Indeed." He rolled onto his other side. "I have a surprise for you."

"What is it?" Excited, she sat up beside him.

He handed her a small wooden box tied with a ribbon. Though she could not see it yet, she examined it with her fingers. She then slid the ribbon off, opened it and felt inside. "'Tis my mother's earrings. Both of them! Where did you find the lost one?"

"I didn't. I had one made to match your original."

"Colin, how sweet you are! That was why my earring disappeared for a few days when I'd thought I lost it."

"Aye. I sent Bryce to Inverness to have one made just like it. He's the only man I would trust with your precious earring."

"I thank you!" She took one earring from the box and put it on, and then the other. "How do they look?"

"Ravishing."

She chuckled at his exaggeration. "Soon, I'll be able to look in the silver mirror and see them myself. To have my vision back is a dream come true! I so look forward to seeing our children's faces one day." She could already visualize their wee blond heads and blue or gray eyes.

Colin was uncharacteristically silent for a long moment.

"Are you holding your breath?" she asked.

"Do you ken something I don't? Are you with child?" His tone was so intense, she had to smile.

"Not that I know of, but I'll ask Deidra if she thinks I am."

He released a breath. "How many children do you want?"

"At least a half dozen."

"Saints! 'Haps we should get busy, then." He chuckled, laid her back on the pillow and kissed her.

Thank you for picking up my book. If you enjoyed it, please leave a short review to help other readers determine if the book is right for them. To learn about my upcoming releases, please join my mailing list at my website: www.vondasinclair.com.

THE HIGHLAND ADVENTURE SERIES

My Fierce Highlander (Alasdair and Gwyneth)
My Wild Highlander (Lachlan and Angelique)
My Brave Highlander (Dirk and Isobel)
My Daring Highlander (Keegan and Seona)
My Notorious Highlander (Torrin and Jessie)
My Rebel Highlander (Rebbie and Calla)
My Captive Highlander (Shamus and Maili)
Highlander Unbroken (Neacal and Anna)
Highlander Entangled (Colin and Kristina)

THE SCOTTISH TREASURE SERIES

Stolen by a Highland Rogue (Dugald and Camille)
Defended by a Highland Renegade (Mairiana and Darack)
More stories will be coming soon!

ABOUT THE AUTHOR

Vonda Sinclair is the *USA Today* bestselling author of award-winning Scottish historical romance. Her favorite pastime is exploring Scotland and taking photos along the way. She also enjoys creating hot, Highland heroes and spirited lasses to drive them mad. She lives in the mountains of North Carolina where she is crafting another Scottish story. Please visit her website at: www.vondasinclair.com

Made in United States
Orlando, FL
19 December 2021